STORMS

OF CHANGE

What Reviewers Say About Radcly*ff*e's Books

"…well-plotted…lovely romance…I couldn't turn the pages fast enough!"—**Ann Bannon**, author of *The Beebo Brinker Chronicles*

"The author's brisk mix of political intrigue, fast-paced action, and frequent interludes of lesbian sex and love…in *Honor Reclaimed*… sure does make for great escapist reading."—**Richard Labonte**, Q Syndicate

"If you're looking for a well-written police procedural make sure you get a copy of *Shield of Justice*. Most assuredly worth it."—**Lynne Jamneck**, author of *Down the Rabbit Hole* and reviewer for The L Life

"Radclyffe has once again pulled together all the ingredients of a genuine page-turner, this time adding some new spices into the mix. Whatever one's personal take on the subject matter, *shadowland* is sure to please—in part because Radclyffe never loses sight of the fact that she is telling a love story, and a compelling one at that."—**Cameron Abbott**, author of *To The Edge* and *An Inexpressible State of Grace*

"*Stolen Moments*…edited by Radclyffe & Stacia Seaman…is a collection of steamy stories about women who just couldn't wait. It's sex when desire overrides reason, and it's incredibly hot!"—**Suzanne Corson**, *On Our Backs*

"With ample angst, realistic and exciting medical emergencies, winsome secondary characters, and a sprinkling of humor, *Fated Love* turns out to be a terrific romance. It's one of the best I have read in the last three years. Run—do not walk—right out and get this one. You'll be hooked by yet another of Radclyffe's wonderful stories. Highly recommended."—Author **Lori L. Lake**, *Midwest Book Review*

"Radclyffe, through her moving text…in *Innocent Hearts*…illustrates that our struggles for acceptance of women loving women is as old as time—only the setting changes. The romance is sweet, sensual, and touching."—**Kathi Isserman**, reviewer for *Just About Write*

Visit us at www.boldstrokesbooks.com

STORMS

OF CHANGE

by

RADCLY*f*FE

2006

CREDITS

EDITORS: RUTH STERNGLANTZ AND STACIA SEAMAN
PRODUCTION DESIGN: STACIA SEAMAN
COVER DESIGN BY SHERI (GRAPHICARTIST2020@HOTMAIL.COM)
PHOTO: SHERI

By the Author

Romances

Safe Harbor

Beyond the Breakwater

Innocent Hearts

Love's Melody Lost

Love's Tender Warriors

Tomorrow's Promise

Passion's Bright Fury

Love's Masquerade

shadowland

Fated Love

Distant Shores, Silent Thunder

Turn Back Time

Promising Hearts

Storms of Change

Honor Series

Above All, Honor

Honor Bound

Love & Honor

Honor Guards

Honor Reclaimed

Justice Series

A Matter of Trust (prequel)

Shield of Justice

In Pursuit of Justice

Justice in the Shadows

Justice Served

Change Of Pace: *Erotic Interludes*
(A Short Story Collection)

Stolen Moments: *Erotic Interludes 2*
Stacia Seaman and Radclyffe, eds.

Lessons in Love: *Erotic Interludes 3*
Stacia Seaman and Radclyffe, eds.

Extreme Passions: *Erotic Interludes 4*
Stacia Seaman and Radclyffe, eds.

Acknowledgments

Provincetown has been inspiring artists for hundreds of years and it continues to inspire me. No matter what I'm writing, I'm always especially motivated when I wake up to the sound of the ocean and fall asleep listening to the foghorn at Long Point.

The village of Provincetown on Cape Cod also forms the foundation for this series, in that this place is as much a character in these stories as the people who populate it. I'm fortunate to be able to spend more time there, now that I am no longer practicing surgery, than I was when I first wrote Safe Harbor one October during Women's Week over a decade ago. Writing and publishing still leaves me with two full-time jobs, but at least they're very portable. If I have a computer, I can work.

My thanks go to my first readers, Connie, Diane, Eva, Jane, Paula, and RB, as well as my editors, Ruth Sternglantz and Stacia Seaman, and the generous proofreaders at Bold Strokes Books for making this a better book.

Thanks also to Sheri for another cover that captures the heart of the story.

Lee, who captured my heart long ago, continues to make all my accomplishments possible. *Amo te.*

Radclyffe 2006

Dedication

For Lee
Beyond the Horizon

CHAPTER ONE

March 2003
Boston, Massachusetts

I hope you're not leaving the party yet," Lorenzo Brassi murmured, his eyes glittering dangerously as he gripped Ricarda Pareto's arm far harder than necessary. With a thin smile that from a distance might have been mistaken as friendly, he pulled her into one of the hallways leading off the grand central foyer in her father's Brookline mansion.

"Let me go, Enzo." Rica kept her voice low and her expression carefully blank, refusing to let him see the pain caused by his fingers digging into the soft flesh above her elbow. She needed to tilt her head only the slightest bit to look into his flat, dark eyes, secretly pleased as she always was to remind him by this gesture that he was only a few inches taller than her own five-eight. Among the many men in her family, her cousin was one of the shortest. The fact that her height bothered him made up for *her* irritation when people thought them siblings on first meeting because of their similar black hair and eyes and sculpted Sicilian features. "I have an early appointment tomorrow for the closing on the new house."

"Ah, yes. Your little hideaway." He leaned close, his breath redolent of whiskey and cigars. "Do you really think you can get away so easily?"

"A twenty-five-minute plane ride is hardly an escape." Rica knew he meant more than just her early departure from her father's birthday party, but she refused to give him the satisfaction of explaining why she wanted to move to the small Cape Cod village. She was aware of guests passing through the foyer only yards away and did not want family business, or family tensions, put on display. She tried to step around him but he blocked her with his body. Her arm throbbed beneath his fingers.

"*Don* Pareto hasn't opened the last of his gifts," Enzo said. "It's fitting that you remain by his side until the celebration is over."

"My father and I don't need you to mediate our relationship," Rica said sharply, wrenching her arm from his grasp, not caring about the bruise that would result. When she heard footsteps in the hallway behind her and realized someone, probably one of the guards, was approaching, she smiled brightly and took advantage of the opportunity to walk quickly away. As she heard Enzo greet the newcomer, she hastened around another corner and slid open the heavy walnut doors to her father's study. As she closed them behind her, she muttered vehemently, "Bastard."

The study occupied the entire length of one wing and was furnished with floor-to-ceiling bookshelves, heavy masculine leather sofas and chairs, and thick Oriental carpets on the dark wood floors. The only light at the moment came from a single Tiffany lamp that stood on an antique table in front of wide French windows. The view beyond was of the circular drive and fountain in front of the mansion. At just after midnight on Saturday night, with her father's sixtieth birthday celebration in full swing, the fountain was illuminated with spotlights, with sheets of sparkling water cascading over carved marble statuary, and the drive was filled with Bentleys, Mercedeses, and the occasional Lamborghini. The muted lighting and the smell of rich leather and old books were a soothing respite to the noise of the well-wishers, sycophants, and enemies disguised as friends.

Rica leaned her head back against the door, her arms behind her, both hands still clasping the doorknob, and closed her eyes. How she hated these events, being forced to socialize with her father's business associates, most of whom looked at her as if she were for sale—just another of her father's *objets d'art* on display for their entertainment. Of course, they never allowed *him* to see their thinly veiled expressions of lust and greed. It was even more trying to behave civilly toward Enzo. She shivered, still feeling the steel of his fingers bite into her skin and the proprietary way his eyes moved over her body as if she were naked.

"Bastard," Rica repeated.

"Forgive me," someone said from the shadows at the opposite end of the room. "I apologize, Ms. Pareto, for intruding on your solitude."

Rica flinched inwardly, but gave no outward sign of alarm. She had been carefully schooled from childhood to keep her emotions under check. She turned her head slowly, unsure whether her unexpected company was male or female. The outline of a slender figure in dark trousers and pale shirt did not immediately answer the question for her. She was certain, however, that she had never heard that voice before. She would have remembered the rich, silky tones that rolled like honey over her skin. "What are you doing in here?"

"One of your father's...assistants...told me I could make a private call in here," the woman lied effortlessly. She pocketed the wafer-thin listening device she had been about to attach to the rear surface of Alfonse Pareto's computer console, where the electronic activity from the other equipment would help conceal it during a cursory sweep of the room for bugs. She stepped forward into the light and extended her hand. "Carter Wayne, Ms. Pareto."

"I'm afraid you were misinformed," Rica said coolly as she perfunctorily shook the surprisingly broad, smooth hand. "This is my father's private study."

"Then I must apologize again." Carter cursed inwardly at the rotten timing. She'd been certain that all the partygoers would be in the ballroom while *Don* Pareto accepted their homage and their gifts.

Rica said nothing, hiding her suspicions as she studied the stranger. A lifetime of growing up in her father's house had taught her that nothing was ever as it appeared on the surface, and oftentimes those closest to you could do the most harm. Up close it was evident that what she had taken for a slender build was actually a sleekly muscular body, judging by the slight pull of the dark charcoal trousers over taut thighs and the stretch of pale linen over arms and shoulders too prominent to be fashionably feminine. She did not see any evidence of a gun, and she was good at recognizing the telltale bulge of a concealed holster or the uneven weight of a revolver in a five-hundred-dollar purse. Taking in the thick chestnut hair that fell almost haphazardly to her collar and the calm, hazel eyes that gazed back at her, apparently unperturbed by her perusal, Rica was quite certain that she had never seen this woman before. This was not the kind of woman that her father's friends brought to social events, which meant that she must be a business associate.

And that was unfortunate, because she was very attractive. "Did you finish your call?"

"I did," Carter lied again, indicating the cell phone cradled in the palm of her left hand. Actually she'd been about to call her contact to check the audio relay in the microphone when Rica had surprised her by coming into the room. The last time she'd seen the Pareto heiress, she'd been fending off the advances of yet another guest. It wasn't hard to understand why, either. Rica elevated the little black dress that every beautiful woman seemed to have in her closet for evening affairs such as this far beyond the realm of *haute couture*. Thin black straps barely broke the elegant lines of her toned shoulders, the neckline slashed down between small, shapely breasts, and the rest of the black silk sheath clung to lithe curves like rain streaming down a windowpane. Small-boned but not delicate, her body beckoned the sweep of a palm and the brush of lips. Realizing that Rica was waiting for her to elaborate, Carter forced the image from her mind. "I was just on my way out when you came in. I take it you were trying to escape someone's unwanted company, and now I've foisted mine upon you."

"Hardly escaping," Rica said, moving a few feet away to put distance between them. There was nothing threatening about the stranger—in fact, just the opposite. Her quiet, intense gaze and unusual directness were unexpectedly appealing. "Just looking for a few minutes of peace and quiet." She regarded Carter thoughtfully. "What is it that you do for my father?"

Carter laughed. "What makes you think I do anything at all for him? I could be someone's date."

"Somehow, I don't think so." Rica smiled, although her eyes remained wary. "The men here tend to have women who look a little… softer…than you on their arms. And that was meant as a compliment, by the way."

"Thank you. I'll take it as such." Carter was unable to decide if Alfonse Pareto's daughter was flirting with her or not. Intelligence indicated she was a lesbian, but now was not the time to overplay her interest, not when she'd been found in slightly suspect circumstances. "You're right, I'm here by invitation of mutual associates. I'm an attorney, but most of my dealings involve brokering imports for several large companies."

Drugs, Rica thought, surprised by the quick surge of disappointment. Why should she care what Carter Wayne's particular illegal activity might be? She was part of the world Rica inhabited by circumstances of birth, not choice, but a world she understood well. Rica walked to the door, pulled it open, and gestured to the hall. "You should return to the party."

It was not a suggestion.

"Of course." Carter stepped past her, careful that their bodies did not touch. "It was a pleasure to meet you, Ms. Pareto."

Rica did not answer but watched until Carter had disappeared before following her down the hall. When she reached the foyer she turned in the opposite direction, away from the revelry. She ignored the faint racing of her pulse as she collected her coat and purse, nodded to the guard at the door, and left the celebration behind. Carter Wayne was undeniably attractive, but like almost everyone else in the house, she was not to be trusted.

Two hours later, Carter completed a circuitous route through the quiet Brookline streets and pulled her black Explorer into the parking lot of one of the few convenience stores in the neighborhood. She stopped next to a dark panel van and watched the rearview mirror for a full minute to see if any vehicles followed her into the lot. After checking out the few cars parked in the well-lit area toward the front of the building, she was satisfied that she had not been followed from Pareto's. She got out and rapped on the side of the van.

The door immediately slid open and she climbed inside. Two men and one woman waited in the cramped quarters, surrounded by electronic surveillance equipment. The older of the men wore pressed chinos, a polo shirt with the Massachusetts State Police logo on the breast pocket, and a thin headset coiled around his neck.

"Since I'm not getting anything over the wire," her partner, Kevin Shaughnessy, said, "I'm guessing you didn't get it planted."

"Ricarda Pareto walked in on me about two seconds too soon," Carter said, squatting down so her head wouldn't bump the ceiling. "That wasn't the way we were supposed to meet."

Marilyn Allen, a sharp-faced blonde wearing the regulation FBI navy suit and a perpetual frown, grunted in displeasure. "Jesus, it's taken us six months to get you in there. All we need now is for you to blow your cover. Or worse, Vincent Rizzo's."

Carter bit back a sarcastic remark, refraining from pointing out that none of the regional FBI agents, including Allen and her partner Bill Toome, had the skill to work undercover, and they never would have gotten *this* far inside without her. Carter, like every other state and local law-enforcement agent, believed that federal agents were nothing but glorified accountants, good for gathering information but a liability in the field. But it was the age of détente when everyone at least paid lip service to working together, and she kept her opinions to herself.

Kevin, in his usual implacable manner, ignored the grumblings of Allen and Toome. "What about Rizzo? Is he holding up all right?"

"He's wasn't happy about bringing me right inside the family, but, considering his other choice is jail, he's managing." Carter rubbed the back of her neck, belatedly realizing that she was far more tense than she'd realized. Tonight had been the first time that Rizzo, a trusted, high-ranking Pareto captain and a very reluctant FBI informant, had actually tied himself to her in public. He had introduced her as a business associate, thereby guaranteeing her legitimacy in the eyes of the organized crime members and sealing his own demise if her cover was ever blown.

"That's good, because he's been acting a little nervous," Allen said with obvious relief. "We want to get him wired before he panics. That will save us months of trying to infiltrate the organization one operative at a time."

"If you put a wire on him, you're signing his death warrant," Carter said. "Sooner or later someone will pick up on it and you'll find him in pieces in the bay."

"As long as it's later, that might save the taxpayers some money," Toome, Allen's fellow FBI agent, muttered.

"Let's call it a night," Kevin said quickly. "We'll meet tomorrow morning with the whole team and go over what we've got." He glanced at Carter. "I think the daughter will be the key to at least one big question—how Pareto's hiding the money trail. She's perfectly situated to move big bucks through those art galleries of hers. She's got to know where it's coming from."

"And from what we've heard," Allen said, not bothering to hide the disdain in her voice, "you should be just her type, Wayne."

Carter stared at her. They hadn't worked together all that long, but Allen had taken an obvious and immediate dislike to her and didn't bother to hide it. *Guess the FBI hasn't heard the directive on détente.*

"Maybe it's not such a bad thing she saw you tonight," Toome offered into the breach. "She might trust you more—you know, since only the upper-level players got invited."

"I guess we'll find out," Carter said as she pushed the door open and stepped out into the dark. There was no point in telling them that the one thing she had *not* seen in Ricarda Pareto's eyes had been trust. For an instant she'd thought she'd detected appreciation, perhaps even a little bit of interest, but that had quickly been eclipsed by suspicion. And oddly, something that had resembled disappointment. It wasn't at all what she had expected from the woman who stood to inherit one of the largest organized crime machines on the East Coast.

As Carter drove toward her apartment in Cambridge, she contemplated the goal of the joint state police, DEA, and FBI task force that she had been part of for almost a year—to shut down one of the major drug portals on the Northeastern Seaboard. With the amount of cocaine and heroin being run through the Port of Boston, the Justice Department estimated that millions of dollars were being laundered and carefully siphoned into the operations of the Pareto family annually. Dozens of agents from almost as many branches of law enforcement were working on the project—tracking cargo ship and truck manifests, money trails, and street-level drug distribution patterns. *Her* assignment was much more up close and personal. She was going to have to seduce Ricarda Pareto, or at least convince the crime boss's daughter that that was her intention. Having met Rica, Carter didn't think that feigning attraction to her would be too hard a task. What might be difficult was remembering that it was all strictly an act.

CHAPTER TWO

April 2003
Provincetown, Massachusetts

A chime sounded in the rear office of Beaux Arts where Rica sat alone with an espresso and croissant, announcing that someone had come into the gallery. Setting aside the pile of invoices she'd been checking against the stock that had yet to be displayed, she rose to greet the visitors. She'd been in her new house in the west end of town only ten days, and the gallery had been open for business for just a week, but she already felt more comfortable than she ever had in the exclusive establishment she'd run in SoHo for the last three years. She ran it, but it never felt like hers. Not really. She chose the art, developed the client list, courted the agents for the wealthiest buyers from coast to coast, but her name wasn't on the deed. The business had been a gift from her father when she'd finished graduate school, and as she'd learned over the years, every gift came with a price. There had been the occasional piece that she would not have carried had her father not requested it of her. *A favor to an old friend.* She never recognized the artists, but she knew better than to ask her father for information. At first, she'd been taken aback at how quickly the vase or statue or painting would sell—almost as if the buyer had been waiting for it to appear on her shelf. As the pattern recurred, she'd stopped being surprised.

"Hello?" a female voice called from the front of the shop.

Rica shook her head impatiently as she pushed the unsettling thoughts away, reminding herself that *this* place was hers. She'd left the gallery in SoHo under the capable direction of the assistant manager, a daughter of a friend of her father's. Rica hadn't thought she'd like Angela Camara when Angie had first come to work for her, expecting another pampered offspring of another rich and powerful man, but she'd been pleasantly surprised. Angie knew the market and was easy to work with, and she had become more than an associate. She was Rica's best friend, and Rica already missed her.

"Sorry," Rica said to the two women who stood in the main gallery surveying the paintings that had arrived just the day before. They looked like locals in casual jeans, boat shoes, and T-shirts. The older woman, a blonde with a year-round tan and piercing blue eyes, had liberal doses of paint splattered on her clothes. "I'm still getting organized."

The blonde turned from the canvas she'd been studying and smiled. "I don't envy you. I have a gallery about half this size, and I know how time-consuming it is. You paint, too?"

Rica shook her head. "I wish I did, but my talent seems to be in selling them, not creating them. I'm Rica Grechi."

"I'm Kate," the blonde said. "My place is just down the street. K&J Gallery."

"I know, I've been in it. I admire your work."

Kate looked pleased and drew her companion forward. "This is Caroline Clark, a good friend and a wonderful artist. I have several of her paintings in my gallery."

"Hello," Rica said, taking the young woman's hand. Blond like Kate, she appeared to be in her early twenties, judging by the bit of smooth abdomen revealed in the space between her short T-shirt and skintight hip huggers and the row of piercings along the curve of one ear.

"Hi," Caroline said. "Great place."

"Thanks. I take it you live here in town?"

Caroline nodded. "I'll be here all summer, and then I have one more year of school in Manhattan."

"Caroline just returned from studying in Paris," Kate said proudly.

"Really?" Rica said with interest. She looked from Kate to Caroline. "Are you two...related? Does painting run in the family?"

"No," Kate said, sliding her arm affectionately around Caroline's shoulders and giving her a hug. "Although I certainly wouldn't mind if she were mine."

"Oh yeah," Caroline said, grinning. "Like anyone would trade Reese for me."

"Who said anything about trading? My daughter, Reese Conlon," Kate said by way of explanation, "is a sheriff here in town and—"

"Completely...awesome," Caroline finished.

Rica laughed. Ordinarily, she didn't find the thought of anyone in law enforcement particularly appealing, but Caroline's obvious crush was endearing. She couldn't remember ever having had an innocent crush on a woman, even when she'd been young. By the time she'd been old enough to recognize her interest in women, she'd already lost her naïve faith in love. "I'll have to come down to the gallery and look at your works again."

"Absolutely," Kate said. "Actually, we stopped by because I wanted to let you know that there's a meeting of the Provincetown Women's Business Association tomorrow night. We'll be talking about advertising, fund-raising events, that sort of thing. I thought since you're new here you might not know about it."

"Thanks," Rica said, surprised by the absence of any overt competition from another gallery owner. That was certainly a refreshing change from what she was used to in New York. "I'll be there. Where and when?"

"Seven at Town Hall." Kate gave a little jump and looked down at the phone on her belt. "Oh, I'm sorry. I should get this." With an apologetic shrug she stepped outside.

"So how was Paris?" Rica asked Caroline.

"It was amazing," Caroline said, her eyes lighting up. "It's so beautiful, and I learned so much." She frowned. "I missed my girlfriend like crazy, though. That was the only thing I didn't like about it."

"Ah," Rica said. "Is she an art student too?"

Caroline laughed. "Not hardly. She's a cop here in Provincetown. She works with Reese."

Mentally Rica shook her head. Perhaps getting out from under the watchful eye of law enforcement wasn't going to be as easy as she'd thought. Thankfully, no one here knew her, and since she wasn't using the family name, hopefully that would continue.

Kate stuck her head back in the door. "That was Reese. She's got an emergency call and needs me to babysit." She waved. "I'll see you at the meeting, Rica."

"I should get going, too," Caroline said. "See you soon."

Rica waved as both women hurried away. She turned in a slow circle, taking in the bi-level gallery that took up most of the ground floor of the building she'd purchased on Commercial Street in the east end—the plain white walls, the counter with a computer and credit card machine tucked into one corner, the pedestals displaying sculptures and hand-blown glassware, and the paintings spotlighted by recessed track lights. The gallery was every bit as fashionable as the one in New York, but it lacked the chic veneer that kept everyone at a safe distance. She had to be careful not to forget that as simple as life here appeared, accessibility would never be an option for her. The distance she maintained was a matter of survival, and went far deeper than the surface.

❖

"Okay, champ," Reese Conlon muttered, tugging cotton play pants decorated with a menagerie of brightly colored animals over the chubby legs of the wriggling, squealing child in her lap. "Almost there. Just hold on for a sec—"

Regina Conlon King laughed joyfully and smacked her mother in the face.

"Ow," Reese exclaimed and then grinned as she saw the nine-month-old studying her seriously, as if trying to determine if what had transpired was a good or bad thing. "Nice left hook."

Seemingly reassured, Regina went back to wiggling. Reese glanced over her shoulder as the door from the side deck ajoining the driveway opened. When she saw Kate, she sighed in relief and stood. "Help is on the way, Reggie. Hi, Mom."

"Here, let me have her," Kate said, holding out her arms. "I thought you worked the night shift. Aren't you supposed to be off today?"

"I am. Well, I was," Reese said, rubbing her face in the hope that she'd wake up a little bit more. "I was going to sleep until Tory went in to the clinic at two, but she got called about some kid who swallowed her tooth about an hour ago. Then Nelson phoned just now and wants to see me in the office right away."

Kate bounced her granddaughter on her hip as she adroitly tucked in the baby's T-shirt and closed the snaps on her pants without looking.

In the process, she regarded her own daughter intently. She couldn't be certain whether Reese was half undressed after ending her shift or partially dressed and ready to return to work, since she wore the dark green T-shirt that went under her protective vest along with her uniform pants, and could be headed in either direction. The pressed khaki uniform shirt was draped over the back of a nearby couch. One thing she *was* sure of was that Reese was tired. Her short black hair was wet from a recent shower, but she was pale and shadows darkened the lids beneath her vibrant deep blue eyes. Now that she looked closely, Kate realized that while still muscular, Reese was thinner than she'd ever seen her. Kate handed Reggie a plastic baby bottle of apple juice and hiked her hip onto a stool in front of the breakfast bar that divided the large living room from the kitchen/dining area. "Is there something bothering you?"

Reese pulled on her shirt. "No, everything is fine. Just a little tired."

"Is Tory feeling all right?" Kate could think of very few things that would distress her daughter enough to make her lose sleep. Any problem that involved Reese's partner or their child was at the top of the list. Tory had had a very difficult pregnancy and emergency cesarean section when Reggie was born, and despite having returned to work in recent months, she was still not totally recovered. And Kate knew that Reese worried.

"Working too hard, as always," Reese muttered, buttoning her shirt. "But she says she's better and handling the patient load okay."

Kate laughed. "You believe her?"

Reese grinned. "She might be exaggerating a little bit, but she's keeping as regular hours as she can, and she's already got someone lined up for the summer. A woman from Providence who wants to downsize her practice. Apparently she's thinking of relocating permanently."

"Good," Kate said. "The clinic is too busy during the summer for Tory to handle it all by herself."

"I expect KT would help out if things got rough," Reese commented, although she suspected that Tory's ex-lover KT O'Bannon, a trauma surgeon who worked in Boston and commuted to Provincetown whenever she was free, would want to spend whatever time she had with her new lover, Pia Torres. Although KT had spent a few months the previous fall working with Tory in the clinic, it wasn't KT's natural environment. According to everything Tory had told her, and what she had observed herself, Reese knew that KT thrived on the adrenaline rush of life-and-death emergency surgery.

"The baby seems great." Kate caught the juice bottle as Reggie launched it into the air.

"She is. I think she's ready to walk." Reese opened the hall closet and took down the lockbox where she kept her gun. "And she's got an amazing vocabulary already."

Kate smiled indulgently as she listened to the baby babble. There might be a few words in there, but she knew better than to disavow her daughter's enthusiasm. "Is it the war that has you losing sleep?"

Reese grew very still for a moment, then removed her service weapon, checked to see the chamber was empty, slid in the clip, and settled it into the holster at her hip. She returned the box to the top shelf and pinned her badge to her shirt pocket. Then she turned and met her mother's eyes, eyes that were the same shade as her own. Despite the fact that she had inherited her black hair from her father, she and her mother looked very much alike. And even though she had spent her adolescence and young adulthood with no contact with her mother, having been raised by her father to be a career Marine and having spent much of her service time under his command, her mother knew her far better than her father ever had. Or perhaps in fairness to him, her mother knew what mattered to her heart far more then General Conlon did, even now.

"I think about it."

"It's escalating, isn't it?" Kate said quietly.

"Seems to be." Reese turned her collar up and threaded a black tie around her neck. She fashioned a small tight knot and settled it against her collar with quick, precise movements. "I don't think anyone who knows anything about this kind of engagement ever thought it would be over in a few weeks. The Middle East isn't all that much different than Southeast Asia."

"Have you talked to your father?"

"Not since he was here last fall to tell me what a great opportunity it would be for me if we went to war," Reese said bitterly. She had asked her father to attend her and Tory's wedding, but he'd refused. Even though he conveniently ignored that she was a lesbian in terms of the potential effect on her career, he would not recognize her relationship to Tory or their child. Selective denial of what mattered most in her life.

Reese shook her head to dispel the anger. It was dangerous for her to go to work with her mind anything less than clear, and she promised Tory every day when they said goodbye that she would be careful.

"I love you," Kate said gently.

Reese's expression softened. "I know. Thanks."

"Not necessary." Kate nuzzled Reggie's neck. "You keep bringing wonderful things into my life."

"Same here." Reese bent down and kissed Reggie's cheek, then her mother's. "Thanks for coming over on such short notice."

"I'll take her home with me," Kate said, "so either you or Tory can pick her up, depending on which one of you finishes first."

"Thanks."

"Be careful," Kate called as Reese went out the door. She waited a few more minutes, listening to the sound of Reese's Blazer revving in the driveway and then disappearing down the highway. She hadn't asked the question that she really wanted answered, which was what Reese would do if the war dragged on and her Marine unit was activated. She didn't ask not because she believed Reese didn't have an answer, but because she wasn't certain she was ready to hear it.

Chapter Three

When Reese drove into the small parking lot behind the single-story, sprawling wood building that housed the sheriff's department on Shank Painter Road, one squad car, a red Honda Civic, and Sheriff Nelson Parker's GMC Jimmy were parked in a neat row. Otherwise it was empty. At one in the afternoon with still a few weeks to go before the tourist season got into full swing, there was unlikely to be much going on other than the daily fare of fender benders, minor thefts, drunk and disorderlies, and domestic disputes. They hadn't yet signed on temporary seasonal help, and only a few officers were on duty each shift.

Reese parked next to Nelson's GMC and let herself in to the main office area through the side door. Their dispatcher and secretary, Gladys, was ensconced behind the array of computers and radio equipment. The matronly, middle-aged woman in a neat cranberry sweater set and dark slacks glanced her way with a look of surprise.

"I thought you weren't due back here until tomorrow."

"The chief called."

"Hmph." Gladys looked over her shoulder at the closed door of Nelson's office. "He's been in there since I got back from lunch."

Reese didn't ask what was going on, because if Gladys knew, she would have told her. And her mild annoyance indicated that she *didn't* know. Gladys had worked in the department for a lot of years and was an integral part of the team, so whatever the chief was doing behind closed doors had to be unusual. "You want to let him know I'm here?"

Gladys punched the intercom, waited a second, and then said, "Reese is here."

Through the static, a deep male voice rumbled, "Send...in."

Reese rapped on the door, then pushed it open and stepped into Nelson Parker's office. The chief, in his fifties with a full head of dark hair laced with gray, a broad face ruddy from a lifetime in the wind and sun, and a waist starting to show the thickness of a few too many years at a desk, sat behind a plain wooden one now on the far side of the room. His eyes were intelligent and quick, and—at the moment— telegraphing a sense of wariness and caution. A visitor occupied one of the two folding metal chairs in front of Nelson's desk, her body angled so that Reese could only see part of her face.

"Chief," Reese said, walking forward to stand behind the empty seat. "You wanted to see me?"

"Take a seat, Reese," Nelson said, tipping his head toward the chair.

Reese obeyed the order although she would have preferred to remain standing. She never liked to be in anything less than a superior position when facing an unknown situation. However, Nelson was in charge. As she sat, she got another quick glimpse of the woman. Brown and hazel, five or six years younger than Reese, dressed in civilian clothes—navy blue crewneck sweater, jeans faded nearly white, and scuffed brown boots. A dark brown leather jacket hung from the back of the wooden chair. Her face was honed down and edgy. Reese had seen her before.

"This is Massachusetts State Trooper Carter Wayne," Nelson said. "Special investigator."

"How're you doing," Reese said, extending her hand.

"Not bad," Carter said as she returned Reese's handshake. "Sorry to call you in."

"No problem." Reese regarded Carter thoughtfully, picturing her getting out of a black SUV, a briefcase in her hand. She'd been wearing the same leather jacket, dark trousers, and a dark shirt. "The sign on that office you opened on Bradford says you're an attorney."

Carter grinned. "You don't miss much. I've only had the office there a month or so and haven't actually done much business yet." In fact, she hadn't done any business, and probably never would. As soon as the investigative unit had learned that Rica had purchased a house in Provincetown, they'd worked out a cover story to make use of vacation property Carter already owned. Posing as an attorney in town would afford Carter a perfect opportunity to make contact with the subject. Carter had waited for Rica to get settled before putting in an appearance. "I really just got moved in this past weekend. Surprised you noticed."

"It's not a very big town." Unlike many local cops, Reese wasn't predisposed to disliking members of other law enforcement agencies. She had spent almost her entire life within the strict hierarchy of the military where the chain of command was absolute. She issued orders that she expected to be obeyed without question, and she followed orders from her superiors with the same volition. The system would not work any other way, and in moments of crisis when the difference between life and death was measured in seconds, the system had to work. Still, she wasn't naïve enough to think that the agendas of other agencies would necessarily benefit her community, so she waited for the state trooper to answer her unspoken questions. *What else are you and why are you here?*

"I *am* an attorney," Carter said. "I got my degree at night. Took me four years. I thought when I finished I'd switch from law enforcement to practicing law, but"—she shrugged—"it hasn't happened."

"I take it you're here about more than opening a law office." Reese looked over at Nelson, whose expression was a mix of concern and annoyance. "Something going on around here we should know about?"

"I don't know yet," Carter said. "I thought I'd check in with you. As a courtesy."

"What would have been a courtesy," Nelson said gruffly, "is if someone had told us you were coming a few months ago, and why."

He was right, and Carter had argued from the beginning that the local law enforcement people should be advised of her presence, but the FBI had vetoed the request. She had agreed in part with their objections, because the more people who knew who she was and what she was doing, the greater the likelihood that her cover would be compromised. On the other hand, Provincetown was geographically isolated, perched as it was on a strip of sand three miles wide on the very tip of Cape Cod. She had no immediate backup, and even though she was used to working under deep cover, it wouldn't do the operation any good if she learned vital information only to be taken out because she had no one to call in an emergency. In the end, after much debate, her superiors and Special Agent Allen had compromised. She spread her hands and told them as much as she could. "I'm not sure anything is going on.

I'm here following a thin lead that may go nowhere. But it's best I not advertise what I'm doing. If anybody were to check, I am a duly licensed attorney. I wouldn't be the first to set up a satellite office here, draw up a few contracts, and spend the rest of my time enjoying the scenery."

"That works fine as a cover for anyone who's not looking too closely." Nelson slid open his desk drawer and fished around for his roll of Tums. He tore off the silver foil, tossed one in his mouth, and chewed it vigorously. "Now you want to tell us why you're really here?"

"We think some of the pleasure boats coming through are carrying drugs. Probably picking them up out at sea and handing them off when they come ashore. One link in the chain, all the way up the coast from Miami." It was the truth, but far from the whole truth. Carter had found that the best way to preserve her cover and her credibility was to tell the truth, but to only tell as much as she needed to. The subterfuge with fellow law enforcement officers bothered her, but her mission was primary. If the situations were reversed, she had no doubt they'd do the same.

Reese contemplated the information. On the surface it was feasible. Provincetown had a year-round population of only a few thousand, and major crime was very unusual. Nevertheless, their proximity to the Atlantic Ocean and the enormous number of wealthy vacationers and part-time residents made the possibility of illegal trafficking a worry. Four summers earlier, when she and Tory had just met, there had been a major confrontation with the crew of a vessel that had run aground while ferrying drugs. Nothing of that scale had happened since, but drug-related problems on the entire Cape were escalating.

"And how do you expect to identify the couriers?" Reese asked.

"I'm hoping they'll come to me," Carter said, a small smile softening the edges of her predatory expression for a fleeting second. "Some distributors prefer to have an agent broker their deals. It keeps them one step removed. That's where I come in."

"You didn't set up those kinds of connections overnight," Reese observed. There was more to this story than they were getting.

Carter was impressed, but not surprised. She knew who Reese Conlon was. Most state police officers did. Conlon had made a name for herself when she'd risked her life to save a fellow officer and got shot in the process. She'd solved some other high-profile crimes but had steadfastly refused any kind of promotion or transfer that would take her out of the small town. "I'm inside a few places. I've been working at it for a while."

Reese looked at Nelson and caught his barely perceptible nod. They'd worked together long enough to almost read one another's minds. "Any major takedowns, we need to be involved. If there's a local distributor, we want the name. This is our town. It's our job to keep it clean."

"Agreed," Carter said. She didn't actually anticipate intercepting any of the drug shipments coming in on private yachts and sailboats because her team wasn't interested in that level of distribution. They wanted a shot at Alfonse Pareto, and they were hoping his daughter would give it to them. But that was the vital piece of information she did not intend to share with Nelson Parker and Reese Conlon. "So, we're agreed. If something comes up, I'll clue you in." She looked from Nelson to Reese. "I don't want to come back to the station again. Which of you should I call?"

"Let's make Conlon your official contact," Nelson said. "She'll keep me advised."

"Done." Carter stood. Conlon, she noted as the other officer stood, was just about her height. "Is there a back way out of here?"

"I'll take her out through the rear holding area," Reese said to Nelson.

"Okay, then head home." Nelson watched them go, two wary allies, and unconsciously unwrapped another Tums.

Reese waited by the Blazer, watching Carter walk away down the sandy path at the rear of the parking lot toward the Grand Union with its large parking lot half a block up the street. She'd probably left her Explorer there and come around to the sheriff's department on foot. No one would notice her coming and going. Her story was plausible, but Reese didn't believe it. No one invested the kind of money and time and training it would take to put an experienced investigator undercover on the off chance that she might stumble on a few shipments of drugs coming into an out-of-the-way port. Reese believed there probably *were* drugs coming in through the harbor, and she intended to have a talk with the harbormaster about it. She also intended to step up the patrols along the wharf, especially at night. But mostly, she planned on watching Carter Wayne.

Reese checked the time. It was the middle of the afternoon, and she was supposed to be at home asleep. Now she was awake and unaccountably restless. She could go to the dojo and train for a while. That always settled her, helped her find her balance. There was only one thing in her life that centered her more.

Minutes later she pulled into the gravel parking lot in front of the East End Health Clinic. At least a dozen cars were parked in front of the low white building, and for a minute, she contemplated backing out and driving away. But she'd been fighting the feeling for weeks that she was running out of time, and all she needed was a minute.

The front door led directly into the waiting room, and it was crowded as it always was, no matter the time. Reese threaded her way between haphazardly placed chairs, the occasional child crawling on the floor, and aluminum walkers. Randy, the handsome blond receptionist, had a phone tucked between his shoulder and ear and was scowling at a computer screen as he typed. Reese took advantage of his attention being elsewhere and sidled around the counter toward the hallway that led back to her lover's office.

When Randy called, "Don't you dare go back there," Reese laughed and kept going. Tory's office was empty, as Reese expected, considering how many patients were in the waiting room. The examining rooms must be full. She went to the large walnut desk that was crowded with file folders, several cups of cold coffee, and a cluster of silver-framed photos on one corner. She smiled at the pictures of Reggie, from newborn right up until the past weekend when they'd taken her out on the ferry for the first time. She looked just like Tory, with red highlights in her golden brown hair and eyes that were blue or green depending on the color of the sky and the water. Reese found a pad and pen and was about to write a note when she heard a sound behind her. She straightened and turned.

Tory stood in the doorway in a white lab coat, blue jeans, and a yellow cotton shirt. She wore sneakers and a light plastic splint on her damaged right ankle. She had a file in one hand and a quizzical smile on her face.

"Sweetheart?" Tory said. "Aren't you supposed to be home asleep?"

"That was my plan before Nelson called me in for an unscheduled meeting. Kate's got the baby."

Tory closed the door and dropped the file folder onto the middle of her desk. Then she leaned her hip against the edge. "But you're done now?"

Reese nodded.

"What are you doing here?"

"I was just…" Reese realized that Tory was in the middle of an incredibly busy day and there was nothing she could tell her that would make any sense. Because all she had were vague feelings and uneasy premonitions, things that were completely beyond her realm of experience. All her life she had been taught to deal with the realities of the moment, to stay focused on the events that she could influence by her actions and reactions. Life was a series of choices, and the wrong ones could mean your life. She didn't deal in *what ifs*, only in what was. Burdening Tory with worries she couldn't even frame in words would be selfish. "I was just going to tell you that Reggie was with Kate."

"You want me to pick her up later?" Tory asked, still confused.

Reese cupped her cheek and kissed her lightly on the lips. "Call me at home when you're done. I'll probably have picked her up already, but if not, we can figure something out then." She hesitated, then kissed Tory again, slowly this time, memorizing her taste. "See you at home." She was almost to the door before Tory called her name.

"Reese?"

Reese turned and looked back.

"Was there something else, sweetheart?"

"No," Reese said softly. "Just wanted an excuse to say hi."

"You never need an excuse. See you later."

"Yeah. Absolutely."

CHAPTER FOUR

Rica slowed her Lexus on the far west end of Bradford Street and turned right onto a narrow private road that twisted up to a wooded crest. She passed several houses partially secluded by trees and dunes before pulling into the driveway behind her new home. Carrying the groceries she'd picked up on the way, she navigated the flagstone walkway in the gathering dusk. There was no sound other than the distant cries of seagulls and the murmur of the waves to-ing and fro-ing over the sand and stones. Balancing the bags on her hip, she unlocked her door and reflected that while true privacy was impossible to attain in a popular resort town where space was limited, she had come close. She'd managed to find a place where, when she sat on the deck outside her living room and looked out over the salt marshes to the bay beyond, she could almost believe she was alone. And that was exactly what she wanted.

She couldn't walk away from her life, even had she wanted to, and it wasn't a matter of how far away she went. Her father and his enterprises were a two-hour drive away, less than a half hour on one of the ten-passenger, two-engine planes that flew regularly from the tiny airport at Race Point. Still, she had managed to extract herself from the gallery in SoHo, and that was a start.

Leaning on the black and gold flecked granite counter in her shiny new kitchen, Rica watched another spectacular sunset through the window, aching with the beauty of it. She recognized the poignant sadness in her heart that echoed the deep blues and purples of the sky as loneliness, but accepted that as the cost of her freedom. Here at least, she was not guarded ever-so-politely by men with guns, not the inadvertent witness to events she did not want to be a part of, and not the object of speculative desire from men and women alike who viewed her as an attractive means to an end. She was not reminded by daily interaction with her father that he regarded her as his heir, whether she sought the position or not.

The phone rang, interrupting her prized solitude, and Rica gave a murmur of displeasure. She hadn't made any acquaintances in town yet, so it had to be the other part of her life exerting its hold on her. For a second, she contemplated not answering, then shook her head and picked up the phone. She'd never known a problem to be solved by ignoring it.

"Hello?"

"Ricarda?" her father said in his deep rumbling baritone. "How is the new house?"

Rica imagined him in his study, a thick cigar held lightly between his long, powerful fingers, a contemplative expression on his hard, dark, handsome face as he watched the smoke swirl and dissipate in the air. "It's fine, Papa. I can see the bay from almost every window. It's beautiful."

"I remember the first time you saw the ocean. You went running right in until the water was over your head. Your mama was screaming and I had to pull you out. You were laughing when I dragged you to the surface."

A deep sigh came through the phone to her.

"You were fearless. Always fearless. Do you remember?"

"I remember, Papa." She'd been two, if that, and the memory was fuzzy, but she remembered sunshine, and warm sand, and the shining blue water stretching forever. Her memories of her mother were less distinct than that of the ocean. She had fleeting images of swirling black hair, warm dark eyes, and gentle hands. It hadn't been long thereafter when her mother had been killed in a car accident on a rainy night on her way home from their summer home in the Berkshires. "You were right, I'm part fish. It feels good to be near the water again."

"There's plenty of water in Boston."

Rica said nothing. They'd had this discussion before. Her father did not understand why, if she wasn't going to live in New York City and run the gallery, she didn't come home. *After all, Ricarda, once you marry, you will be living here anyhow. Why move twice?* When she'd tried to explain to him yet again that she was not interested in marriage, he waved his hand dismissively, as he did with any problem not worthy of his time. *We all think that way when we are young,* cara mia, *but you will change your mind soon enough.*

"And the business?" Alfonse Pareto said after a moment of silence.

"Just getting going," Rica said casually. "It won't be like New York. Something smaller, less formal."

"That may be, but it's an interesting community, this new place of yours. Not so very far away, and there are many people of wealth and influence who pass through." His voice took on a musing quality. "In many ways, the cloak of invisibility is a welcome aspect of your little town."

Rica shivered, although the room was warm. "Nothing goes unnoticed here, Papa. Everyone knows everyone else."

Pareto laughed. "People only see what they are allowed to see, Rica. That is true no matter where you live. Never trust what you see. There's always another story."

"I know."

"I thought I would send Johnny T. over to help—"

"No!" Rica drew a breath and tried to quiet the surge of panic. "I don't need a guard. I haven't needed one since I was sixteen."

"Not to guard you," Pareto said, sounding wounded. "Just to… assist you. Whatever you might need, in the gallery or around the house."

"I'm fine, Papa. Really. Thank you."

"Of course, if that's what you want."

Rica could see him sitting forward in his chair, stubbing out his cigar, the meeting ended. She didn't wait for him to dismiss her.

"I'm sorry, I have to go. Groceries. I just got home."

"We're having the Memorial Day party as usual. Just the family and a few friends. Plan to be here, Rica."

"I will. Goodbye, Papa."

Rica disconnected, smiling ruefully at her own earlier self-delusion. She loved her father, she was who she was, and a large part of her was shaped by the world she had grown up in. She couldn't change the past or deny her heritage. The best she could hope to do was decide her future for herself.

❖

Carter carried an ice-cold bottle of Dos Equis out to the small balcony that extended from her second-floor apartment above the law office. The building stood on a corner a block from the center of town, and if she angled her head just right, she got a pretty good view of the harbor. A few sailboats were moored offshore, swaying indolently on the quiet water as the sun and moon exchanged places. Fractured rays of sunlight slanted across the water, close to being swallowed by the glassy surface, and the indigo blue sky above was edging toward black. A brisk breeze caught her shirt and whipped it around her torso. She sipped her beer and thought about Rica. Or rather, exactly how she was going to get close to her. The don's daughter wasn't the only member of the organization under surveillance, but she was one of the closest people to him. No one was certain how deeply she might be involved in the day-to-day or even the long-range workings of the organization, but it was common knowledge that she was looked upon by Pareto and everyone else in his crime family as the heir. That alone made her a key figure in the investigation. The move to Provincetown had been a surprise and made the job of observing her all that much more difficult. Routine field surveillance was out of the question in a community so small and geographically restricted. Fortunately, if Rica bought Carter's cover story, she would be in a unique position to gain access to Rica in a way that she might not have been able to previously.

All things considered, this unexpected turn of events might be advantageous. Carter smiled. Certainly she'd had less desirable assignments.

Her cell phone rang and she unclipped it from her belt. She recognized the readout, and her smile broadened. "Wayne."

"What are you wearing?"

"Nothing. I'm lying on my bed, imagining you starting at my toes and licking—"

"Stop!"

Laughing, Carter drained the bottle of beer and set it on the wooden deck by her foot, picturing the voluptuous redhead on the other end with a pleasant stirring in the pit of her stomach. She hadn't had sex in almost a month, and she was edgy because of it. When she was this involved in an investigation, she couldn't spare the time to meet someone, even casually. That's why it was nice to have a woman in her life who understood her priorities. Susan Price worked in the DA's office, so she appreciated the unpredictability and demands of the job. And fortunately, she wasn't interested in anything more serious than good friendship and excellent sex. "So when did you get back?"

"Just a few hours ago," Susan said. "And before you ask, Aruba was gorgeous, and I highly recommend it. It's everything they said—white sandy beaches, tall cool drinks, and the women...God, the women."

"Did you get any sleep at all?"

"Carter, sweetheart, you don't go on vacation to sleep."

"Well, you obviously enjoyed your vacation more than I did."

"Miss me?" Susan asked with a teasing lilt.

"More and more every day."

"Once in a while it's fun to explore new territory, but there's something to be said for the familiarity of home."

"Are you trying to say I'm predictable and boring?" Carter asked, feigning indignation.

"Mmm, no. I'm trying to say you still make me come better than almost any woman I've ever met."

Carter sucked in a breath, the image of Susan's fingers digging into her shoulders as she cried out in pleasure making her instantly aroused. "Jesus. It isn't fair to tease me after you've left me high and dry for weeks."

"Aww, poor baby. No one else around to ease your suffering?"

"No one and no time."

"Where are you? Maybe I can remedy this regretful situation."

"Out of town."

Susan murmured sympathetically, "Working?"

"Uh-huh."

"Long-time thing?"

"Could be," Carter said, turning to rest her back against the railing. She contemplated another beer, but the evening was so beautiful and her apartment so barren that she didn't want to go back inside, even for another drink.

"There's phone sex," Susan suggested.

Carter laughed. "Make sure you have your cell phone at all times. I might take you up on it."

"Any time, sweetheart." Susan sighed. "I should go. I need to unpack and think about getting my head into working again."

"Okay. If I can, I'll try to drop in one of these nights."

"Do that. I've missed you. And Carter?"

"Hmm?"

"Be careful, wherever you are."

"Always. Night, Susie."

When Susan hung up, Carter felt an instant pang of loneliness. She wasn't entirely certain why, because she and Susan had never been in love. She stepped inside the sparsely furnished living room and closed the sliding glass doors behind her. She went to the refrigerator in the adjoining kitchen, pulled out another beer, and swiveled off the top. While she tilted the bottle to her lips and let the sharp, cold liquid stream down her throat, she contemplated her next meeting with Ricarda. She was looking forward to it, and in all honesty, she had to admit that the anticipation wasn't completely due to professional reasons. Rica was a beautiful, intelligent, intriguing woman. It had been a long time since she'd met a woman with just the right combination of brains and charisma to interest her. And, unfortunately, Rica had it all.

When the phone rang, Reese lunged for it, thinking it was Tory. She flipped it open with one hand while simultaneously scooping Reggie off the floor and under her arm with the other.

"Thought I'd better catch you before you rumbled right outside and off the deck," Reese muttered to Reggie as she crossed the living room to close the sliding glass doors. "Hello? Tor?"

Reggie tugged at the buttons on Reese's shirt, valiantly trying to liberate them.

"Hello?" Reese repeated.

She stiffened at the first sound of the familiar voice. Unconsciously she tightened her arm around Reggie's middle, making the child squirm and protest. Instantly, she relaxed her grip and settled Reggie more securely against her chest. "Yes, sir. Go ahead, please."

She listened for a full five minutes and asked no questions. Instead of closing the doors to the deck, she walked outside, the phone that linked her to one world against her ear, and her daughter, who anchored her in another, against her heart. Reggie, as if she understood the gravity of the moment, rested her head against Reese's shoulder and went to sleep.

"I understand. Yes, sir." Reese took a deep breath and did something she had never done before in her life. She asked a favor of the general, because he was her father. "If I could have twenty-four hours, sir."

The silence was the longest of her life.

"Thank you, General."

She closed the phone and slid it into her pants pocket, then folded both arms around Reggie, whose small body was warm and soft. She stood at the rail and watched moonlight play over the surface of the water, her cheek resting against the top of Reggie's head. Everywhere she looked was beauty. Her heart was full of precious wonder at the child in her arms and the woman who had brought love and meaning into her life. Tory, Reggie, and the life they shared among family and friends were the miracles she would carry with her wherever she went. They were her greatest strength, and she knew because of them, she could do what she needed to do.

The wind blew in, crisp and sharp off the water, and ruffled the baby's hair. Reese cupped Reggie's face in the palm of her hand to shield her from the night air and went inside. She slid the phone from her pocket and opened it one-handed. The first number on the speed dial was Tory at the clinic. She pressed two.

After a moment, she said, "Mom, I need a favor."

Chapter Five

Tory closed the door behind her and scanned the living room, trying to sense what was different. It was just past nine p.m., but the house seemed very still. The only light came from a single lamp turned down low on the far side of the room. The glass doors leading to the deck were open, and the smell of the sea filled the air.

"Reese?"

Tory dropped her keys and wallet on a small table by the door and started toward the stairs that led to the second floor and their bedroom. Just as she did, Reese came in from the deck.

"Hey," Tory said. "It's so quiet, I thought you'd all gone to bed."

Reese put her arms around Tory and pulled her near, burying her face in Tory's thick, silky hair. "Not without you." She kissed Tory's neck. "What would be the point?"

"God, you feel good," Tory murmured. She curved her arms around Reese's shoulders and relaxed against her body. Her planned six-hour shift had turned into nine, and she was dead tired. Her leg ached, as it often did after she'd been standing for an extended period, and her back felt as if she'd been lifting fifty-pound boxes all day. What she wanted was to soak in a hot tub, curl up next to Reese, and fall asleep. "Is the baby asleep already?"

"She's with Kate and Jean."

"Really?" Tory laughed. "They don't get enough of her, babysitting almost every day?"

"I asked them to keep her." Reese moved her hand to the back of Tory's neck and worked her fingers into the tight muscles on either side of her spine. "I've got an open bottle of Merlot out on the deck and some nibbles if you're hungry."

"You do, huh?" Tory ran her hands up and down Reese's back. "One lounge chair or two?"

"One." Slipping her fingers higher into Tory's hair, Reese massaged her scalp. "And a blanket."

"Oh, it's that way, is it?" Leaning back, Tory kissed the tip of Reese's chin. "You do realize we both have to work in the morning?"

"I won't keep you up too late."

"Don't make promises you might not be able to keep." Tory kissed Reese, savoring the way Reese smelled—warm sunshine, salty ocean spray, and Reggie—all the things Tory loved. Reese's body was firm beneath her hands, a sculpted landscape of strength and certainty. As she took the kiss deeper, skimming her tongue into the smooth, warm recesses of Reese's mouth, she heard Reese moan softly and felt her tremble. "Are you all right, sweetheart?"

"Perfect," Reese whispered. "You're here."

"Where else would I be?" Tory placed her hand over Reese's heart. It beat wildly beneath her fingers. "This is my home."

Reese turned her face away and pressed her cheek to Tory's hair, not wanting her to see the tears that came quickly and unbidden. Hoarsely, she said, "How about some of that wine?"

"I can see that you've got plans. So why don't you just lead the way."

"Remember you said that." Reese grasped Tory's hand and guided her out onto the deck. She settled into a lounge chair and drew Tory down so that she rested with her back against Reese's chest, nestled between her outstretched legs. With one arm curved around Tory's waist, she leaned sideways and filled two glasses from the bottle of Merlot she had left open on a small table. "Here you go."

Tory sipped the smooth, dry wine, sampled the crackers and cheese Reese had assembled, and watched the moon flit in and out of the clouds. It was heaven. She sighed, content.

"Cold?" Reese asked.

"No, not with your arms around me."

"You know what I think about, every time I lie out here with you like this?"

"No, what?" Tory shifted so she could lean her head back and see Reese's face. In the moonlight, her dark hair and bold profile were edged in silver, like an image on an ancient coin. Tory felt a surge of arousal and smiled inwardly, pleased that time and the common joys of daily life had not diminished her desire.

Feeling Tory's gaze upon her face, Reese met her eyes. "Of the night we made love out here and afterward, you told me you wanted to have a baby."

Tory smiled softly. "I remember. And I remember you telling me that you wanted it, too. That it would make you happy. I don't know why I ever thought you wouldn't understand." Tory kissed her gently. "You always have."

"The only thing in my life that's made me happier than having Reggie was finding you."

"Reese?"

"What?" Reese whispered, reaching out without looking to find the table and setting down her wineglass. Before Tory could respond, Reese turned sideways so they were facing each other and tugged Tory's blouse from her jeans. She smoothed her palm over Tory's belly, her fingers tracing the sweep of her ribs. "What?"

Tory arched into her touch and closed her eyes. "I...is..."

Reese released the clasp on Tory's bra and danced her fingertips over the full curve and tight, round nipple. "What?"

"Nothing. I can't remember. Can't think when you touch me like that."

"Good, don't think. Feel me." Reese lowered her head as she pushed Tory's blouse higher and circled Tory's nipple with her tongue. It hardened at the caress, and she sucked it in, scraping the edges carefully with her teeth before soothing the tingling spots with her lips. She was aware of Tory fumbling with her belt and she lifted her hips, giving her room to release it. "Don't distract me."

Tory laughed and held Reese's head more tightly to her breast. "No chance. You started it. Now you have to finish."

Reese bit down and Tory cried out. The sound made Reese's mind swirl, pulsing red with the rush of hot blood and thick lust through her limbs. She moved from one breast to the other, licking, sucking, biting, while she unbuttoned Tory's blouse, pausing only long enough to strip off the offending garment. She leaned away and absorbed the sight of Tory, her head thrown back, her breasts—heavier now after Reggie—

flushed and swollen with desire. Tory's chest rose and fell rapidly as her lips parted with the silent pleas only a lover could hear. *Touch me, take me, claim what is yours.*

"I love you," Reese murmured.

Tory opened her eyes, her vision hazy, her body ripe and ready. "No one else ever has—not like you. Never wi—" She jerked and lost her breath as Reese cupped a hand between her legs. "Oh!"

Reese shifted until she was kneeling on the deck by Tory's side. "I always will." She opened Tory's jeans. Slid the zipper down. "You're the only one I've ever wanted." She curled her fingers around the waistband, waiting for Tory to rise up so she could ease them over her hips and down her legs. "All I've ever needed."

"Reese," Tory whispered. Reese's face was in shadow, her body curved over Tory's like the blade of a knife, hypnotically dangerous. "Sweetheart, what—"

"I live for you, for this." Reese leaned down, kissed the curve of Tory's thigh where it blended into the soft folds of her sex. "And Reggie." She brushed her fingertips through silky wetness and Tory whimpered. "Our life."

Reese cupped Tory's buttocks and guided her down the chaise, opening her thighs with gentle insistence. "You see the stars up there?"

Tory's hand trembled in Reese's hair as Reese lowered her head and kissed between her legs again. It was so hard to think.

"Yes."

Tory's voice was high and thin, tremulous with need.

"When I see them"—Reese caught the crystal droplets of Tory's passion on the tip of her tongue—"I think of you." She eased her fingers along the path her tongue had taken, sliding smoothly inside. "Of the beauty and peace you bring into my heart."

Tory braced her arms on the sides of the lounge and pushed up so she could watch Reese make love to her. She strained against Reese's hand, taking her deeper than she ever had. "Go inside me more. Fill me up." Her head fell back as Reese pushed slowly forward. Her arms shook and her voice broke on a sob. "Oh God."

"More?"

"Yes. Yes."

Sweat drenched Reese's back and her stomach tensed as she fought back her own aching need. She focused every ounce of concentration on Tory's breathing, Tory's body, Tory's small sounds of pleasure. She pushed, Tory opened, and she pushed higher. "Oh Jesus, Tor, you're so hot inside. You feel so amazing."

Tory wrapped her arms around Reese's shoulders and pressed her face to Reese's neck. Panting, she gasped, "I want you all the way inside. Keep going. Oh, more."

"Sure?"

"Uh-huh. Uh-huh."

Reese slowed, waiting for the tense tissues to relax. "All right?"

"Good," Tory groaned. "So good." She took a long breath and willed her body to soften even as the pressure spiraled in her depths. "Do it. Let me feel you make me come."

Reese supported Tory with an arm around her waist and steadily, carefully, relentlessly worked her hand within the slick, hot muscles. "Hold on to me," she whispered. "Hold on, baby."

Tory closed her eyes and gave herself over to Reese's embrace, her legs around Reese's hips as Reese rocked her arm between her thighs. Every thrust drove her a little bit closer to the edge, but she held back, wanting the sensation to go on forever. Wanting Reese so far inside of her that nothing could ever come between them. They were one, and nothing had ever felt so right.

Reese felt it, the first spasm, before Tory jerked in her arms and cried out, "I'm coming."

Reese covered Tory's mouth with hers, drinking her passion, swallowing her cries of pleasure as she curled her fingers forward and pressed the spot that always made Tory explode. She wasn't prepared for the force of Tory's orgasm and cried out in surprise as Tory stiffened in her arms, clamping down around her hand and dragging her to the brink of coming.

"Oh Tory," Reese moaned. "You're so beautiful."

Tory couldn't speak, she could barely breathe. She'd never come this way before, with Reese inside every cell of her body, every molecule of her consciousness. She hadn't thought they could be any closer. but somehow they were. She pulled her hips back and then pushed down hard on Reese's hand, and came again.

"Oh my God," Tory gasped when she caught her breath. She laughed weakly. "What did you do?"

"Me?" Reese flung her head back, spraying sweat into the air like tears. "Me?" She slowly inched her fingers from within Tory's body.

"Jesus Christ—you said more." She kissed Tory hard, a possessive, hungry kiss.

"True." Tory stroked Reese's face, then began to unbutton her shirt. "More is never enough." She pushed the material aside and kissed Reese's chest, then slipped her hand inside to caress her breast. "But that was damn close."

Reese shivered.

"Cold?"

"No."

"You didn't come then, did you?" Tory kissed Reese's throat and toyed with her nipple. "I can usually tell but I was so...so gone, I couldn't tell up from down."

"I'm okay. It was amazing."

Tory sucked on Reese's lip, then bit it gently. "Okay? *Okay?* Oh, that is just not good enough." She pushed against Reese's chest. "Help me stand up. I'm not sure I can walk."

"What—"

"I want to make love to you. Inside. On a bed."

"Oh. Well." Reese stood and guided Tory up into her arms. She pulled a blanket from the neighboring chaise and draped it around Tory's shoulders. "I'll carry the wine."

"Tory, Tory. stop," Reese groaned. She tried to roll onto her side, but Tory held her firmly in place. "I'm done, baby."

"That's what you said the last time. And the time before that." With a smug smile, Tory caught Reese's clitoris between her teeth and tugged gently. When it hardened instantly, she sucked slowly.

Reese's hips jerked and she tightened her fist in Tory's hair, pulling her more tightly to her center. She couldn't tell where she ended and Tory began, where her heartbeat stopped and Tory's took over. She only knew she wanted, *needed*, never to leave this place. This sanctuary she had found, this bright shining focus of all that mattered in her life. "Tory," she breathed as she slipped into orgasm, surrendering with total trust.

Tory felt the change in her breathing first, beneath her hand where it lay between Reese's breasts. There was a subtle shift in the cadence, signaling not pleasure, but pain. She lifted her eyes to Reese's face and gasped when she saw tears. Reese so very rarely cried.

"Sweetheart," Tory exclaimed, crawling quickly up the bed and gathering Reese into her arms. She kissed her forehead, her eyelids, her mouth. "What is it? What is it?"

"Nothing." Reese managed to keep her voice steady though her throat threatened to close around more tears. "Just love you. So much."

Tory pulled a sheet over them and pillowed Reese's head against her breast. "I love you too. With all my heart."

Reese closed her eyes, waiting for sleep to come. She wanted these moments, these impossibly perfect moments when they were as close as they could ever be, to remain untarnished by what was to come. No matter where she was, she would never be far from this moment when Tory filled her heart and her body. Filled her until there was no room for fear or sadness.

Tory awakened from a sound sleep with the sense that something was terribly wrong. She sat up quickly and felt for Reese beside her. The bed was empty. She threw back the covers, pulled her robe from the back of the bedroom door, and put it on as she hurried down the hallway toward the stairs. She stopped when she realized a light was burning in Reggie's room. She pushed the door open and looked in to see Reese, dressed in jeans and a T-shirt and sitting alone in the rocking chair they used to coax Reggie back to sleep in the middle of the night.

"It's time for you to tell me what's wrong," Tory said gently. She wrapped her arms around herself, beneath her breasts, as if that could keep the bitter chill from stealing into her heart. She leaned against the door and watched an agony of emotion play across Reese's handsome face. "Now. I can't stand waiting, knowing you're hurting so much."

Reese looked into Tory's eyes, hers filled with apology. "My father called tonight."

Tory's grip tightened on the material of her robe until her fingers were white.

"My unit has been activated. I'm sorry, baby. I have to go."

"When?" Tory whispered.

Reese glanced at her watch. It was 4 a.m. Friday morning. She should have been on her way.

"This time tomorrow."

Twenty-four hours. Tory blinked, fighting the dizziness that threatened to take her to her knees. "Oh my God."

"I'm so sorry, Tor," Reese murmured. "I—"

Tory held up her hand. "Hush. Come back to bed."

Wordlessly Reese rose and took Tory's hand, following her back to the bedroom. She stood by the side of the bed as Tory sat on the edge and unsnapped her jeans. She lifted her T-shirt over her head while Tory skimmed her pants down to the floor. When she was naked, she slid beneath the sheets and opened her arms to Tory. She held Tory, and Tory held her, arms and legs entwined.

"Thank you for tonight," Tory whispered. "For loving me that way. Thank you for knowing I'd need it."

"I needed it too."

Tory kissed Reese's throat, then the corner of her mouth, then her lips. Tenderly, with infinite care. "I know. But somehow, when *you* need, you give. I've never known anyone so unselfish."

Reese laughed bitterly. "I'm leaving you and the baby. And you can still say that?"

Tory leaned away, her eyes dark with sorrow as she searched Reese's face. "There are so many things I love about you. Your honesty, your bravery. Your tenderness. Maybe most of all, I love that I can always trust you to keep your promises." She pressed her fingers to Reese's mouth when Reese would have protested. Gently. Every touch was precious and she wanted each one to stay in her memory forever. "We've talked about this before, and we both knew what you would do if this happened. You made promises a long time ago, before you made them to us."

"If I'd known—"

"Maybe it would have been different. Maybe." Tory drew a shaky breath. It felt like she was breathing crushed glass. Everything inside of her was ripping apart. "But you made a pledge, gave your word. I knew who you were when I fell in love with you."

"You didn't bargain on this," Reese pointed out. She'd do anything in her power to keep Tory and Reggie from being hurt. Do anything, *give* anything, including her life. And now she was causing Tory pain, and knowing that was torture.

"Reese, my darling," Tory said quietly, cleaving to Reese along every inch of their bodies, "every day when you leave this house to go to work, I know the risk. I know what I might lose. I knew that when I watched you put yourself between that man trapped out on the jetty and hundreds of pounds of rock. And when you were shot saving a fellow officer—God, when you almost died saving *me*. I knew and I chose loving you because *nothing* in my life has ever been as good as being with you."

"I love you so much, Tor." Reese framed Tory's face and kissed her, first softly, just a hint of heat skirting over her lips, then a stroke of her tongue, then the weight of her mouth, claiming her. Tory's arms came around her, and they reached inside one another until they were breathless. Reese rolled onto her back and drew Tory against her chest. She stroked Tory's hair, listened to Tory's soft breathing, and felt their hearts beating close together. "I was going to tell you in the morning."

"I know." Tory smoothed her hand over Reese's chest and down her abdomen, drawing one leg up over Reese's thighs to keep them connected. "You didn't want me to be sad when we were making love."

"No."

"Were *you*?"

"Just a little. Once or twice." Reese stroked Tory's back, circling her fingers along her spine and into the hollow above her hips. Her body was warm, soft and pliant, with strength and resiliency below the surface. Just like Tory herself. "When I'm making love with you there's nothing in my mind except you. Tonight...I just needed to have you, all of you..." Her voice trailed off and she swallowed. "To take with me."

Tory pushed up on her elbow and looked into Reese's eyes. "You are never going anywhere without me." She kissed Reese's chest where a pulse beat steadily. "Here. In your heart. No matter where you are, no matter what you're doing, I'll be here. Right here. Because I will love you through anything, no matter what."

"I'm counting on it," Reese said hoarsely.

"Good," Tory said. "You can." She kissed her again, then settled back against Reese's shoulder, one arm around her chest. She held her close. "Now close your eyes. You need some sleep."

Reese was certain she couldn't sleep, didn't want to spend a moment unaware when she could be with Tory or Reggie. But as the heat of Tory's body, and the soft caress of her hands, and the gentle cadence of her breathing permeated her consciousness, she drifted off.

Tory felt Reese slip into sleep. She wouldn't cry, not just for fear of waking her, but for fear of hurting her. She would keep her own anger and sorrow and terror buried, and she would let Reese go believing that she was not dying inside. That would be her gift.

CHAPTER SIX

Carter lay awake, eyes tightly closed against the brilliant sunshine that insisted on brightening her bedroom, and tried to place the unfamiliar sounds. After a second she sorted it out—seagulls and the distant low of the foghorn off Long Point. She'd slept with the windows open and the air was chilly, but she didn't mind. The brisk breeze might help chase away the cobwebs left over from one too many beers the night before. She rarely drank more than two these days, but somehow the number had morphed to four when she hadn't been looking.

She opened her eyes, wondering just what caused the gritty sandpapery sensation when she blinked. Which she did, several times, as her mind drifted back to the previous night. She could blame the beer on not enough to do. Inactivity always made her edgy. She'd taken to undercover work immediately because the adrenaline rush that came from the danger of living or dying by her wits kept her mind occupied and her body satisfied, just like good sex. She grimaced, aware that if she wasn't in the field, involved in some action, she didn't have much else in her life *except* sex. And she was running on empty there.

But this time, the case was preying on her mind, and that was odd. It wasn't the potential danger that concerned her—she'd been in situations before where, if her true identity had become known, she'd have been a target for extermination. No, it wasn't the case itself, it was the subject. The woman. Reluctantly she admitted that her brief and unplanned encounter with Rica had been unsettling. In those few moments when Rica hadn't known she was being observed, she had revealed a hint of weariness and vulnerability that was never obvious in her public persona. Quite unexpectedly, Carter had seen a woman, not a mobster's daughter, and the image lingered even weeks later.

"So what?" Carter muttered, throwing off the sheet and rising rapidly despite the protest pounding in her head. "She's still the target. *Just* the target."

After a shower dispelled the last of her fuzziness, she dug an old pair of gray chinos out of her suitcase, pulled on a washed-out Red Sox T-shirt, and headed out into the disgustingly gorgeous spring morning. At 7:30 a.m., the streets were still fairly empty. A rollerblader passed her heading west down Commercial Street at literally breakneck speed, the usual bevy of workmen in pickup trucks were clustered around the Coffee Pot Café on MacMillan Wharf, and a few preseason tourists ambled along, peering into the still-closed shop windows.

Carter turned east on Commercial without any conscious plan, until, fifteen minutes later, she was leaning against the corner of a building opposite Rica's new art gallery. To her surprise, she detected shadowy movement through the large plate glass window. She checked the cars parked up the street and saw Rica's Lexus.

"You're working early," Carter mused, grateful there weren't many people around to see her talking to herself. She hadn't yet worked out exactly how she was going to reintroduce herself to her target after the premature meeting at Alfonse Pareto's birthday celebration. No matter how she devised it, Rica was likely to be suspicious. "Well, there's no time like the present."

Not one to dwell on a decision made, Carter retraced her steps until she reached the Wired Puppy, one of the specialty coffeehouses in town. She ordered two double espressos and scones. Five minutes later, she tapped on the door of Beaux Arts. At first, she thought her knock would go unanswered, but thirty seconds later Rica came into view. The don's daughter stopped just on the opposite side of the closed door and frowned at Carter through the glass. Then she shook her head and tapped her watch, as if suggesting that Carter come back later.

Carter held the cardboard carrier containing the coffee and pastries aloft and mouthed the words, "Breakfast."

"You just happened to be in the neighborhood?" Rica said when she opened the door, holding it ajar with her arm and blocking the entrance to the main gallery.

"Actually, yes. Are you ready for your second espresso?"

"What makes you think I've had a first?"

"The sign on your door says the gallery opens at eleven, but it's not even eight o'clock." Carter shrugged. "So you're working at the crack of dawn, and who does that without coffee?"

Rica narrowed her eyes, taking in Carter's casual clothes and just-showered look. Obviously, she was staying in town. And just as obviously, she hadn't stumbled on Rica by accident. "Well, I suppose you're a better choice than Johnny T."

Carter, through years of practice, hid her surprise despite the spurt of adrenaline that coursed through her. Johnny T. was one of Alfonse Pareto's musclemen. The fact that Rica referred to him so casually in Carter's presence was a first step toward trusting her. She made a decision. In her undercover persona as a friend of the "family," she would be expected to know Johnny T.

"I'm glad you think so. Johnny's a nice guy, but he lacks for a bit of polish."

"I don't need you here. I told my father that."

Carter tried to decode that information while hoping she looked as if she knew what Rica was talking about. Obviously Rica was not pleased to see her and assumed that she was performing some duty for Rica's father. She couldn't imagine— *Oh, Christ. She thinks I've been sent here to check up on her. A female version of Johnny T. That's not likely to get me into her good graces.*

There were times when the truth was the best approach.

"I'm not working for your father."

"And I'm supposed to believe that you would tell me if you were?"

"Look, Ms. Pareto—"

"Grechi. It's Grechi here."

"Ms. *Grechi*," Carter said, extending the package in her hands. "Can we talk about this inside over coffee and scones?"

Rica wanted to say no. She hated being manipulated by her father, and the fact that he had sent an attractive woman when she had turned down his offer of Johnny T. infuriated her. As if a woman bodyguard, or spy, or whatever function Carter might be performing would be more acceptable just because Rica might find her attractive. Her father steadfastly refused to acknowledge her lesbianism, until it suited him. Then, when he thought it might get him what he wanted, he tried to use it to his advantage. So what if Carter Wayne was a charming, gorgeous woman—that was supposed to make her accept being spied on?

"I'm sorry. I really am quite busy. Now, if you'll excuse me." Rica swung the door closed.

Carter could have blocked the door with her knee or shoulder, but she knew that would only prove to Rica exactly what she already suspected—that Carter was there to strong-arm her into doing something she didn't want. So instead, she said quickly as the door closed in her face, "He didn't send me. I swear."

Through the glass, Rica studied Carter's face. Her eyes were intense, unwavering. Surprisingly, they were completely unguarded, and Rica almost believed she saw truth in them. Even though she knew better, she found herself opening the door. "My first cup of coffee *wasn't* espresso, and it was three hours ago. Come inside."

"Thanks."

Carter followed Rica through the surprisingly spacious and impressively well-stocked main gallery to a small office in the rear. That room opened through a set of sliding glass doors onto a ground deck that sat right on the beach. Rica guided her to a small, round gray granite-topped table and matching sling back chairs.

"Whoa," Carter exclaimed as she sat down. "How did you manage to score this place?"

Rica removed the top from her espresso and sipped it appreciatively. "Good timing."

Carter handed her a scone. "I thought I got lucky getting a single on Bradford."

"You bought a house?" Rica said with surprise.

"Office-apartment combination," Carter replied. She bit into the scone and brushed crumbs from her pants. "Nothing to compare to this, though."

Carter was serious. Fifty feet away the water shimmered, a perfect mirror for the perfect clouds in the perfect blue sky. The vista was so beautiful it hurt to look at it, and she was finally awake enough to appreciate it. What made the picture memorable, though, was the sunlight glinting on the loose, midnight black waves framing Rica's face. When the wind caught them and whipped them about her cheeks and neck, Carter had the sudden image of Rica in the throes of passion, her head flung back—

"What kind of an office?"

"Law." Carter forced herself to focus.

"Oh, I remember now," Rica said. "You're an attorney."

"That's right."

"And what is a high-powered Boston attorney doing in a quiet little place like this?"

Carter laughed. "And what is a high-powered New York City art gallery owner doing in a quiet little place like this?"

Rica smiled. "I asked you first."

Carter had never seen a spontaneous smile from her before, and it nearly stopped her heart. It had always been obvious that Rica was a classically beautiful woman, but she'd never appreciated the sensuous fullness of her mouth or the deep allure of her dark eyes before this moment.

"Are you going to answer the question?"

Carter gave a start and shook her head. "Sorry. Late night. I bought the building some months ago, thinking I'd spend part of the summer over here. I'm just now getting everything set up."

"Somehow you don't seem the type to summer in this kind of place."

"Really? Why is that?"

"Come now," Rica said scornfully. "A woman who spends her time with powerful men, dealing with them on their terms, and winning, I'd wager." She lifted her hands as if to say that was answer enough.

"What you see isn't always the whole story," Carter said, skirting dangerously close to the truth. For some reason, she didn't want Rica to casually dismiss her as just another player in an unsavory game. Even though that's exactly who she needed Rica to believe her to be.

Rica stared, momentarily unnerved by the echo of her father's words of the night before. She couldn't help but think that they were having an entirely different conversation than the one their words would suggest, but she couldn't quite understand it. She also couldn't explain to herself why she didn't want Carter Wayne to be who she knew her to be. Another handsome, charming liar. She stood abruptly.

"I'm sorry. I have a great deal of work to do."

Carter rose as well and collected the trash, rolling up the bag and holding it in her fist. "I imagine you do. You have some beautiful pieces on display already."

"Thank you."

"Would you like to join me for dinner this evening?"

"You have quite a different approach than Johnny T., too," Rica said, turning to walk back inside.

Carter followed. "I thought we already got that settled?"

"No," Rica said, sitting down behind her desk. "You only said you weren't sent here by my father. I didn't say I believed you."

"Come to dinner, then, and let me convince you."

Smiling despite herself, Rica shook her head once more.

"I'm sorry. I don't have time for games. I came here to start a business, and that's about all that I have time for." She lifted a thick sheaf of papers. "Thank you for the coffee."

"You're welcome."

Without another word, Carter turned and left the gallery. She'd been dismissed, and she sensed that any further attempt on her part to prolong the meeting would only alienate Rica completely. Not only was it necessary to the investigation for her to foster her association with Rica, but an amicable relationship was something she very much wanted. If for no other reason than to see Rica Grechi smile that astonishingly beautiful smile again.

CHAPTER SEVEN

Bri Parker leaned across her girlfriend's naked body and grabbed the portable phone. Caroline gave a mild mewl of protest and burrowed more deeply into Bri's side, wrapping an arm and leg securely around Bri's body.

"'Lo," Bri croaked. She curved an arm beneath Caroline's shoulder and stroked her back, squinting against the sunlight that streaked through the skylight above their heads. The sliding glass doors at the far end of the second-floor loft apartment were open, and the morning sounds and scent of the sea wafted in. It was just about a year since she'd decided to leave college and return to her hometown to follow in her father's footsteps in the sheriff's department. And not just her father's footsteps, but Reese Conlon's. She'd known Reese since she was seventeen. In those nearly four years, Reese had become her mentor, her role model, her friend. Reese was everything she'd ever wanted to be. Bri tightened her hold on her girlfriend as she listened to the request.

"Oh, man. This morning? I worked the late shift."

"What?" Caroline mumbled. "Tell them no."

Bri laughed. "No, sir. I didn't say a word. I'll be there in under an hour. Yes, sir." She dropped the phone onto the floor beside the bed. "I gotta go in, babe."

Caroline groaned and scooted on top of Bri. She propped her head in her hand and regarded Bri with a combination of annoyance and invitation. "I've only been back in town a week, and I don't think we've had a chance to get properly reacquainted." To emphasize her point, she insinuated her thigh between Bri's and pushed down against her crotch. Then she rolled her hips and made a low humming sound of pleasure.

"Oh, hey, babe," Bri protested weakly. "You know I don't want to." She arched her back as Caroline hit a particularly sensitive spot. "I mean, I want to. With you. Work. I was talking about work. Oh, Jesus, Carre. Mercy."

"You know, all the time I was in Paris," Caroline said, leaning down to kiss Bri, "I was sort of afraid you would fall out of love with me or not want me so much anymore when I came back. Eight months is a long time."

"Tell me about it," Bri murmured, catching Caroline's small, firm breasts in her hands as they swayed above her and fanning her fingers over the smooth flesh. When Caroline's nipples knotted against her palms, her clit tightened and she got wet. "I thought I was going to explode a million times before you got back." She squeezed and flicked Caroline's nipples with her thumbnails, making Caroline whimper. "I want you more than I ever did, not less."

"Oh that's good," Caroline said, breathless. "That you do. What you're doing. Don't stop, baby."

Bri replaced her fingers with her mouth and sucked on Caroline's breasts, hard enough to make Caroline writhe and dig her fingers into Bri's shoulders.

"Work or not, you're gonna have to make me come," Caroline warned, her eyes partway closed, her stomach quivering. "You're getting me too excited not to."

Wordlessly, Bri pumped her hips and flipped Caroline onto her back, following her over to resume her attentions to Caroline's nipples. Even as she bit and sucked them, she slid her hand up the inside of Caroline's thigh. When she cupped Caroline's sex, Caroline covered her hand and pushed her fingers inside.

"Just fuck me. Fuck me hard."

Bri groaned and closed her eyes tightly, locking out everything except the sensation of Caroline, inside and out. The heat of her skin, the pounding of her heart, the small cries of pleasure, the slick grip of muscles closing around her fingers. They fit together perfectly, heart to heart, body to body. They always had, since they were kids. Bri knew her—what made her cry, what made her happy, what made her come— and every time they were together like this it was as if she'd never experienced her before. She took her hard, the way Caroline wanted, the way she liked it, and felt Caroline's orgasm flood her hand.

"Oh yeah," Bri whispered. "Just like that, babe."

Caroline twisted her fingers into Bri's short black hair and pulled her head up so she could bite down on Bri's neck as she climaxed, her whole body stiffening with one electrifying jolt after another. She moaned and shivered and finally laughed.

"I don't know how you always make me do that so fast," Caroline gasped.

"'Cause," Bri said with a grin, brushing her thumb over Caroline's clitoris and making her twitch, "I'm the world's best lover."

"Mmm, yeah, true," Caroline said lazily, smoothing her fingers over the mark she'd left on Bri's neck, then gently tracing the scar next to it. "Lucky me."

Bri relaxed against Caroline's body, enjoying the way Caroline's face always got all soft and dreamy right after she came. She loved being able to do that. Knowing that she was the cause of that look. That happiness. "Lucky me too." She sighed. "I gotta go to work, babe."

Caroline blinked to clear the fog of pleasure from her brain. "You really do?"

"Uh-huh."

"Then we'd better hurry if we're going to take care of you," Caroline said, scraping her nails down the center of Bri's back until she reached her butt. She squeezed Bri's ass, planted her foot on the bed, and wedged her knee between Bri's legs. "You ready to go for a ride?"

Bri sucked in her breath, clenched her jaws, and eased her hips away from Caroline's leg. "I can't. I really *really* gotta get a shower and go."

"Oh, hey," Caroline crooned, feathering Bri's hair with her fingers. "You gonna be okay?"

Shaking her head, Bri rolled off her and sat on the edge of the bed. "No. I'm going to walk around with a stiffie all day." She looked over her shoulder at Caroline and grinned. "But I'm gonna like thinking about you taking care of it later."

"You do that." Caroline stroked Bri's thigh. "Because I'm going to, the minute you walk in the door."

As Bri searched through the closet for a clean shirt and uniform trousers, Caroline asked from the bed, "How come you got called in?"

"They need me to take Reese's shift."

"Reese? Why?" Caroline threw the covers aside and got up. She pulled on sweats and a T-shirt of Bri's from a nearby chair. "Reese is never sick. What's going on?"

"I don't know." Bri pushed down the quick surge of anxiety. "My dad just said for me to come in."

"Call me, okay? Something's not right."

"Yeah," Bri muttered. "I know."

Reese tucked her wallet into the back pocket of her jeans, slid her badge into the front, and clipped her holster to her waistband. Then she turned to face Tory, who sat at the breakfast bar in loose cotton pants and an old, stretched-out sweater that dipped low in the front and made her look impossibly sexy. "I'll be back just as soon as I can."

"I'll go by the clinic and talk to Randy about rearranging my schedule," Tory said. "I should be back here in an hour, and then we can pick up Reggie from Kate and Jean's."

"I wish you didn't need to cancel patients," Reese said. She crossed the room, put her arms around Tory, and kissed her softly. "I can pick up the baby myself, and you can work for a few hours."

Tory shook her head. "I never take a day off. We rarely leave town for more than a week on vacation, and"—she laughed unsteadily—"I'd say this is an emergency."

"Tor," Reese whispered, pulling her close and rocking her. "I hate for you to be hurting."

"I'm all right. I just don't want to waste any of today. Go talk to Nelson, and then come home."

"I'll be quick."

Tory kissed her and gave her a gentle shove. "Go ahead now. I'll see you in a little while."

Reese stepped away but waited to leave until Tory disappeared upstairs. She could tell by the ever-darkening shadows in Tory's deep green eyes and the way her smile flickered shakily how hard she was trying to keep her worry and sadness a secret. Reese hated knowing she had put the pain there, and was at a loss as to how to fix it. That was the worst part. The helplessness.

For most of her life she'd been a career Marine, and an order had been just an order, a duty to be performed. She did not consider the consequences to herself because she had accepted whatever might result when she'd taken an oath to uphold the honor of the Corps and to serve her country. It had been simple and clear. Now, for the first time in her life, her duty was at odds with her responsibility. Tory's willingness to accept the hardship of their separation was all that allowed her to leave at all. Even so, she felt pulled in two directions, and something inside was tearing apart.

She walked to her car, knowing that in less than twenty-four hours she would have to put everything aside except what she needed to do to keep those under her command safe and to carry out her duty. Until then, she was going to give everything she had to Tory and Reggie.

Since Carter had nothing to do after having been dismissed by Ricarda Pareto—Ricarda Grechi, as she apparently preferred to be called now—she decided she might as well walk down to the harbor and take a look at the area she was supposedly interested in investigating for signs of drug smuggling. The place couldn't look less like a drug corridor than it did on this sunny morning. The commercial fishing boats had already left for the deeper ocean waters, but there were plenty of small pleasure craft, under sail and motor, coming and going in the harbor off MacMillan Wharf. Carter sipped a second cup of coffee she'd picked up along the way and leaned against a chest-high wooden piling, playing tourist and contemplating Rica Grechi.

The feds hadn't actually provided any hard evidence tying the daughter to the father in terms of illegal activity. There had been a fair amount of interest in Rica's gallery in Manhattan because photo surveillance had recorded shots of two upper-level drug couriers making purchases there in the last six months. That was damning, but not something you'd want to go to court on. Still, it was an intriguing piece of the puzzle and warranted continued surveillance. The fact that Rica had opened another gallery where there was already suspicious drug-related activity was a huge red flag that had practically sent Special Agent Allen into paroxysms of excitement.

Carter drained her coffee cup and tossed it into a nearby wastebasket. As she did, she noted out of the corner of her eye a gunmetal gray sedan edge along the pier and stop. She'd seen it parked up the street from Rica's gallery that morning and she'd also seen it following her as she'd walked down Commercial Street. The driver evidently thought that because no one ever drove more than five miles an hour along the single lane one-way street, she wouldn't notice him tailing her.

Carter decided to disavow him of that notion. She walked over to the car and tapped on the window. When she saw who was inside, she smiled.

The automatic window slid down and she leaned her forearms on the door, smiling at the man and woman in the front seat. "Hello, Agents."

Agent Allen, her features—which would have been pretty had she ever thought to smile—set into a mask of annoyance, leaned across Toome, who was in the driver's seat. "What do you think you're doing?"

"I was about to ask you the same thing."

"Oh, for God's sake. Get in the car before someone sees us."

Carter glanced around the wharf. A line was queuing for the Boston ferry, and harried families with too much luggage and wayward children milled about among the gay and lesbian couples leaving after their week of enjoying majority status. The most nefarious individuals in sight were a pair of male street performers dressed like Cher and Celine Dion.

"I don't actually think there's anyone around who would care about—"

"Just get in the car."

"Okay," Carter said as she slid into the backseat. "But it would be a lot less conspicuous if you, Special Agent Allen, got out and we went for a stroll. Anyone who was really looking for an undercover team would pick up on this vehicle right away."

Allen snorted. "Oh really? And just what would they think the two of us were doing walking around in plain sight?"

"They'd probably think we were lovers." Carter smothered a smile at Allen's look of horror. She lifted her shoulder. "But if you want to take a chance—"

"All right," Allen seethed. "We'll *walk.* Get out of the car."

Apparently the once distasteful idea was suddenly more appealing, because Allen bolted from the car and Carter had to sprint before catching up with her halfway down the wharf in the center of town. She gripped Allen's wrist to slow her down.

"What's going on?"

"I wanted to get a look at the place, in case any kind of action develops here."

"You mean you've never been?"

Allen slanted her eyes in Carter's direction. "Why would I?"

"Well," Carter mused, "it's one of the most beautiful places on the East Coast. It's got miles of national seashore. It's got great history, excellent food, fine art, good entertainment, and beautiful women—"

"Your problem, Carter, is that you can't keep your personal life separate from your work."

Carter raised her eyebrows. "Is that so? And how exactly would you know that?"

"It's not *exactly* a secret that you've slept with witnesses, and for all I know, probably suspects."

Carter laughed. "The only entertaining I've done with witnesses has been after a case has closed. As to suspects, well, it's one instance where handcuffs are a turnoff."

Allen stopped dead. "If I didn't think you had the best chance of getting into Ricarda Pareto's bed, I would've had you pulled off this investigation a long time ago."

"It's Grechi."

"What?"

"Grechi. She's going by Grechi, not Pareto."

"Her grandmother's name?"

"And her mother's maiden," Carter pointed out.

"Why? Has she ever done that before?" Allen reached into her pocket for a small notebook, but at Carter's look of amusement, changed her mind. "All right, then. What's your theory?"

"I got the sense that she came here because no one knows her. Maybe she doesn't want to be the don's daughter."

Allen gave Carter an incredulous look. "That's ridiculous."

"Why? What do you really have on her that says otherwise?"

"That's your job," Allen said acerbically. "It would be nice if you actually did it for a change. So just do whatever it is that you do, and get to the pillow talk."

"Maybe she's not my type."

"Make the sacrifice."

"Maybe I'm not hers," Carter said, realizing the thought bothered her.

"So charm her."

After their brief encounter that morning, Carter wasn't certain that charming Rica was going to be all that easy, but she liked the prospect. She regarded Allen seriously. "Look, this town is too small to have you hanging around. If Rica's father does send someone over here to keep an eye on her, they're going to be on to you and Toome right away. Stay out of town."

"I'm not leaving you unsupervised," Allen said. "But the next time, I'll come alone and book a room somewhere. I'll play tourist."

Carter shook her head. "You're the boss."

"You'd do well to remember that."

Allen turned her back and marched back down the wharf toward the gray sedan. Carter wondered who had been telling Agent Allen that she would sleep with suspects to get information. She actually never had, although she'd done drugs with a few to prove her cover story. It wasn't a moral issue, since fabricating entire existences was part of her undercover work and using sex as a ploy to get what she needed came under the heading of "doing what was necessary to get the job done." She'd always been able to find out what she needed short of getting completely up close and personal, and she'd actually never been tempted to take what was frequently offered. She just hadn't been interested.

Watching the federal agents drive away, Carter stuffed her hands in her pockets and headed west down Commercial Street, opposite the direction she really wanted to go. She wanted to go east, back to Rica's gallery. Carter didn't relish the idea of lying her way into Rica's bed, and she wasn't sure why. The woman was beautiful and desirable.

Still she remembered the way Rica had searched her face through the glass, as if looking for truth. Making her believe she'd found it, when it was all a lie, was going to be harder than Carter thought.

CHAPTER EIGHT

Bri parked her brand-new Harley Roadster next to Reese's Blazer and took the stairs up to the office two at a time. When she shouldered through the door, she saw her partner Ali already at her desk and Gladys in her usual place at the call station.

"Hey. What's going on?" Bri asked of no one in particular. She dropped her motorcycle gloves and helmet on her desk.

Ali shrugged and Gladys pointed to Nelson's office.

"They're in there."

Bri looked from one woman to the other, sensing a disturbance in the air. Tiny fingers of dread trickled along her spine, and she shrugged the apprehension away. Needing somewhere to aim her uneasiness, she strode to her father's office door and knocked sharply. When she heard a rumble that approximated *Come in*, she pushed it open and stepped inside. Reese sat in one of the chairs in front of her father's desk. She didn't look sick, but she did look odd in her civilian clothes. Bri was used to Reese always being command perfect when at work, her uniform crisp and clean, her attitude focused and certain. Again, she had the feeling that something was out of place. Off kilter. As if the world had tilted just a little bit.

With a note of bravado in her voice, Bri said, "What gives?"

Reese turned ever so slightly in her chair and locked gazes with Bri. Her face was expressionless but her eyes were sharp and hard. "Do you want to rephrase that, Officer?"

For a second, Bri was tempted to resist the authority in Reese's voice. For a second, she was the same angry, belligerent teenager she'd been the first night Reese had come upon her and Caroline making out in a dark alley. She'd been ready to fight then, and she was ready to fight now. Because she felt threatened and afraid. She took a breath and looked from her father to Reese, and could find no enemy. She squared her shoulders and faced her father.

"You wanted to see me, Chief Parker?"

"I need you to take Conlon's shift."

"Yes sir."

Reese stood. "And I need you to come for a ride with me."

"Yes ma'am."

Nelson stood as well and stretched his hand out across the desk. "I'll see you soon, Conlon." His voice was husky and he cleared his throat before clasping Reese's hand. He shook it firmly and added, "And give them hell."

"Yes sir," Reese said to the standard exhortation. "I will, sir."

Bri didn't say anything as she and Reese walked through the squad room, but she felt Ali's and Gladys's eyes on them. Her stomach burned and her legs felt wobbly, and she didn't have the slightest idea why. There was nothing visibly wrong, except her father looked sad in a way he hadn't since that night she'd been attacked in the dunes. When she'd been beaten and—

"Is Tory all right?" Bri stopped dead in the middle of the parking lot. "She's not hurt, is she?"

Yes, she is. And I'm to blame. Reese shook her head. "No, she's fine. Come on, get in the truck and I'll explain."

Bri climbed into the passenger seat and sat with her hands clasped between her knees, staring straight ahead as Reese pulled out of the lot, turned left and then left again onto Route 6. They were going to the parking lot at Herring Cove. They always seemed to go there when Reese wanted to talk to her. Knowing that made her both comfortable and uneasy. Something was coming, something she probably didn't want to hear. But this was Reese, and she trusted her in a way that she trusted no one else in her life. She trusted her father to care for her and about her, but not to understand her. She trusted Caroline to understand and to love her, but she felt protective of Caroline and wanted to always be strong for her. With Reese, she knew she was understood, and loved, and if she needed it, protected.

"You can just go ahead and say it," Bri said.

"That was my plan." Reese smiled and stopped the vehicle midway down the long narrow parking lot, away from any other vehicles. The tide was coming in and white froth bubbled along the water's edge, tracing a lacy border where sand met sea. She turned off the ignition, released her seat belt, and swiveled until her back was against the door. She waited until Bri did the same.

"My reserve unit has been called up, and I'm going to be deployed to the Middle East." Reese said it matter-of-factly, because that's exactly what it was. She was a lieutenant colonel in the United States Marine Corps Reserves. And whether this particular involvement was called a war or not was of no consequence to her. She had pledged to serve and to fight, if asked to, and that's what she was going to do.

"When?" Bri's throat was dry, but her voice was steady, and she was pleased about that.

"I'm leaving tomorrow at four a.m. I'd like you to drive me to the airport."

"Sure." Bri closed her fingers tightly into fists. "Tomorrow?"

Reese nodded.

"How do you know you'll be sent...you know. Where there's fighting?"

"My father knows my orders. He told me."

"Oh." Bri looked away from Reese out the windshield toward Cape Cod Bay. She'd seen the scene a thousand times. She'd seen the waves stretch endlessly across the horizon, seen the white slash of gulls diving through a crystal blue sky, seen clouds float by like wishes, impossible to catch. She tried to imagine being surrounded by endless miles of scorching sand and blistering sun and sudden death. "Someplace bad?"

"There's no place that's safe," Reese said quietly, "but I've got a top-notch unit."

"When will you be back?"

"I don't know."

Bri jerked her head around. "The television says it will be over soon. Weeks, maybe a few months."

"I know. But sometimes..." Reese lifted a hand, blew out a breath. "Sometimes things change. It's better not to think about how long it will be."

"It doesn't work," Bri said sharply. "I tried that when Carre went to Paris...I know it's not the same, but—"

"It was hard, just the same. I know." Reese tapped her closed fist on Bri's knee. "And you did well."

Bri snorted. "You didn't see me sometimes."

"I saw you do what needed to be done," Reese said quietly. "You stood strong for her."

"How's Tory?"

"Standing strong." Reese brushed a hand over her face. "I have a favor to ask of you."

Bri sat up, her feet flat on the floor, her back straight. It was as close as she could get to coming to attention in a seated position. "Anything."

"I'm putting you in charge of the dojo until I get back."

"Tory outranks me."

"I know, but she'll be busy with the baby, and"—Reese smiled—"we both planned for you to take over someday."

"Just until you come back," Bri said insistently.

"Just until then," Reese affirmed. "And one more thing."

"Tory."

"Yes." Reese met Bri's unwavering gaze, proud of the strength she saw there. "She won't lean on anyone, but she loves you and I know you love her. If there comes a time when she needs to lean, even if she doesn't want to, I need you to be there."

Bri's throat moved convulsively and she swallowed back a sudden swell of tears. "I will, but nothing's going to hap—"

"Good enough." Reese started the engine. "Thanks for taking my shift today."

"Sure."

"And Bri," Reese said gently before backing out of the space. When Bri looked over, Reese brushed a hand over Bri's cheek and through her hair. "It'll be okay."

"Pia," Tory said into the phone as she dropped the last file on the corner of her overcrowded desk. "It's Tory."

"Hi," Pia Torres said. "What's up?"

"Is KT coming in this weekend?"

"She's here now. She came in on an early plane and is just taking a shower. Do you need her?"

"Would it be okay if I stopped by for just a minute? I know she's probably tired if she worked all night, but—"

Pia laughed. "We're talking about the same KT, right? The tall, dark-haired surgeon with the endless energy who's never happier than when she's working?"

Despite the million things on her mind, Tory smiled. It was still hard to believe that KT, her once and long-ago lover, the woman who had turned her life upside down and nearly torn her heart out in the process, was back in her life again. Back in her life and happily involved with a friend of hers, and it didn't bother Tory a bit. In fact, she and KT had finally made peace and with it, a great deal of her past had finally been laid to rest. "Unless you've gotten a new girlfriend since the last time I saw you, that would be the one."

"Then she's wide awake and I was just about to fix her something to eat. Come on over."

"Thanks. I promise I won't keep you."

"Tory, just hush and get over here."

Six minutes later, Tory parked in front of Pia's bungalow, a classic white Cape Codder set back from the street on the far west end of Commercial. KT didn't live there; she worked in Boston as a trauma surgeon and spent as much of her time off as possible with Pia. Today, Tory was especially glad to have KT back. Despite all the pain, KT was one of the most important people in her life.

Pia, her jet black curls framing a dark-eyed, sensuous face that typified her Portuguese heritage, came out the front door onto the small, neat porch as Tory made her way up the walkway between the flower gardens. She regarded Tory with a concerned smile. Impromptu visits were not common. "She's in the kitchen."

"Thanks." When Tory realized that Pia was going to wait out on the porch, she added, "This is about you, too. Come inside."

KT O'Bannon, tall, dark, and proverbially handsome, rose from her seat in the kitchen that looked out over Pia's rear gardens. She was barefoot, in jeans and a frayed white T-shirt, and her dark hair was wet from her recent shower. "Hey, Vic. What's going on?"

Tory smiled at the old nickname that she had once asked KT to stop using because it was so painfully intimate. Now she found it warmly familiar. KT reminded her of Reese in some ways. They were devilishly good-looking, strong and commanding, and beneath the charisma, tender. KT, however, through no fault of her own when Tory looked back on it now, had never provided the solid, unshakable foundation that Reese brought to Tory's world. And Tory had never been able to give KT the freedom she needed along with the certainty of always having a safe place to return, as Pia was able to do.

Tory kissed KT's cheek. "It's good to see you."

KT frowned and pulled out a chair at the table. "Sit. Let me get you some coffee. You look beat."

"Why, thank you. I think." Tory laughed shakily and pushed her hands through her hair.

"*You* sit," Pia said, brushing her hand over KT's back. "I'll get you both some coffee."

"Thanks, honey," KT said before turning her attention to Tory. "What's wrong?"

"I hate to do this to you two, because I know you worked last night and you're probably looking forward to a weekend off, but I need you to cover my practice tonight and maybe part of tomorrow."

"Sure," KT said immediately. "Why?"

"Reese's reserve unit has been called to duty. She's leaving tomorrow morning." Even as she said it, Tory found the words hard to absorb. She and Reese hadn't been apart except for the once-a-month weekends and the few weeks every summer when Reese had to fulfill Marine reserve responsibilities. Even sitting across the table from KT, a woman she had loved for years, she couldn't remember a time when Reese had not filled her heart and her mind. "I don't want us to be disturbed tonight."

"Of course we want to help," Pia said.

"Jesus." KT turned her coffee cup in her hands, frowning. "Isn't her father some big deal in the military?"

"He's a general."

"Can't he do anything about this? Get her some kind of deferment or something?"

Tory laughed, a short harsh sound. "KT. He's been waiting for this to happen. He's never forgiven her for leaving active duty, and he sees this as her chance to advance."

"You're kidding."

Pia came to stand behind KT and rested her hands gently on KT's shoulders. She leaned down and kissed the top of her head. "Sweetheart, maybe Reese doesn't want a deferment." She looked over KT's head at Tory. "Reese strikes me as the kind of person who would go if it was required of her."

"Oh come on," KT said. "She's got a wife and child to think about. Why would she—"

"You're right, Pia," Tory said softly. "I wouldn't say that Reese *wants* to go, but she wouldn't be Reese if she didn't feel compelled to carry out her duty."

"That's bullshit," KT snapped. "*You're* her duty."

Pia cupped one hand on the back of KT's neck and squeezed gently, massaging the muscles that had turned to iron. "Tory's going to be fine."

Tory shook her head, amazed by Pia's ability to read beneath the surface of KT's anger and arrogance. She leaned across the table and took KT's hand. "I appreciate you being upset for me. It's complicated. *Reese* is complicated. But she loves me and Reggie more than anything in the world, and this is hard for her too."

"Good," KT muttered, but the edge had gone out of her voice. "I can take your patients all weekend, if you need me to."

"You need a break sometimes, too. Just until tomorrow afternoon." Tory stood and gave Pia and KT a grateful smile. "Thanks for being such good friends."

KT rose and walked Tory to the door, one arm around her shoulders. "You sure you're okay, Vic?"

"Scared," Tory admitted. She stopped in the doorway and rested her head against KT's shoulder. "It might all be over in just a few weeks. I just don't know what I'd do if—"

"Don't," KT said gently. "Reese Conlon has the best reason in the world to keep her ass out of trouble. She's got you and Reggie. She'll be back before you know it."

"God, I hope so," Tory said fervently.

KT kissed Tory's forehead. "Thanks for letting me help."

"Thanks for being here." Tory looked past KT's shoulder to where Pia stood in the kitchen doorway, watching them. "Both of you." Then she took a deep breath and smiled. "Now, I've got to go. I've got a date with my lover."

CHAPTER NINE

I made sandwiches," Kate said to Tory and Reese when she opened the door. "Go on back to the kitchen. Jean has Reggie outside."

Reese held Tory's hand as they walked through the house her mother shared with her lover Jean. She couldn't help thinking of the first night she had arrived on her mother's doorstep after their twenty-year separation. She hadn't quite known what to expect, because she had never been entirely certain why her mother had broken off contact after her divorce from Reese's father. When Kate revealed that her ex-husband had forbidden her to communicate with Reese upon learning that Kate and Jean were lovers, Reese was more sad than angry. She loved her father, and that would never change. But he had made his anger her punishment, and in her heart she knew he had been unfair. She would never be able to replace the years she had lost with her mother. Unconsciously, she pulled Tory closer.

"What is it?" Tory said gently, wrapping an arm around Reese's waist as they stopped in front of the glass doors leading out to the deck. Jean and Reggie sat together on the weathered wooden surface, a jumble of building blocks scattered between them. Reggie, her hair the same red-gold-brown as Tory's, wore a baby-sized Red Sox cap that shielded her fair skin from the sun.

"She's going to walk soon," Reese said.

Tory frowned, trying to decipher the source of the pain riding just below the surface of Reese's voice. She caught her breath, understanding. "She's going to be the most videoed baby on the planet." She turned

Reese to face her, slid both arms up to her shoulders, and kissed her softly. "You're not going to miss a second. I promise."

Reese nodded, not trusting her voice to be steady. She rested her forehead against Tory's and angled her head to watch Reggie. She was just in time to see Reggie fling a block off the deck with an exuberant squeal. "She's got a pretty good arm already."

"If this had to happen," Tory said, "this is the perfect time. You'll be back in plenty of time to teach her everything she'll need to know."

From the doorway, Kate said, "You were about Reggie's age when Roger started his second tour in Vietnam." She indicated the table and the sandwiches she'd made earlier. "Sit. Have something to eat. I know what these days are like, right before you ship out. The minutes drag and the hours fly by. Neither of you has probably had anything except coffee all day."

"Thank you," Tory said, drawing Reese with her to the table. She kept hold of Reese's hand as she reached for a sandwich. "Was he gone a long time?"

Reese stiffened but said nothing. Tory deserved the chance to share her uncertainty with someone who understood.

Kate sat down with them. "A little over a year the first time. Almost two the second."

"My God," Tory breathed. "How did you cope?"

"First of all, I knew when I married him that we might be separated frequently and for extended periods of time, so I was at least mentally prepared. I also lived on base, and there were lots of other young wives in the same situation. We banded together around our shared insecurities." She clasped Tory's free hand and smiled at Reese, her eyes calm and certain. "Reese inherited one very important thing from her father's side of the family. Conlons make great Marines. Reese is going to be fine."

Reese laughed softly. "*You* must've made a great Marine wife."

"I did," Kate said archly. "Until I ran off with Jean."

The three laughed, and the atmosphere in the room lightened. Reese and Tory finally started in on the sandwiches. Jean came in from outside and passed a wriggling Reggie to Tory. She kissed first Reese and then Tory on the cheek before taking the remaining seat at the table.

"How are you two doing?"

Reese glanced at Tory, who smiled back.

"Pretty well," Tory said. "It just came up so suddenly, but I'm catching my breath now. Reese?"

Reese hesitated. She wasn't sure anyone would understand her answer, but if not these women who loved her, then who? She raised Tory's hand and brushed her lips over Tory's knuckles. "I'm not concerned about going. I'm only having a hard time leaving."

The room was silent until Kate said matter-of-factly, "I think that's exactly the way it should be. There'll be no need for you to worry about anything while you're over there except doing your job. Everything here at home is going to be fine."

"I'm sure of it," Reese said, knowing that even as she was doing whatever she had to do, part of her would always be thinking about Tory and home.

"Are you sure you don't want us to keep Reggie tonight?" Jean asked. "You know she's no trouble at all."

Reese held out her arms and Reggie squirmed toward her. Reese settled Reggie in her lap and brushed her hand over the top of her head. "Thanks, but I want to put her to bed. I promised to finish this story we've been reading."

"Excuse me," Tory said, abruptly rising.

"Tor?" Reese said with concern.

Tory turned away, gesturing toward the adjoining room. "Bathroom."

Once behind closed doors, Tory leaned her head back and squeezed her eyes tightly, biting down on her lower lip to stop the flood of tears. Kate was right. Reese was trained for this. There was no one better than Reese at what she did. Reese would go and do what she needed to do and then she'd come home. And their life would go on.

Please, Tory thought, *please just let her come home so we can have our life back.*

Rica slid into the back row of the meeting room on the second floor of Town Hall just as the president of the Women's Business Association called the meeting to order. She looked around the room at the other women, who were dressed casually and ranged in age from early twenties all the way up to well past conventional retirement age. She had decided to attend to show that she was a serious part of the business community. And even though, unlike most of the business owners in town, she wasn't dependent on the income she could earn during the four to six months of the tourist season, she still wanted to acquaint herself with the economic realities of the seasonal market.

She leaned back as a newcomer moved down her aisle to an empty chair next to hers.

"Excuse me. Sorry."

Rica shifted sideways and eyed Carter as she settled next to her. Leaning close, she whispered, "Are you following me?"

"Yes." Carter grinned. It was the truth, after all. She hadn't had anything better to do than watch the gallery, and she had just about decided to go in when Rica had come out. So she'd followed her. "You wouldn't go to dinner with me, so I thought I'd make a pest of myself until you relented."

"That's called stalking."

"Not if I admit it."

Smiling, Rica shook her head and faced forward.

Carter feigned interest in the proceedings, but all of her attention was riveted on the woman next to her. Rica had changed out of the silk blouse and slacks she had been wearing earlier into jeans and a dark red sweater. It looked like cashmere, soft and subtly clinging to the gentle curves of her breasts. She smelled of something warm and breezy, like sunshine on summer sand.

"You're staring," Rica said quietly without moving her gaze from the woman who was discussing the issue of diverting traffic down Commercial Street during business hours.

"Sorry," Carter whispered. "You look terrific."

"Whatever you think you know about me, you're wrong."

Carter settled back in her seat and waited for the meeting to end. Twenty minutes later, it did, and when participants began to fold up the metal chairs and stack them against the wall, she took advantage of the noise to lean close to Rica.

"Even if I heard wrong, and you're not a lesbian, I'd still like to take you to dinner."

Rica flipped up the seat of her chair sharply and walked away. Carter closed hers and followed.

"You know where I work," Rica said, "and I'm sure it's not difficult for you to find out where I live. If you want to shadow me, fine. But I already told you I don't need you around, and I'm not going to make your job easier."

"And I already told you I'm not working for any of our mutual acquaintances." For a second, Carter forgot that she was lying. All she really wanted in that moment was for Rica to believe that she wanted to spend time with her. Because that *was* the truth. "So just pretend I'm a stranger."

"I'm not in the habit of going anywhere with strangers. Especially not out to dinner."

"Look, I don't know anyone in town," Carter said, holding her hands up in an "I'm harmless" gesture. "Just some food and a little conversation. Have you eaten? I bet you haven't." *Not unless you snuck out the back door sometime in the last three hours when I wasn't looking.*

"I was going to stop for something at one of the takeout places on the pier."

"Excellent. So let's do that and you come over to my place. It's just around the corner, and I've got cold beer and a fairly decent bottle of wine."

Rica sighed. "No business. Of any kind."

Carter crossed her heart. "Deal."

Despite herself, Rica laughed.

Fifteen minutes later, Carter led Rica up the outside staircase to her second-floor apartment, unlocked the door, and held it open with her shoulder for Rica to pass inside. She flipped on the light with one hand and carried the takeout bag she held in the other into the kitchen.

"Beer or wine?"

"Wine, if it's not too much trouble."

"No trouble at all." Carter pulled plates from the cabinet above the sink and looked over her shoulder into the living room. "We can eat out on the deck. It's got a tiny bit of a view."

Rica opened the doors to let the heat out and the breeze in, and then walked back inside to help Carter. "What are you really doing here?"

Carter paused, trying to look unfazed while scrambling for an answer. Rica continued to surprise her. She was disarmingly direct while frustratingly distant. It was a tantalizing and intriguing combination. "I thought we said no business."

Rica felt a flash of disappointment. Of course, whatever the reason Carter was in town, whether it was to report to her father about her activities or not, it was still most likely to be related in some way to the far-reaching tentacles of her father's enormous organization. "I'm sorry, you're right. I'm afraid that doesn't leave us very much to talk about."

Carter finished pouring the wine and handed Rica the glass of Bordeaux. She opened a beer for herself. "On the contrary. Now we're free to talk about anything we like. No codes required."

Rica grimaced. "You don't seem to have the usual paranoia of most…business associates. Or the obsequiousness."

"Really?" Carter laughed. "You don't think following you around town and begging you to have dinner with me was just a little ingratiating?"

Rica smiled that secretive, sad smile that made Carter's heart tighten. "Maybe just a little."

"Good. Maybe before the night's over, I can win a few more points." Carter opened the takeout containers and transferred the food onto plates. She handed one to Rica. "Let's sit outside and enjoy the sunset."

Wordlessly, Rica followed Carter, wondering exactly how she had come to be in a stranger's apartment. A strange *woman*, who was very obviously trying to seduce her, and who was just the kind of person she had vowed never to get involved with. She had to admit, though, that Carter's annoying arrogance was counterbalanced by her refreshing lack of concern for who Rica was. Or more precisely, who her father was. And that was unusual.

So many people in her life had a hidden agenda. They wanted to claim some kind of relationship with her, believing, falsely, that this would gain them favor in the eyes of her father. Men refused to accept the fact that she was not interested in them as bedmates; women pretended friendship or, on occasion, attraction, to move closer to the inner circle of power through her. She'd learned to keep people at a distance, not only because they were often disappointing but because they could be dangerous.

"Your food's going to get cold," Carter said softly. She wondered what had put the slightly pensive, slightly faraway look on Rica's face and resisted the urge to touch her. The physical pull she experienced when she was anywhere near Rica was far stronger than just the ordinary response to a beautiful woman, and she silently reminded herself to be careful.

"I'm sorry." Rica sighed. "I'm not even particularly good company, and that was half the reason for your invitation."

"I lied about that."

"Really?" Rica sipped her wine and eyed Carter curiously. "Which part?"

"I don't know anyone in town. That's true." Carter grinned sheepishly. "But I don't really care if we talk about anything at all. I'd like to, at some point. But for tonight, I'm happy just to sit out here with you."

"I don't know why, but I believe that." Rica stretched out her legs and tilted her head back, watching the stars suddenly blink on as if a switch had been turned. "It's amazing, that instant when night falls."

"You never see it in the city. Too many lights."

"This place does have a slightly otherworldly feel to it." Rica nibbled at her sandwich, contemplating the strange sense of freedom she'd had ever since arriving, even though she knew reality was just minutes away. "I can almost believe that I've escaped."

Carter balanced her beer bottle on her knee, watching moonlight dance in Rica's hair. She didn't have to see her eyes to know the sadness in them. She'd already seen it more than once, when Rica had been unaware, and she suspected that it was never far from the surface. She found herself wanting nothing more than to make it go away. Counter to all her objectives in getting to know Rica Grechi, she said, "Who knows. Maybe you'll be able to, here."

"It would be nice to think so." Rica shook her head with a rueful smile, then straightened, as if forcibly banishing unwanted thoughts. "I truly am terrible company. I should go."

"I'm glad you stopped by." Carter, for the second time that day, had the feeling that the slightest bit of pressure would send Rica fleeing permanently. "I'd like to do it again."

"Are you always this persistent?" Rica rose and started back into the apartment.

Carter followed. "Always."

Rica set her wineglass on the counter along with her plate of barely touched food. Then she turned and regarded Carter seriously. "I don't know what it is you're really after." She held up her hand when Carter started to protest. "But whatever it is, nothing of consequence is going to happen between us."

"Define *consequence*. Does that include sex?"

"No, it doesn't. Not necessarily. But you might as well know right now that *if* anything of that nature were to happen, it would be casual and nothing more."

Carter leaned back against the counter and folded her arms. "I can see that you're used to making all the rules. Does everyone always play along?"

The corner of Rica's mouth twitched. "Usually. Yes."

"Well, I can agree to the *casual* stipulation." She suddenly took a step that brought her very close to Rica. Without touching her with her hands, she closed her mouth over Rica's and kissed her. When Rica didn't pull away, she skimmed the tip of her tongue lightly over Rica's bottom lip before pulling back. "But I intend for it to have very memorable consequences."

Rica's eyes swept down Carter's body and back up, a slow appraising survey, languid as a caress. "We'll see. Good night, Carter."

"Ms. Grechi," Carter murmured, watching her walk out the door. She listened to her footsteps on the stairs, then let out a long breath. *Jesus Christ, what the hell just happened?*

Nothing about the evening had gone the way she had planned, especially not the way her body had ignited at the first touch of Rica's mouth. She opened another bottle of beer and tried to tell herself everything was under control. But she knew she was lying.

CHAPTER TEN

As Rica walked back from Carter's to the gallery, where she had left her car, she appreciated once more that nothing in Provincetown was very far from anything else. Commercial Street followed the curve of the harbor for three miles, defining the main business and tourist heart of the little village. Though it was after nine at night and all the businesses were closed, people still strolled down the middle of the street, drinking a last cup of coffee, window shopping, or making their way to one of the few restaurants or bars open during the off-season. She disregarded the man standing in front of her gallery, apparently perusing the items visible through the window, until she was close enough to recognize the sharp profile and thick, dark hair that always seemed on the verge of needing a cut.

"What are you doing here, Enzo?" Rica said as she stepped up beside her cousin.

Enzo leaned down and kissed Rica's cheek. "Your manners are no better now than they were when you were six."

"Maybe that's because you're still a bully."

Enzo laughed and put his arm around her shoulders, forcing her to face him. "You wouldn't think that if you weren't so determined to be independent." He brushed his mouth over her ear as he murmured, "With me, you might even like it."

"I think I've made it plain to you why I wouldn't." Rica put her hand against his chest and tried to push away. His grip tightened and the expression on his face went from amused to angry. For the first time, Rica realized just how vulnerable she was outside the immediate sphere of her father's influence and the ever-watchful presence of his trusted employees. Even in Manhattan, "friends" of the family were in and out of her gallery constantly, and some of them had undoubtedly been dispatched to monitor her welfare. She hadn't liked the attention, but some part of her had not found the protection unwelcome.

Now she was very much aware of being alone. Fleetingly, and for no reason she could imagine, she saw Carter's face. Then it was gone and she was doubly aware of Enzo's unwanted touch. Determined not to let him sense her uneasiness, Rica kept her voice low and steady. "You don't have anything that interests me. You should know that by now."

"That won't always be the case, little cousin," Enzo snarled. He tilted his hips forward until his crotch brushed against her pelvis. "Your father thinks more highly of me than you do."

Rica felt his erection press against her lower abdomen but she didn't pull away. She knew from experience that struggling would only excite him more. She kept her eyes firmly on his. "I'm not one of my father's assets, to be awarded to the highest earner. Whatever payment you think you have coming, it won't be me."

"He wants grandchildren. I'm sure you can tell, I'm ready and able to give him some." Enzo moved his arm from Rica's shoulders to her waist, holding her even more firmly against his body. "As for the women you *think* you want..." He lifted a shoulder and smiled unctuously. "That might prove interesting for all of us."

"No matter what my father wants," Rica said, "he would never condone you putting your hands on me when I didn't want it."

Enzo relaxed his grip slightly. "One thing I know about you, Rica, is that you fight your own battles. You never told him about our childhood games. You won't tell him anything now."

"Games?" Rica had a quick flash of being twelve and angrily telling her older cousin that she wasn't interested in him *that way* because *she* preferred girls. Laughing, the fourteen-year-old Enzo had held her down with the weight of his body, forcing her to kiss him while he ground his pelvis into hers. She had bitten him, and he'd slapped her before trapping her hand between their bodies and making her caress him. Then, like now, she never moved her eyes from his. "He would have killed you then, just like now." She braced both hands against his chest and shoved him back a step, knowing he would not create a scene in the middle of a public thoroughfare.

"You never told," Enzo said musingly, dropping his hands. "Maybe because you didn't really mind."

Rica shook her head. Enzo was baiting her, and she wouldn't give him the satisfaction of her anger. It would have created a family schism had she complained to her father of Enzo's actions, and Enzo had known then, as now, that she would never do that. The family came first, before anything else. "I'm going home."

"I have some business to discuss with you."

"I'm neither discussing nor doing any kind of business with you."

"This message comes from your father." Enzo glanced up and down the street, then took her arm more gently this time. "Let's go for a walk and have a friendly conversation. Like loving cousins, eh?"

Reluctantly, Rica fell into step beside him. It was normal for her father to use Enzo or some other trusted associate to contact her about anything business related. He never discussed such matters on the phone. They walked silently into the center of town and then out onto MacMillan Wharf. The wind knifed across the water and she shivered from the slashing cold. The sweater that had been sufficient to keep her warm a few hours earlier was woefully inadequate now, but she said nothing. Enzo was like a wild animal, preying on the weaknesses of others. She would never give him that advantage.

"What did my father say?"

"Look," Enzo said, pointing to a vessel rounding Long Point and entering the harbor.

The double-decker ferry stood out against the nighttime sky, blazing with lights on every level and approaching the pier at what looked like an impossibly fast speed. Under other circumstances, Rica enjoyed watching the captain guide the huge ship against the dock with barely a bump. Tonight, Enzo's presence tainted even that small pleasure.

"From here to the pier at the World Trade Center in Boston in ninety minutes." Enzo indicated the harbor where a number of yachts were moored. "And so accessible to visitors. You couldn't have picked a better place to live."

"Yes," Rica said, pretending she didn't follow his conversation. "It's beautiful here."

"I'm sure your gallery will do very well. Some friends are very anxious to display their works there, and it's so easy for them to deliver the merchandise."

Rica shook her head. "I'm sorry. I have limited space. The gallery in Manhattan would be better suited for that."

"Your father doesn't think so."

Rica wasn't surprised that Enzo was relaying this cloaked request. She and her father never talked of the family enterprises, which allowed them to avoid confrontation over areas where they disagreed. "I'm sure my father will understand I'm very busy with the work I already have on consignment. Please give him that message for me."

When she turned to leave, Enzo caught her shoulder and swung her back to face him. She pulled away, her voice as icy as the wind: "Is there something else?"

"There may come a time when you'll need a favor from me." Enzo trailed his fingers along the edge of her jaw and down her neck. "There are many who believe a man is the rightful head of a family." He half closed his eyes and bowed his head. "If anything should happen to Don Pareto, God forbid."

Rica resisted the urge to clasp her arms over her breasts, although her instincts screamed for her to shield herself from his fury and his thwarted lust. "My father is still a relatively young man. You're likely to find yourself in the same position as Prince Charles—too old to rule *if* the time ever comes."

Enzo laughed. "I'll have you in my bed long before then. You'll think differently of matters after that."

"I'll kill you before I'll ever let you touch me."

Rica turned and walked away before he could touch her again. When she was far enough away that he couldn't see her, she gave in to the cold that chilled her body and soul. Shivering uncontrollably, she wrapped her arms tightly around herself and hurried into the dark.

Tory set the book that she hadn't been reading onto the bedside table as Reese walked into the room. Reese wore an old T-shirt and shorts with the Marine Corps insignia on them, as she often did at night around the house. In fact, everything about the evening had been so routine since they'd returned from Kate and Jean's, Tory could hardly believe that her entire life was about to change in six hours.

"Did you get to the end of the story?"

Reese smiled. "Nope. She fell asleep with half a chapter to go." Reese stripped off her T-shirt and shorts and climbed naked into bed. She pulled the sheet up to her waist, turned on her side, and rested her palm in the center of Tory's abdomen. "I'll finish it when I get back."

"Good." Tory covered Reese's hand where it lay on the cotton nightshirt she had pulled on while waiting for Reese. In an automatic response, Reese laced her fingers through Tory's. "What happens tomorrow after you leave here?"

"I'm flying to North Carolina to meet with my father and then shipping out right away. The rest of my unit will follow in the next week or so."

"Is he going too?"

Reese shook her head. "Not yet, and maybe not at all. I didn't get the sense he was happy about that, either. They want him here for strategic planning, apparently."

"But he would rather be commanding a combat unit." Tory couldn't help but keep the bitterness from her voice. Rationally, she knew it wasn't Reese's father's fault that any of this had happened. Reese had made her choice years ago, and for reasons that were inherently good, as good as Reese herself. Honorable, valorous reasons. Sometimes that made it the hardest of all. She could hardly resent her lover for being a courageous and noble woman. "He would rather be going, and if he can't, you're a good substitute."

"I don't know about that part," Reese said quietly, recognizing Tory's anger and not begrudging it. She let go of Tory's hand and skimmed beneath the cotton to rest on flesh. "No one wants war, but for some people—career Marines like my father—it's a matter of training your whole life for something that may never happen. So when it does, you want the chance to prove your life has meant something."

"Do you feel that way?"

"My life is you and Reggie. Right here, every day."

"But what about before us? When you thought *you'd* be a career Marine forever. Did you…want to fight?"

Reese shook her head. "No. I never did. I mostly had the opportunity to do what I wanted to do without that. First I enforced the law, then I adjudicated it. I didn't need war for that." She laughed thinly. "All you need for that is people."

"What are you going to be doing over there?"

"Tor," Reese said gently. She leaned down and kissed the hollow at the base of Tory's throat. "I'll probably be sitting around in a tent getting bored to tears most of the time."

Tory knew that the military police unit Reese commanded would not be sitting quietly anywhere. She spread her fingers through Reese's hair and guided her face lower, to her breast. "I love you even when you lie to me."

Reese chuckled and swept her cheek back and forth over Tory's nipple, which was erect beneath the thin cotton. "That's a very odd statement." She pushed up the nightshirt and ducked her head to kiss Tory's breast. Then she looked up, her eyes serious. "You know I wouldn't, don't you? Lie to you? It's just that knowing isn't always—"

"I know." Tory stroked Reese's cheek. "When you're sitting around being bored in that tent, or doing…whatever else you need to do, remember that we're waiting for you, and that we need you."

"I never forget that. It's the constant of my life." Reese kissed the tip of Tory's chin. "I'll be careful, just like I am here, every day." Reese clasped Tory and rolled onto her back, settling Tory against her side with Tory's cheek on her shoulder. She stroked Tory's hair and her shoulders and her back. She pulled Tory's shirt up again so that she could run her fingertips up and down Tory's spine in a slow caress. "You have to promise not to worry and not to work twenty-four hours a day because I'm not here to nag you."

"Will you be able to call?" Tory sat up and removed her shirt, then snuggled down again.

"Yes, but probably not regularly. I'll be able to e-mail, too."

Tory shifted further on top of Reese, resting her thigh between Reese's legs. "How long do you think, really?"

Reese sighed. "I'm not sure. Best guess—three to six months."

"Keep thinking three," Tory murmured. She skimmed her fingertips over Reese's face, touching her brows, her cheeks, her lips. "I love you."

"I love you," Reese whispered. "Try not to worry, okay?"

"I'll give it my best."

"Do you think you can sleep?"

Tory rested her head on Reese's shoulder and fit her body to Reese's, circling her waist with one arm. "I don't know that I want to. I'd rather just lie here with you." She kissed Reese's breast. "I can still feel the way we made love the last time. It was perfect, but if you need—"

"No," Reese said quietly. "I always want you, but right now, this is enough."

"It's all right to sleep if you need to. I'll be here."

Reese nuzzled Tory's hair, breathing in her essence, warming everywhere inside. "Every time I go to sleep, I'll feel you just like this."

Tory nodded wordlessly, giving her every bit of strength she had. Until that moment, she hadn't realized how hard it was to truly love. "I wouldn't change one single thing about you, Reese."

"Thank you," Reese whispered. She closed her eyes and emptied her mind of everything except Tory. With love came peace.

CHAPTER ELEVEN

Lieutenant Colonel Reese Conlon, USMCR—her duffel bag packed and ready downstairs by the front door—stood by the side of the bed and looked down upon the sleeping woman and child. The sky outside the windows gave no hint of dawn. Tory slept curled on her side, her hair nearly obscuring the elegant lines of her face. Only the corner of her full, wide mouth was visible. Reggie lay with her face pillowed between Tory's breasts. Long gold lashes lay against creamy cheeks. Her lips, rosebud pink, were pursed in a tiny smile of innocent bliss. No painter had ever captured the image of an angel as perfectly as in that moment.

Absently, Reese turned the plain gold band on her left ring finger, smiling as her daughter made a small cooing sound and nuzzled against Tory's breast. When Reese had risen after dozing for a few hours to shower and put on her uniform, Reggie had started to fuss, almost as if she too understood that a momentous change was about to befall their lives. That and everything else about the night was unusual enough that Reese had rescued the baby from her crib and brought her to Tory. The fact that Tory had fallen back to sleep was just one more indication of how difficult this was for her. She was clearly exhausted, and Reese felt a surge of anxiety knowing that circumstances were not likely to improve.

As if reading her troubled thoughts, Tory opened her eyes and instantly fixed on Reese's face. "Is it time?"

"Yes." Seeing the pain in Tory's eyes, and knowing that she'd put it there, was enough to break Reese's resolve. Six months ago, she would have sworn on her life that she would never do anything to hurt the only woman she had ever loved. She'd been wrong, and she wondered if she would ever be able to make up for putting Tory through this.

"Let me put her back to bed," Tory said quietly, starting to rise.

"Here," Reese said, extending her arms. "Let me take her."

"She'll muss your uniform."

"I don't care. Besides, you know she's got a stomach like mine. Cast-iron. She won't spit up."

Tory slid from bed, still naked, and passed their sleeping daughter to Reese. She skimmed her hand down Reese's chest, fingering the rows of service ribbons, and smiled shakily. "You look so goddamned sexy in this."

"Good to hear." Reese's voice was husky as she gently cradled Reggie against her shoulder, knowing it might be months, possibly longer, before she would be able to hold her this way again. Contemplating missing a *day* in her daughter's life was torture, but imagining weeks or months passing in her absence was nearly unbearable. As the agonizing realization of all that she stood to lose struck hard at her heart, she tenderly stroked the baby's soft hair, straightened her shoulders, and forced a grin. "Wait til you see me in camo."

Tory turned away, fumbling at the foot of the bed for her robe, the tears in her eyes making it difficult for her to focus. She'd promised herself she wouldn't cry. She would not allow Reese to leave them with anything other than the sure and certain knowledge that they loved her more than life and would be there when she came home. *When she comes home. Please, God. Please.*

"Tor?"

The faint note of uncertainty in her lover's voice solidified Tory's determination. She blinked once and turned back, her eyes clear and her face composed. "It's all right, baby." She brushed her fingers over Reese's cheek and leaned forward to kiss her softly. "It's all right."

The crunch of tires over the seashells lining their driveway reverberated like gunshots in the still room. Despite herself, Tory jerked at the sound. Her eyes met Reese's.

"That's Bri," Reese said unnecessarily.

"I want to come with you to the airport." Tory's voice shook.

Worry, not anger, Reese thought. She started toward the bedroom door, Reggie asleep on her shoulder. With her free hand she caught

Tory's. "We already decided, Tor. It'll be easier for you and the baby if—"

"*Nothing* is going to make it easier for us." The quick flash of pain in Reese's face stopped the next words before they could be spoken. *Nothing except you not leaving.* "I'm sorry."

Starting down the stairs, Reese shook her head. "No. Don't say that." At the front door, she turned and held out the sleeping child. "I'll call you as soon as I can. I don't know when that will be."

"I understand."

Bending, Reese kissed Reggie's forehead, then gently encircled Tory's waist, drawing her near. She brushed her lips over Tory's once, then again, lingeringly, as she smoothed her hands up and down Tory's back. "I love you. Both of you—so much."

Then Reese stepped back and reached for her duffel.

"Wait!" Tory carried Reggie to the sofa, where she laid her down and nestled a cushion beside her to prevent her from rolling off. Swiftly, she returned to Reese and put both arms around her neck, pressing close. With her hands in Reese's hair, she found Reese's mouth, cleaving to the long hard lines of the familiar body. With a soft moan, Tory kissed her, a deep probing kiss that spoke more of promises than passion. When she lifted her mouth away, she searched the blue eyes that held her soul. "I love you. I *need* you. Reggie needs you. You be safe, and you come home. Do you understand?"

"I will," Reese said, her voice hoarse and her body trembling. "I promise. I will."

A moment later, Tory stood in the doorway, the baby in her arms, watching her lover stow her duffel bag in the back of the police cruiser, thinking of the things they hadn't spoken of. In less than an hour, Reese would be on her way to the Marine base at Camp Lejeune, pending deployment of the 8th Battalion of the II Marine Expeditionary Force. In a matter of days, she would be in Iraq. As an experienced ranking officer with training in the military police force, Tory knew that Reese would be in the heart of the battle zone.

The police cruiser turned left from the driveway onto 6A, heading toward Provincetown and the tiny airport at Race Point. As the taillights faded from sight, a terrible sadness settled in Tory's chest. The baby stirred in her arms, and Tory gently kissed her forehead.

"It's going to be all right."

She wasn't certain how that could be, when it felt as if her heart were breaking, but she would never stop believing in Reese and the life they had made. Reese would come home, because anything else was unthinkable.

❖

Bri switched off the ignition, popped the trunk with the inside lever, and jumped out of the cruiser almost before the vehicle had come to a complete stop. She was hauling the duffel out of the trunk when Reese reached her.

"Let me give you a hand," Reese said.

"I got it," Bri said in short, clipped tones.

Reese covered Bri's hand where it gripped the canvas strap and squeezed gently. "Hold up a minute."

Bri stood still, her body stiff, her face averted.

"What's on your mind?" Reese asked.

"Nothing."

"Bri." Reese's voice was gently chiding.

"We should go. Get you checked in."

Reese glanced through the glass doors into the main room of the tiny airport. The lights inside seemed unnaturally bright, illuminating the plastic chairs and serviceable all-weather carpet with harsh honesty. The room was empty save for two airport employees and a security officer. "Not much of a line."

Bri shrugged.

"This is no time for silence between us." Reese rested her hand on Bri's shoulder, and as had happened only once before when Bri had been much younger, she was taken off guard when Bri launched herself into her arms. Reese circled Bri's narrow waist and held her hard against her chest while she stroked the back of her head with her other hand. "Hey. Hey, it's okay."

"Everyone is always leaving."

It must feel that way sometimes, Reese thought. *Your mother. Caroline. Me.* Bri's face was turned away so that Reese couldn't see her, but she didn't need to to know her blue eyes would be clouded with misery. "Caroline came back. So will I."

"I know. Sorry," Bri mumbled.

Reese pulled away just enough to let Bri stand on her own, but she kept her arm around her. "I'm going to miss you something fierce." She tapped Bri's chin. "Look after yourself."

Bri nodded. "I know you'll be really busy, but maybe sometime—"

Reese patted her chest pocket. "I've got a list of important e-mail addresses right here. Yours is on top."

"Yeah?"

"Yeah."

Bri straightened. "So I'll be talking to you."

"You will." Reese bent down and hefted her duffel. "Ready?"

"Yes ma'am."

Carter heaved herself out of the deck chair where she'd been sitting most of the night. After Rica had left, she couldn't sleep, so she'd opened another beer and returned to the deck, trying to sort out her thoughts. Allen was playing the odds as far as Rica was concerned—betting that because Rica was the only child and the presumed next in line to head the Pareto family that Rica was actually involved in the business. It was a reasonable assumption, but there was very little hard evidence to substantiate the theory. A few surveillance photos showing known mob affiliates entering Rica's gallery, making purchases or deliveries, was hardly proof of anything. Rica was on a first-name basis with some pretty heavy hitters, but her primary interaction with them was at family gatherings, precisely because they *were* friends of the family whom she had known since she was a child. Not damning in itself.

Despite having gotten close to some of Pareto's highly placed captains, Carter had yet to hear anything suggesting that Rica was giving orders or involved in any of the Pareto enterprises.

"Christ, *I've* been at more important meetings then she seems to have been," Carter muttered. At some point when she had finally admitted that she just couldn't face her empty bed and her tangled thoughts, she had gotten up to get a jacket. She'd sipped her beer, watched fingers of clouds flirt with the moon, and replayed the feel of Rica's mouth against hers.

Despite the cold, she'd dozed on and off, and now the first blush of pink teased along the horizon. She went back inside, changed into shorts and running shoes, and headed toward Herring Cove. She needed to run off the beer and sweat out the heat that Rica's kiss had stirred in her belly, because she had a feeling it might be a long time before she got that close to the elusive Mafia heiress again.

Rica struggled beneath Enzo's suffocating weight. His breath was hot on her neck, his hands rough on her skin, his hard lust bruising her flesh. She jerked her face away from his mouth and came awake with a gasp.

Shivering, she threw the covers aside and pulled a robe from a nearby chair. Wrapping it quickly around herself, she opened the French doors to her deck and stepped out into the dawn. The sky flamed purple and orange as the sun rose over the water. She braced her hands on the wooden railing and breathed the crisp salt air, letting it cleanse her. Closing her eyes, she touched her lips and remembered the soft glide of Carter's mouth.

For just a moment, she regretted not sleeping with Carter the night before. If she had, she would not have met Enzo and been reminded of his unwelcome touch. If she had let Carter complete her seduction, she could have lost herself for a few hours in the comfort of shared desire. It wasn't something she allowed herself often, and usually she limited the liaisons to women she knew only casually. Somehow Carter felt like more than that already.

As the erratic beat of her heart steadied and the queasiness left her stomach, Rica took in the peaceful vista that stretched from below her home to the ocean. A lone runner jogged along the footpath that snaked through the dunes on the water's edge. In the distance, a needle-thin red kayak crested the waves, headed toward Race Point. Overhead, a small twin-engine plane climbed into the sky on its journey to Boston.

Alone on her deck, Rica felt an inexplicable connection to those solitary souls as they shared the beauty of the dawn.

CHAPTER TWELVE

Carter stopped in the nearly empty parking lot at Herring Cove to catch her breath and to watch the last of the sunrise. A few RVs and a Jeep Cherokee were the only vehicles in sight. As she bent forward slightly, breathing deeply, inhaling salt and spray and the indefinable taste of the sea, she watched a kayaker paddle to shore. The kayaker climbed out into the surf when the craft was a few feet from shore, stumbling a little before grabbing the edge of the cockpit for balance. Carter saw then that the kayaker was a woman, and it looked as if she was having difficulty getting the craft onto the beach.

Carter started across the sand, and, as she came closer, realized that the moisture on the woman's face was more than sea spray. She was crying.

She was also very beautiful. Waves of auburn hair fell to her shoulders, surrounding an oval face with delicately arched cheekbones, a fine straight nose, and a sculpted jaw. Despite the early hour and the predictable chill, she wore shorts and a sleeveless T-shirt beneath her PFD. When she stripped off the vest and tossed it into the cockpit, her damp T-shirt clung to her high, full breasts. Her arms and legs were nicely toned and the rest of her figure followed suit. She had some kind of brace on her right ankle. Carter lifted a hand in greeting. "Can I help you with that?"

Tory blinked and brushed at the tears on her cheeks. When she'd seen the taillights of the cruiser disappear into the dark and realized that Reese was really gone, she'd known she wouldn't sleep. She had bundled up the baby and taken her to Jean and Kate's. They were used to her showing up at all hours when she had an emergency call and Reese was working, so they had taken Reggie and spared her any questions. Kate had given her a long look, and maybe whatever she had seen in Tory's eyes had been answer enough. The tears had been very close to the surface even then.

Once out on the water and settled into her rhythm, she had been fine, really. When the plane had lifted off and climbed slowly in a low arc above her head, she had watched, paddle resting across her bow, and imagined Reese looking out the window. "Be safe, baby," she had whispered.

Even on her way back she'd held on to some of the harmony she always achieved when her mind and body became one with the sea. It wasn't until she'd scanned the parking lot, unconsciously expecting to see Reese's cruiser as she had almost every day in the years they had been together, that the vacant spot where Reese should have been waiting blossomed inside her chest to leave her feeling hollow. And she had lost her battle with the tears.

"I'm sorry," Carter said gently and started to back away when she got no answer. "I didn't mean to intrude."

"No," Tory said hoarsely, "that's all right." The churning waves dragged at her kayak as she awkwardly pulled it higher onto the sand "You're not."

Carter reached for the strap on the nose of the kayak. "It's pretty cold out here. Aren't you freezing?"

"I'm still warm from paddling. I've got a jacket in the car." Tory held out her hand. "Tory King."

"Carter Wayne. Hello." Carter took note of the gold wedding band, still wondering about the tears. Since she couldn't think of any way of asking that wouldn't be awkward and embarrassing, she kept silent as they carried the kayak the rest of the way up the beach and lifted it onto the roof rack of the Jeep Cherokee she had passed in the parking lot.

"Thanks. I've got it from here," Tory said as she looped the tie-down straps through the front and rear handles and secured them to the bumpers.

"Okay. Nice meeting—" Carter stopped when a police cruiser slammed to a stop behind the Jeep and a young woman in uniform jumped out. Carter wasn't sure why, but the look on the officer's face was decidedly mistrustful.

"Everything all right, Tory?" Bri said.

"Yes. Bri, this is Carter Wayne. Carter, Officer Bri Parker."

Parker. The sheriff's daughter? Carter extended her hand. "Nice to meet you. I'm an attorney here in town. Just getting moved in."

"Hi," Bri said, her attention on Tory. "Reese said you'd probably be here. She said she'd call from the base when she gets in if she can."

Tory smiled. "Thanks." She glanced at Carter. "My partner. Her Marine reserve unit was just called up."

And there goes half my backup. Carter looked from Tory to Bri, who still regarded her suspiciously. "That's tough."

"Well, it was sudden," Tory agreed. "We're just getting adjusted." She touched Bri's cheek gently for a second. "I've got to get home and change. I'll be at the clinic later. Reggie is at Kate's." She opened the car door and smiled at Carter. "It was nice meeting you. Welcome to Provincetown."

"You too." Carter met Bri's steady stare and nodded. "Officer."

Bri touched her cap and climbed back into her cruiser. Through the open window she said, "Have a nice day."

Carter kept her smile in check as the cruiser backed out and sped away. Parker wasn't a rookie, but not far from it. And with Reese Conlon out of the picture, she'd have big shoes to fill. *Great. Nelson Parker is a desk jockey and Parker the Younger is hardly seasoned. And she looks like she has a temper. Terrific.*

Carter clenched her jaw, becoming increasingly uneasy about the entire assignment. It just didn't feel right. The target didn't feel right. Well, actually, she did. *Too* right, and that was part of the problem. Because Rica wasn't the first woman Carter had needed to get close to while undercover, but she was the first that it bothered her to lie to. And now her primary contact had just taken off for parts unknown. She took a deep breath and tried to dispel the feeling that something was off. She glanced up at the million-dollar houses sitting on the overlook facing the bay. Rica lived up there somewhere. She wasn't certain which house was hers from this vantage point, but she caught a glimpse of movement out on one of the decks. She squinted in the sunlight but was barely able to make out the figure of a woman. Her heart kicked in her chest and her stomach tensed as she felt the heat of Rica's mouth again.

"Get a grip, Carter. Jesus." With a shake of her head, Carter looked away from the shadowy figure and started to run.

❖

"Hello?" A sleepy voice said when the phone was answered.

Rica smiled. "Hi, Ang. What are you doing?"

"It's six thirty in the morning, Rica. What do you think I'm doing? I'm sleeping."

"Alone?"

"At the moment, yes. Three hours ago, I wasn't sleeping. And I wasn't alone."

"Was he worth losing sleep over?"

A sound that was half purr, half moan came through the line. "Oh, yeah. Big broad shoulders, big strong thighs, big thick—"

"I get it," Rica said, laughing. "Was this a regular or just a one-time side dish?"

"I don't know. He's got the potential to be a steady menu item." Another lusty sigh, and then Angie said, sounding much more alert, "So what are *you* doing?"

"Remember those super high-powered binoculars you got me for bird watching when you knew I was moving here?"

"The ones you informed me you would never use because you never go bird watching?"

"Those would be the ones."

"I remember."

"Well, I'm using them to spy on *people* instead."

"Really?" Angie said with interest. "Who?"

Rica leaned her elbows on the railing and held the powerful Zeiss binoculars to her eyes with one hand and the phone to her ear with the other.

"At the moment, I'm watching a very sexy woman run along the beach. Great shoulders, excellent thighs, and a nice tight—"

Angie's laughter interrupted her.

"Well, she's worth whatever you paid for these," Rica murmured.

"Do you know this woman or are you just turning into some kind of peeping Thomasina?"

"I don't actually know her." Rica watched Carter disappear into the scrub at the far end of the parking lot where the bike trail started its course through the dunes. "But I can tell you that she's a great kisser."

"Whoa. Back up. You don't *know* her, but you've kissed her?"

"I met her at my father's house a few weeks ago, and I had—almost had—dinner with her last night."

"Rica, you're not making any sense. How can you almost have dinner? And since when do you date family friends?"

"We're not dating," Rica said, her attention still focused on the dune trail where she expected to see Carter reemerge. "I told you, we barely know each other."

"But you're watching her at six thirty in the morning through binoculars. What aren't you telling me?"

"Nothing. There's nothing to tell."

Was there? When Rica had first glimpsed the runner, she'd gotten the prickly sensation that she recognized the figure. Just out of curiosity, she'd found the binoculars she'd tossed into a kitchen drawer and taken a closer look. When she had seen it was Carter, she couldn't look away. The little interlude on the beach with the very attractive kayaker still left her mildly...perturbed. She'd followed Carter on her trek down the beach, and then back up in the company of the woman carrying the kayak. And then the little conversation by the Jeep. Carter had leaned against the vehicle, all tight-bodied and wind-blown, looking spectacularly sexy.

Since Rica couldn't tell anything from the body language and she couldn't read lips, she was left to imagine the conversation. It was perfectly clear that Carter was being gallant, and what woman wouldn't enjoy that kind of attention from someone as good-looking and charming as Carter? If they were anywhere else in the world, Rica might not have thought anything of it, but this was Provincetown and two women lingering together on a beach at sunrise most often spelled mutual attraction.

And what of it? She'd already made it very clear to Carter that she wasn't interested in pursuing anything of a personal nature with her. Well, not anything beyond a pleasant interlude. Or two. Still, the image of the other woman smiling at Carter kept intruding on her thoughts.

"Rica?"

"Hmm? Sorry, what?"

"I said it sounds like this one has gotten under your skin."

"Not at all," Rica said with certainty.

"So what's the story with the kiss?"

Rica sighed. "Oh, it was just one of those things. She was just testing the waters."

"And did you invite her in for a dip?"

"No," Rica said with a laugh. "I informed her that I *might* be interested in something casual. And the operative word was *might*."

"How long has it been since you've had a serious relationship?"

Rica frowned. Angie might be her best friend, but Rica still didn't like to be interrogated about her personal life. It had been hard enough as a teenager trying to have friends when they learned exactly what it was her father did for a living. She had been embarrassed by her friends' curiosity and the need to offer explanations. As an adult, intimate relationships were even more problematic, and it was just so much simpler to avoid them. But she wasn't thinking about a relationship. She *was* thinking about Carter in bed. "More to the point, how long has it been since I've had sex."

"I take it she's at least a good candidate in that department?"

"If the kiss is any indication of the rest of her skills, most definitely."

"So? Why don't you do something about it?"

"I don't know," Rica mused. "If I hadn't first seen her at the house, maybe."

"Well, you're not in Boston now, so why don't you just think of this as a little side trip. You can keep it separate from everything else."

"That's a nice fantasy, but you know it's impossible."

"I can't remember the last time you mentioned a woman who even interested you. This one sounds like it's more than that. Take a chance."

Rica shook her head ruefully. Taking chances was exactly what she couldn't afford to do. "Are you coming out to visit soon?"

"You're changing the subject."

"You noticed."

Angie laughed. "As soon as I can. Call me with updates. I want to hear everything."

"I'll call you, but there won't be any updates."

When Rica hung up, she scanned the dunes with the binoculars again, but she saw no sign of Carter. *Take a chance.* When was the last time she'd done that? When was the last time she'd wanted to?

On impulse, she hurried inside.

❖

Carter swiped at the sweat on her brow with her bare forearm and stared at the woman walking toward her on the side of the road. She slowed and tried not to appear as if she were short of breath.

"Is this just a lucky coincidence?" Carter asked.

Smiling, Rica shook her head. "Actually, no. I happened to notice you when I was standing out on my deck."

Carter turned in a circle, frowning. "Where?"

Rica gestured to the hill behind them. "There."

Carter whistled, even though she had known that's where Rica lived. "Nice view."

"At times."

Grinning, Carter said, "I hope this morning was one of them."

Rica did another of those slow sexy scans, starting at the top of Carter's head, moving down over her sweat-stained T-shirt to the expanse of long, lean bare legs. "It had its memorable moments."

"So are you heading to the beach?"

"No. I realized that I was a terrible guest last evening and I thought I'd make up for it by offering you coffee and something to eat this morning."

Carter tried to ignore the jolt of anticipation that shot straight to her groin. This was the opportunity she'd been waiting for, and she couldn't let her hormones cloud her judgment. Nevertheless, she indicated her T-shirt and shorts. "I'm not fit for company right now. Maybe—"

"You can shower while I make coffee. I've got old sweats that will fit you."

Although the invitation might be a prelude to seduction, and a welcome one, Carter had the feeling that wasn't what Rica was doing. Trying to tread carefully and not overplay her hand, she lifted her shoulder. "You sure?"

"Yes," Rica said contemplatively, "I am."

Carter squelched the sudden image she had of Rica joining her in the shower. She got her mind under control, but her body was way ahead of her. She'd have to make the shower a cold one.

"Okay. Great. Let's go."

CHAPTER THIRTEEN

The bathroom is right down the hall." Rica pointed to the guest bathroom. "I'll start the coffee."

"Thanks," Carter said.

Still trying to figure out what was behind Rica's invitation and, more importantly, exactly how she had come to be undressing in Rica's bathroom, Carter shed her T-shirt and shorts and discarded them in a pile on the floor by the shower. Her skin was still tingling from Rica's earlier appraisal when she reached in and turned on the water. She kept it just this side of warm.

When she lathered her hair, she caught a whiff of the scent she'd smelled the night before when she had kissed Rica. The memory of the taste of Rica's lips sent tremors through her, and she struggled not to imagine Rica's fingers skimming over her body in swirls of soap and lust. She didn't do a very good job of banishing the fantasies.

The only thing the shower accomplished was sluicing off the sweat, because she was still just as hot as she had been when she stepped in. Her adrenaline was pumping as it always did when she was in the midst of an undercover case, and this time, she had the added boost of sexual excitement. She felt like a rocket ready to launch.

Christ, you'd think you were the rookie. The Parker kid could probably do a better job of it. Disgusted, Carter slicked her hair back with both hands and slid the glass shower door open. As she stepped out, the bathroom door opened and Rica slipped in.

Rica stared into Carter's eyes, then deliberately dropped her gaze. Carter felt her nipples tighten. Even when her clit throbbed, Carter didn't move a muscle. Wordlessly, Rica carefully placed a pair of sweatpants and a T-shirt on the counter, turned, and walked out.

Sucking in a shaky breath, Carter leaned back against the shower door and closed her eyes. She'd just been naked and two feet away from a woman who had looked at her more than once with open appreciation. Today Rica's gaze had held an invitation. Her assignment was to gain the woman's trust, by any means possible, and she'd stood there and done nothing. What the hell was wrong with her?

Carter pulled on baggy sweatpants and a Boston Bruins T-shirt, slid on her running shoes, and made her way into the kitchen. Rica stood at the counter with her back to the room, assembling breakfast.

"I'm sorry. I knocked," Rica said without turning.

"No problem," Carter replied. *I wish you'd done more than look. And since when do I wait for a woman to make the first move?*

"I thought we'd eat outside," Rica said, lifting the tray.

"Here, let me take that." Carter reached for the tray and their hands brushed. She swore she could see sparks jump into the air.

Rica backed up a step and relinquished the tray. "Thanks."

Carter followed Rica onto the deck and set the food in the middle of the round, beveled-glass table. As she settled into one of the wrought-iron chairs, she indicated the Bruins logo on the shirt. "Are you a fan?"

Rica shook her head as she poured coffee. "No. But my father is. You?"

"I have six brothers. Of course I'm a fan."

"Six?" Rica stared. "My God."

Carter smiled. Although a basic tenet of undercover work was to tell the truth whenever possible, because veracity always sounded more believable than lies and you were less likely to get tripped up down the road, she didn't usually extend that rule to disclosing information about her personal life. But then, none of the rules seemed to apply to her and Rica. "My father kept trying for girls."

"So you're the youngest?"

Carter shook her head. "Next to the youngest. My parents decided after my baby brother Charles was born that I was a fluke. They gave up on making me a sister."

"What was it like? Growing up with all those brothers?"

"I learned survival skills at an early age."

Rica laughed.

"It was fine," Carter said, sipping the coffee. "God, this is good. They were tough, but fair. If I didn't cry when I got hurt and didn't tattle to my parents about *anything* ever, they let me play whatever they were playing."

"Did you ever win?" Rica asked with an oddly thoughtful expression on her face.

"Once in a while. I got to be very fast. And sneaky."

"Really?" Rica gazed at Carter over the top of her coffee mug, which she cradled between her long, slim fingers. "Funny, you don't strike me as the nefarious sort."

Carter's stomach clenched. For the first time that she could remember, she hated her job. She felt a flush rise to her face and was helpless to stop it. "I try not to be when it really matters."

"Good." Rica indicated the tray of bagels and spreads. "You should eat something. You must be hungry after that run. Is that your normal routine?"

"Not really," Carter said as she broke a bagel in half. She looked up to find Rica's intent gaze on her. "I was trying to run you out of my system."

Rica's lips parted in surprise and her eyes widened slightly. A smile played across her mouth. "Did you learn that line from one of your brothers?"

"No." Carter took a bite of the bagel, chewed, and swallowed. "They got it from me."

Laughing, Rica tossed her head back, and sunlight shimmered over her hair in ebony waves. "You must be an excellent attorney."

"When I need to be." Carter decided that she liked Rica's laughter even more than her beautiful smile. Knowing she should push the flirtation, but inexplicably backing away from it, she changed the subject. "There's just you, isn't there? I mean, no brothers or sisters?"

"Just me," Rica said. "My father didn't remarry right away, and when he did, there were no further children."

"I used to be jealous of my friends with no siblings."

"And I used to envy my friends with big families."

Carter was rewarded with another one of Rica's rare smiles. "How's business?"

Rica raised an eyebrow.

"The *gallery*," Carter said with exaggerated emphasis. "I'm assuming our deal is still on."

"What deal?"

"Not to discuss other business when we're together."

"Business is good," Rica conceded. "I built a strong client list in New York, and many of the artists are happy to expand to another market. I'm going to have an open house as soon as I get a little more organized. Probably early June. You should come. Wine and cheese, some of the local artists will be there."

"I will. Thanks." Carter reached for the coffee carafe and refilled her own cup and Rica's. "But that's almost a month away. I'm going to see you before then, aren't I?"

"When are you going back to the mainland?"

Carter did a silent mental assessment, trying to sort out how quickly she should try to move things ahead. Her body said one thing and her professional judgment another. She went with the surge of heat rippling through her nervous system. "I'm back and forth pretty much all the time. That's the nice thing about working for yourself. I set my own schedule."

Rica reached across the table and took Carter's hand. "Well, I hope you intend to make room for me."

The morning grew very still. Even the seagulls quieted. Carter stared at Rica's fingers closed loosely over hers. It was the first time she'd ever truly heard her own heartbeat. She should have had a cool response, but her throat was dry and whatever came out was going to be anything but cool. She looked into Rica's eyes. She had never realized that black could come in so many shades, and then she realized that Rica's irises were comprised of subtly shifting shades of dark purples and grays, and not black at all. She wondered how many other things she'd been wrong about. "Does this fall under the category of casual and inconsequential occurrences?"

"It falls under I'm very attracted to you and I'm hoping that I'll get to see you in my bathroom without clothes again," Rica said.

Carter fought to keep her expression nonchalant. "It hasn't escaped me that you didn't answer the question. Casual and inconsequential?"

Rica smiled. "That didn't matter to you last night when you kissed me."

"That kiss kept me awake all night."

"Me too." Rica skimmed her thumb over the top of Carter's hand. "You seem to have an unforgettable mouth."

Carter found herself in the inexplicable position of sitting outdoors under a clear blue sky and feeling uncomfortably short of breath. She couldn't get enough air. Her chest squeezed down until her head was swimming. She was about to drown in the invitation in Rica's voice. Very carefully, she pushed to her feet, afraid she might stumble and pitch backward right over the railing.

"Thanks for breakfast." Carter gripped the railing to steady herself. "If I stay another minute, you're going to have to take me to bed and put me out of my misery."

Rica leaned back in her chair, her breasts rising and falling rapidly. "Would that be so bad?"

"Ask me again when my brain cells are functioning." Carter leaned down and braced her arms on either side of Rica, curling her fingers over the cool iron of the armrests. She kissed her, because she had to, or explode. She kissed her as she had the night before, without touching her with anything but her mouth, exploring the soft smooth surface of her lips with the tip of her tongue, slowly probing inside, deeper this time, losing herself in the inner heat. She moaned and broke the kiss when Rica slid a hand beneath her T-shirt and trailed her fingers over Carter's abdomen.

"The next time," Rica said, leaning her head back against the chair and letting her hands fall palms up onto her thighs, "a kiss, even a *great* kiss, is not going to be enough. Not when you take me halfway there just from the feel of you inside my mouth."

Carter closed her eyes for a second, fighting to keep her legs under her. "Jesus."

"You're going to have to make up your mind, Carter," Rica said. "This time yesterday morning you wanted me in bed. Now you don't."

"Rica," Carter said with a shake of her head, "it's not—"

"I don't need to know the reasons. And I'm not asking for them." Rica stood and stepped so close that her breasts pressed lightly against Carter's chest. She skimmed her mouth along the rim of Carter's ear. "But if you're going to play with me, don't quit until we finish the game."

Carter desperately wanted to hold her. She wanted to kiss her again. She wanted to lie down next to her and touch every inch of her body. She wanted to make her laugh and moan and cry out with pleasure. She wanted her so badly she ached in her bones. And she was afraid to touch her when a lie stood between them, and she didn't know what the hell to do about it. "I'm not playing."

Rica touched a finger to Carter's lips. "Of course you are."

Then Rica turned and disappeared inside the house, leaving Carter, stunned and so aroused she could barely move, to wander down the outside stairs to the street and make her way home. She needed the walk to figure out why she couldn't do what she'd been sent there to do, and she knew with certainty that a couple of miles was not going to be enough.

Tory walked down the narrow path beside the clinic and let herself in the back door. She didn't want to see Randy, because she knew the look of sympathy in his eyes would only make her sadness deepen. What she needed was to settle into routine, to focus on her patients and their problems to the exclusion of her own. In the years after she and KT had parted, she'd sought forgetfulness, if not solace, in her work. Eventually she had achieved a modicum of peace. She didn't expect that now, but she hoped that she would at least be able to keep the pain at bay.

What she hadn't expected was the tenderness and understanding in KT's eyes when they met in the hall.

"Hey, Vic," KT said softly, closing the chart she was studying and sliding it into a slot on the closed door beside her. "How are you doing?"

Tory shook her head and walked past her into her office. When KT followed, she held out a hand behind her. "Go back to work. I'm all right."

KT closed the door. "That's crap." She carefully took Tory by the shoulders and turned her to face her. Then she skimmed her fingers over Tory's cheek and into her hair. "You never could lie to me."

Tory smiled shakily. "You're such an arrogant bastard."

KT grinned. "And you always loved that about me."

"True." Tory looped her arms loosely around KT's waist and rested her head against her shoulder. "I don't know why I'm so scared. There are thousands of men and women over there. Trained to do this job. The casualty rate is very low."

"Because you and I know that statistics are meaningless." KT lightly stroked Tory's hair. "We deal with tragedy every day. Meaningless events that defy rationalization. We know that one in a million is an empty statistic if it happens to you or someone you love. It's an occupational hazard, Vic. That's what's got you so bent out of shape." She skimmed her hand down Tory's back and up again, a gentle caress. "That and the fact that you love her like crazy and you've never been apart before."

Tory leaned back, her hands on KT's hips. "Pia has been very good for you."

KT pretended to be affronted. "Now that hurts."

"You're right, about all of it. But the part about us never being separated before—you wouldn't have gotten that a year ago. It's because you understand"—she touched KT's chest above her heart—"in here, about being in love."

"Tory," KT said tenderly, her eyes troubled. "You know I lo—"

"Loved me?" Tory touched KT's cheek. "Of course I know. I loved you. Still do." She laughed. "I wouldn't have been able to say *that* a year ago. So maybe we both found places inside ourselves these past years that let us love differently."

"Okay," KT said, her voice tight. "I can buy that. Differently. Not better."

Tory smiled. "Speaking of Pia, why don't you go now and spend the rest of your weekend with her."

"There's a hell of a patient list still to go through. I can stay."

Tory shook her head. "No. It's good of you, really. I know what your days are like in the trauma center. You need this time to unwind. And you need to be with Pia." She rested her fingers against KT's chest again. "And she needs you. Go home."

"Thanks, Vic." KT kissed Tory's cheek and then shrugged out of her lab coat. "When do you expect to hear from Reese?"

"Today, I hope. When she arrives. She said she'd call if she could."

"*If* she could? What the hell does that mean?"

"I gathered things are moving quickly, and she's going to be right in the thick of it as soon as she arrives. She can't always—"

"Oh, that's just cra—"

"Why you so angry with her?" Tory asked mildly.

"Because she hurt you, God damn it. This whole war business, it's just ego and politics."

"That may be," Tory said, "but it's not Reese's doing or her fault."

KT scowled. "She should've gotten out when the baby was born."

"Maybe," Tory conceded. "Neither of us wanted to believe this was really going to happen, and I couldn't ask her to give up something that was part of her."

KT made a disbelieving sound.

"I know you don't understand it, but part of the reason I love her is because she believes in things like duty and responsibility."

"I get that," KT said. "Sort of."

"You should. I fell in love with you for the same reason."

"Oh, unfair."

Tory smiled. "Go home, KT. Go home and tell Pia how much you love her."

"Okay," KT said grudgingly. "Tell Reese I said hi, and to get her goddamn ass back here soon."

"Oh," Tory said softly as KT left. "I surely will."

CHAPTER FOURTEEN

Tory closed her eyes and dropped her head onto the back of her chair. The headache that had been threatening for the last three hours had finally erupted as a staccato burst of light and fury behind her eyes. She groaned softly and tried not to think about the fact that she had three more patients to see and it was almost nine p.m. Somehow the afternoon and evening had gotten away from her, but despite the breakneck pace, she had not been able to keep Reese out of her thoughts. Whenever she stepped away from a patient to jot a note in a file or search for a lab report, she remembered that when she finally went home, Reese would not be there to hold her. She hadn't realized how much she had come to depend upon Reese's strength and utter constancy. Without Reese near, she felt frighteningly unsteady.

Opening her eyes, Tory reached for the next chart. She had patients who relied upon her, a daughter who needed her, and a lover who trusted her to get through whatever lay ahead for them. And that's exactly what she intended to do. She opened the chart and withdrew the patient's most recent EKG. When the phone rang, she reached for it absently, her attention on the report.

"Dr. King."

"Hi," Reese said.

Tory dropped the chart and sat up straight. "Reese? Are you at the base?"

"For a few more hours, then I'm shipping out. How are you?"

"Oh God, I miss you." It hadn't been what she'd meant to say, but the sound of Reese's voice made her forget her resolutions.

"Same here. I don't suppose that's going to change any time soon."

"No, I guess not," Tory said with a small smile. "I'm *so* glad you called."

"Still seeing patients?"

"Mmm."

"Tor," Reese said, her voice low and husky, "it's late. You should be home."

"Almost. Just a few more minutes," Tory said, feeling a little bit of her world slide back into place with the familiar sound of Reese's concern. "How about you? Is everything all right?"

"Fine. Just a little hectic."

"Is your father there?"

"No," Reese said. "I have a message to call him as soon as I arrive."

Tory laughed. "Insubordinate already, Colonel?"

"I needed to hear your voice."

Tory caught her breath. "Oh, sweetheart. Me, too."

"So," Reese said after a few seconds of silence, "I guess I can expect Reggie to be spoiled beyond recognition, what with all the time she'll be spending with Kate and Jean."

"Undoubtedly."

Reese laughed. "Small price to pay. I'm glad you have them. That *we* have them."

"I'd be lost without their help."

"I'm sorry, Tor—"

"We're past that now, sweetheart. We love you. All of us, so much."

"I love you too, baby."

Tory closed her eyes, imagining Reese's face, absorbing the sound of her voice as if it were a touch. "Can you tell me anything? Where you're going? What you'll be doing?"

"I'll be onboard ship for the next week or so until we reach Mosul, and then our unit is headed for Baghdad."

"Well," Tory said, clenching the pen she held in her right hand so hard her fingers ached, "I'm not surprised."

"We'll mostly be doing cleanup, Tor—transport, escort, and containment. The main resistance is broken."

"Of course. I know." Tory didn't believe her. She watched television. She listened to the news. She knew it wasn't that simple, but she wasn't going to argue. Reese was trying to protect her, and she needed to believe that she could. She needed to be secure in the knowledge that Tory was all right. Tory inhaled slowly and forced a note of lightness into her voice. "Still, you'll probably be busy polishing whatever it is that you Marines polish with such devotion, so I won't worry if you don't call every day."

Reese laughed. "Phone calls might be tricky, but everything is computerized. I'll e-mail as often as I can. Just don't worry if you don't hear from me—"

"I understand," Tory said quickly, wondering how in God's name she was going to stand not knowing what was happening to her over there. "I've got a message for you from KT."

"Oh yeah?"

Tory smiled at the faint edge in her lover's usually calm voice. Although Reese and KT got along well, they were too much alike not to feel the tiniest bit competitive. "She said to tell you to get your ass back...no...your *goddamn* ass back as soon as possible. I agree."

"You can tell her from me that's at the top of my list." After another pause, Reese said, "I've got to go, Tor."

The sinking feeling in the pit of her stomach hit so fast, Tory was nauseous. She dropped her pen and pressed her hand hard against her abdomen, waiting for the sensation to pass before trying to speak. "I love you."

"That's just what I need." Reese cleared her throat. "Kiss Reggie for me."

"I will."

"I love you, Tory. I'll talk to you soon."

"Bye, darling."

"Bye, baby."

The line went dead and Tory dropped the receiver onto the desk. She pressed both hands to her eyes and took deep breaths, willing the sick surge of panic to dissipate. *She's going to be fine. She won't get hurt. She'll come home soon. Nothing will happen to her.*

"Tory?" Randy said tentatively from the doorway. "You okay?"

Tory brushed her palms over her cheeks and sat up. She smiled at her receptionist, who looked worried. "Yes. Just tired."

"I can reschedule the last three. They're all regulars."

With a shake of her head, Tory braced her hands on the desk and pushed herself upright. "No. I'll see them."

"Was that Reese?"

"Yes."

"Is everything okay?" Randy asked softly.

"Just fine." Wondering when, if ever, she would begin to believe her own lies, Tory lifted a chart from the desk. "Don't worry. Everything is fine."

Carter wanted to see Rica. She hadn't thought of anything else all day. Somewhere in the last twenty-four hours she'd gotten completely off track. In her line of work, she was used to events moving rapidly. She'd learned to shift alliances in the blink of an eye, had become adept at altering her cover story just enough to divert suspicion at a moment's notice, and could fake almost anything, from anger to an orgasm, with little effort.

Now, she couldn't find her groove. She couldn't get her mind off the many images of Rica—weary and vulnerable that first night at her father's, reserved and aloof in the gallery, sensual and seductive that morning. The memory of Rica's voice, her touch, drew Carter along Commercial Street toward the gallery like a salmon struggling upstream to die. She couldn't stop herself.

She walked with her head down, her hands in her pockets, mentally arguing with herself. She knew she needed to back away, because every atom in her body wanted to take up where that kiss had left off. And she couldn't afford to be thinking with her hormones in the middle of a case. Not just for the sake of getting laid. And obviously that was what Rica was interested in. Her remarkable turnabout since the day before—*her very, very sexy change of heart,* Carter thought—was clear evidence that was *all* Rica was interested in.

And what the hell is wrong with that? That's exactly what you want, Carter muttered under her breath. *Let her call the shots. Let her think she's in control. It's a perfect setup to gain her trust and find out what you need to know.* Carter laughed. *Who are you kidding? She* is *in control. You don't know what the fuck you're doing, and she's got you tied up in knots.*

Carter tensed when a hand closed around her arm, and she automatically pulled away. The grip tightened, and surprised, she stopped to face the interloper.

"Jesus Christ, what are you still doing here?"

Special Agent Marilyn Allen dragged Carter out of the stream of pedestrians into the mouth of a narrow unpaved alley that led down to the beach. "*You're* the one who's walking around talking to herself. What the hell is wrong with you?"

"Nothing." Carter glanced worriedly across the street. They were in direct eyesight of Rica's gallery and the lights were still on, which meant she was still there. "Look, this is a bad idea. We can't be seen together."

"We need to talk."

"Fine. But not—aw, shit."

The lights went out in Beaux Arts and Rica stepped out the front door.

"What?" Allen said, her voice rising.

"Quiet," Carter snapped and yanked Allen a few feet further down the alley into the shadows. She risked one look back toward the gallery and cursed again. Then she shoved Allen against the nearest building, treated her to a full body press, and clamped her mouth over Allen's open, astonished one.

Rica pushed redial on her cell phone as she cut diagonally across Commercial Street toward the path to the beach. It was one of those early May nights that felt more like summer than spring, and she'd rather walk home along the water than dodge the unseasonable late night crowds.

She frowned as she listened to Carter's phone ring unanswered, annoyed that she didn't even know her cell number. The only listing that directory assistance had available was for the law office, and it probably didn't ring in Carter's apartment.

On the other hand, it was ridiculous that she was even contemplating chasing after a near stranger when they didn't know each other well enough to have exchanged telephone numbers. She turned down the alley toward the harbor, snapped the phone shut in disgust, and dropped it in her shoulder bag. A low moan drew her attention to two figures in the shadows. There was barely enough light to make out the shapes of two women writhing in the heat of passion, arms and legs twisting about one another, hands frantically grappling for purchase. One yanked the other's shirt from her pants, exposing a pale patch of skin to the moonlight.

Quickly, Rica averted her gaze, but not before she'd seen enough to send a searing bolt of arousal through her. She imagined Carter as she'd seen her that morning, sleek-bodied and strong, with her narrow hips pumping between Rica's spread thighs, pounding against her swollen sex until Rica came screaming beneath her.

"God," Rica whispered, walking faster until she sank into the warm, soft sand. She stopped a few feet from the water's edge and opened the top button of her blouse. Her body was flushed with heat. She tilted her head back and let the damp breeze wash over her face and neck.

She had wanted women before in her life, some with hunger, some with need. Some for hours. Others for far longer, or so she had thought at the time. Some she'd considered friends, other strangers. Carter was all of them, and like no one she'd ever met before. Sitting out on the deck with her the evening before and that morning, she'd found Carter easy to talk to—charming and open. Unassuming and even a little bit uncertain. And then a look that was more raw than simple desire had come over her face, a dark shadow had eclipsed her clear gaze, and something dangerous had leapt to the surface. Her mouth had been hard and demanding, yet she had held back. Even as they kissed, Carter hadn't pushed, hadn't tried to take from her more than she was ready to give. Hadn't even tried to take what Rica *wanted* to give. Rica had felt desire tremble between them, had felt the swift clench of muscles when she had brushed her fingers over Carter's abdomen. There was want there, every bit as urgent as her own. And still Carter had hesitated.

"Why?" She wrapped her arms around herself, suddenly chilled. *Take a chance,* Angie had said. Rica wasn't certain she even had a choice.

She thought about calling Carter's number one more time but decided that she didn't want to hear the unanswered phone. She didn't want to wonder who Carter was with. Whose mouth she might be tormenting with irresistible, unbearable pleasure.

❖

Groaning, Agent Allen dug her fingers into Carter's back and plunged her tongue into Carter's mouth. Carter felt as if the air was being sucked from her lungs as Allen threatened to consume her with the voracious kiss. A hand snaked between her legs and squeezed down so hard she grunted in surprise. Then just as quickly, Allen elbowed Carter viciously in the ribs and jammed her knee between Carter's legs in the exact spot her fingers had just been exploring.

"Oh, fuck," Carter gasped as she released Allen and staggered away, collapsing against the wall. She locked her knees to keep from falling while she doubled over and struggled not to vomit.

Allen gripped a handful of Carter's hair and yanked her head back. "What the *fuck* do you think you're doing?"

Carter found herself staring into Allen's furious face. "Trying not to puke. Let go."

"Jesus," Allen said in disgust and stepped away. She pushed back her hair with trembling hands and stared into the street.

Carter braced a palm against the crumbling planks of the building and slowly straightened. She squinted down the alley, blinking tears from her eyes. She couldn't see Rica. Her groin pulsed with pain, but the nausea was subsiding.

"That was Rica who passed us a minute ago," Carter muttered through gritted teeth.

Allen swung her head around. "What?"

"Rica. I didn't think…it would be a good idea if she saw us together."

"I didn't see her."

No, you were too busy trying to swallow my tongue. Who would have guessed you were that kind of hungry. Carter rubbed her ribs. "Nice shot."

"You could have faked it. You didn't have to assault me."

"Believe me, I didn't enjoy it."

Allen stiffened. "You're not only ineffective at your job, Wayne, you're dangerously unbalanced."

Carter straightened up, wincing at the lingering ache in her crotch. "I'm so happy we shared this time together. Have a nice night."

When Carter started to step around Allen, who stood between her and the street, Allen gripped her arm again.

"I said we needed to talk."

"It can wait. I need a drink. And some aspirin."

"You can have all the alcohol you want as soon as you're debriefed. Then I couldn't care less what you do."

Carter stopped. "Debriefed? What are you talking about?"

"I said, not here."

"Christ." Reluctantly, Carter followed Allen across the street and up one of the narrow streets that connected Commercial to Bradford. Toome was parked halfway up the block in the familiar gray sedan. Obviously, they'd never left town.

"If you two keep hanging around, you're going to blow my cover," Carter said as she slid carefully into the backseat. Allen packed a lot more power than her thin frame suggested.

"You're not going to have to worry about that any longer," Allen said as she lifted a briefcase onto her lap and extracted a folder from inside. "And it's lucky for you that we *did* stay in town. At least someone involved is gathering vital information."

Carter leaned her head back against the seat. "And I'm sure you're going to tell me."

"We're taking you off the case. This part at least."

"What?" Carter snapped, jerking forward. She was pleased to see Allen recoil even though the front seat was an effective barrier between them.

"It's come to our attention that the initial intelligence on Pareto's daughter was wrong."

"You mean Rica isn't going to lead us anywhere because she's not involved with the business," Carter said, a surge of relief rushing through her.

"No," Allen said sharply, "we have no evidence that Ms. Pareto is not part of the organization. But our new information makes it very clear that you're not going to be of any use to us as far she's concerned."

Carter shook her head, wondering if the kiss had deprived Allen of essential oxygen. "You want to try speaking English?"

"She's not a lesbian, Wayne. She's Lorenzo Brassi's lover."

Carter laughed. "Wherever you're getting your information, it's wrong." She wasn't about to tell them about the near tryst she'd had with Rica that morning, because she didn't intend to tell Agent Allen anything that she didn't have to. And for some reason, the time she'd spent with Rica had felt personal. It wasn't about business.

Allen leaned between the seats and dropped a file folder into Carter's lap. She shone her Maglite on it. "Open it."

"Christ," Carter muttered, shaking her head. She flipped the folder open and blinked as the glare of the intense light reflected off the shiny surface of the photograph. Lorenzo Brassi stood with his arms around Rica, one hand nearly cradling her breast. His mouth was against her neck. The bastard looked like he was one step away from fucking her standing up. Carter recognized the gallery in the background.

"That was last night," Allen said with a hint of triumph in her voice. "I'd say they look rather *friendly*, wouldn't you." She flipped the photograph aside with one neatly trimmed fingernail to reveal another underneath.

This time Rica's hands were on Lorenzo's chest and their hips were almost fused together. Carter couldn't see Rica's face because her hair had fallen forward to cover most of it, but Brassi had a look of arrogant pleasure on his. Carter wanted to kill him. She closed the folder.

"This doesn't mean anything."

"We followed them while they took a lovers' stroll through town and out onto the pier. They were very cozy the entire time."

Carter looked at Toome. "You take the photographs?"

Toome nodded.

"You agree with her?"

Again, the agent nodded. "It's been rumored that Brassi and Ricarda might marry. The old man is in favor of it."

Carter felt another swell of nausea, and it had nothing to do with the blow to her groin. She hadn't been wrong in what she'd seen in Rica's eyes, or in what she'd felt when they'd kissed. If marriage was in the works, she couldn't believe it was anything other than family business. "That doesn't change anything."

"It makes it less likely that you're going to get anything substantial from her," Allen replied. "You've already got a strong contact with Rizzo, and there's no point in risking that. You're to back off on the daughter. We've got surveillance on Brassi. That will be enough."

"I don't take orders from the FBI." Carter opened the door and stepped out. "I'm not changing anything until I talk to my team."

Allen powered down her window. "Talk all you want. It's already been decided." She smiled at Carter. "Have a nice night. And take care of that...headache."

Carter watched them drive away. She wasn't thinking about her sore ribs or her throbbing groin. She was thinking about the image of Lorenzo Brassi with his hands all over Rica Grechi. It was just as well she hadn't been the one to see it, because even now she wanted to wipe that smug look off his face with her fist.

CHAPTER FIFTEEN

Carter slid into a booth in a roadside diner in Eastham, thirty miles up the Cape from Provincetown. Her partner, State Investigator Kevin Shaughnessy, sat across from her with a plate of eggs, sausage, and pancakes and a look of unbridled lust on his florid Irish face. "You're early."

"Don't let me interrupt," Carter said sarcastically, "because I've only been trying to reach you for three days." She managed a smile for the young waitress, who magically appeared at her side, and turned her coffee cup right side up. "Just coffee, thanks."

"You sure?" The blond waitress wore a short black skirt and a white blouse that was so tight it gaped open between her breasts, displaying a lovely expanse of creamy cleavage. She cocked her hips and gave Carter a special smile. "We've got a great menu here."

"I believe it," Carter replied, grinning despite her irritation at being made to cool her heels for three days before getting some decent information about what was happening with Rica and the investigation. "But nothing for me right now."

"Well, if you change your mind"—the waitress slowly ran her fingers over her chest and tapped the plastic badge that said *Kylie*— "you be sure to ask for me."

As Kylie sashayed away, Kevin swallowed noisily and said, "Jesus. That never happens to me."

"Maybe that's got something to do with your wedding ring." Carter sipped her coffee. "Eat before your eggs get cold."

"I can eat and talk." To prove it, Kevin swiped his toast through the egg yolk on his plate and took a huge bite. "So what bug is biting your ass?"

"It's not a bug, it's more like a piranha. By the name of Allen."

Kevin made a face. "Her. What exactly did you do to her, anyway?"

"Me? Nothing…" Carter couldn't help but smile at the memory of Allen going native during that kiss, even though her crotch was still sore from the backlash. She bet Allen was still thinking about it too, unless Allen's powers of denial were even better than Carter imagined. "…much."

"Sorry I couldn't get here sooner, but I was tied up meeting with the brass and the state's attorney the last couple of days."

"Not your fault," Carter said with a sigh. "Look, Allen says they're pulling me in. At least from this part. What do you know about that?"

"You know the feds never tell us everything, and what they share with the higher-ups doesn't trickle down to us." He held up a hand when Carter growled. "*But*, I do know that attention has shifted from the daughter to the nephew."

"Why?"

"Since the daughter has been in Provincetown, there's been more activity in the Manhattan gallery—especially after hours. And the interesting thing is, they're not all Pareto people."

"You sure?"

"Positive IDs." Kevin shoveled in another forkful of breakfast and washed it down with coffee. "At least two *customers* have been Pareto competitors."

"That doesn't make a lot of sense."

"It makes even less sense when they show up on the same day that Lorenzo Brassi pays a visit."

"Brassi again," Carter said with disgust, immediately remembering the photograph of him with his arms around Rica and his fingers splayed beneath her breast. "What's your read on that? You think he's branching out on his own?"

"Maybe, but if he is, he's dumber than he looks. There's already a rumor that some highly positioned people want him to succeed Pareto, and not Ricarda. He'd be crazy to risk that."

"Some men don't like to wait for power."

Kevin laughed. "You got that right. Still, he's got a sweet deal for a guy who's not a blood relative."

"What do you mea—oh, right. He's a nephew by Pareto's second wife. He and Rica aren't blood cousins." *Which makes a marriage even more feasible*, Carter thought sourly. "He's been out here sniffing around Rica. If there's interest in him, why pull me off?"

"Who knows, maybe they think you'll get in the way of something he's got going with her." Kevin smirked and made a suggestive hand gesture. "Business or otherwise."

Carter put her hands flat on the table and leaned forward, her eyes flashing. "I'm telling you, she's not in it that way. Allen's got nothing."

"Whoa," Kevin said, sitting back. "Take it easy. I'm just saying maybe she and Brassi are—"

"And *I'm* saying, they're not."

Kevin narrowed his eyes, all trace of frivolity gone. He hunched closer, his big body casting a shadow across the table. "What's going on? Did you get up close and personal with her already?"

"No," Carter said sharply.

"But there's something."

Carter stared stonily past Kevin out the window.

"Oh, for fuck's sake." Kevin made a sound like a load of gravel hitting the pavement. "All the women you've blown off after a night or two, and *this* one is the one that gets to you?"

"Leave it alone, Kevin."

"You're the one that has to leave it alone. Leave *her* alone." Kevin shook his head. "It's a damn good thing Allen wants you to back off before you get your ass in a boatload of trouble. Stay away from her, Carter."

"It looks like I don't have a choice."

"I'll have that crated and shipped to you by the end of the week," Rica said, handing a receipt to the woman who had just purchased one of the most expensive paintings in the gallery. When the chime over the front door jingled, she glanced up automatically. It had been a busy morning, and after finalizing this last sale, she had planned to close for several hours and catch up on the attendant paperwork. She needed an assistant, but she enjoyed filling her time with work. She paused with the receipt extended when she saw Carter. Then she looked quickly back to her customer. "Thank you and I hope you stop by again."

"Oh, don't worry. I will. I love your selections."

As the woman swept out, Rica followed in her wake and flipped the small sign on the front door to *Closed*. She snapped the lock and turned to face Carter. She hadn't expected to see her again. It had been three days with no contact, and even though she'd risen early each morning to scan the path along the beach, Carter had not returned to jog along the beach trail.

Rica understood the signals perfectly well. Any woman who was interested would have contacted her by now, especially after the blatant invitation she'd made the last time they were together. In retrospect, she was glad she hadn't reached Carter by phone that night. She would have been humiliated by a polite refusal from Carter after her own none too subtle actions that morning. She'd been motivated more by lust than by reason, and that embarrassed her.

Still, in her own defense, it was very easy to lust after a woman who looked so good in jeans and a faded denim shirt. Carter's hair was nicely windblown and she looked ever so sexy. Rica couldn't help but smile. "I'm sorry, we're closed."

Carter grinned. "Then my timing's perfect." She hefted the paper bag she held in the crook of one arm. "I brought lunch."

"You're always trying to feed me."

"I'm trying to ingratiate myself, remember?"

Rica laughed.

"Besides," Carter said, "this time we're going to play tourist first, *then* have lunch."

"Oh, are we? You've got it all planned."

"Absolutely," Carter said, lying with conviction. She hadn't the slightest idea what she was doing, but she knew she wasn't leaving town without seeing Rica again. Kevin had said the bosses wanted her back on the mainland, focusing her efforts on Rizzo and her inside connection. She hadn't been exactly *ordered* to stay away from Rica, but she wouldn't have much chance to see her either. So when she'd left the diner she didn't think about what she was going to do next, she just acted. "We've got an outboard waiting for us at Flyer's, and I'm taking you to Long Point for lunch on the beach. Have you got a jacket here? It's going to be chilly on the boat."

Rica stared. "In case you haven't noticed, it's the middle of the day in the middle of the week. I'm running a business here."

Carter hooked a thumb in the direction of the door. "Says *closed* to me."

"I'm in heels, Carter, and this"—Rica indicated her royal blue silk blouse and slacks—"is not picnic wear."

"We'll swing by your place. You can change and grab a windbreaker." Carter took a step closer and kissed Rica lightly on the mouth. "Please."

Rica felt a warning flutter in her stomach, far far more than she should be feeling from just a simple kiss. "You have to stop doing that."

"What?" Carter asked, her voice husky.

"Kissing me."

"Please tell me you're lying."

"All right," Rica said, easing her arms around Carter's waist. "I'm lying." She kept her eyes open as she slid her mouth slowly over Carter's. With a soft sigh, she pressed closer and teased her tongue along the inner surface of Carter's lip, tugging ever so gently with her teeth.

"Rica," Carter gasped when Rica pulled away.

"Hmm?" Rica unbuttoned the first button on Carter's shirt and skimmed her fingertips inside.

Carter, feeling as if she had been washed in fire, broke out into a full body sweat. Even her vision was red. "We're crushing the sandwiches."

Rica struggled to make sense of the words, because she was seconds away from dragging Carter down to the floor. The reality of her, the hard length of her thighs, the soft press of her breasts, the hot taste of her mouth, was so much better than the dreams that had brought her to the edge of orgasm more than once in the last few days. She'd never been so helpless to resist a woman in her life. "Well," she gasped, putting her palms flat against Carter's chest and pushing back a few inches. She searched Carter's eyes and smiled, satisfied when she saw her own desire reflected there. "We wouldn't want that, would we?"

"You have no idea what I want."

"Oh, I think I do." Rica brushed a single fingertip along the edge of Carter's lower lip and stepped away. "Let's go for a boat ride and find out."

Twenty minutes later, Rica had changed into casual tan slacks and a burgundy pullover. They'd collected some sunscreen, towels, and a blanket at Rica's, and Carter was now steering the outboard away from the dock at Flyer's boat rental.

"Cold?" Carter shouted above the wind and the roar of the motor.

Rica sat in the middle of the boat, facing Carter, her hands curled around the edge of the aluminum seat. She tilted her head back so that her hair streamed behind her in the breeze and the sun warmed her face. "Not at all. It's great out here."

"You look beautiful."

"Thank you," Rica said, meaning it. She'd heard it before, almost all her life. From boys and then men, and women. She rarely if ever believed them. It wasn't their words she distrusted, but why they'd said them. Carter stood with her legs braced in the back of the boat, hips thrust forward, one arm stretched back behind her on the motor. Her shirt was wet from spray and plastered to her chest. When she wasn't checking the water ahead for other boats, she was looking at Rica. Not just an idle glance, but an absorbing gaze that suggested she was trying to memorize everything about her. Rica shivered. "Watch where you're going."

The corner of Carter's mouth flickered. "That's exactly what I'm doing."

Rica tilted her head back again and closed her eyes. She couldn't keep looking at Carter because just the sight of her was making her excited. Her arousal was fast overtaking her common sense, and as much as she enjoyed the sensation, she needed to remember who she was, and more importantly, who Carter was. Sex was one thing. A very nice thing, to be sure. But what she was starting to feel when she looked at Carter felt dangerously like something else.

The motor quieted and alerted Rica to the fact that they were approaching the beach. It was still too early in the year for it to be crowded, and as she glanced toward the lighthouse at the very tip of Long Point, she could see that they were alone.

"Do you need me to get out and guide us in?" Rica asked.

Carter shook her head. "No. If you get wet, you'll be too cold. I'll just coast us up onto the beach."

A minute later they grounded and Carter jumped out. She grabbed the bow of the boat and pulled it farther up onto the sand. "Toss me the gear."

Rica did, and then climbed onto the small platform at the bow. Before she could jump off, Carter grasped her waist and swung her down. When she landed, they were body to body again, and it was the most natural thing in the world to wrap her arms around Carter's neck and kiss her.

"Thanks," Rica said when she finally broke the kiss. She skimmed her fingers through Carter's damp hair. "It's too cold to make love in the surf, so I'd suggest we take a walk instead."

"Whatever you say," Carter said, taking Rica's hand and grabbing the gear with the other. Rica was in control and Carter knew it, and she didn't know what to do about it. After leaving Kevin and knowing she was going to see Rica, regardless of anyone's orders, she had finally stopped pretending that she was doing her job. Being with Rica had nothing to do with Rica's father or Carter's being an undercover investigator or Allen's FBI sting operation. It had everything to do with the fact that Rica was an intriguing woman and just thinking about her made Carter ache to be close to her. Yes, she wanted her. Desperately, urgently. But just as much as she wanted to taste her again, to run her hands over the sleek lines of her body, she wanted to know what drove a young, intelligent, vibrant woman to leave everything in her life behind and seclude herself in a sleepy little town by the sea. Because that's exactly what Rica had done. "You're the boss."

"Actually," Rica said playfully, leaning close to brush a kiss along the edge of Carter's jaw, "I'm not."

It was the first time Rica had ever directly alluded to her father's business, and Carter knew she should follow up on it. Instead, she swung their joined hands and pointed toward a natural cul-de-sac in the dunes where they would be shielded from the worst of the wind by the rising swells of sand on either side. "We can spread the blanket out in there and continue the conversation you started by the boat."

"Not until I've had lunch and...did I see champagne in that gear bag of yours?"

"You did." They stopped and Carter handed one end of the blanket to Rica. Together they spread it out on the sand and weighted it down at the corners with items from the bag. "Go ahead and get comfortable, and I'll serve you."

Rica stretched out on the blanket, leaning on her elbows to watch Carter put out their lunch. "This just gets better all the time."

Carter shot her a grin. "Wait till we get to dessert."

Rica was afraid she wouldn't make it through lunch without begging Carter to touch her. She so desperately needed to get control of herself, and yet she loved the way being around Carter made her feel. For the first time in her life, she felt not only wonderfully alive, but completely herself. "I'll try. But I'm not making any promises."

"I'm not asking for any." Carter knelt beside Rica on the blanket, the bottle of champagne cradled between her palms, and leaned down to kiss her. She kept it light and easy because she wanted it to be anything but. And it just wasn't possible. "Let's just enjoy it."

"Yes. Let's."

Chapter Sixteen

Tory fumbled for a towel and wiped at the smear of puréed carrots on Reggie's cheek. "Come on, honey, two more bites and we're done." She glanced at the clock. Ten minutes to two. She was going to be late for work. Again.

"Never mind," Tory murmured. "It's not your fault." If she'd been sleeping better, the few extra hours she needed for child care without Reese home to help wouldn't have mattered. But the bed was too large and achingly empty, and sleep just wouldn't come.

"My schedule is just off, that's all. Things will be fine in a few more days."

Reggie smiled and blew carrot bubbles.

The crunch of tires over shells in the driveway drew Tory's attention, and she set the spoon aside, wondering as to the identity of her unexpected visitor. She took three steps toward the screen door and jerked to a stop with a small gasp. She could just make out the dark-haired officer in the patrol car, and for a second, all she could think was *Reese!*

When Bri climbed out, the disappointment was sharp enough to make her moan softly. Still, she forced a smile as Bri rapped on the door.

"Come in," Tory called, turning back to Reggie, who was making impatient noises. "We're about done with lunch and then I have to take her over to Kate's."

"Are you working today?" Bri tossed her hat onto the counter, followed by her keys.

Tory watched the familiar action, thinking of how many times she'd seen Reese do exactly the same thing. Bri, with her thick, jet black hair, brilliant blue eyes, and confident walk, seemed more like Reese every day. Tory was glad to see her, but on some irrational level, it hurt.

"I'm due in the clinic in about five minutes."

Bri looked at Reggie, who was eagerly reaching for the next spoonful of baby food. "Want me to finish that so you can get ready?"

"Are you on your lunch break?"

"Yeah."

"I'd love for you to take her, but I'm warning you right now, you'll probably end up with carrots on your uniform."

Bri shrugged. "No problem."

Tory smiled, knowing that Bri was every bit as particular about the appearance of her uniform as Reese was. *God, could they be any more alike?* She touched Bri's shoulder lightly on her way to wash her hands. "Thank you."

"Uh, Tory?"

"Mmm?"

"Have you heard from Reese?"

Tory dried her hands and folded the towel with more care than necessary. "I had an e-mail two days ago. She said she was about to ship out, and that it would be a while before she could contact me again. You?"

Bri shook her head. "I got an e-mail then too. She said everything was okay, that she was really busy, and wanted to know if everything was okay here."

"Here, here?" Tory asked quietly. "Meaning me?"

"She didn't say, exactly," Bri said, looking uncomfortable. She adroitly avoided Reggie's flailing hands and guided a spoonful of baby food into Reggie's mouth. "She probably just meant work."

"Probably." Tory slid her arm around Bri's shoulders. "I'm really glad that you came by. I've been going a little crazy just talking to Reggie, although it *is* nice that she never argues or contradicts me."

Bri laughed. "So how are things."

"I'm doing okay. You can tell her that, okay?" Tory rested her cheek against the top of Bri's head for a second. "I really miss her, though."

"Me too."

"Are things all right with her gone and the busy season coming?"

"My dad rearranged the schedule some. It'll be okay until Reese gets back. She won't be gone that long."

Tory gave Bri a squeeze. "I'm going to change, honey. Can you stay with her a few more minutes?"

"I can take her to Kate's, if you want. She loves to ride in the cruiser." Bri blushed. "The baby seat's in the trunk."

"Has anyone ever told you that you're incredibly sweet?"

Bri grinned that cocky grin that had had her breaking hearts since she was sixteen years old. "Caroline does. Now and then."

"I'll just bet she does." Laughing, feeling lighter at heart than she had since Reese left, Tory lifted Reggie from her high chair. "I'll get her things together while you fix the car seat. And Bri? Thanks."

"You know, I was sort of screwed up when I first met Reese, but she trusted me anyhow. Then the two of you took me in when Caroline and I had that bad spot last year," Bri said quietly. "I think I might have been in trouble if you hadn't." She settled her hat low on her brows. "That makes us family, right?"

"Oh honey," Tory whispered, kissing her cheek. "Yes, it does."

Carter slid behind Rica on the beach blanket, extending her legs outside of Rica's thighs, and wrapped her arms loosely around Rica's waist. She nuzzled Rica's neck just below her ear. "You're shivering."

Rica settled back against Carter's shoulder, turned her head, and kissed Carter's throat. "I'm not cold."

"Sure?" Carter leaned to one side and retrieved the champagne bottle that she had propped up in the sand while they ate the sandwiches she'd picked up earlier. She refilled Rica's plastic cup and then her own.

"Mmm." Rica grasped Carter's forearms and drew them securely around her middle. "The tide's going out."

Carter eased forward until her breasts and abdomen were tight to Rica's back. "We've got a little bit of time."

Rica tilted her head to see Carter's face. "Do we? Funny, it doesn't feel that way."

"I *do* have to go back to the mainland for a while." Carter had been wondering how to bring up the subject of her leaving, but now that the opening had arisen, she didn't want to talk about it. She didn't want to think about it.

"For how long?" Rica's voice was steady, almost emotionless.

"A few weeks. There are some important meetings I've been putting off, and now they've caught up with me." She slowly caressed Rica's stomach with one hand, stopping just below her breasts. "But it's close enough for a visit now and then."

"What is it that you do for my father?"

Carter sucked in a breath. "What happened to our deal?"

"The rules have changed." Rica shifted around in Carter's arms, drawing her legs up over Carter's thighs as if she were sitting sideways in a chair, her torso nestled against Carter's chest. Her eyes were wide and serious.

"Have they?" Carter asked, brushing her mouth over Rica's.

"I'm afraid so."

"Why?"

"Because we've been here for over an hour, and you've asked me about my work, and where I went to school, and what I like to do to relax." Rica ran her tongue along the pulse that beat in Carter's neck. "And because I told you."

"Were they secrets?" Carter lifted the lower edge of Rica's sweater and slipped her hand underneath. Her camisole was silk and glided beneath Carter's fingers. Carter was grateful for the thin barrier that kept her from touching the firm, warm flesh beneath it. If she had been able to run her palm over Rica's skin, she wouldn't have been able to stop until she held Rica's breast in her hand. Even as the muscles in her thighs trembled and twitched, she contented herself with pressing her mouth to the hollow at the base of Rica's throat. "I just want to know you."

"Why?" Rica didn't ask accusingly, but more curiously. She covered Carter's hand, placing hers outside the sweater, and guided Carter's fingers upward to her breast. She arched her back at the first touch. "Isn't this enough?"

When Rica's nipple tightened into a knot beneath Carter's fingertips, the sensation was like a fist in her midsection. Carter groaned softly. "It's wonderful." She rubbed her hand in a gentle circle over Rica's breast and then back down her abdomen, breathing deeply until she could think again. "You must know I want you."

"I do. It's been in your eyes since the first time you looked at me." Rica hooked her nails on the edge of the seam along the inside of Carter's thigh and dragged her fingers up until they rested in the vee of Carter's crotch.

"Jesus, Rica." The sun was starting to go down and the wind had picked up. "We can't make love out here."

"I know. We should've slept together already, and we haven't." Rica squeezed the denim gently in her hand and rocked her wrist in a slow, steady circle. "I could make you come like this, though, couldn't I?"

A muscle jumped along the edge of Carter's jaw. "Yes."

"Do you want me to?" Rica's mouth hovered above Carter's, her eyes so intense Carter felt feverish from the heat.

"Yes," Carter gasped. "No. I mean, not—"

Rica relinquished the pressure. Her breasts were tight-nippled and distended beneath the cotton of her sweater. "That's what I mean," she said breathlessly. "You keep holding back. You want me, but you keep holding back."

"It's just—"

"I swore I'd never get involved with someone who worked for my father." Rica gently removed Carter's hand from beneath her sweater and eased back until her hips were no longer cradled against Carter's crotch. "You make me forget things I shouldn't."

"This doesn't have anything to do with that." Carter knew she should let it go. That she should let Rica go now, but she couldn't. "This is personal. It has nothing to do with your family."

"It has everything to do with it, Carter. My whole life—everything I do—it all comes back to who my father is."

"It doesn't have to."

"You know that's not true."

"It's true if we say it's true." Carter didn't know what she was talking about anymore. Rica's father, her own job, the untruths between them—they all merged into one confusing tangle. She didn't know which thread, if tugged even gently, would unravel the entire tapestry of secrets and lies. "Please, Rica, it's just us here."

"We should get back." Rica stood and walked a few feet away, gazing out to the ocean, her arms wrapped tightly around her midsection.

"Damn it, Rica. Just talk to me."

"About what?" Rica asked, her back still turned.

"Anything. Everything." Carter stood, feeling helpless and frustrated. She wanted to make Rica understand things she didn't understand herself. "I want to know who you are—every damn thing from the time you took your first breath."

Rica laughed. "There's nothing to tell."

"Tell me about the first girl you ever kissed."

"I was seventeen and she was in college. And we didn't kiss—we fucked in the bathroom at a friend's wedding. You?"

"I was twenty and so was she. I was so nervous I bit her lip and she bled on my shirt. I didn't wash it for a month."

"You're not nervous when you kiss me."

"Yes, I am." Carter raked her hands through her hair, cursing herself for not being able to control her body. Not wanting to. She went to Rica, gently encircling her from behind again. She kissed the nape of Rica's neck where the wind blew her hair away from her shoulders. "I don't do anything for your father."

Rica stiffened. "I know that's not true."

"I don't, not directly. I've had some dealings with an associate of his."

"It's the same thing."

"No. It isn't." Carter's smoothed her hands over Rica's shoulders. "I swear, it's not what you think."

Rica turned and studied Carter's face. "I'm not sure that makes me feel any better."

"I know. I'm sorry."

"So am I." Rica smoothed her hand over Carter's chest. "It's probably good if we don't see each other for a while."

The arousal that had been churning in Carter's stomach tightened into a heavy ball of disappointment. "Why?"

"Because then when we *do* see each other again, maybe instead of talking, we can just have sex and get it out of our systems."

"I like talking." Carter kissed her. "But I like this too. I'll call you when I get to Boston—"

"No. I don't want to talk to you when you're there. Doing whatever it is that you *don't* do for my family." Rica took a step back, breaking contact with Carter completely. "I'll see you when you get back here. Where it's just us."

"It might be a few weeks."

"I know."

Carter watched helplessly as Rica packed up the remains of their meal and started toward the boat. She quickly rolled up the blanket and towels and followed. She was shivering now too. She found the jacket she'd left under one of the seats and handed it to Rica. "Here. You're going to freeze."

"Thanks." Rica pulled on Carter's jacket and wrapped her arms around her knees. She watched Carter push the boat off the sand and jump adroitly in. She rested her cheek against her knee and studied the woman who was still so much a stranger, but who seemed with each passing hour to be more and more a part of her world. And that's what she hadn't wanted to happen.

From the time she had been old enough to understand what it was her father did, she had carefully separated herself from all that entailed. As she'd gotten older, it had become even harder to do. She'd come to recognize that every family gathering was always more than that. Men took her father aside for whispered conversations in the midst of a wedding party, birthday gifts were bestowed like tithes, and guests subtly vied for the coveted seats at the tables closest to her father's. There was always an undercurrent of unrest and danger.

She wanted none of it, and she had distanced herself as much as she could considering her father's agenda for her. Now she found herself almost totally alone.

Until Carter. Carter threatened to draw her right back into the very arena she'd fought so hard to leave behind. She couldn't let that happen. Time was what she needed. Time to close the doors Carter had opened.

CHAPTER SEVENTEEN

"Hi, good morning. Hello, how are you?" Tory greeted the patients already gathered in her waiting room as she hurried toward her office.

"You have a nice holiday now, Dr. King," one elderly gentleman called.

Memorial Day weekend. The start of the busiest time of the year. Oh yes, it will be wonderful.

"Thank you. You, too, Mr. Durkee." Tory gave Randy a harried smile. "Everything okay?"

"Dr. Burgoyne is here," Randy said. "I sent her back."

"Thanks," Tory said, checking her watch. For once, she wasn't late. "Give me fifteen."

"You got it."

When she reached her office, Tory found her new associate perusing the photographs of Tory during her Olympic rowing days. Reese had done the same thing, the morning they'd met, but the similarity ended there. Bonita was a petite African American woman of thirty, with almond skin and warm brown eyes. "Good morning. Have you been waiting long?"

Bonita Burgoyne turned with a smile. "No, not really. I was early. I've forgotten what it's like to live in a small town where it just takes a few minutes to get from one place to another." She laughed. "I'm still on big-city time. In Rhode Island I had an hour commute and needed to get ready two hours early for anything."

"Did you get settled in?" Tory dropped her briefcase on her desk and gestured to the chair in front of it. She sat down and glanced automatically at the framed photograph on the right-hand corner of her desk. Reese was right, she looked gorgeous in her desert camouflage BDUs. For just a second, Tory forgot what she was doing and thought back instead to their last phone call, which had been almost a week before. The connection hadn't been great, but it was clear enough for her to hear that Reese was tired, and more than that, troubled. Troubled by the things, Tory imagined, that she had seen or perhaps done. Things that she hadn't told Tory, and might never tell her. Unconsciously, she reached out and ran her fingers along the edge of the silver frame.

"How long has she been gone?" Bonita asked quietly.

Tory looked up with a start, then shook her head ruefully. "I'm sorry. Just about a month." *Actually, thirty-one days, five hours, and seven minutes.*

"I saw the picture on your desk when I was looking at the ones up on the wall. I don't mean to pry, but I've got a cousin there, too. I can relate."

"It's all right," Tory said. "I hope we'll be friends as well as colleagues." She added quickly, "But you're not required to share anything that you don't want to."

Bonita laughed. "I don't have any deep dark secrets. As I told you during the interview, I don't like the pace of city living and I don't like the kind of medicine I'm being forced to practice with all the restrictions and bureaucracy in a big hospital. I want a quiet life, and I want to practice medicine that matters."

Tory noticed that Bonita neatly managed to avoid mentioning what she wanted in her personal life. Tory knew she was single. She didn't know if her new associate was a lesbian. Indeed, she knew very little about Bonita beyond her professional credentials, which were exemplary, and the fact that she was easy to talk to and seemed to have a calm, centered personality. Just what Tory needed in a medical partner.

"That's pretty much what you'll get here," Tory said. "Peace and predictability." She looked at the photo of Reese standing outside a tent in the desert. She could feel the heat on her skin just looking at it. "Most of the time."

"How's she doing? Does she say?"

"She's a Marine," Tory said with a small smile.

"Ah. One of my sisters and two of my brothers are cops, just like our father." Bonita shook her head. "And they never talk about how hard it can be, either."

"How did you escape the call, then?" Tory wondered at the trace of bitterness in Bonita's voice.

"Never even heard a whisper. I had enough of the tough-guy attitude growing up. It's the last thing I wanted in my life once I became an adult."

"I think I can understand that. But we don't choose who we fall in love with. And I wouldn't change anything about Reese."

"Good for you," Bonita said sincerely.

"Yes. I know."

Carter snagged a drink from a passing tuxedoed waiter and moved off to one side of the stone patio into the shade of a huge flowering dogwood. At seven p.m., under the golden glow of the setting sun, the expansive gardens behind Alfonse Pareto's home were a riot of color and fragrance. Their beauty, however, was eclipsed by that of the woman Carter watched as she sipped her 1995 Krug. She hadn't seen Rica in three weeks, and while she hadn't thought it was possible to forget how striking she was, she had been wrong.

Rica wore a white two-piece evening dress—a sleek sleeveless silk top subtly styled like a bustier and a floor length fishtail skirt—with heels that brought her close to Carter's height. Her hair was pulled back from her face and held with a comb at the base of her neck. She looked exotic and untouchable. Every time she gazed in Carter's direction, her eyes passed over Carter's face as if they were strangers. Each time it happened, Carter felt the affront as if she'd been slapped. Finally, she couldn't take it any longer.

Against her better judgment, she eased her way through the crowd and waited until Rica had stopped speaking to yet another of the men Carter recognized as Pareto's captains. Then she closed the final gap between them.

"Ms. Grechi," Carter said quietly, her eyes sweeping the crowd, relieved when she saw that no one was paying any particular attention to them. It wasn't the smartest move for her to approach Rica in full view of people who might take notice, but she couldn't help herself. Up close she could see that the top of Rica's ensemble laced in the back, leaving her skin tantalizingly displayed beneath the thin silk strands. Carter's fingertips tingled with the need to caress the small bare patches of skin.

"Carter," Rica said.

When it seemed that Rica might not say anything else, Carter murmured, "You look amazing tonight."

Rica slanted Carter a glance, then fingered the sleeve of Carter's plain, black, tab-collared shirt while she slowly perused the belted trousers. "You're probably the only woman in my father's entire acquaintance who could manage to show up wearing this and not cause a stir. Prada?"

"Uh-huh."

"I like the look."

"I'm glad." Carter sipped her champagne. "I called you when I was out on the Cape." She'd only been able to get away once for more than a day in the last few weeks, and although she could easily have made the short trip out to the Cape with a smaller window of time than that, she was afraid she might be called back when she was there. She hadn't wanted to rouse Rica's suspicions by making another abrupt departure, so she had forced herself to stay away. But the longer she had gone without seeing Rica, the harder it had been to sleep. The harder it had been to concentrate. The harder it had been to do *anything* except think about Rica and how much she wanted to see her again. "I left a message."

"I had to go back to Manhattan unexpectedly."

Carter nodded. That didn't explain why Rica hadn't returned her call, but it was neither the time nor place to push her for further explanation. "Everything all right?"

Rica smiled fleetingly. Angie had called because she'd been worried about some odd transactions which they still hadn't sorted out. "Business is good."

"Glad to hear it."

"I didn't know you were coming today."

"Neither did I," Carter said, which was the truth. She wasn't happy to be there, because she hadn't wanted Rica to see her with Rizzo or anyone else related to Pareto's organization. But Rizzo had reported to Special Agent Allen that something was happening. Apparently the captains had all heard various forms of a rumor that the competition was gaining strength, and Rizzo felt some kind of retaliation might be coming. Allen had fairly salivated at the news and had insisted that Carter get an inside look at who seemed to be in Pareto's favor. "I wouldn't have come if I could've avoided it."

Rica gave Carter a curious look. "Why?"

"Because you don't want me here. And I don't want to put another roadblock in front of—" Carter gave an exasperated sigh. "Whatever we have going."

"That's very eloquent," Rica said, but her eyes were smiling. "I'm sorry I missed you when you were in town."

At that, some of the tension eased from Carter's chest, and she was able to take a full breath again. "Good. Are you going to be here for a few days?"

"I don't know. And I won't see you here anyway. I told you that."

"All right, but—" Carter swept the crowd again and this time locked eyes with Lorenzo Brassi, who stood directly opposite them across the patio, watching them with the stillness of a great cat judging the distance to its prey. Just knowing that he was watching Rica caused Carter to clench her fists. "What about next weekend? If I come to you?"

Rica regarded her thoughtfully. "Call me and we'll see."

Carter tried to look unperturbed as Rica turned and walked away, because she knew Brassi was watching them. It took all her willpower not to follow Rica into the house, because now that she'd seen Rica, she ached to touch her. It was as if she'd been starving and hadn't been able to identify the source of her pain until just that moment. Now, with surcease so close, it was agony to wait. She narrowed her eyes as she watched Lorenzo Brassi walk briskly into the house after Rica.

Rica slowed once she was inside and turned down the hallway toward her father's study. Even as a child she had gone there for comfort and to escape from whatever troubled her. The cool dark room still held the smells she associated with her father, her childhood, and more innocent times. Though she was too old now to believe that there was any place where she could truly escape, this was still her favorite room in her father's house.

"Is that dyke what you think you want?" Enzo said from behind her.

Rica stiffened, angry at herself for relaxing her vigilance. She had been taken off guard by seeing Carter. Not just seeing her, but realizing just *how much* she had wanted to see her. It had been so hard to maintain her cool facade while under the watchful eye of her father and his men when all she'd wanted was to kiss her. As if that were possible when there were at least a dozen men observing her. The last thing she wanted was to incite curiosity about her relationship with Carter, because if it reached her father's ears, he would have Carter investigated at the very least. Worse, if he had any doubts about what was happening between them, he would order one of his trusted lieutenants to shadow them.

While she had been struggling not to reveal how much she had wanted to be alone with Carter, she hadn't noticed Enzo. And now she would pay for that lapse.

"Does she make you come, Rica?" Enzo whispered harshly.

Even before she felt Enzo's hand on her arm, Rica stopped. She had to divert his attention from Carter at all costs. She hoped her expression was civil as she said lightly, "I don't know what you're talking about, Enzo. Can we please have just one family gathering without an argument?"

He ran his finger along the edge of her jaw. "You've always been a terrible liar, *cara*." He moved closer, forcing Rica back a step. "But the way your...friend looks at you, she would have given you both away, anyhow."

Rica's heart sped up. She hated the thought of Enzo knowing anything about Carter. "Whatever you think you saw—"

"If she had balls, I would say that you have hers in a vise. She is dying to fuck you, isn't she?"

"I'm going back outside." Rica tried to sidestep him, but he crowded her into an alcove off the main hallway. "Enzo."

When she tried to ward him off, he caught both wrists and shoved her against the wall, dragging her arms above her head. He crushed her hands together and gripped both wrists in one of his large hands. "You tease women like you do men," he snarled. "But she won't take what she wants, will she? I can see it in her face, how much she wants you. She's sick with it. But you offer it in one breath and refuse her in the next. Bitch."

For a fleeting second, Rica asked herself if that's what she did with Carter, but then his body crushed hers, and her only thoughts were of survival. Her wrists screamed with pain and her fingers went numb. She jerked her head away as his mouth closed on her neck.

"Stop it," she said urgently, trying not to raise her voice in case one of her father's men was nearby. It was just like always. The horrible fear and humiliation—that he could do this to her over and over, and that only by admitting her helplessness could she escape. "Enzo. For God's sake."

He fisted her dress and raked it up her thighs to her hips, nearly exposing her completely. Rica struggled, writhing beneath him in a frantic parody of lovemaking, and he slapped her sharply with his free hand. The blow rocked her head back and she tasted blood on the inside of her lip.

"Hold still."

She twisted and tried to drive her hipbone between his legs, but he slapped her again. He'd never been like this before, so wild, so crazed. Rica's stomach clenched with a rush of pain and nausea as she thrashed against his weight.

"Do you fight her too?" Enzo rasped. He bit her neck and drove his hand between her thighs. He squeezed her tender flesh until she whimpered. "You want women because you can control them," he grunted, forcing her legs apart. "You won't make me like them."

Rica felt his hand fumbling between them, and a terrible chill ran through her at the sound of a zipper opening. "You can't rape me. Enzo, you can't—"

"It's not rape when you want it," he snarled, transferring his hand quickly from her wrist to her throat.

He pinned her to the wall with his vise-like grip on her neck, and her vision dimmed while she struggled to breathe. She gathered all of her strength in one last effort to fight back, and then, miraculously, he was gone. She gasped for breath and, through tear-filled eyes, saw Carter.

"You *son of a bitch*," Carter raged, driving her fist into Enzo's throat. He gagged and dropped to his knees, both hands clamped to his neck. She pulled his head back with a fistful of hair and made sure that he saw her face. "Touch her again and I'll kill you next time."

She spoke quietly, with deadly calm, and stared into his eyes until she was sure her words had registered. When she was certain that he had heard her, she slammed her fist under his chin. He dropped unconscious to the floor, and she gathered Rica into her arms.

"I'm sorry," Carter murmured, stroking Rica's hair. "I should've come sooner. Jesus. Rica."

Rica fisted Carter's shirt and pressed her forehead hard to her shoulder, willing back the tears, struggling not to tremble. "It's all right. He didn't...he didn't."

Carter gently lifted Rica's face, her eyes turning to stone at the sight of the angry red marks on Rica's face. "The bastard hit you."

"Carter, you have to get out of here." With trembling hands, Rica smoothed down her dress and tried to tame her hair, which had fallen loose in the struggle. "Enzo. When he wakes up, he'll come after you."

"Fine."

"No, you don't understand. He's my father's second in command. You can't do to him what you just did."

"The hell I can't." Carter flexed her fist, which was starting to stiffen. "He was going to rape you, Rica."

"He would have stopped. Even he wouldn't do that." Rica wasn't certain, but she'd say anything to get Carter to settle down. Because Carter had a look on her face that was frightening in an entirely different way than Enzo had been frightening. Rica had never really understood the meaning of the words *cold fury* until now. "You can't go against him this way, Carter. Please."

Carter had never heard the edge of fear in Rica's voice before, and she hated that she might have been responsible for even part of it. She cupped Rica's cheek and very softly kissed her bruised mouth. "All right. But you're coming with me."

Rica shook her head. "I can handle him."

"He's crazy, Rica. To try to do what he just did?" Carter brushed a stray lock of hair off Rica's cheek. "I'm not leaving you alone, especially not with him anywhere in the vicinity."

Enzo moaned and twitched, and Rica caught her breath.

"All right," Rica said impatiently. "All right. Where are we going?"

"Come on." Carter took her hand. "I'll take you home."

CHAPTER EIGHTEEN

W here are we going?" Rica tugged her seat belt forward and shifted sideways in the bucket seat. With each mile that Carter put between Enzo and them, Rica regained a little more of her self-control. Still, every time she remembered the venom in his voice and the cruel indifference of his hands roaming her body, a wave of loathing washed through her. Looking at Carter helped banish the horror.

"Back to Provincetown."

"That's the first place Enzo will look." Rica pulled the blue blazer she'd snatched from a closet closer around her. She had been in such a hurry to get away that she hadn't said good night to anyone, not even her father. Carter had urged her to tell him she was leaving, at the very least, but Rica had feared that Enzo would intercept them at any moment. "He won't care that you're a woman. He'll hurt you, Carter."

"You're shaking." Carter turned on the heat, then reached across the gap between them and took Rica's hand. Her fingers were cold. "He'll *want* to hurt me. But he didn't get where he is by being stupid. He won't do anything until he knows what all the consequences might be. He's not coming tonight."

"But he *will* come." Rica shivered despite the blast of hot air. Enzo had threatened her before, even physically accosted her, although he'd never come as close to raping her as he had that evening. Still, she'd never been so frightened, and it was more than the near rape. He had almost succeeded in stripping her of the one thing she clung to, her ability to define herself by her own rules and desires. She was not a pawn in her father's game or a victim of circumstance if *she* controlled who touched her life, her body—her heart. "He won't forget this."

"Neither will I." Carter's hand tightened on the wheel as she remembered coming around the corner and seeing Enzo molesting Rica. Her dress had been bunched around her thighs, and he was grinding himself between her legs. Rica's cheek was flaming from where he'd struck her, and her eyes were wild with panic. Carter knew if she'd had her gun, she would have put it to the back of his head and pulled the trigger without a second's remorse. She still wanted to. And because she knew that Rica would sense her anger, just as *she* sensed Rica's lingering panic, Carter forced the image from her mind. All that mattered was that Rica feel safe. "How's your cheek? Should I stop for ice?"

Rica tentatively probed her left cheek. Her entire head throbbed. "My jaw hurts a little when I move it, but I think it's just swollen."

"Maybe we should have it checked."

"No. No doctors."

"Rica, if you're hurt—"

"I'm not. I'm fine. Please, just take me home."

Carter heard the panic just below the surface, and the sound tore at her. She knew that Rica had to be hurting in more than just her body for her control to slip enough for her fear to show "Hey, it's okay. Why don't you put your seat back and try to get some sleep. We'll be there in about an hour."

"You should stop somewhere and I'll rent a car. There's no need for you to take me home."

"Rica," Carter said softly. "What do you take me for? I'm not leaving you alone."

Rica studied Carter's face, which was obscured by shadow. Who was she really, this woman who had come into her life and made her feel safe? She knew nothing of her except things she wished were not true. "You just said he wouldn't come tonight."

"He won't. But I'm not leaving you alone after what happened."

"I'm all right. It's not the first time Enzo has been…difficult."

Carter's fingers tightened around Rica's. "How long?"

"Since we were teenagers."

"*Bastard.*" Carter glanced at Rica. "Did he force himself on you then?"

"He tried," Rica said, her expression distant. "I always managed to stop him."

"I'm surprised your father let him live." Carter's voice hardened. "He didn't blame you, did he?"

"I never told him."

"Why?" Carter lifted Rica's hand and brushed her lips over Rica's fingers, hoping to soften the question.

"He would have killed Enzo," Rica said with certainty. "And I didn't want that."

"I'm not following, honey," Carter said gently.

"Because even when we were young I could see that Enzo was the son my father had never had." Rica stared at Carter. "Don't you see? As long as he stays in my father's favor, *Enzo* will take his place, not me. Most of the family will welcome him as successor."

"Jesus," Carter murmured. "So you kept quiet all these years so you wouldn't be pressed to take over?"

"Yes."

"And now I've made things a lot more difficult for you." Carter thought bitterly of the irony that by investigating the suspicions that Rica was connected to organized crime, she'd made Rica's efforts not to be involved even harder. Everything was turned around. "Jesus, I'm sorry."

Rica leaned over and kissed Carter on the corner of her mouth. "No. You've made everything better, if just for a little while." Then she leaned her head against Carter's shoulder and closed her eyes.

Carter drove on, wondering how long it would take Enzo to make his move on her, and if she could make things right for Rica before he did.

"Rica." Carter stroked Rica's shoulder and kissed her forehead. "We're here."

"Mmm." Enjoying the sensation of Carter's arm around her and the heat of her body, Rica rubbed her cheek against Carter's shoulder. The stabbing pain brought her awake and she jolted upright. "Oh, God."

"What is it? Your jaw?"

"Cheek."

Carter swore. "I'm going to find someone to check that. There's gotta be a doctor in this town."

Rica curled her hand around Carter's thigh, restraining her as she pushed her door open. "No. Please. It just startled me. It's not that bad."

"We'll take a look at it inside where we can get some light on it." Carter added frustration and helplessness to her long list of confused emotions where Rica was concerned. But none of her discomfort was Rica's fault, and she carefully kept her unease from showing. "Just wait here for a few minutes while I check the house. Let me have your key."

"For what? I thought you said you weren't worried about Enzo." Rica gripped Carter's forearm. "God, he could have been here by plane an hour ago. You're not going in there."

Carter took Rica's hands in hers. "He's not inside. There's no way he would have left your house early. He wouldn't risk missing a meeting with your father or rousing his suspicions. Just the same, I'm not letting you walk in there until we're certain that he didn't send one of his friends."

"You don't know who might be in there," Rica said urgently. "You might be brave, but you're no match for Enzo's muscle." She slipped one hand behind Carter and patted her back and hips. "You're not even armed."

"Don't worry." Carter gently pulled away from Rica and reached for the trunk release. "Let me have your key, Rica. Please."

"I don't even have my purse."

"No spare key under the flower pot?"

Rica managed a small smile. "They're inside, but the keypad next to the garage door opens it with a code. It's not very noisy."

"Well, if there's anyone inside, they already know we're out here. What's the code?"

"0-7-0-5."

Carter slid out of the car. "Be right back."

Carter retrieved her Glock semiautomatic from the compartment in the side panel of the Explorer's cargo area, taking care to tuck her badge and ID down out of sight before closing it again. Then she walked quickly toward the house, staying in the shadows and avoiding the seashells that liberally lined the drive. She wasn't quite as certain as she had professed to Rica that Enzo hadn't sent one of his boys to scare them, or, if he was as crazy as she suspected, to manhandle Rica back to Boston. No cars were parked on the street, and none in the nearby driveways looked out of place, but that didn't mean someone couldn't have parked a few blocks away and walked. If they had come over by plane from Boston, they wouldn't have arrived much sooner than she and Rica.

Carter keyed in Rica's security code and ducked quickly underneath the garage door as soon as there was clearance. By the time the door was all the way up, she was inside the kitchen in the dark. She steadied her breathing and listened, hearing nothing but the sounds of an empty house. The refrigerator running, the wind rattling the windows, the tick of a clock. But then, anyone who was any good would not be making any noise. She moved methodically from room to room, checking closets, shower enclosures, and the dark recesses of the hallways. The house was empty.

She pushed her gun beneath the waistband of her trousers at the small of her back and turned on the outside lights. By the time she started down the driveway, Rica was almost to the porch.

"There's no one here," Carter said.

Rica regarded her contemplatively, then nodded. "Thank you."

When Rica walked past her into the house, Carter followed. She wasn't surprised that now that Rica was home, she was starting to withdraw. Carter had seen enough traumatized victims to know that most of them just wanted to be alone in safe surroundings. She had no intention of intruding, but she wasn't leaving.

The kitchen was empty when Carter walked in. She stood still for a few minutes, listening, and when she heard the shower running upstairs, she went through the counter drawers until she found a plastic bag. She checked a few more cabinets, then filled the bag with ice and sat down at the kitchen table until she heard the shower go off. She waited a few more minutes and then went upstairs.

"Rica," Carter said after tapping on the closed bathroom door, "I'm leaving some ice out here for your face. I didn't see any aspirin in the kitchen, but if you've got some in there you should take—"

The door opened and Rica, wrapped in a towel, her hair wet and tangled about her shoulders, pointed down the hallway to the right. "The bedroom is at the end of the hall. I'll be right there. Can you find a bottle of wine in the kitchen and bring it up?"

"Sure." Carter made a concerted effort not to look anywhere

except at Rica's face, but she was painfully aware that the plush sea green towel knotted above Rica's breasts slanted open a few inches as it fell, revealing a slice of tanned thigh. The swell of unbidden arousal was tempered by the sight of the bruise that marred Rica's cheek. Rica didn't need to be groped by any one else that night. Carter looked away. "I'll give you a few minutes."

"Just get the wine and come upstairs." Rica skimmed her fingers over Carter's shoulder as she passed. "Thanks for the ice."

❖

Rica stood in front of the open French doors, listening to the sound of Carter's steady footsteps approaching down the hall. She'd toweled off her hair and pulled on a robe. She hoped the wine would warm her, because she seemed to be frozen all the way through. Where she pushed her hands inside the sleeves of her robe, her body felt warm under her fingertips, but just beneath her skin where she couldn't touch, she was cold.

Carter stopped inside the door, a wine bottle in one hand and a glass held by its stem between the fingers of her other. "I could only find red. Is that all right?"

"Yes," Rica said, turning. She'd switched on a reading light in the far corner of the room and Carter's face looked softer than usual in the lamplight. When Carter's eyes swept down her body and then quickly back to her face, the look left a thin trail of heat in its wake. Surprised by the odd burning sensation, Rica moved toward her, out of the cold.

"I'll just leave it here." Carter backed up a step and set the wineglass and bottle carefully on a bureau next to the door. "You really should get some res—"

"Look at me," Rica said, opening her robe.

"Rica," Carter whispered, glancing down despite herself. Rica's breasts were flushed, as if from the warmth of the shower, and her nipples tight pink buds of invitation. Carter's stomach clutched.

"I don't feel anything." Rica swept her fingers over her chest and cupped her breast. She strummed her thumb across her nipple. The pink turned to red. "Nothing. Except where you look at me."

"You need to rest," Carter said gently. She knew it was some kind of shock, some reaction to the assault. She knew that. She *knew*, but her body was doing crazy things as Rica moved to within inches of her, her long, slender fingers continuing to play over her breasts and down her abdomen. Carter took another step back and hit the door.

"Enzo said you were dying to fuck me," Rica whispered, her naked thighs brushing Carter's pants.

"Enzo is an animal." Carter brushed her thumb tenderly over the bruised cheek. "Listen to me. You need to lie down. You're in pain, and frightened—"

"I know what I'm doing, Carter," Rica said. "My face hurts like hell or I'd kiss you right now. I'm not trying to block out what happened." She grasped Carter's wrist and guided Carter's hand to her breast. She smiled when Carter groaned. "I'm cold because I've had to be for so long—to fight Enzo and the rest of them—and now I can't get warm. I can't feel anything. Except where you touch me. Touch me."

"No," Carter whispered. Everything in her screamed *wrong time, wrong place, wrong reasons*, while her hands shook and her stomach knotted with the delirious scorching need to feel her.

"Please." Rica covered Carter's hand and squeezed Carter's fingers down around her nipple. She tilted her head back and moaned.

"Oh, Jesus." Somehow Carter's other hand found its way into Rica's hair, and she held her head gently while she raked her teeth down the center of Rica's exposed throat. The sound of Rica whimpering vibrated against her lips, and she couldn't think of anything except hearing, touching, tasting more of Rica's pleasure. She cupped Rica's breast with her whole hand, continuing the rhythmic pinch of thumb and fingers on the swollen peak. Harder and harder, twisting and tugging, until Rica slumped against her.

"Oh, so good." Rica clutched Carter's shoulder to steady herself and pressed her sex against Carter's thigh. Heat flooded through her even as it flooded from her, drenching Carter's pants. "So good, Carter."

Carter took a nipple in her mouth.

Rica gasped. "I've dreamed of you making me come."

Carter lifted her head and looked into the depths of Rica's wide, dark eyes. Then she was swirling and tumbling and about to drown in the vortex of pure and simple desire. Rica's lips trembled as she pumped her hips in long, hard strokes over Carter's thigh.

"I'm afraid I will," Rica whispered, her eyes glazing. "I'm so close to coming already. Oh Carter, don't let me come before you touch me."

Carter's heart squeezed painfully. Rica was so beautiful, so open, so...trusting.

"Rica, I can't," Carter groaned, and released Rica's breast. But she was too late.

Rica caught Carter's hand and thrust it between her legs, her breath hitching on a thin cry. "I'm going to..." She plunged Carter's fingers into her aching sex, took her deep inside, and drove down against her palm in short, hard thrusts. She came on Carter's hand with a broken wail.

Carter wrapped an arm around Rica's waist and caught her as her legs gave way, lifting her into her arms. "It's okay, baby, it's okay," she murmured as Rica whimpered with the last ravages of her climax. "It's okay."

But just like so many times in her life when she'd held a woman in moments like this, she was lying. And this time, the lie was tearing her apart.

Chapter Nineteen

Rica awakened cold and naked. The room itself was warm, and she was covered by a light sheet, but Carter was gone and she'd taken the heat with her. Rica remembered sleeping in Carter's arms. She remembered the faintly rough texture of Carter's shirt beneath her cheek and the surprisingly erratic beat of Carter's heart somewhere in her distant dreams. It had been months since she'd awakened with anyone in her bed, and longer than that since she'd allowed anyone to actually hold her while she slept. Dropping into an exhausted stupor next to the woman who had just made her come was a far cry from what had happened with Carter.

And what *had* happened with Carter? Oh, she knew what had happened, at least the easy part. Rica skimmed her hand down the center of her chest. She could remember Carter's mouth and hands on her breasts. Her nipples were still swollen and pleasantly sore. Her skin was nothing but raw nerve endings. She tensed, remembering how desperate she'd been to be filled, so wild to come with Carter inside her that she couldn't think at all. Her whole body was still loose and languid after climaxing harder than she could ever recall. She slid her fingers along the inside of her thigh and over her sex. She was still wet. She wanted Carter again. Her body, no, not just her body, *all* of her, was out of control.

With a sigh, Rica rose and found her robe where it lay pooled in the sunlight by the bedroom door. She remembered the rest of it too. Carter had tried to stop her, but she'd been too far gone to hear. Carter had tried to stop her, and now Carter was gone. It shouldn't have mattered, but it did. She shouldn't have slept with her, but she hadn't been able to get her out of her head all the time they had been separated. Three weeks had felt like three years. She should have been glad Carter was gone, because she didn't need the complication now. Enzo's demands, business and personal, were becoming harder and harder to turn aside. And now Carter was in the middle, and that was a very dangerous place for her to be.

"It's just as well she's gone."

When Rica walked into the kitchen and saw Carter outside on the deck, talking on her cell phone, her heart leapt. A twist of desire nearly made her stumble and she stopped just inside the door to look at Carter. Just look. Carter still wore the clothes she'd had on the previous evening and her face was drawn and tired, as if she hadn't slept. Even though she was rumpled and windblown, she looked beautiful. A wash of desire flooded Rica's thighs.

"Oh God," she whispered. This was far more than she had wanted to feel, and she feared there was no turning back.

When Carter turned sideways to lean her hip against the railing, still speaking urgently, Rica saw the Glock tucked into the small of her back. Rica flashed on Carter opening the cargo area the night before and then moving stealthily up the path to her house, her steps certain and sure. As if she'd done it before. A small note of warning sounded in Rica's mind.

Carter glanced into the house and, meeting Rica's gaze, quickly ended her call. She stepped back into the kitchen and kissed Rica softly, just a gentle brush of lips. "How are you feeling?"

"Like I owe you an apology," Rica said, folding her arms over her breasts.

"No," Carter said softly, "you don't."

"I don't unusually throw myself at women."

"Rica, last night was—"

"No." Rica held up a hand, knowing Carter thought that the sex had been an attempt to block out the attack. "Last night was not about Enzo. It was about wanting you so much that I—"

"*Last night* was great." Carter caressed Rica's neck. "Last night was amazing."

"Yes." Rica smiled fleetingly. "I notice you didn't stick around for seconds, though." At Carter's look of surprise, Rica grimaced. "God, I don't know what's wrong with me. I'm sorry."

"Maybe it has something to do with fighting alone all your life. Don't apologize."

Rica shrugged. "A bit late now. I should call my father and let him know where I am. At least he won't send anyone out looking for me."

"Good idea."

"If you've got friends in my father's favor, now would be the time to call on them. Before Enzo twists this around and makes you out to be a threat to someone besides him."

There it was. The opening Carter needed to press for details about the organization. *Who are the important people? Who should I call? Who are Enzo's enemies? His friends?* Carter said nothing.

Rica laughed bitterly and then winced at the sharp twinge in her jaw. Her face pulsed with pain. "I'm sure I don't need to tell you how to handle these things. You've probably already called."

"Yes," Carter said, but it hadn't been the call Rica imagined.

"Kevin? We've got problems."

"That's a fucking understatement. Where the hell are you?"

"Cape Cod. What have you heard?"

"That someone put Brassi on the floor at a family gathering last night and left him with his dick hanging out."

"Who'd you hear it from?"

"A friend. You're not the only one inside," Kevin said. "It was you, wasn't it?"

"Yes."

"Motherfu—Jesus. Allen is busting a nut over this. She's been trying to call you all night. Where's your phone?"

"I'm talking to you on it."

Kevin laughed. "Funny. Why didn't you answer?"

"I was sleeping."

"Sleeping. With a certain dark-haired princess?"

Carter was silent.

"Fuck me." Kevin sighed audibly. "Allen went over our heads. Says you've compromised the whole operation. Says your judgment's impaired. You're off the case, Carter, all the way off. You'll be lucky if you don't end up with a suspension."

"He was going to rape her."

"So you had to ride to the rescue?"

"You would've done the same thing."

"Yeah, maybe," Kevin muttered. "Allen thinks it was probably just a lover's spat and you got in the middle of it. After she warned you away from Grechi."

"It wasn't a spat."

"You gotta come in, partner. Allen's after your head. She already put Rizzo in witness protection, just in case Brassi makes the connection when he starts gunning for you."

"Rica is not involved, Kevin. She's not part of the organization."

"Maybe she is, maybe she isn't. And maybe your head's not in the right place for this job right now."

"I'm telling you, she's clean," Carter said. "I'm not leaving her alone for a few days. Brassi's probably going to show up."

"He's probably going to be looking for your head on a platter, not hers. If he doesn't get it, Allen will."

"Brassi's probably got people here in town already—watching Rica while they're taking care of his other business. Allen can't come in here and pull me out without raising suspicions. I'm safe here for a while."

"You're putting your job on the line for this woman, Carter."

"I put her in a tough place, Kev. I'm not walking away from her."

Kevin groaned. "Jesus, you're stubborn. Maybe you've been doing this too long. Maybe you need a brea—"

Carter had disconnected when she'd realized Rica was awake and watching her from the kitchen. She would have hung up anyway; there was no way she could explain to Kevin why she wasn't going to follow Allen's directive. The kind of investigation Allen was running could go on for years without an arrest. Men like Pareto were rarely indicted even with testimony from insiders. Allegiances ran deep and betrayals were dealt with swiftly and mercilessly. In all the months she'd been working the case, she hadn't uncovered one single bit of evidence to suggest Rica was involved even peripherally in her father's organization or doing anything illegal. And now, with Rizzo out of the picture in WITSEC, her primary contact was gone. Her part in Allen's operation was over. And even if it wasn't, it didn't matter anymore. She was done betraying Rica's trust.

"Enzo won't do anything hasty, Rica." Carter carefully touched her fingers to Rica's cheek. "Hurt?"

"Some." Rica covered Carter's hand with hers. "Still, you need to be careful."

"I will be."

Rica circled Carter's waist and felt the Glock tucked into her waistband. She'd made a lot of assumptions about Carter, assumptions that might be wrong. Suddenly that mattered. "Are you really an attorney?"

Carter flinched. "Yes."

"And what else?"

"Rica, we agreed—"

"Things have changed now, haven't they?" Rica slid back a few steps until they were no longer in contact. She had to know. She'd broken her own rule when she'd let Carter get close, and she needed to know just how badly she had overstepped her own boundaries. "Tell me."

A dozen replies came to mind. Lies she'd told so often they felt like truths. What was truth? Maybe it was something as simple as a woman sleeping in her arms. Carter didn't know. She didn't need to. She only knew there was only one answer now.

"I'm a cop, Rica."

Rica sucked in a breath, her eyes never leaving Carter's face. She wavered for just a second and then straightened. "Well, that makes things easy. I can stop worrying about Enzo. He'll kill you, and that will take care of my mistake." She slid past Carter, being careful that their bodies did not touch. "Get out."

"I need you to know something," Carter said to Rica's back. She held her breath, waiting.

Rica turned at the doorway, her face a careful mask. "I should call my father now and tell him who you are. I'm sure he could find out who brought you inside. Who has betrayed him."

"There's no one to find, Rica."

"Did you really think you could fuck me and I'd betray my father?"

"I know you wouldn't." Carter wanted desperately to go to her. To touch her for just a second. The cold disdain in her eyes was worse than anything she'd ever imagined. Anything except losing her. "I also know—"

"You don't know anything about me if you think there's anything in the world that would make me turn against my family. Especially"—

Rica shrugged—"not for something I could get anywhere, anytime I wanted it."

Carter absorbed the words as if they were blows. Her body ached. Her heart bled. "I don't want you to betray him."

"Then what are you doing here?"

"I'm in love with you."

Rica laughed. "If you come anywhere near me again, I won't wait for Enzo to do the job."

Carter closed her eyes, knowing that when she opened them, Rica would be gone. Rica was still inside the house where they'd come for sanctuary and to make love, but she was as unattainable now as if they'd never met. The gulf that stretched between them echoed with recriminations and broken trust. She'd always known how the story would end, but even knowing, she'd been helpless not to play her part. Still, the empty room and the silent house hurt far more than she'd thought possible. After all the lies, it was the truth that would finally break her heart.

I'm in love with you.

Rica walked directly upstairs, through her bedroom, past the bed where she'd lain only hours before in Carter's arms. She opened the French doors and stepped out onto the deck. The sky was heavy with clouds, thick gray layers of impending rain that obscured the shoreline and draped the lighthouse at Race Point in shrouds of fog. The air was dank and cold. She'd been wrong. Her earlier chill had had nothing to do with Carter abandoning her in the aftermath of their hasty passion, but only with the weather. Nothing had changed except the color of the sky. Women had come into her life and passed through with barely a notice before, leaving nothing in their wake but blurred memories. Pleasure was a fleeting sensation and after a time, empty.

I'm a cop, Rica.

Why hadn't she known? Why hadn't she sensed that something was terribly wrong? How had she allowed a handsome face and a little bit of attention to cloud her judgment so badly?

I'm in love with you.

She'd heard the words, but she refused to consider their meaning. Nothing Carter said could be trusted. She was a liar and a threat.

I'm in love with you.

Carter had asked her about her life. *Her* life. Not her father's. She'd been interested in her work, her plans for the gallery, her struggle to build a future all her own. They'd never talked about her legacy. Carter had never asked about her father.

I'm a cop, Rica.

Nothing Carter had said mattered now. Her only reason for being in Rica's life had been to destroy it. This was the reason that opening up to anyone but family was dangerous. At least family could be trusted.

Rica shivered, feeling the weight of Enzo's body pinning her to the wall, his hard fury pounding between her thighs. Family.

I'm in love with you.

Rica closed her eyes, trying to erase the images of Carter driving her home through the dark, shepherding her to safety, pushing her to orgasm. Carter's hands, tender and demanding. Her mouth, gentle and fierce. Her eyes, compassionate and devouring.

I'm a cop, Rica.

Why had Carter told her? Why risk the truth? Why had she held her all night?

Rica fought back tears and brutally contained her pain with fury and denial. The effort made her head scream; her face was a throbbing agony. Nearly blind with the pain, she stumbled into her bathroom and pawed through the medicine cabinet for painkillers. Nothing.

She curled up on top of the sheets, her arms clutched around her middle, her knees drawn up, her eyes tightly closed. The pain in her head and the ache in her heart threatened to consume her. She wished for oblivion but sleep wouldn't come. She moaned as her stomach revolted. She smelled Carter on the pillow. With a cry, she pushed herself up and fumbled for the phone.

When she pulled out of her driveway thirty minutes later, she was too busy fighting back the nausea to notice the vehicle that fell into line a discreet distance behind her.

Chapter Twenty

Tory lifted the chart from the rack on the back of the door. When she didn't recognize the name, she thumbed through to the intake form. *Chief complaint: headache.* The rest of the information was sparse. No significant past medical history, no drugs, no allergies, no unusual illnesses. She knocked on the door and walked into the examining room.

"Ms. Grechi? Hello, I'm Dr. King."

The woman who sat on the examining table was sheet white, the skin around her luminous dark eyes tight with obvious pain, her lips pale. A noticeable hematoma marred her left cheek and a bruise discolored her flawless skin as far down as the edge of her jaw. Tory reached to the wall beside her and turned off the overhead fluorescents, leaving only the small lights under the cabinets for illumination.

"Thank you," Rica said.

Tory gestured to the chart. "It says you have a headache."

"Yes. An enormous one. I took some ibuprofen last night, but I don't think that's going to be enough today."

"Do you have a history of headaches? Migraines?"

Rica started to shake her head, then stopped quickly with a wince. "No."

"Any other symptoms besides the headache? Changes in vision—wavy lines, spots, blind areas?"

"No. I'm a little nauseated just at the moment. I'm sure if I can just get some sleep, I'll be fine. I was hoping you could give me something for the pain."

"Let me get a look." Tory removed a small penlight from her lab coat pocket, examined Rica's eyes, and then performed a complete head and neck exam. When she finished, she made a few notes, then set the chart aside. "How did you get the bruise on your cheek?"

Rica's expression did not change as she contemplated Tory and the closed folder. The message was clear. Off the record. Not that it mattered, because she didn't discuss private matters with strangers. She heard the words in her head and would have laughed if her face hadn't been about to explode. When had she started lying to herself *about* herself? She had discussed a great many personal things with Carter with hardly a moment's worry. She hadn't even worried about letting her into her heart. Oh God, was that what she'd done? No. Of course she hadn't. She might have been blinded by lust, but…She realized the doctor was waiting, regarding her with calm, accepting eyes. Whatever mistakes she'd made with Carter, she wouldn't pretend it was only lust between them. That lie hurt too much. "Someone hit me."

"When?"

"Last night." Rica felt unexpectedly relieved at the opportunity to say the words out loud. She didn't ask herself why, blaming the pain as an excuse for her lapse in caution.

"How many times?"

Rica thought back to the frantic encounter. She couldn't remember the exact sequence, only her initial anger giving way to escalating panic. She hated him more for the fear than the violation of her body. He'd hit her when she'd struggled, and then again when she still wouldn't give in. It was hard to remember it. Hard to relive it, but she recalled quite vividly the fury in Carter's eyes as she'd confronted Enzo. And, after she'd hit him, the gentleness in Carter's touch when she'd taken Rica into her arms. It was so much easier to recall the tenderness than the brutality. "Twice."

"Did you lose consciousness?"

"No."

"Has this person done this before?"

Rica grimaced. "No, he hasn't."

"Did you report it to the police?"

"No." She met Tory's eyes. "It's a family matter."

"Ms. Grechi," Tory said gently, "in situations like thi—"

"Dr. King," Rica said, "I know what the procedures are, and I know what you're thinking. I'm not an abused partner. I don't have a romantic relationship with this man and, believe me, I'm not trying to protect him. You'll just have to believe me that it won't happen again."

"All right," Tory said after a moment. Her new patient did not have the frantic, almost apologetic demeanor of the chronically abused. There was also something about her careful phrasing that made Tory believe this wasn't the result of a love affair gone bad, either. "Did he assault you in any other way?"

Rica closed her hands tightly around the edge of the vinyl cushion that covered the examining table. She felt his hands on her thighs, his erection thrusting between her legs. She hated him and everything he represented in her life. His arrogant entitlement, his cruel dominance. All her life she'd lived in the shadow of men like Enzo. Her father was blind to the fact that his power made her nothing more than an object of desire, a prize to be won. Whereas his power defined him, it obliterated her. From the moment they'd met, Carter had seen only her, not Alfonse Pareto's daughter. At least, that's what she'd believed. Until this morning. Rica swallowed around the sudden constriction in her throat. Her voice was soft when she spoke. "No. He didn't have a chance to."

"But you believe you're safe from him now?"

"Yes."

Tory rested her fingertips on the chart and spun it slowly on the table, searching Rica's face. "Part of your headache is due to the fact that your temporomandibular joint is badly inflamed as a result of the blows. I don't see any evidence of intracranial injury, but you were lucky. The next time he could do far more serious damage."

"It won't happen again. Please take my word for that."

"I can't force you to file charges, and I do understand how difficult it can be, especially when it's a family member. Will you call me if there's another problem?"

Rica stared, surprised. "Why does it matter so much to you? You don't know me."

Tory smiled. "No, I don't. But I care that someone hurt you, because no one has the right to do that."

"Is it that simple for you?" Rica asked curiously. Nothing in her life had ever seemed to be black and white. Some of the things her father did for a living were illegal, but he was her father and she loved him. So she pretended that if she didn't acknowledge what he did, she wouldn't have to judge him. He had given her a life that appeared on the surface to be one of privilege, but underneath, it had been a prison. Carter had lied to her, and yet she'd felt more like herself with Carter than she ever had with another person. There was nothing simple about the truths of her life. "Do you always find the right and wrong of things so clear?"

"No, not always." Tory's eyes grew distant as she thought of Reese and wondered what she was doing at that moment. Some people believed soldiers like Reese blindly followed orders as if every decision was black and white, but Tory knew that wasn't true. She could tell from their often aborted conversations that Reese questioned what she was doing in a country half a world away fighting for an agenda that was far from apparent. Reese believed in the ideals of the Marine Corps, but Tory knew her allegiance came with a personal price. Reese paid it, and so, now, did she. Tory looked into Rica's eyes. "But this is one of those times when I think the right and wrong of it are very clear. He has no right to touch you, ever, unless you want him to."

"It won't happen again, but," Rica said quickly, sensing Tory's objection, "I'll call you if I'm wrong."

Tory nodded, satisfied. "Good. The medication I'm going to give you will make you sleepy. Do you have someone who can stay with you?"

"Yes," Rica lied. *Not anymore.*

"Don't take these until you get home if you're driving."

"No, I won't. Thank you."

As Tory wrote out the prescription, she said, "Call me tomorrow if the pain hasn't improved or if your jaw gets stiffer. We may need to x-ray it."

"Yes, of course," Rica said, taking the prescription. "I appreciate your help."

"Just take care of yourself, Ms. Grechi."

"I will." Rica made her way outside, steadfastly ignoring the pounding pain behind her eyes. *Take care of yourself.* Yes, that was just what she intended to do, and her first stop, even before the pharmacy, was going to be her gallery, where she kept a .25 caliber Beretta in the desk.

She was so focused on fighting off the headache until she could finish what she needed to do that she didn't even notice the car that pulled out behind her again or the official-looking vehicle with the insignia on the doors that passed her on its way into the parking lot.

❖

Tory didn't look up at the sound of her office door opening, but continued making notes in a patient's chart. "I'll be ready for the next one in a minute."

"Tory," Randy said, his voice oddly hollow.

"Hmm," Tory said tiredly, glancing toward the door. She dropped her pen and stood slowly, her eyes riveted on the man standing next to Randy in the doorway. She'd heard his voice several times over the phone, but she'd never seen him. He was very handsome, and with his dark black hair, laser-bright blue eyes, and strong bold features, he looked more like Reese than she'd expected. The chin was different; that Reese got from her mother. "Oh my God."

The officer in the impeccable uniform smoothly closed the office door as Randy reflexively stepped back into the hall. Then he advanced swiftly until he was standing opposite Tory with his hand extended. His voice was a rich baritone. "Dr. King, I'm General Roger Conlon."

Tory recognized the large gold ring with the Marine Corps insignia he wore on his right hand. Reese had one just like it, but she didn't wear it. She kept it in a box in the top drawer of her dresser. She didn't wear any jewelry, except for her wedding ring. Tory couldn't bring herself to take his hand. She didn't want him in her office. She didn't want him in her life. She didn't want him to say whatever he had come to say.

"I know who you are." Tory braced her fingertips against the top of the desk. Her arms were shaking. She stared into his eyes, which were cool and unwavering. Hers stung with fury. "You couldn't be bothered to come here before, when she was happy. When *we* were happy. Don't you dare come in here now and tell me she's dead."

"We have no confirmation that is the case." Not a muscle in his handsome face flickered. His voice was smooth and hard as granite. "I am here to inform you that Colonel Conlon is missing in action."

Missing in action. What did that mean? That she was dead but they couldn't find her body? That she was lost in the desert without radio contact? No, it couldn't be something as simple as that, or he wouldn't be there. It was something worse. Something she didn't want to know. She wanted him gone. She wanted his war to be gone. She wanted Reese at home where she belonged, with the people who loved her, doing the work that mattered to so many every day. She wanted Reese beside her in the night, holding the baby, guiding Bri into adulthood with a sure and steady hand. She wanted her lover, her partner, her love, in her arms.

"Where is she? God damn you, where is she?"

"Colonel Conlon was in command of a unit escorting several high-ranking officials from Baghdad to a secure facility when her convoy was attacked by insurgents. Her vehicle and several others were separated from the main body during the firefight."

Tory struggled to decipher what he was saying. "Separated. Where did they go?"

"The vehicles have been recovered along with a number of casualties. Colonel Conlon's body was not among them."

Casualties. *Body.* A wave of dizziness threatened to take her legs out from under her. Tory sat heavily and pressed trembling fingers to her mouth. She breathed deeply several times and called upon every bit of fortitude she had to think her way through what he was telling her. "So she might be alive."

"Colonel Con—"

"Reese. Her name is Reese."

Reese's father nodded. "Reese and three others are presumed captured."

"Do you know where she is?"

"Not as of yet."

"But you *are* looking for her, aren't you?"

Tory thought it impossible that Roger Conlon could look any harder than he already did, but his face transformed before her eyes into an unyielding wall of stone.

"Reese is a Marine. We don't leave our people behind."

With effort, Tory pushed herself up. "Then you find her, General Conlon. You find her, you get her out, and you bring her home. I've had enough of your war. Reese has done her duty, now you do yours."

For just a second, Roger Conlon looked taken aback. "You have my word."

"Does Kate know?" Tory asked, feeling hope replace despair. Reese was smart. Reese was tough. Reese would not leave them. She wouldn't, not when she knew how very much they needed her.

"No. Colonel Con—Reese listed you as her next of kin."

"I am." Tory wondered fleetingly what it cost him to say that, but found that she didn't really care. All that mattered was that he use whatever power he had at his disposal to find Reese. She scribbled on a piece of paper and handed it to him. "This is my cell phone number. When you find her, call me. If she's hurt…" Her voice broke and she closed her eyes. After a second, she went on, "If she's hurt, I want to know immediately…and I'll want to talk to the doctors. You make that happen."

"I'm in constant contact with the officers in command over there. I'll know the moment there's news."

"Good. That's good."

"Try not to worry, Dr. King."

Tory glanced around the room as if she weren't certain where she was. Then she straightened, and her voice was stronger. "I'll be at Kate's for the next few hours. Our daughter is there." She held Roger Conlon's gaze. "Regina will be glad when Reese comes home. She misses her. We all do."

"I understand."

"I don't imagine that you do, but I don't need you to. I just want her home."

"I'll see to it."

Tory waited until Reese's father had left the room before slumping into her chair. She wasn't certain who to call. She needed to tell Kate. She needed to arrange for the rest of her patients to be seen. Bonita couldn't handle them all alone. She could call KT. No, KT was in Boston. Wasn't she? Pia would know. She pressed her fingertips to her temples and closed her eyes. It was so hard to think. Why was it so hard to think?

She opened her eyes and saw the picture of Reese in her desert fatigues. Her hat was tucked under her arm and the wind blew through her hair. She was smiling.

"Oh God, baby, please come home. I love you so much."

CHAPTER TWENTY-ONE

Tory knocked on Kate's front door, her mind a blank. On the drive over, she had tried to think of the right words to say, but none had come. None that would make the message any easier. It had all come down to one simple, unimaginable truth. *Your daughter is missing.*

She had delivered difficult messages before. *I'm sorry, there's nothing more we can do. I know this is difficult, but the medicine doesn't seem to be helping. I wish I had better news…*but this was Reese. Reese couldn't be missing, not when Tory could feel her with every beat of her heart.

The door opened and Tory met Kate's eyes. "Kate, I…oh, God, Kate—"

Kate pulled Tory into her arms and hugged her. "I know. Roger was just here."

Tory held on, her eyes closed, her cheek against Kate's shoulder. She let herself be comforted for another few seconds and then gently pulled away. Kate was pale. "I'm sorry, I should have called to let you know, but I wanted to tell you in person. I didn't think he'd come here."

"No, it's all right. Roger was decent." Kate held the door wide, recalling the shock of seeing him at her door after more than twenty years. When she'd recognized pain and not anger in his eyes, she'd known immediately why he had come. Before her heart had the chance to break, he'd said, *Missing. Not dead.* Three words she clung to. "It was good of him to come. If she weren't his daughter, we wouldn't even know she was missing. We'd be left to wonder why we weren't hearing from her until there was some official word."

"He'll find her, won't he?"

"Yes," Kate said firmly as she led Tory through the living room to the kitchen. "He will."

Jean sat at the kitchen table with Reggie dozing on her lap. Her eyes were red rimmed but resolute. "Hello, honey."

Tory lifted Reggie into her arms and rubbed her lips against the silky hair, wondering at the innocence of childhood. "Hi. How are you doing?"

"Fine, considering. Roger didn't shoot me, which was what he threatened the last time he saw me." Jean kissed Tory's cheek. "Reese is going to be all right. Don't think for a second that she isn't."

"I know," Tory said thickly. She said the words because she had to believe them, but how could any of them be sure?

"Have you eaten?" Kate asked briskly, caressing Jean's shoulder on the way to the refrigerator. "We're not going to know anything for a little bit, and no one is going to get sick while we wait."

"I can't right now." Tory shifted Reggie onto her hip. "Would you mind awfully if I went home for a while? I have some calls to make and I'd just like to be around...Reese. Us." She smiled just a little unsteadily. "Does that make any sense?"

"Perfectly." Kate gave her another hug. "Is there anyone you want me to call?"

"Would you mind finding Bri and asking her to meet me at the house? Just tell her I need to talk to her."

Jean went to the kitchen phone. "I'll do it."

"Thanks. And I'll call you the second I hear anything," Tory said, gathering the bright yellow plastic tote with Reggie's things.

As soon as Tory arrived home she put Reggie down to finish her nap and called Pia. She had just hung up after explaining what had happened and asking Pia to call KT when a cruiser slammed to a stop in the driveway and Bri bolted from the vehicle. Tory steeled herself to repeat the news that she knew was going to cause unbearable pain.

"What's wrong?" Bri said as she burst through the door, her eyes automatically scanning the room as if expecting an intruder. Her right hand rested on the butt of her holstered automatic. "Jean said you needed to see me right away. Is the baby okay?"

"Reggie's fine." Tory put both hands on Bri's forearms and said gently, "Something went wrong with a mission that Reese was on, and she's missing, honey. Her father just told me a little while ago."

Bri stiffened. "Missing. Jesus." Her eyes went a little wild. "Oh, Christ, Tory."

Then, before Tory had a chance to offer the comfort she had planned along with the now-familiar, if empty, words of reassurance, Bri gathered Tory into her arms and held her against her chest. She stroked her hair and murmured, "Don't worry. She'll be okay."

Bri wasn't as tall as Reese or as muscular, but there was no mistaking her power now. The gesture was so different than the maternal embrace that Kate had bestowed and so much like the automatic protective response Reese would have made that Tory nearly broke. There had been so few people in her life that she had leaned on. KT, so long ago, and Reese. The two women in her life she had loved with all she was. The only two she had ever trusted completely; the only two whose strength she had ever accepted when her own had faltered. Now, it seemed, there was another.

"I am so damn scared," Tory whispered.

"Yeah," Bri murmured, seeing no point in pretending she wasn't, too. She kept her arm around Tory's shoulder and guided her to the sofa, where she continued to hold her even after they were seated. When Tory leaned her head against her shoulder, Bri experienced a swell of pride and terrible affection. She wanted to make Tory's hurt and fear go away so badly she ached. She'd never felt this need to care for any woman other than Caroline, and even though this was different, she understood that it was love. "What happened?"

Tory told her what little she knew, realizing there were questions she should have asked that she hadn't been able to think of when Reese's father had been in her office. All she'd been able to think of then was that Reese might be hurt. That someone, for reasons she would never be able to understand, had wanted to kill the woman she loved. There was no way for her to understand that, to rationalize it, or to ever accept it, because she could not fathom anything, beyond protecting her child and Reese, that she would kill for. Beneath her confusion and pain, she was furious at the insanity of it.

"I'm sorry, I didn't ask…" Tory trembled. "All I could think was that Reese…" She searched Bri's face, wondering if she'd been right about the strength she'd imagined. Bri met her inquiring gaze calmly, her blue eyes dark with worry but steady. So steady. "I feel so helpless. Waiting. Not knowing if she's hurt."

"I know. It sucks."

Tory laughed through her tears. "Oh God, sweetie. It really does."

"Reese's father was here?" Bri asked.

"Yes, he came himself to tell me what happened. He said he'd call me as soon as anything...as soon as... God, I don't know what's supposed to happen next."

"Did he leave a number? Do you think he'd talk to me?"

Tory shook her head. "I don't know. Maybe he gave something to Randy. God, I was so rattled I didn't think..."

"You're not supposed to have to." Bri kissed Tory's cheek and stood. "I'm going to call my dad. He needs to know about Reese, and I bet he can find out what's going on."

Tory smiled, touched by the faith Bri had in those she loved. Warmed by it. "You go ahead and do that, sweetie. Thank you."

"I'm just doing what Reese would tell me to do, if she were here."

"She wouldn't have to tell you," Tory said. "You already know."

Bri blushed. "I'm going to call Caroline, too."

Tory nodded, understanding the need to touch the ones you loved in the midst of life's pain.

Half a block down the street from Rica's gallery, Carter sat in her parked vehicle with the engine running, wondering what was so important that Rica would have gone directly there from the clinic instead of home. Every few seconds she checked her mirrors and scanned the streets on both sides looking for anyone else who was also watching Rica. So far she hadn't seen anyone, but she expected to at any moment. She'd been trying to puzzle out exactly what Enzo's next move would be, but putting herself in the mind of a psychopath was difficult despite all the practice she'd had playing them on the job. She wasn't as certain as Rica that Enzo would seek retribution, because the last thing a man who'd been embarrassed by a woman wanted to do was call attention to it. She doubted that more than a handful of people even knew about the incident, if that many. In all likelihood, Enzo had crawled off to lick his wounds, figuratively speaking. Still, she didn't believe that Enzo would give up in his quest for Rica, especially not now.

"So all right, so maybe it wasn't the smartest move to challenge him," Carter muttered, hating to agree with Allen even obliquely. "It's not like I had a choice."

No man wanted to be bested in a competition for a woman's affections, and Carter had known very few men in her life who could tolerate losing to a woman. Enzo was not going to let that affront go, and she didn't intend to give him the opportunity to vent his bruised ego on Rica. Unfortunately, she hadn't quite figured out how she was going to watch Rica twenty-four hours a day, especially now that Rica wanted nothing to do with her.

If you come anywhere near me again, I'll do the job myself.

When Rica had said those words, Carter had no doubt that she had meant them. Her face had been pale, but cold and hard as marble.

"You fucked this one up royally." Carter rubbed her face and stretched her cramped legs beneath the dashboard. It wasn't Rica's anger that continued to gnaw at her, but the memory of those few seconds of shocked hurt that she had glimpsed in Rica's eyes before Rica had locked her feelings down. She'd proven to Rica that she was just like everyone else in her life—someone who used her, someone who lied to her, someone who pretended to care about her, because of who her father was. That's what Rica believed. Ironically, that's what Carter should have done, but she'd made a fatal error. She'd caught a glimpse of the woman behind the mask, and she'd wanted her.

Carter tensed as the door to Rica's gallery opened. Rica came out, locked the door, and walked briskly to her car, which she had left with the hazard lights blinking in the loading zone out front. Grateful for any activity to take her mind off the hollow ache in the center of her chest and the sick feeling she got every time she remembered Rica telling her to get out, Carter eased into traffic five cars behind Rica. She followed her as Rica drove directly home, slowing when Rica turned onto her street and driving past until she could make a U-turn in a motel parking lot a few blocks away. When she turned into Rica's street and passed her house, Rica's car was nowhere to be seen.

Probably already in the garage.

She made a thorough survey of the street and saw no one. The few cars parked in front of houses appeared to be empty. She stopped three houses away and settled in to watch.

❖

At 9:30 p.m., Tory opened the door to Nelson Parker. She put her arms around his neck and kissed his cheek. "Hi."

"Hi," Nelson said gruffly, bestowing a quick hug. He followed Tory into the living room and nodded in the direction of the others congregated there.

Pia was in the kitchen making a pot of coffee. Kate and Jean were upstairs with the baby. They had arrived at suppertime, insisting upon fixing a dinner that Tory had not been able to eat. KT, who had flown over from Boston as soon as her shift had ended at eight p.m, was outside on the deck. Bri and Caroline were on the couch. Bri was no longer in uniform but wore a skintight black T-shirt and jeans with motorcycle boots and sat splayed in one corner with Caroline curled up in her arms. They looked like young lion cubs, ready to fight or make love with equal fervor.

"Is there any news?" Tory asked, trying not to sound as anxious as she felt.

"Well," Nelson said, turning his cap in his hands, "I got through to General Conlon. It took me a couple of hours. You'd think I was trying to talk to the president."

Tory took one step forward and faltered, knowing from the look on Nelson's face there was no good news.

"He wouldn't tell me anything at first, but I finally got him to come across with a couple of things."

"Let me get Kate and Jean," Tory said.

"We're right here," Jean said as they came down the stairs. "Reggie's asleep."

Jean settled into one of the overstuffed chairs and Kate perched on the arm. KT came to stand in the doorway between the deck and the large living room. Her eyes drifted across the heads of those seated to where Pia stood in the kitchen. Pia smiled softly and tilted her head in Tory's direction. KT nodded, walked to Tory, and took her hand.

"Why don't you sit down, Vic."

"I don't want to si—" Tory stopped, hearing the anger at the same time as the panic edged a little closer to the surface. She squeezed KT's hand. "Thanks."

KT and Tory sat on the sofa, and KT kept Tory's hand in hers. Nelson perched on a stool he pulled over from the breakfast bar. He looked at his watch.

"This is what I know. Reese has been missing for just about twenty-four hours."

Tory unconsciously drew KT's hand into her lap and clasped it with both of hers. Twenty-four hours. If Reese was wounded, twenty-four hours could make the difference between life and death. If she'd been captured, God, what could they do to her in that amount of time?

"Don't start thinking about maybes, Vic," KT murmured. "Let's just deal with the facts."

"Keep telling me that," Tory said.

"No problem."

"Do they know where she is?" Tory asked.

Nelson shrugged. "If they do, he wasn't going to say. He *did* say that it was standard procedure to prepare an extraction team. They're going to go get her—all of them—as soon as they get a fix on them. That message was clear."

"Are they going to tell us when?"

"I don't think so," Nelson said. "That's SOP, too."

"So we wait." Tory wondered how long she could stand it.

Bri unwrapped herself from Caroline and stood abruptly. "I'm going out for some air."

"Don't take that motorcycle of yours," Nelson said automatically. "Not when your head's not on right."

"My *head's* just fine." Bri glared.

Caroline grasped Bri's hand and gave Nelson a small smile. "Don't worry, I'll go with her. We'll be back in a little while."

Nelson watched them walk out. "Damn kid."

"She'll be all right, Nelson," Tory said, knowing that he had never really gotten over almost losing her. "She's been a rock, and now she just needs the chance to get a handle on being scared. Caroline will help her with that."

"Good thing. I don't seem to be able to."

KT clapped him on the shoulder and caught Pia's eye. "Some of us take longer than others to get the message."

Nelson grinned and even Tory smiled. Then they all found seats and settled down quietly to wait.

Just before one a.m., the last light in Rica's house went out and Carter decided she'd turned in for the night. There'd been no activity on the upscale residential street since shortly after midnight, when a car full of partygoers had tumbled out and weaved their raucous way into one of the nearby houses. If anyone was watching Rica's house besides her, they weren't doing it from a vehicle. Street surveillance in this part of town made no sense, because if Rica were to leave in her car, she'd be gone before anyone could make their way to a vehicle without being obvious about it. Carter decided Rica was safe until morning, started her car, and headed home.

Bone tired and emotionally worn out, she pulled her SUV into the alley next to her building. The building next door, a converted garage that was now the office for one of the whale watch concessions, was dark. Still in the clothes she'd worn to the party the night before, she was hungry, she smelled, and she needed a shower. She just made it to the bottom of the stairs leading up to her second-floor apartment when a blow from behind caught her in the kidney and sent her sprawling onto the stairs. As she fell, she yanked the automatic from her waistband and twisted, trying to land on her back so she could get a shot off at whoever had hit her. She landed hard on her shoulder just as a foot connected with her wrist. Her hand went numb and she dropped her gun. Two dark shapes loomed above her.

"Get smart, bitch," a gravelly voice grated. "Stop sniffing around pussy that don't belong to you."

Carter tried to place the voice. "I don't know wha—"

A boot drove into her midsection, and she gagged as bile flooded her throat.

"Sure you do," the other one said. "You've got good taste in cunts. You're just trying to eat at someone else's table." He laughed, as if pleased with his own joke.

Carter kicked him in the knee and he howled. She almost got her feet under her when something flat and hard rammed her temple. Her vision dimmed and her legs wobbled. The next blow took her down for good. A short, harsh flash lit up the alley and her world went black.

CHAPTER TWENTY-TWO

Rica lay awake in the dark, listening to the wind and the night sounds. The codeine had helped ease the throbbing in her face, and she had dozed on and off throughout the evening. Now, well into the night, her head still pounded, but that wasn't the pain that kept sleep away. And nothing that came in a bottle was going to dull the ache that had settled around her heart.

She had *almost* convinced herself that the previous night had been a dream. That the incredible rightness of Carter's hands on her body, *inside* her body, had only been a perfect fantasy. A wish and nothing more. But it wasn't just the heat of Carter's mouth or her firm body and soft hands that she couldn't forget, but the quiet way Carter listened when Rica spoke of her past and the hard fury in Carter's eyes when Enzo had touched her.

Rica had changed the sheets, but she imagined that she could still smell her. And with that single fragile memory, all the rest came flooding back. The wanting, the yearning, the incredible freedom of being known. The rightness.

I'm a cop, Rica.

Furious with herself for being taken in by the understanding in Carter's eyes, Rica threw the crisp, clean sheets aside and grabbed the bedside phone to call her father. She hesitated, her finger poised to speed dial, and considered what she would say. *Papa, I've discovered an impostor who is trying to hurt you.* That was Carter's aim, wasn't it? Her father needed to know, didn't he?

She knew that her father, whose friends and allies could just as easily become enemies in the menacing world of shifting allegiances, was well protected. *This time it's different, Papa. She's not one of us, she's a cop.* Surely the threat Carter posed was greater than that of the men who tried to wrest control from her father every day. *Not one of us.* When had she joined her father's camp? Perhaps she hadn't, but she couldn't stand by and let him be hurt.

She stared at the phone. If she told him about Carter, what would he do? She wasn't certain, because she had never wanted to know what orders her father issued to protect himself and his empire. Ignorance was innocence, or so she had let herself believe. More lies of her own making. Lies she had built her life upon. Would her father kill the woman who had held her in her arms? She shivered. She didn't know.

One thing she did know. She wouldn't be able to live with herself if she exposed Carter and Carter suffered for it. Right or wrong, enemy or friend, she could still smell Carter on her sheets. She had wanted her last night, last week, last month, and she wanted her now.

But what of the danger to her father? God, her head hurt. Carter had said there was no one else inside to find. Did that mean there was no danger, either? Why should she believe her? There was no reason to, but she did. She *did* believe her. But he was her father.

"Papa?"

"It's late, *cara*. Are you all right?"

"Yes, I know. I'm fine." Rica closed her eyes, although the room was dark. "I'm sorry."

"You left without saying goodbye yesterday."

"Something came up. An emergency here at the gallery."

"Taken care of now?"

"Yes. Yes, I think so." Rica steeled herself, knowing the phones could be monitored, choosing her words carefully. "I couldn't sleep. Bad dreams. Can I tell you a story? That always makes me feels better."

"Yes. Tell me what you...dreamed."

"It was about friends who weren't, one in particular. Someone we...I...trusted, who betrayed us. Hurt you."

"Ah, broken loyalties. Infidelity of the worst kind." Her father's voice was soft, pensive. "This friend—he was secretly working with the enemy?"

"She." Rica's heart ached. "In my dream, it was a woman. I don't know how, exactly, but I'm afraid—"

"I had a similar dream," Alfonse said, "of a man I loved like a brother. He turned against me because he was weak and afraid. Don't worry, *cara*. Dreams can't hurt us." He laughed softly. "When you were small, I would leave the light on so that you wouldn't be afraid of the shadows in the corners. There will always be shadows, but you don't have to worry about them. Go to sleep, *cara*, and forget about the dream."

"You're all right?"

"I'll keep the light on for a while, but I'll sleep well."

"I love you, Papa," Rica said softly, because it was the truth.

"I love you, *cara*. Come home soon when we aren't giving a party. We'll talk."

"I'll try. Good night, Papa."

"Good night, Ricarda *mia*."

Rica hung up, her head pounding mercilessly. As she lay awake, wondering who the man was her father had spoken of, she heard a car slow and stop somewhere nearby. She thought nothing of it until the crunch of shoes on shells penetrated her awareness. Listening more intently, she tried to discern if it was just a neighbor returning home. When the uneasy sensation of something not quite right became too much to tolerate, she crept to the window and looked down into the driveway. There was nothing but darkness.

She went back to bed and eventually fell into a restless half sleep, only to dream of running through endless dark streets from some formless horror that grew closer with each step.

"You should try to get some sleep," KT said as she slid the screen door closed behind her and crossed the deck to where Tory stood at the railing. The slice of moon hanging over the water was nearly obscured by cloud, but she didn't need moonlight to see Tory's face. She'd lain down beside her countless nights, and every curve and plane of Tory's being was carved into her soul. She rested her hand lightly on Tory's lower back. "Reese will be pissed as hell if she comes home and you're worn down to the bone."

Tory stared at the harbor, but she wasn't seeing the ebony surface, broken here and there by teasing slivers of starlight. "Do you think she'll come home?"

"Yes," KT said immediately. The terrible pain in Tory's voice brought back memories of another time when the hurt had been of her doing, but she swiftly pushed those thoughts aside. The wounds she had caused Tory were in the past, and if she were to hope for absolution it would come not from apologies, but from whatever comfort and friendship she could offer her now. "She's not dead, Vic. If she were, they'd have found her body by now, and we'd know."

Tory shuddered but KT went on. She was no stranger to delivering hard messages, and she trusted Tory's strength. "That means she's a prisoner, because she's too damn smart to just be lost and wandering around somewhere."

"She could be hurt, lying out there in the desert." Tory's voice was an agonized whisper. "I can't stand the thought of her being hurt and alone. I can't."

"They've got all kinds of aerial and ground surveillance equipment. Christ, they can put a missile down a chimney in the middle of a city. They don't lose people." KT slid her arm around Tory's shoulders and squeezed. "Her father told you what happened, and I believe him. She's been captured."

"She's a woman, KT," Tory said in a strangled voice.

"She's a fucking Marine. And even if those military types didn't pride themselves on never leaving their people behind, her father's a goddamn general. You can bet they're tearing up the desert looking for her."

"But it's been so long. Anything could have happened—"

KT turned Tory to face her just as the moon escaped its cover. She framed Tory's face as their eyes met. "Don't. Don't torture yourself thinking of things you can't change. She'll get through it, no matter what. So will you."

"I've never felt this helpless." Tory closed her eyes and pressed her cheek to KT's palm. "So weak."

"Oh, bullshit. Any one of us would be crazy out of our minds if it was our lover. Jesus, Reese would be ripping her way through the Pentagon by now."

Tory laughed shakily. "She would."

"It's going to be okay. They'll find her or she'll get out. She'll come home." If it was a lie, KT knew it didn't matter. In this moment, what mattered was hope. If the time came when there was none, they'd deal with that, too.

"I know you're right. It's just so hard not to be able to do anything." Tory reached up and covered KT's hand where it rested on her cheek. "You should go home. Don't you have to go back to Boston tomorrow?"

"I traded a few days. I'll be here for a bit."

"Did Pia leave?"

"About an hour ago. She's got early clients she couldn't cancel."

"She's good for you," Tory said.

"Yeah. She is."

"She knows you're not really so tough, doesn't she?"

KT laughed. "Yeah."

"In case you don't know," Tory said, "I'm glad you're here."

KT tilted her head until her forehead touched Tory's. "Me too, Vic."

"Good. Now that we have that settled, go home."

Tory sounded stronger, and KT felt a little of her own worry lift. "Make a deal with you."

"Oh no, I know what your deals are like."

"I've changed."

"Not *that* much."

"I'll go home if you go to bed." KT touched a finger to Tory's chin. "Please."

"All right," Tory said with a sigh. "You win this time. But don't get used to it."

"Not a chance." KT kissed Tory's forehead. "Thanks."

Arm in arm, they walked into the house.

"Come back to bed, baby," Caroline said softly. Neither she nor Bri had wanted to go home, so they'd bunked in the first-floor guest room at Tory's.

"In a second," Bri said, standing naked in the shadows by the window looking out. The low murmur of voices outside on the deck had drawn her from bed, and now she watched KT and Tory disappear into the other part of the house. After a second, she slid back into bed, propped some pillows behind her back, and pulled Caroline into her arms.

"If we split up, would you still love me?" Bri asked, combing her fingers slowly through Caroline's hair.

Caroline drew her leg up over Bri's and rubbed her palm over Bri's abdomen. "No, because you'd be dead."

Bri laughed. "How do you know *I'd* be the one who left?"

"Because I know." Caroline shifted on top of Bri and kissed her. "Besides the fact that you're the sexiest girl I've ever seen, so why would I leave you for sex that wasn't as good, I love you."

Even before she'd come back to bed, Bri had wanted to make love. She'd hungered to feel Caroline, to know that she was there and wouldn't leave her, that the person she counted on most in life wouldn't disappear. She'd had an ache deep inside all night, a burning urgency to touch and be touched, to feel Caroline arch beneath her hands and come with a cry against her mouth. She was wet and hard, wanting her.

I love you, Carre had said.

Bri had never quite been able to believe her luck, never quite gotten over worrying that Caroline would find someone else—someone stronger, someone braver, someone better.

I love you.

Suddenly the enormity of how much she needed that love washed over her, and out of nowhere came the tears. Bri buried her face in the soft warm curve of Caroline's neck and cried.

"Oh, hey. Baby." Caroline wrapped her arms around Bri and held her as tightly as she could. She didn't tell her not to cry, because it was such a rare event for Bri that she knew it must be necessary. Instead she murmured, over and over, "I love you. I love you so much. Don't worry, Reese will come home. It's all right, baby. Everything is going to be all right."

"Fuck," Bri gasped, finally pulling away. "Oh man, Carre, I'm sorry."

"For what?" Caroline stroked the tears from Bri's face. "For not being tough all the time? For letting me take care of you?" She punched Bri lightly on the arm. "I'm a lot stronger than you think."

"I know." Bri heaved a deep breath and felt her insides settle. She brushed Caroline's hair back from her face, then traced her thumb over Caroline's mouth. "I know just how strong you are. Sometimes, I wonder why you're even with m—"

"Baby. Shut up." Caroline sealed her mouth to Bri's, plunging her tongue between her lips while she snaked a hand between them and into Bri's crotch. She gave a deep murmur of approval when she found her hot and wet and open. She didn't wait but slid through the heat and inside her.

Bri jerked and moaned and writhed while Caroline drove into her and drove out her fears and her uncertainties. When she came, stifling her cries against Caroline's breast, Caroline whispered, "I love you."

While all around her was chaos, Bri clung to Caroline and let their love be her strength.

Carter came awake to a world of pain. Something warm and thick ran down her forehead, into her eyes. Blood. She recognized it from the smell. When she tried to raise her arm to wipe it away, she couldn't. She blinked and her vision swam.

"Fuck."

She turned her head and vomited.

Bits and pieces of the beating came back to her. She was still on the stairs. It was dark. Still night. How much time had passed? Her ears were ringing. She tried hard to listen for sounds in the alley. She thought she was alone. Had they gone? She was dead if they came back now.

She struggled to isolate her pain. Shoulder. Hand. Stomach. Back. She took a breath. Hurt. Not too bad though. She shifted her legs. Knees were okay. Sweat broke out on her face, ran down her back. Cold, sick sweat.

She wasn't certain she could feel her hands and feet. Hard to tell through the agony that screamed along her nerve endings every time she moved. Had to get up. Inside. Call Kevin.

Rica. Jesus, Rica. Sickness flooded her. If they'd touched her. Kill them.

"Time to get up," she gasped.

She got one hand braced against the stairs but when she tried to push upright, the world did a slow circle in front of her eyes. She vomited again, slumped over, and passed out.

Just before dawn, Rica gave up her restless battle with sleep and dragged herself from bed. She showered, hoping to wash the weariness from her mind as well as her body. She felt more awake afterward, but no less sad.

What she needed was coffee and work. Dwelling on mistakes was not her nature. She had done her duty, although it seemed her father already knew something of what was happening. Still, now she could forget about Carter and all the rest of it.

Feeling resolved if not particularly better, she dressed casually in jeans and a blouse for a day of office work and went downstairs. When she opened the kitchen door, an envelope that had been pushed into the space between the door and the jamb fluttered to the deck.

With trembling hands, she opened it and extracted a Polaroid photograph.

"Oh my God," she moaned.

She dropped the photo in horror and raced from the house.

CHAPTER TWENTY-THREE

Rica's lifelong vigilance against doing anything that might attract the attention of the police prevented her from speeding down Bradford, despite her frenzy to get to Carter's apartment. The image in the Polaroid print kept flashing through her mind. The harsh light had captured Carter's unconscious body with brutal clarity. With her eyes closed and uneven trails of blood streaming down her face, Carter looked smaller, broken. She might have been dead.

No. No, of course she isn't. That's impossible. They wouldn't. He wouldn't.

She had no idea who had ordered the retaliation. It might have been Enzo, furious at having been physically rebuffed by Rica and bested by a woman whom Rica favored over him. That seemed most likely, but she couldn't help wondering if it had been her father's order that had resulted in the devastation. She couldn't allow herself to believe that. She couldn't believe that one person she loved could do that to another she lov—

No. That's not what I feel for her. It isn't. It can't be.

Feeling physically ill with apprehension at what she might find, Rica careened into the alley next to Carter's building. Carter's Explorer was there. She slammed to a stop behind it, jumped out, and started for the stairs. Then she saw her.

"Oh my God, Carter," she cried, rushing forward. When she reached her, she wasn't sure if she should touch her. Carter lay as she had in the photograph, her legs on the ground and her upper body twisted sideways on the stairs. There was blood on her face and her clothes and on the stairs. For one terrible moment, Rica feared she really was dead. Moaning, she whispered Carter's name again and tentatively touched her cheek. Her skin was warm, and Rica felt a flood of relief.

"Carter?"

Carter twitched.

"Oh thank God." Rica fell to her knees beside her and stroked her face. "Carter. Carter, darling. Can you hear me?"

Carter's eyelids fluttered and she groaned.

Rica looked over her shoulder toward the street, wondering if anyone could see them now that the sun had risen. She wanted to go for help, but it was so hard to break the habits of a lifetime. She hesitated to involve the authorities when she wasn't certain what had happened. She was relieved to see that they were still alone.

"Rica," Carter whispered.

Rica felt almost dizzy as a tiny bit of her fear subsided. "Oh, Carter. What happe—"

"Go…away." Carter tried to turn onto her back, but the motion sent a shaft of pain through her. She groaned again and lay still, breathing heavily. "Not safe here."

"Don't be silly," Rica said sharply, fear and fury warring within her. She wanted to kill whoever had done this. She'd never felt such hatred in her life. "You need help. I'm going to call for EMTs."

"No. Don't." With supreme effort, Carter rolled over onto her back and fought to bring Rica's face into focus. "Help me upstairs."

"You need a doctor."

"I'll be okay." She could breathe, she could see, and most of her parts were working. She could even finally think a little. Carter was pretty sure nothing was irreparably damaged, but she didn't know if her late-night visitors were still lurking around. She didn't want Rica endangered. "Go. Please."

"No. I need to find a phone." Rica was frightened by how pale Carter looked and how much blood had pooled beneath her face on the stairs.

"My cell. Belt," Carter whispered. "Need to…call my…partner."

Rica checked Carter's belt, but there was nothing there. "It's gone. Maybe it fell off when they…" Pressing her lips tightly together, Rica peered into the alley and underneath the stairs. She saw Carter's phone and retrieved it.

"My gun. Lost it."

"I didn't see it." Rica looked again, even bending down to search underneath Carter's vehicle, but she couldn't find it.

Carter closed her eyes, exhausted.

"Carter?" Rica knelt again. "Darling?"

"Sounds good," Carter muttered.

Rica smiled unsteadily and caressed Carter's shoulder. "It's going to be all right."

Carter opened her eyes and braced her good hand against the stairs. She was weak, but some of the nausea had subsided. "Help me up."

"I don't think—damn it," Rica exploded, hastily wrapping an arm around Carter's shoulder as Carter pushed herself into a sitting position. "God, you're so stubborn."

Winded, Carter rested her cheek against Rica's shoulder. "Ditto."

"Can you walk to the car?" Rica cradled Carter's face gently against her breast, feeling the sticky blood beneath her fingers.

"Rather go upstairs."

"Yes, I know, but you're not going to until a doctor has seen you. You either let me drive you somewhere or I'll call 911."

"Rica," Carter said as firmly as she could. "We need to keep this quiet. You'll be exposed…if this is documented."

"I don't care."

"Clinic." Carter was too weak to argue.

Tory snatched up the phone on the first ring. "Hello?"

"Dr. King? This is Rica Grechi. I'm sorry to disturb you so early, but this number is listed at the clinic for emergencies."

Tory had been so prepared to hear the sound of Roger Conlon's voice that she struggled to orient herself. She couldn't place the woman's name. "I'm sorry. I don't remember…"

"I saw you yesterday afternoon. I had some injuries to my face."

The image of the beautiful young woman who'd been seriously battered snapped into place. "Of course. I'm sorry. You're at the clinic now?"

"Yes. I'm afraid it's a bit of an emergency."

"What's the problem?"

"It's rather complicated, but…there's been an assault."

So Rica Grechi was wrong that he wouldn't come after her again. Tory glanced at the clock in the kitchen. 6:30 a.m. She'd been up since five, feeding Reggie and pacing. She could call KT or Bonita to run over to the clinic. Either one of them would be willing to see an emergency patient for her.

"I'm so sorry to call like this," Rica said, her voice trembling. "It's my lover. She's been hurt, and we can't go anywhere else."

Two battered women. Whatever was going on, it had the potential to be very dangerous for one or both of them. "Is she conscious?"

"Yes, but…it looks bad."

"Is there any chance that you've been followed? That he'll attack you again?"

"No. I don't think so."

"All right, but keep an eye out and be prepared to leave if you need to. I'll be there in ten minutes." Tory hung up and went to the guest room. She tapped on the door. "Bri?"

"Yeah?"

Tory opened the door and then quickly averted her gaze when a naked Bri jumped from bed. It didn't matter that Bri was twenty years her junior, she was a beautiful young woman and Tory was *not* her mother. "Sorry. Can you watch the baby for a little while? I've got to go to the clinic."

"Now?" Bri frowned as she searched for her jeans. "I mean, I don't mind watching Reggie." She pulled up her pants, zipped them, and tugged on her T-shirt. "But isn't it awfully early?"

"Emergency."

"Jesus, Tory." Bri ran a hand through her thick, unruly hair. "Can't you let someone else do it? You must be beat."

Tory smiled softly. Obviously, everyone she knew thought she was fragile. "I've got my cell phone. I gave that number to Reese's father, so when…when he calls, I'll get it. I won't stay. I just need to see this one patient."

"Okay. I told my dad I wasn't coming in today unless he really needs me. I want to be here when they find Reese."

"Good. I want you to be here, too."

Bri's certainty was almost contagious, and Tory allowed herself to believe in it as she left for the clinic. It had been just over thirty-three hours since Reese had disappeared. Surely it wouldn't be much longer.

When Tory turned into the clinic parking lot she saw a silver Lexus idling by the side entrance to the clinic. It was the only vehicle in the lot and invisible from the road. She pulled up nearby and got out at the same time as Ricarda Grechi jumped from the Lexus. They met by the front passenger door.

"Thank you so much for coming," Rica said. She opened the door and bent down. "Carter? The doctor's here."

Tory peered into the vehicle. "Let me take a look before we try to move her."

Carter carefully turned her head and squinted. The woman looked familiar. "I can walk. Slowly."

"Is your neck okay?" Tory asked.

"Seems to be. Head hurts like a bastard, though."

Tory eyed the three inch laceration running along the woman's right temporal hairline. Her hair was matted with dried blood. "I'll just bet it does."

"Sorry about all of this."

"No need for apologies." Tory scooped an arm around Carter's waist as Rica helped ease Carter from the car to an upright position. "Here, let's take it slow." Five minutes later she and Rica helped Carter onto an examining table in the quiet, empty clinic. As Tory washed her hands, she said, "Fill me in on the details."

Rica, who stood by the side of the examining table with her hand on Carter's shoulder, looked down at her inquiringly.

"It happened about one o'clock this morning. I took a couple of shots to the back, a couple to the stomach, a kick to the right wrist, and blunt force trauma to the head. A sap, I think. Twice. Knocked me cold."

Rica moaned softly and stroked Carter's hair with trembling fingers. "Who was it?"

"Don't know." Carter lifted her uninjured hand and caught Rica's. "It's okay."

"That's where you're very wrong, Carter."

Tory studied Rica, surprised by the anger and resolve in her voice. This situation was not what she had expected. These were not lovers battered by an angry spouse or boyfriend. They seemed to be lovers, but there was some other tension between them. And Rica Grechi looked ready to exact vengeance from someone. "Have you called the police?"

Carter held Rica's eyes. "I'm a Massachusetts State Police detective."

"I see." Tory sighed. "And I assume there's a reason why you're here instead of calling for backup and an ambulance?"

"Several," Carter replied, still looking at Rica.

"All right. Let's worry about you first. *Then* we'll talk."

After completing her examination, Tory said, "I'm going to need a urine specimen. Can you make it to the bathroom?"

"I'll help her," Rica said.

"Just help me get over there," Carter said. "I can handle it from there."

Tory smiled. "Not too sick to forgo pride, I see. Cops are all alike." At Rica's curious expression she said, "My lover is the sheriff here."

"Conlon?" Carter asked. At Tory's nod, she started to shake her head and then winced. "I remember you now. That day at the beach. You had some young kid riding bodyguard detail."

"Bri Parker. Family friend."

"Conlon due back soon?"

Tory struggled to keep her expression neutral. "Soon. We hope soon." She took Carter's elbow. "Come on. Let's get you to the bathroom."

Rica paced uneasily in front of the closed door. "I don't think we should leave her alone in there."

"She'll be all right for a few minutes, but she's in no shape to be making decisions, Ms. Grechi." Tory kept her voice low. "She has a concussion. The two of you are obviously in danger, and she's not going to be able to protect you."

"I can."

Tory believed her. "I know that if Reese were here and something like this happened, there'd be hell to pay if Carter kept quiet about it. Whatever's going on, Carter should be able to get all the help she needs from the local authorities."

"She's worried about me," Rica said softly.

"I gathered that. Try to convince her to get some backup in case there's more trouble."

"I will."

The bathroom door opened and Carter leaned against the door frame. "Mission accomplished, but I don't think I can make it back to the table."

Rica rushed to her and put an arm around her waist. "Lean on me. Come on."

"I'll be right back." Tory took the specimen cup and went next door to the small lab.

In the few minutes it took Rica to get Carter settled again, Tory completed her analysis. "You've got traces of blood in your urine, which probably is due to a bruised kidney."

"Should we go to the hospital?" Rica said immediately.

"It would be the prudent thing to do, yes," Tory said, watching Carter's face take on a set expression. "But Detective Wayne isn't going to. Which means, *Detective*, you are going to go home and get into bed. You are to drink plenty of fluid. Tylenol only for pain. I'll give you a small dose of codeine to augment it. No aspirin. No ibuprofen. Nothing that could increase the chance of bleeding."

"Okay," Carter said.

"And," Tory went on sternly, "you need to be observed for at least twenty-four hours. You've got a serious concussion and all too frequently we see other problems develop as a result. You need to be on the lookout for visual changes, confusion, increasing nausea, dizziness, weakness. I need to know about it immediately."

"I'll stay with her," Rica said.

Carter said nothing.

"And I need to suture that laceration on your temple." Tory looked at Rica. "I assume you want to stay while I do that?"

Rica kept her eyes on Carter. "Yes."

When Tory finished, she found two business cards among the pile of prescription pads in a drawer and handed one to each woman. "Call me if anything changes. I won't be in for the rest of the day. Possibly not for several." She wrote a prescription and handed it to Rica. "One every four hours. No more for the first twenty-four, then you can double the dose."

"I understand."

"If I hear that there's any further violence involving either of you, I'm going to Sheriff Parker. I don't care what this investigation is all about."

Carter held out her hand. "Thank you, Dr. King. I can promise you there won't be any further problems."

"Just go home and go to bed, Detective."

❖

Carter slumped into the front seat of Rica's car with a faint groan. "Jesus. She's not happy with us."

"I got the feeling she's well versed in cop bullshit," Rica said as she headed toward town.

Carter smiled faintly. "Yeah. I got that too."

"I'm going to get you settled first, and then I'll pick up your prescription."

"I don't need it. Tylenol will be fine."

"Uh-huh."

Carter narrowed her eyes against the bright sunlight and checked the street signs. "Where are you going?"

"I'm taking you home."

"This isn't the way to my apartment. "

"No," Rica said calmly. "But it is the way to my house."

Carter swore. "Rica, you can't be seen with me."

Rica turned her head briefly, gave Carter a measured look, and then turned her attention back to the road. "Carter, you are in no position to be giving orders."

"You don't have any idea how dangerous the situation is. If these guys come back—Christ, I don't even have my weapon."

"Somehow," Rica said conversationally, "you've gotten the wrong impression. I'm not a pampered rich girl. I've had to protect myself my entire life. And I know how to do it."

"Why are you doing this?"

"What makes you think I'll tell you the truth?"

"Because there's no point in lying anymore," Carter said wearily.

"I suppose you're right." Rica turned into her driveway and shifted to meet Carter's eyes. "I don't know why. Let's just say I don't want any more of your blood on my hands."

Carter wasn't certain what she had hoped to hear, but she was in no position to ask for more. "Twenty-four hours. Maybe that will give us enough time to sort this out."

"Maybe." Rica shrugged. "Either way, tomorrow we say goodbye and call it even."

"Right." Carter watched Rica come around the front of the vehicle to help her out. They could pretend all they wanted that none of this had ever happened, but she wasn't going to be able to forget.

Chapter Twenty-Four

It's probably just as well that we don't see one another in the future," Rica said as she slowly guided Carter upstairs to her bedroom. "Our relationship doesn't seem to be very good for our health."

Winded, Carter settled onto the side of the bed. "You think?"

Rica forced herself to relinquish her hold on Carter, even though she had an almost obsessive desire to keep touching her. The terror of finding that photo and thinking for an instant that Carter was dead still haunted her. She folded her arms around her middle. "The last forty-eight hours would indicate that."

"What happened to me isn't your fault," Carter said. "It's mine."

"Someone nearly beat you to death because of me."

"We don't know that." Carter closed her eyes, absurdly glad that she hurt in more than one place so that she couldn't actually focus on where the pain was greatest. "I need a shower."

"You can barely stand. Get some sleep, and you can shower later."

"I'm not getting into bed without one."

"God, Carter," Rica exploded. "Can't you do anything the easy way? Do you have any idea how bad you look right now?"

"It looks worse than it—"

"Don't. Just...don't." Rica walked quickly to the other side of the room, afraid that Carter would see the tears that had taken her by surprise. God, she didn't want to feel any of this. She flinched at the light touch on her shoulder.

"I'm sorry. For all of this."

"I don't want to talk about it now," Rica said, her back still turned. "Can you manage the shower by yourself?"

"Yes." Carter hesitated. She should contact Kevin and tell him what happened. She should heed Allen's call to come in. She should be anywhere but in Rica Grechi's bedroom. And all she could think of was easing the pain she could hear in Rica's voice. "I never lied to you about how I feel about you."

"Just about everything else." Rica couldn't keep the bitterness from her voice. She turned, refusing to allow the sight of Carter's injuries to assuage her anger. "Is that supposed to make it all right that you deceived me for weeks?"

"No," Carter said quietly. "I can't make it all right. I should've backed off when I realized I was falling in love with you, but I didn't want to admit it."

"I don't care what you feel or don't feel about me."

"I know." Carter touched her fingertips lightly to the bruise on Rica's cheek. "This is looking a little better."

Rica said nothing as Carter slowly made her way into the bathroom and closed the door quietly behind her. She wanted to follow. She wanted to help her undress and bathe her wounds. She wanted to wash the blood from Carter's hair and from her own memories. She forced herself to stay where she was, because she wanted so badly to touch her.

"Here you go, babe," Bri said with a flourish, sliding an only slightly burned grilled cheese sandwich onto a plate in front of Caroline, who sat at the breakfast island with Reggie on her lap. "You sure you don't want one, Tory?"

"No. I'm fine. Thanks." Tory stood at the open door to the deck, staring at the cloudless blue sky and wondering if Reese could see the sky from wherever she was. It was night there already. Dark. Forty hours. She'd been missing forty hours.

The cell phone on her belt chimed. Tory snatched it off and stared at the readout. Private caller. She knew it could be anyone. Her mother had promised to call at midday to see if there was any news after Tory insisted that her parents not make the ten-hour drive just yet. She'd given her private number to quite a few patients in case they had questions about new medications or needed to report a change in an unstable medical condition. It might just be a wrong number. Her hand shook.

"Hello?"

She heard a garbled voice. A male voice, she thought. Then faint static gave way to silence. Something in Tory's face brought Bri hurrying around the counter, but Caroline caught her arm and stopped her.

"Hello," Tory said urgently. "This is Victoria King. Hello?"

"Hi…baby…me."

Tory covered her mouth to stifle a cry. She stared at Bri and Caroline, both of whom seemed to be frozen in mid-motion, like figures in a snapshot.

"Reese?" Tory's voice trembled. "Sweetheart? *Reese?*"

Six thousand miles away, Reese Conlon motioned for the medics to hold off lifting her stretcher into the UH-60Q Black Hawk medivac helicopter. "I'm okay. Tory, baby, can you hear me? I'm okay."

"Where…you?"

"Germany. I love you."

"Hurt? …you hurt?"

"Nothing much. Don't worry. Tory, I love you."

The connection went dead and Reese swore.

"Time to go, Colonel," the medic said.

"Just try again," Reese pleaded.

"Load her up. *Now,*" a familiar voice snapped.

Reese turned her head, gritting her teeth as the movement pulled at the burn on her shoulder and arm. Her father's face was in shadow, his body outlined against the night sky by the spotlights from the helicopters. "If I could just try the call one more—"

"We need to move. You got your call." Roger Conlon squatted beside the stretcher and rested his hand on the blankets covering Reese's thighs. In a softer tone, he said, "And you need to have those wounds seen to."

"I'm fine, sir. How are my Marines?"

"The others are already airborne. They're all going to make it." He touched her hair, then drew his hand back. "You did a fine job. I'm proud of you."

"Thank you, sir." Reese fought to stay awake. "Thank you for the call, sir."

"I'll see you in Germany, Colonel."

Reese fumbled for her father's hand. "Call her, Dad…please."

General Roger Conlon stood and waved to the medics. "Get this Marine to the hospital."

"Yes, sir," the men called back.

By the time the medics secured her stretcher and the last of the Special Ops Black Hawks were in the air, Reese was asleep.

Tory stared at the phone, afraid to believe the words she had just heard. *What if it was a dream?* Her legs suddenly felt rubbery and she braced a hand on a nearby chair. She looked up, dazed, when Bri gently removed the phone from her hand and cupped her elbow.

"Was it Reese?" Bri's voice was a hushed whisper.

"It was." Tory's eyes glistened with tears. "Oh my God. She called me." Laughing now, she threw her arms around Bri's neck. "She *called* me."

Letting loose with a whoop of joy, Bri lifted Tory and swung her in a circle. "Oh yeah. Oh yeah oh yeah."

Reggie giggled and clapped as Caroline danced her about.

Breathless, Tory gasped, "We have to call Kate and Jean and—"

"Not on your cell phone." Bri reverently handed it back to Tory. "Reese might call again soon. Caroline and I will call everyone on ours."

"She's alive." Tory sat on the sofa. "My God. She's alive."

Caroline slid down beside her and handed Reggie to her. She slipped an arm around Tory's waist. "Did she say where she was?"

"I…Germany, I think," Tory said, puzzled, still replaying the fractured call in her mind. Then she stiffened. "That's where the main military hospital is."

"Hey. You just talked to her, remember? She's all right."

"She must be hurt." Tory jumped up. "Reese wouldn't tell me if she was hurt. She must be, if they're taking her to the hospital." She stared around the room as if seeking an answer. "God. This is driving me crazy. Why can't they just tell us what's happening?"

"It's probably only been a little while since they found her," Caroline soothed, grasping Tory's hand and tugging her back down to the sofa. "Reese's father said he'll call. Do you think he will?"

"He raised her. He taught her some of the things I love most about her," Tory said almost to herself. "He'll call."

Three hours later the phone rang again.

Every person in the room went silent. Kate took Jean's hand. Pia wrapped an arm tightly around KT's waist. Bri hugged Caroline from behind, cradling her against her chest. Nelson patted Reggie's back as she slept on his shoulder.

Tory watched her family and friends, drawing strength from their love. "Hello? This is Tor—"

"General Conlon, Dr. King."

"How is she?"

"Colonel—uh, Reese—is resting comfortably at Landstuhl Regional Medical Center in western Germany."

"What are her injuries?" Tory asked with a calmness she didn't feel.

"Second- and third-degree burns scattered over her torso, and a fractured clavicle, sustained when her vehicle ran over a land mine." He sounded as if he were reading a laundry list. "Nothing life-threatening, the doctors assure me."

"She's conscious? No head injury?"

"They sedated her to treat the wounds, but she was quite alert in the field."

"I appreciate all you've done, General," Tory said, "but I'd like to ask another favor. Can you arrange for me to see her at the hospital? I'll try to get flights for tomorrow. I can be there—"

"That won't be necessary, Dr. King. Ordinarily, she would go from here to a stateside military hospital as soon as possible for whatever rehab is needed. If the doctors clear it, I'll see that she comes home." He paused. "Reese's request."

Tory took a long breath to steady herself. "I can assure you, General Conlon, that she will get all the care necessary right here."

"I don't doubt that, Doctor. I'll be in touch."

"Thank you." Tory ended the call and regarded the anxious faces watching her. "Well. I didn't think I'd ever say this, but it's very nice to have a general in the family. Reese is coming home."

Amidst the cheers, Kate made her way to Tory and gave her a hug. "One thing I never doubted was that Roger loved her. I'll always be grateful to him for this."

Tory nodded. "So will I." Then she laughed. "She's coming home. God, Kate. She's coming home."

Carter knew Rica was there before she opened her eyes. She could smell her, a faint whiff of mandarin and spice.

"Opium," Carter murmured.

Rica laughed. "No, but that's very good. It's a custom fragrance but there are some similarities."

Naked beneath the sheets, Carter gazed at Rica, who sat nearby in a white wicker chair, framed by the colors of sunset beyond the open French doors. A breeze teased her hair and a hint of a smile lingered. She looked so achingly lovely that Carter wished with all her heart that she could stop time.

"How long have I been asleep?" Carter vaguely remembered falling into bed after her shower. Rica had not been in the room then.

"About four hours. How are you feeling?"

"Cleaner." Carter studied Rica's remote expression. They might have been strangers. "Why am I here?"

Rica drew her legs up and sat sideways in the chair with her feet tucked beneath her. "You're in no shape to travel or defend yourself. If they come back, they'll kill you."

"If they wanted to kill me, they would have last night."

"Maybe," Rica said. "But I'm not willing to take the chance."

"You didn't feel that way yesterday morning."

"This isn't about you and me," Rica said sharply. "If I wanted you dead, I wouldn't hire thugs to beat you. I'd hunt you down and shoot you myself."

Despite the fact that she hurt more than she'd imagined possible in every bone of her body, Carter laughed. "I believe you."

"Good." Rica regarded Carter intently, ridiculously relieved that she was awake and seemed stronger. She'd watched her sleep for hours, irrationally terrified that she'd stop breathing. She wondered if she'd ever be able to get the image of Carter lying in her own blood out of her mind. "Do you know who did this?"

"I might recognize one of the voices, given a little time. Head's too fuzzy just yet." At Rica's expression of alarm, Carter added quickly, "It wasn't Enzo. Him I would know." Very carefully, she inched her way up until she was sitting upright against the pillows. It didn't register in her still slightly befuddled mind that the sheets had fallen away, leaving her chest exposed. "I'm pretty certain it was someone I met...doing business."

"My father's people," Rica said tonelessly. And now she knew the answers to so many of her questions. What her father was capable of. What price her loyalty would exact. What toll love would demand. "I'm sorry. It wasn't what I wanted to happen. I never wanted you hurt."

Carter considered the words. "You told your father."

"Yes. Did you think I wouldn't?"

"No," Carter said quietly. "I thought you would."

"And still you told me. *Why?*"

"I told you the reason."

Rica laughed bitterly. "Because you love me."

"Yes." When Rica looked away, Carter said, "It might not have been your father."

"Enzo would have killed you," Rica said.

"Not necessarily. I'm not certain Enzo has the clout to order a hit on his own. I doubt your father wants that kind of attention drawn to him or any of his people. Chances are Enzo just wanted to teach me a lesson. Or teach you one."

"Then he would have sent them after me."

"No. He'd never do anything so blatant. Your father would kill him and he knows it. He's probably regretting the marks he left on your face right about now, believe me." Just thinking about Enzo striking Rica made Carter's heart hammer with rage. Jesus, she still wanted to kill him. "You wouldn't tell your father about the sexual assaults—" At Rica's sound of protest, Carter said harshly, "That's what they *were*, Rica. He knew you wouldn't go to your father with that, but bruises can't be hidden."

"He's never hit me before. Now I understand why."

"How did you know to look for me?"

"A photograph." Rica closed her eyes. "Someone sent me a photograph of you lying…" *in your own blood.* "Unconscious."

"Let me see it."

Even though she never wanted to see it again, and would never need to, not with the image so clearly branded in her memory, Rica went downstairs to retrieve it. It still lay on the floor next to the envelope. For the first time, Rica realized there was a message scrawled on the envelope. The photograph had been so horrific it was the only thing she had been able to see.

"I think you might be right," Rica said, handing the envelope to Carter.

Carter read the message, *Next time, say yes.* Then held out her hand. "Where's the photo? Hand it to me by the edges."

Rica hesitated.

"I'm not going to put it on the record, Rica. Jesus. But it would be good if we know who Enzo's using to threaten you. I doubt there are any prints, but we can check."

"If this *was* Enzo's way of warning you away from me," Rica said, passing Carter the Polaroid, "or showing me what would happen if I refused him again, you could still be in danger from my father. He may want you…out of the way…for completely different reasons." She stared around the room as if expecting someone to burst through one of the doors at any second, then rose and walked to the dresser. She took out her Beretta and returned to the chair.

"I'm going to pretend I don't see that." Carter slid the photo into the envelope and set it on the bedside table. "Eject the clip and stash that somewhere."

"You don't give me orders, Carter."

"What are you going to do, Rica? Shoot someone?" Carter leaned her head back and closed her eyes. "Did you tell your father I was a cop?"

"No."

"Did you tell him my name?"

"No."

Carter opened her eyes. "What exactly *did* you tell him?"

"I tried to warn him that he'd been betrayed, but I got the feeling that he already knew."

Rizzo. He must know Rizzo is missing by now, so he figures he's turned. Carter said nothing, but she thought it possible that Pareto knew nothing of her involvement.

Rica didn't want to, but she asked a question she been thinking about for twenty-four hours. She didn't know why it mattered, but it did. "Is Carter Wayne really your name?"

"Carter's my first name, but Wayne is my grandmother's name. You won't find a cop officially listed by the name of Carter Wayne, if you or anyone else goes looking."

Rica didn't care what Carter's last name was. She was just absurdly glad that the name she had screamed in her mind...or was it out loud?... when this woman had been inside her was the truth. "And the part about being a lawyer?"

"True."

"The place in town?"

"I really own it."

Relieved, and irritated that any of it mattered, Rica snapped, "Would you mind very much covering up?"

"What?" Carter looked down and realized for the first time that she was bare to her hips. "Oh."

"Thank you," Rica said, relieved when Carter drew up the sheet, as if that would erase the image of Carter's body from her mind. Carter was beautiful. Firm upright breasts, defined arms and shoulders, and a long tapered waist beneath arching ribs that called out for a caress. She had felt that body through her clothes, sensed the power of it by watching her move, but she hadn't expected the graceful combination of femininity and strength. She wanted to touch her, and reminded herself of all the reasons why she couldn't.

"I'm in no shape to make a pass," Carter said gently.

"How much does it hurt?" Rica hated the purple discoloration that spread over Carter's ribs from just below her left breast to her navel. She hated the person who had put that mark there even more.

"I'll live."

"That's convenient, because I don't want your death on my conscience."

"Nothing is going to happen, but even if it did, you're not responsible."

"Perhaps you've forgotten what happened at my father's house with Enzo, and here when I *begged* you to fuck me," Rica said angrily. "But *I* haven't. I can't. If I'd known who you were I never would have let you touch me. I certainly wouldn't have let you touch Enzo. God, Carter, what were you thinking?"

"I was thinking that I didn't want his hands on you. Not then, not ever." Carter held Rica's gaze. "And I'm very very glad you let me touch you."

"Well, now it doesn't matter anymore."

"You're wrong, Rica," Carter said quietly. "It still matters to me."

Rica rose and slipped the small Beretta into the pocket of her tailored silk slacks. "As I predicted when we first met, what happened between us is of no consequence to me."

Chapter Twenty-Five

The sun was shining the next time Carter woke, and she had no idea what time it was. Or even what day it was. Her cell phone, wallet, and keys were on the bedside table along with a white envelope Rica had given her. Stretching carefully, wincing at the pain that burned down the center of her back and burrowed into her pelvis, she palmed the phone and eased back against the pillows. To her relief, it still held a charge, and she focused long enough to speed-dial.

"Kev? It's me."

"Jesus Christ and all that's holy. Where are you?"

"Still on the Cape. I had a bit of trouble."

Kevin sucked in air. "Define trouble."

"I'm still breathing. Just a little beat up."

"When?"

"What day is it?"

"Christ, Carter. It's Tuesday afternoon."

"Uh...about thirty-six hours ago, I guess."

"I'll come and get you."

"Yeah. I don't think I can drive just yet."

"Where exactly are you?"

"Rica's."

"Where's your head? She could be behind—"

"No. Look—"

"Forget about it. Give me the address."

"They could be watching the place."

"So they know you're there. If she moves you, they'll know that too. Stay put."

"Yeah. Okay."

Carter gave him directions, closed the cell phone, and then carefully swung her legs over the side of the bed. She closed her eyes against a wave of dizziness and fought to breathe slowly until it passed. Her clothes were folded in a pile on a nearby chair. It took her fifteen minutes to dress. It took her almost that long to get downstairs.

Rica met her at the bottom of the stairs. After a moment of silence, Rica brushed her fingertips over the stains on Carter's silk shirt. "I couldn't get all the blood out of your clothes. This is ruined, but I thought you'd prefer it clean."

"That's okay. Thanks." Carter steadied herself with a hand against the wall. Rica wore jeans and a white sleeveless tank top. She looked tired. "I'm going to get out of your hair in a couple of hours."

"How?"

"My...brother is picking me up."

"Your brother." Rica searched Carter's face. "Don't lie to me. There's no reason to any longer."

Carter cupped Rica's neck and skimmed her thumb along the edge of her jaw. She wasn't going to identify Kevin as a cop, on the chance someone was watching the house. "I wouldn't, if it were just me. If I could go back and do things differently—"

"Don't." Rica pressed her fingertips to Carter's lips. "You can't change who you are any more than I can. And I don't think you would have done anything differently."

"You're wrong." Slowly, Carter leaned forward, and when Rica did not move away, she gently kissed her mouth. She let her lips linger on Rica's, softly savoring the taste and the heat. She felt Rica's hands come to her waist, and Carter tangled her fingers in Rica's hair, carefully, tenderly, holding her close. Her body ached, her mind was a confused miasma of conflicting allegiances and desires, but this kiss... This was right. *They* were right. "God, Rica. Tell me you can feel it, too."

"No," Rica lied, even as her heart said yes. Enzo would kill Carter the next time. Regardless of whether her father sanctioned it or not, regardless of how long or how often Rica refused Enzo's demands, Enzo would kill Carter because he had seen what Rica had resisted for weeks. She loved Carter, and Enzo knew it. It didn't matter that Rica was not his to claim. He believed, had always believed, that eventually she would be his. He'd said he could tolerate her affairs with women, and maybe he meant it. But he would never accept her loving another woman when he knew that she would never love him. "It's just sex, Carter. Nothing more."

"You have to tell your father about Enzo," Carter murmured, stroking Rica's cheek. "He's crazy, Rica."

"My family matters aren't your concern." Laughing bitterly, Rica stepped back. "Of course, that's not true, is it? I should have said my *personal* business is not your concern."

"I'm not interested in your family business anymore."

"No? It's that simple?" Rica gestured with her head toward the living room. "Go sit down. You're not going to be able to stay upright much longer."

"I'm okay."

"Just do it. I don't have the patience for your stubbornness right now."

Carter grinned. "Okay."

Rica pressed her hand to Carter's back as they moved to the sofa, then sat beside her. "I don't want to know what you're going to tell your associates about me or my father. But I know you can't just walk away. And that's why I want you to walk out of here and out of my life."

Carter rarely believed what people said, because it was easy to tell lies and, after a while, even easier to believe them. For a minute, when they had kissed, she'd thought she'd felt the truth in Rica's touch. But whatever had been there then, it was gone now, and she owed it to her to go.

"I'll go, Rica. And I swear, I won't hurt you."

Rica shook her head and rose, her face a careful mask. As she left the room, she said steadily, "Don't make promises you can't keep. Just go."

Carter waited alone in silence until she heard a car pass by slowly on the street and then return a minute later. She went to the front window, looked out, and saw Kevin parked at the curb in his battered Jeep Wrangler. It was going to be a long, bumpy, painful ride home, but she didn't care. She didn't feel much of anything any longer except numb. She let herself out and quietly closed the door behind her. She didn't look back when Kevin pulled away.

"You look like shit," Kevin said.

"Yeah. Thanks. See anything in the neighborhood?" She checked the side mirror and didn't see a tail.

"There's no one watching the house unless they're sitting in a tree. Been to a doctor?"

"Yeah. Just bumps and bruises." Carter pointed. "Slow down up there and pull into that alley behind my car. I think they got my weapon, but we should check again."

Kevin parked and got out. "Stay put. I'll look."

A minute later, he slid back in, started the car, and backed out onto Bradford. "Nothing except some old blood on the stairs. I guess that's yours."

"Uh-huh."

"Fuck, Carter. You're lucky they didn't kill you. Do you think Pareto is on to you because we pulled Rizzo in? If Allen almost got you killed, I'm gonna—"

"No. I don't think it was Pareto. It was Enzo Brassi, and it's personal. He's got a thing for Rica, and he's nuts."

"Great. And you're fucking her."

"Easy, Kevin," Carter said softly.

He glanced over. "Oh, perfect. She's really got you messed up."

"No, she doesn't." Carter turned to watch the town disappear, feeling the hollow ache inside her expand until she was nearly choking on the emptiness. "I'm the one who messed it up."

"You're not going to be able to dodge Allen much longer, partner."

Carter sighed. "I know." She eased her seat back and tried to get comfortable. "Jesus, can't you get a car made for adults?"

"I didn't plan on needing an ambulance," Kevin snapped. He rubbed his face. "Sorry. I'm used to you disappearing, but it's the first time you've ever showed up looking like…you might not have showed up."

"They knew what they were doing." She reached across the narrow space between them and squeezed his forearm. "They didn't intend to kill me."

"Nice. Glad to hear that." The muscles along the edge of his jaw bunched. "What did they want, do you think?"

"It was a message to Rica. Don't cross Enzo, especially for a woman."

"Sorry."

"Yeah. Me too."

❖

"Do you think she'll come home in an ambulance?" Bri asked Tory as she hopped up onto the deck. She glanced at her watch. "When do you think she'll get here?"

"I don't know, sweetie. The transport left Germany early this morning, our time. I'm not sure how long it takes for that kind of flight." Tory had to force herself not to pace. The hours crawled by. She'd gone to the clinic in the morning, knowing that Reese couldn't possibly arrive before nightfall. Even then, she was always aware in the back of her mind that Reese was on her way home. Home for good, if she had anything to say about it.

"I know she's probably not gonna want to see anybody for a while," Bri said, echoing her father's gentle warning, "but do you think maybe you could call and let us know she's home?"

Smiling, Tory gave Bri a quick hug. "I know that Reese will call you first thing. She's going to want a report on everything that's happened while she's been gone."

"I should still plan on running class at the dojo for a while, right?"

Tory nodded. She hadn't mentioned to anyone what Reese's father had said about her injuries. Reese would share what she wanted to. "She's probably pretty tired, honey. I think it's a good idea for you to take care of everything there for a while."

"No problem." Bri colored slightly. "I like teaching class."

"I can tell." Tory squeezed her hand. "You're very good at it too. I enjoy your classes."

"Thanks." Bri stuffed her hands into the pockets of her uniform pants. "Well, I should go, so you can...you know, be alone with Reese."

"Come on. I'll walk you down to your cruiser."

Tory watched Bri back out and stood in the driveway watching until the car disappeared. It was eight p.m., and she didn't think she could stand another night alone. She returned to the deck and stretched out in one of the lounge chairs, watching the sky grow dark, and waiting.

The crunch of tires brought her bolting awake. She jumped up and nearly fell. She didn't wear her ankle brace around the house anymore, but her damaged lower leg wasn't strong enough to tolerate even a normal level of sudden stress. She hissed in a breath and waited a second for the sharp stab of pain to relent, while her heart pounded wildly. Headlights flashed through the trees and shrubs between their rear deck and the driveway, but she couldn't make out the details of the vehicle. It might be Kate. It could be Bri, too impatient to wait for a phone call. It might be Nelson. Moving quickly but more cautiously, she hastened down the steps. The security lights over the garage came on, illuminating the scene like a movie set.

A big black car with a small American flag waving on the front fender idled in the drive. She caught a flash of an insignia on the shiny black surface before the rear door opened and obscured it. A man exited the front passenger side and walked around the front of the car toward her, but she didn't even look at him. It could have been the president of the United States and she would not have cared. She didn't wait, couldn't wait, and hurried toward the open rear door. Then, she halted abruptly as Reese slowly climbed out.

"Hi, baby," Reese said softly.

She was in uniform, the desert camos that she'd worn in the picture on Tory's desk. That was the only similarity between how she looked in that photograph and now. Tory had never seen her so thin. The harsh light from the security lights accentuated the hollow shadows beneath her eyes. A row of black sutures ran across her forehead. Tory knew without asking that the wound was caused by a blow from a rifle butt, and she felt fury like she'd never known. When Reese had been captured, Tory thought she had understood the white-hot rage to kill, but now she knew with absolute certainty that she could kill with a cold clear mind. Somewhere in the depths of her consciousness, she knew she would be frightened by that knowledge later, but not now. Now her wrath only made her tender. She took a slow step, then another, and another until she gently framed Reese's face and brushed the lightest of kisses over her mouth.

"Welcome home, darling."

Reese curved an arm around Tory's shoulders and held her against her chest, brushing her cheek against Tory's hair. "I missed you so much."

Tory curled her arms around Reese's waist, every motion careful, because she knew she was hurt, but she didn't know where or how badly. Reese's heart beat against her breast, something she had missed every day that Reese had been gone. She had managed without her, would have managed for herself and for Reggie for as long as it took, forever if necessary. But without the beat of Reese's heart steadying her world, she would have bled for eternity missing her. "I'm so glad you're home. I love you."

"I love you," Reese whispered. She tilted Tory's chin up with her left hand and kissed her again. "Is the baby here?"

"Asleep. But you can wake her."

Reese smiled. "I can wait awhile." With her arm still around Tory's shoulders, Reese turned slightly away to face the man who stood nearby. "I understand you've met my partner."

Roger Conlon nodded. "Dr. King."

"General. Thank you for bringing her home."

"She earned it, Doctor." He started back around the car. "Good night, Colonel. Dr. King."

"Sir," Reese called. "Would you like to come inside?"

The general hesitated. "Not tonight, Colonel. I need to get back to Washington. There's a war on."

"Some other time, then," Reese said. She released Tory and saluted with her left hand. "Good night, sir."

He returned the salute as he slid into the car. Reese and Tory stepped back a few feet while the car backed out, turned onto Route 6, and disappeared.

"Let's get *you* inside," Tory said gently. Reese was trembling, and Tory knew that only part of it was the emotion of homecoming. Reese was physically weak, something that Tory found incredibly frightening. "Come inside and hold me."

"Oh yeah. That sounds good." Reese rested her forehead against Tory's and closed her eyes. "So damn good."

Chapter Twenty-Six

Rica poured the last of her wine, set the empty bottle beside her, and sipped without tasting. After preparing a meal that she hadn't eaten, she'd settled into a lounge chair on the first-floor deck—the one that faced Herring Cove and the beach trail along which she had watched Carter run weeks before. The sunset blazed above the water, a glorious canvas she didn't see. Now it was dark. The sky was a riot of stars, the air tart enough to sting. Perhaps it was the wine, but she didn't feel cold. Carter had been gone twelve hours. In those twelve hours, Rica had gone to work and accomplished nothing. She'd come home and tried to go about the daily routine that usually satisfied her. Simply doing things when she wanted, how she wanted, always gave her a comforting sense of control. It also allowed her to live a lie of her own choosing.

Perhaps coming to Provincetown, opening the gallery, had been the ultimate lie. Self-delusion at its finest—pretending that forsaking her father's name would somehow make her less a part of who he was, what he was. But she was still her father's daughter, whether she gave the orders or not. Whether she acknowledged what went on around her or not. And when the ultimate test had come, she had chosen family over everything, including love.

Carter had been gone twelve hours, and in that time, Rica had tried very hard to convince herself it was for the best. There was no future for them. How could there be? Carter was sworn to destroy the very foundation of Rica's life. And if she didn't, that life would destroy her.

Rica sipped her wine, wondering whether the lies Carter had told her were any worse than the ones she told herself.

❖

Her arm still around Tory's shoulders, Reese stopped just inside the door and looked around the living room. The doors to the deck were open, just screens holding out the night. A single light burned under a counter in the kitchen, but she didn't need light to see every inch of the space. She'd seen it over and over again in her mind, every day that she'd been away—she remembered coming home from work just a few days before Reggie had been born and finding Tory stretched out on the couch, complaining of feeling like a whale and looking so beautiful that Reese had wanted to get down on her knees, press her face to the swell of Tory's belly, and weep for the miracle within. Sitting in a rocker with Reggie in her arms, watching her suck on a bottle, her blue eyes wide with wonder and promise. The sun slanting in at dawn to illuminate Tory's face while she slept, an image Reese carried in her heart like a treasured photo. This house sheltered her family, and her family was her heart.

"Good to be home," Reese said, her voice still hoarse from the searing heat of the desert and the days without water and the tubes they had put down her throat when they'd cleaned her wounds.

"Yes." Tory waited, listening in the silence for the things she knew Reese wouldn't say.

"Did the baby walk yet?"

"No," Tory said gently. "She's pulling herself up and she's teetering for a few seconds, but no forward motion." She hugged Reese carefully. "She's waiting for you."

Reese pressed her face to Tory's hair. "Let's go to bed."

"That would be perfect."

Upstairs, they paused in the doorway to Reggie's room. Reese stood at the threshold, listening the way she had listened in the desert for the sound of metal on metal, for the approaching thunder of explosive rounds, for the whir and thump of rotor blades, and finally, for rescue. She listened with all her mind and body to the steady, soft breathing of her daughter as she slept, safe and secure and innocent.

"She's a wonder, isn't she," Reese murmured.

"Yes, she is."

Inside the bedroom, they stopped by the bed. Earlier in the evening,

Tory had turned the sheets down, leaving it open and welcoming, and had switched on a lamp on the dresser. She pressed her palms to Reese's chest. The stiff, starched material was rough against her skin. The muscles beneath were hard. The heart beneath was wounded. "Can I help you undress?"

"Yes." Reese cupped Tory's face. "Please."

A slanted swatch of material above the right breast pocket said *Conlon* in large block letters. A similar patch above the left breast said *U.S. Marine.* As if those few words defined her completely. At one time they had. Tory opened the first button, then the next, and the next.

"How high can you lift your right arm?" Tory asked.

"About shoulder level, if I go slow."

"Then don't try. We'll get the left out, and I'll slide it off." Tory moved around Reese, first to the left, then behind, then to the right, carefully removing her shirt. Underneath she found an Ace wrap holding bandages in place over Reese's right shoulder and upper chest. Tory's stomach clenched, but her voice was steady. "Burns?"

"Some." Reese flashed on the blazing Humvee, of running across open ground that seemed endless while bullets snapped around her, of grabbing the unconscious driver and jerking him out of the mangled wreck. Of lying on top of him while the sky ignited into a scorching inferno. She shivered.

"Am I hurting you?"

"No." Reese touched Tory's hair. It was soft, silky, smoother than anything she could remember touching for weeks. "There was a firefight. It split us up. A ground-to-surface missile took out one of the Humvees. It burned."

Tory sat down on the edge of the bed, her legs weak, and quickly covered her reaction by reaching for the button on Reese's waistband. "That sounds terrifying."

Reese looked down, watching Tory open the buttons on her pants. Tory had beautiful hands. Her fingers were narrow and long. She had calluses on her palms from the kayak paddle. Her hands were steady. "Only for a second. Then you're just too damn busy to think about it."

"That's good, then." Tory curled her fingers around the thick canvas and rocked the pants down Reese's hips and let them fall around her ankles. "Sit down, darling. What about your collarbone?"

The air was alive with shouts and screams and the roar of automatic rifle fire. Flames writhed into the night sky, giant tongues of fury. "I fell. Tripped carrying the driver over my shoulder. I took the fall on my right. Hit a rock."

"Lift your foot so I can get your boot." Tory wanted to ask about the driver. Was he—she?—alive? But she was afraid to take Reese somewhere she wasn't ready to go. Reese was one of the strongest women she'd ever known. Reese would tell her what she could, when she could, and whenever that might be, Tory would listen, no matter how much it made her want to scream and rage. The desert combat boots were dark brown leather—rough rather than shiny—as if the boots had been turned inside out so they wouldn't reflect beneath the brilliant desert sun. She unlaced first one, then the other, and pulled them off and placed them side by side beneath the bed. "There's a bandage on your leg."

Every breath was like swallowing fire. She managed to get to her feet, despite the stabbing pain in her chest and the scorching agony of the burns. She couldn't lift the driver but suddenly another Marine materialized beside them and, between the two of them, they dragged the limp body toward the shelter of darkness. She stumbled when her leg buckled.

"It's nothing much." Reese regarded the wound on her thigh. "Bit of shrapnel caught me in the leg."

"Did they get it out?"

The Marine who had come to her aid swore as the projectile lodged in his calf, but he kept running. They both kept running, half carrying their comrade. "Passed through."

"Lie back, and I'll get your briefs off." She searched Reese's face. She hadn't stopped thinking about what some nameless, faceless monsters might have done to Reese in those hours when Reese had been helpless. As a physician, she had been trained to push doubts and uncertainty aside in order to function, but this time she had not been able to completely block the terrible fear. "Okay?"

There was nowhere to go, no way to reach sanctuary. It had only been a matter of a few minutes before the five of them had been surrounded by three times as many men with more firepower than they could repel. Reese softly kissed Tory. "They threw us in the back of a truck at first, then locked us up in some kind of shack. They didn't give us food or water and were quick to use a rifle butt. Just the same, they didn't even want to touch me or the other female Marine. We weren't clean."

"I hate them," Tory whispered.

"I'm sorry for scaring you."

Tory stood and rested her hands ever so lightly on Reese's shoulders. "Lie down. Don't apologize. You didn't do anything except what you had to do." She eased the cotton briefs over hipbones that were far too prominent, taking care not to snag the material on the clear plastic that covered the sutures on Reese's thigh. Another scar. Another battle. Too many. Too many.

"Baby," Reese said quietly, catching Tory's hand and urging Tory down beside her. "I'll heal."

Tory dropped the last piece of the uniform on the floor and lay down to claim the Marine as her own again. She curled on her side against Reese's left shoulder and drew the sheet up over them both. It felt awkward, because she always slept on Reese's right side. But that was where Reese was hurt. She knew Reese's body would heal because Reese was strong and fit, and the wounds, her physician's mind said, were painful but not dangerous. She worried, agonized over, the wounds she couldn't see and would never see. And wondered how they would heal and what scars they would leave. "I love you."

The sheets were so soft. Tory's body was so warm. Reese caressed Tory's shoulders and arm, then held her close. "I love you."

Tory curled her arm around Reese's middle. Her ribs arched starkly beneath her skin and her stomach hollowed down to the curve of her pelvis as if someone had carved parts of her away. "It's good to have you home."

She'd been disoriented from the blow from the rifle butt, and it had been hard to keep track of time. They were all frightened. But they were together, and when the guards were far enough away not to hear, they whispered encouragement to one another. Reese reminded them that they were alive, and they were Marines. Their fellow Marines would not abandon them. And in her private moments, she reminded herself that Tory was waiting. That Reggie had a lifetime of discovery ahead of her. And that she needed to go home, because she had promised she would.

"It's good to be here. Better than anything else in the world."

❖

Carter rolled over in the grip of an uneasy sleep, and the pain in her back jolted her awake. "God damn it."

After Kevin had dropped her off at her apartment in Cambridge, she'd swallowed three pain pills and crawled into bed. She squinted at the clock. Seven hours ago. Now it was the middle of the night and she wasn't exactly awake, but was too sore to find a comfortable position and slide back into sleep. She could swallow another handful of pain pills and that might do the job, but she knew without checking that the blinking red light on her phone was a message, probably *many* messages, from Special Agent Allen. And she was going to have to face the Special Agent in Charge in the morning, and she'd need a clear head if she was going to save any piece of her ass or some part of her career.

When she'd first stumbled into the apartment and seen the blinking light, she'd had the crazy idea it was Rica. The way her heart had swelled so big, so fast, it actually hurt inside her chest. Hurt in a good way. And then just as quickly the pain settled in the pit of her stomach, because she'd realized that Rica did not know her home number. And even if she had, she would not be calling.

Carter curled on her side and closed her eyes, even knowing that sleep wouldn't come. It was starting to be easier to ignore the pain in her body than the one that ached ceaselessly in her soul.

CHAPTER TWENTY-SEVEN

Tory sat at the breakfast counter sipping coffee, as she did every morning. This morning, even the mundane felt extraordinary. She'd never tasted a better cup of coffee. The air was fresher, sweeter, than she could ever remember. Excitement hummed through her body. It took feeling truly alive to make her realize that she hadn't been. The thought was both exhilarating and terrifying.

At exactly 7:30 a.m., she heard a car pull into the driveway. She smiled to herself, having expected it an hour earlier. Wondering how painful that hour of waiting had been, she went to the door and greeted her visitor. "Hi, sweetie."

Bri quickly doffed her cap and turned it restlessly between her fingers. "I...uh...so, is she here?"

Tory held the door open and gestured Bri inside. "She's sleeping."

"Oh. Okay." Bri bent down and picked up Reggie, who had crawled over to them. She bounced the baby once or twice and settled her against her hip. "So. How is...everything?"

"She's doing fine," Tory said. "Come on in and have coffee. She'll be up soon."

"Nah. I should probably get back out—"

"Hey," Reese said as she slowly came down the stairs. Her thick black hair, shorter than she usually wore it, was slicked back and still damp from the shower. Her jeans and a short-sleeved pullover were loose. She grinned at Bri with sharp, clear blue eyes. "How you doing?"

Bri grinned back, rocking ever so slightly on her heels as if trying not to run forward. "Not bad."

Reese's attention fixed on Reggie. "Hey, sweetheart."

Reggie started squirming and Tory quickly plucked her from Bri's arms. "Let me take her." Then she carried her to Reese. "I don't know if you should hold her just yet."

"It'll be okay," Reese said hoarsely. When Tory passed the baby to her, she held her against her left side and nuzzled her neck. Reggie giggled and Reese closed her eyes, shivering lightly.

After a minute, Tory gently took her back. "She's too heavy for you to hold with your collarbone the way it is, darling."

Wordlessly, Reese let her go. Then she glanced over at Bri, who looked embarrassed and uncertain. "Come on in."

"Maybe I should come back."

"No." Reese edged a hip onto a stool on the living room side of the counter that separated the kitchen from the living area. "Have a seat. Tell me what's been going on."

When Bri cast a quick, doubtful look in Tory's direction, Tory nodded encouragingly. Then Bri rushed the final few feet, skidding to a halt beside Reese, looking as if she wanted to hug her. Reese tossed her left arm around Bri's shoulders and pulled her in for an embrace. She held her without saying anything for a long moment while Bri gently threaded her arms around Reese's waist.

"Missed you," Reese said.

"Oh yeah. Man, me too."

Bri's voice wavered and Reese clapped her on the back before loosening her hold. "So. Bring me up to date."

Tory slid a cup of coffee across the counter to Bri, who picked it up automatically as she launched into an excited recounting of everything that had happened in the sheriff's department since the day Reese left. While they talked, Tory grabbed the portable phone and carried Reggie out onto the deck. She checked that the gate was closed, went back inside to quickly retrieve her coffee, and once outside again, speed-dialed.

"She's up," Tory said when Kate answered the phone. She leaned against the railing and looked back into the house, watching Bri and Reese together. It was a sight she'd seen a thousand times, but it took losing that little piece of family to make her realize how much she needed it. They looked so much alike, even more so now that Reese was thinner. But there was no mistaking the stark contrast between Bri's youthful buoyancy and Reese's fatigue. It saddened her, to know that Reese had once been like Bri, fresh and eager and optimistic. She'd lived long enough and lost enough to know that there was no going back, but in loving Reese she'd found more than she'd ever lost. Now what she wanted most of all was to give Reese a place to recover her faith in the things that made her who she was. Honor, duty, principle.

"What, Kate? I'm sorry. I...I can't quite believe she's home."

"How does she seem?"

"She's worn out. Quiet." Tory had lain awake for a long time, listening to Reese's breathing and trying to determine if she was sleeping. Usually she could tell, but something had changed in the cadence of Reese's breathing while she'd been gone. It was as if even while asleep every now and then she would stop and listen. Tory wondered what she was listening for and was afraid she knew. There was no respite from danger, when death came in the silent seconds between heartbeats. And as much as Tory wished that she could, she knew she could not protect Reese from the threats that haunted her sleep.

"Is she badly hurt?"

Tory could tell from the tight, flat sound of Kate's voice just how difficult it had been for her to ask that question. "She's mostly banged up. I don't know what's worse, a nice clean bullet wound or all these damn minor injuries."

Kate laughed shakily. "You're starting to sound like a Marine's wife."

"Don't even think it." Tory bent down and removed a leaf from Reggie's mouth. "Don't eat that, sweetie."

"Do you need me to come and get her?"

"I'll call you later. I need to go into the clinic, but I don't want to leave Reese just yet."

"I know. Jean and I both want to see her, of course, but I think she needs you for a while first."

Tory watched through the wide glass doors as Bri put her hat on, obviously getting ready to leave. Reese squeezed her arm and said something that made Bri nod seriously. Some order of business, Tory surmised. "I need her for a while, too."

"When you think of it, tell her we'll be by later."

"Thanks, Kate. For understanding."

"She's home. That's enough for us right now."

"Yes." Tory smiled as Reese swiveled on the stool and met her eyes. The heat that flooded through her came as a surprise. She hadn't realized just how cold she'd been. "We'll see you later."

When Kate rang off, Tory collected Reggie and went back inside. "Hungry?"

"Some."

"How about I fix you something to eat, then we all go back to bed."

Smiling, Reese nodded. "Let me go lock the doors."

"You ready?" Kevin said, eyeing Carter speculatively. "You still look like shit."

"Thank you. That makes me feel so much better." Carter knew just exactly how bad she looked. The stitches Dr. King had put in didn't show much in her hair, but the bruise had seeped down along her jawline, discoloring the right side of her neck. The purple hues matched the circles under her eyes.

"Don't smart-mouth Allen," Kevin warned. "She's royally pissed at you."

Carter sighed, thinking not for the first time that she didn't really care what bug Special Agent Allen had up her ass that morning. She had more important things on her mind. Like whether Enzo had contacted Rica. Or if Rica was still in Provincetown. Or if Rica thought of her at all. "I know how to handle suits like her."

"Yeah. That's obvious. You've been doing such a good job so far."

"Listen, Kev," Carter said seriously. "No matter how this goes, don't put your ass on the line for me. Not this time. Because..." She shrugged. "It's just not that important."

Kevin studied her. "You mean that, don't you."

"Yeah. I do."

"Okay. So let's go see what the feds want from us."

Allen was alone. Carter had expected either her immediate superior or a representative from internal affairs to be there, too. Instead, Allen stood by the window in the small, featureless room, her back partially turned to the door. As usual, she wore a dark navy pantsuit and a cream-colored silk blouse. Her blond hair was stylishly but simply cut. Her shoes were expensive but functional. She was pretty, but she worked hard to make sure it didn't show. Carter looked at Kevin, who shrugged.

"Have a seat, Detective." Special Agent Allen glanced once at Carter and ignored Kevin. As Carter pulled out a straight-backed chair in front of the rectangular metal table, Allen added smoothly, "Your presence is not required, Detective Shaughnessy."

"Now wait a minute," Kevin protested.

"That's okay, Kevin." Carter settled into the uncomfortable chair, smothering a wince as a tender spot on her hip connected with the unpadded seat. "Go get coffee or something. I'll call you when we're done."

Kevin hesitated in the doorway, looking back and forth between the two women, his jaws working as if he were chewing glass. Then he muttered something that was just garbled enough to be unintelligible, which was probably wise, because Allen was regarding him as if he were an alien specimen in a zoo.

"Okay. Sure."

When they were alone, Allen pulled out a chair opposite Carter and sat down. "I've been trying to reach you for over three days."

"I was indisposed."

"Yes. I can see that." Allen slid a file folder in front of her, opened it, and extracted a single sheet of paper. "This is your last report. It was filed almost two months ago."

"I'm not much for forms."

Allen closed the folder and pushed it away. Then she leaned forward and laced her fingers together on the table top. "Rizzo is getting forgetful. Ever since we picked him up on Sunday he's become more and more vague about all kinds of information he was very certain about before. He's not our only informant, but a large part of the case we're building against Alfonse Pareto hinges on his testimony."

"He's probably scared shitless," Carter said. "He's been part of that organization for forty years. He knows what happens when someone talks. It's one thing to have secret meetings with you in a car under a bridge somewhere, feeding you little tidbits to keep himself out of jail and you satisfied. But climbing up into the witness box and ratting out one of the three most powerful organized crime heads east of the Mississippi? Come on."

"You're right. Men like him are often unreliable." Allen shrugged. "Which is why your report is even more critical."

"I don't have a whole hell of a lot to report just now, Special Agent."

"You've had several months to get a handle on Ricarda Pareto's place in all of this. If you can turn her, then—"

"Rica?" Carter laughed. "*If* she were involved, which I've told you she isn't, there's no way she would betray her father."

Allen sat back and said conversationally, "Not even for you? Not even for the woman she's sleeping with?"

"We're not sleeping together. And if we were, it wouldn't matter. Rica isn't part of it."

"We have evidence to suggest otherwise."

Carter shook her head. "What you have is rumor and wishful thinking."

"Pareto is using the daughter's gallery in SoHo as a front for money laundering. It's relatively small scale for him, but significant enough for us to bring her in. They may be moving drugs through there as well."

"Not Rica." Carter's hands fisted beneath the table, but she forced herself to sit calmly. "Whatever you've got, Rica isn't the one behind it."

"It's her gallery. That puts her name on the warrant."

Cold sweat broke out between Carter's shoulder blades as sick worry churned in her stomach. If Rica were arrested, the press would have a field day. Her picture would be in every tabloid in the country. She'd never have a moment's peace or privacy again. "You should be looking at Enzo. You said you had him in the surveillance photos going in there, sometimes when Rica wasn't even there. It's probably his sideline. Damn it, Allen, you know it isn't her."

"Then get her to give up some information. I want her father's connection at the port. We're not just talking drugs. We're talking automobiles, electronics—maybe even girls."

"If someone's moving human traffic, it's not Pareto. Maybe one of his lieutenants has gone independent. Pareto's old-school. You know that." Carter stood, too agitated to sit. She paced in the small room, thought of her barren apartment, and yearned for the feel of salt air on her skin and the beach at dawn. "You can't get to Pareto through Rica, because I don't think she knows anything. And even if she did, she'll never turn."

"A woman will do a lot of things for love. Or what she thinks is love."

At the unexpected sound of pain in Allen's voice, Carter halted abruptly. She caught a glimpse of sadness and regret in Allen's face before her features reformed into her normal professional facade. Briefly, she wondered if Allen had been the one to compromise herself for love, or if the nameless woman had betrayed her. Because it was clear there had been a woman. But knowing that, even feeling sympathy, did not make them allies. Allen was threatening the woman Carter loved. "If you name Rica in this, I'll go on record against it. She's innocent."

"Your convictions aren't going to mean very much. Especially since you nearly blew months of work by attacking Lorenzo Brassi."

"I didn't attack him. I pulled him off a woman he was trying to rape."

"You don't know his advances were unwelcome. We have photographic evidence—"

"Fuck your evidence. Rica was a victim."

"Your judgment leaves something to be desired."

Carter laughed. "Why don't you just admit that you were wrong about her. Whatever information you had, whatever you *think* you saw in those surveillance photos, Rica is not involved with Enzo Brassi. She's not part of her father's organization. She's not responsible for her father's actions."

"Well," Allen said, shrugging as she stood. "I guess we'll find out just how much she knows when we bring her in."

"If you can even get a warrant with what little you've got, all you're going to do is tip your hand to Pareto. He'll know what you know, and then he'll just cover his tracks. You're jumping the gun."

"If we can't get anything from the daughter, we'll at least be a step closer to Brassi, and Brassi sits at Pareto's right hand. One way or the other, we'll be closer than we are now."

Carter knew she wasn't going to be able to reason with Allen, because for whatever reason, Allen was fixated on Rica. Maybe she wanted Rica to be guilty. Maybe on some level she *needed* Rica to be guilty. Just because Allen was supposedly one of the good guys didn't mean her motives were pure, or rational. Carter didn't really care. All she cared about was getting Rica out of Allen's line of fire. She wasn't certain quite how she was going to do that, but she knew she had to. An arrest would ruin Rica's life.

"If there's something going on at the gallery in New York City, Rica is obviously not involved. She hasn't been there for weeks."

"She was there about a month ago." Allen walked to the door, then paused as if in afterthought. "By the way. Unless you bring me something on Rica, you may find yourself on the bad end of an obstruction of justice charge."

Carter watched the door swing closed behind Allen. She might have no official role in Rica's life any longer, but nothing that had happened between the two of them had been about the case. Nothing that mattered. And now, Carter realized, keeping Rica from being destroyed because of her family ties was the only thing she cared about.

CHAPTER TWENTY-EIGHT

S o?" Kevin pounced the minute he saw Carter exit the station's rear door to the parking lot. "What's the word?"

"How'd you know I'd come out here?" Carter asked, stalling.

He snorted. "Come on, you and I have been ducking out on meetings this way for the last four years. What did she say? You were in there long enough."

Carter squinted in the bright noon sun. Her head ached. Her heart ached. "Let's go for a beer."

Kevin stopped and stared, his big open face revealing surprise and concern. "Kinda early."

"It's either that or a pain pill," Carter said as she wove her way through the departmental and private vehicles baking on the tarmac. "What would you choose?"

"Good point. The Shamrock?"

Carter nodded, thinking that the dark, dingy hole-in-the-wall bar suited her mood perfectly. Plus, it was a cop bar, but not the kind where whole squads got together to celebrate. It was a place for solitary drinking when the waste and insanity that was a cop's daily fare got to be too much. No one would bother them, or even notice them. Cops went to the Shamrock to try to forget, not for company.

The couple of men who sat at the bar didn't look up as they walked in. A woman, blond, thirty, looking as if she hadn't slept in a week, was slumped over a glass she cradled in both hands in a booth against the wall. She glanced once in their direction and quickly looked away. She was still new enough to be embarrassed at not being able to handle another dead child, another senseless vehicular fatality, another rape. Carter tried to remember how old *she'd* been when she'd passed from caring to numbness. It'd been a while ago. Before this case. Long before Rica.

"Two beers," Carter said to the bartender. She handed a longneck to Kevin, and they ambled into the darker recesses at the rear. She slid across the cracked red vinyl seat to the far corner of a booth, turned sideways to rest her sore back against the wall, and stretched her legs out into the aisle. Kevin pulled at his beer, sitting across from her and waiting.

"Allen wants to get a warrant on Rica for whatever's going down at the gallery," Carter said at last.

"Huh. I don't think we've got enough hard evidence on that to go after anyone, not yet. I agree there's *something* there—probably a little bit of cash cleaning. Small-time, though. I'm surprised Pareto would risk his daughter for something like that."

Carter drained half the bottle in several deep swallows. "It's not Pareto. It's Brassi."

"Yeah, that would make more sense—Brassi setting up a little sideline and using Rica as a front. You think she knows?"

Carter shook her head. "Pareto doesn't give those orders himself. Brassi is his messenger, so Rica would think that anything Brassi told her to do was coming from her father."

"Well, if Pareto doesn't know about it, Brassi's risking his neck. All the daughter has to do is tell Daddy that this guy is fooling around with her business, putting her at risk. Do you think Brassi's really that crazy?"

"Oh yeah. He thinks he's got Rica in his pocket because he's important to her father. And some other reasons. It goes back a ways."

"All this family shit makes me nuts," Kevin muttered. "Loyalty only goes so far, you know?"

Carter regarded Kevin silently for a long moment. "You agree with me, then? That Rica's not part of this?"

Kevin shrugged. "You're good police. Good instincts. Even if you are thinking with your…whatever, right now."

"My whatever," Carter said, grinning sadly, "doesn't come into this. Rica doesn't want anything to do with me."

"If your dick's anything like my dick, that doesn't matter."

Kevin didn't always wear his wedding ring when he was working undercover. None of the undercover detectives did. But Carter had never known him to fool around on his wife of a dozen years. They had three kids. She tried to imagine what it would be like to go home after a day or week or a month of being someone else, of living another life, and then putting all that aside for the semblance of normality. She'd never needed to. She didn't have another life besides the one she assumed until the next assignment. "So you think Allen's off base with this plan of hers?"

"Yeah, I do," Kevin said slowly. "She's jumping the gun—and might blow any chance of getting at Pareto by going for the small fish first. Even if she got something to stick on Brassi, he'd never turn. Just doesn't make good tactical sense."

"Yeah, I think Brassi's a dead end as far as getting to Pareto. Glad you agree."

Kevin frowned. "Why is it so important what I think?"

"Because you're my partner and someone needs to keep an eye on Allen," Carter said quietly. "And because I turned in my shield today."

Kevin banged his beer bottle down with a thump. "Jesus Christ, Carter, what the fuck's wrong with you?"

"Nothing." She grinned just a little unsteadily. "Well, if you don't count the bumps and bruises."

"Don't try to laugh this off. We're talking about your goddamn career here."

"No we're not. We're talking about Allen's personal agenda and the fact that we both know it's wrong."

"Okay. Fine. We'll go over her head. Together." He started to slide out of the booth. "Come on. Right now."

"If I could move fast enough I'd haul you back down, but I can't. So just sit. Please."

"Fuck," he muttered, but he settled back into the seat.

"It's more than Allen. It's me, too, Kev. Things used to be really clear to me. Black and white. Right and wrong." She drained her beer and set the bottle gently on the tabletop. "Now it's not."

"That's because of Rica. You're all twisted up about her, but it doesn't make what her father does right."

"No, it doesn't. But it doesn't make her wrong."

Kevin rubbed his face furiously, then sighed loudly. "What are you going to do?"

"You don't have to worry about it."

"Like hell. I don't want to end up coming after you one of these days."

Carter smiled, and hoped this once, she was telling the truth. "I'll make sure you never need to."

Reese marveled, not for the first time, at how memory blunts the fine details of beauty. She knew every inch of Tory's face as her own, but the images she'd replayed in her mind dozens of times while she'd been in Iraq were nowhere near as breathtaking as the reality. The midday sun slanted through the window and haloed Tory's face as she slept. Her hair held a little more gray, her skin carried a few more lines around her eyes and mouth than when they'd first met, but she was only more lovely with the passage of time. Reese traced a fingertip along the edge of her jaw and smiled when Tory murmured with pleasure.

"You're supposed to be sleeping," Tory whispered, her eyes still closed.

"I was."

Tory opened her eyes and regarded Reese with professional focus. "How do you feel?"

"Lazy."

"Silly me," Tory said, laughing softly. "Here I thought you'd be home for at least a couple of days before you started chafing about the inactivity." She ran her fingers gently over Reese's collarbone. "What about this?"

"If I lie on my left side like now, it doesn't really hurt. I can even move my right arm pretty comfortably."

"You're still not going to be able to carry the baby for a while." At Reese's sound of protest, Tory hastened to add, "Back and forth to the crib like this morning is fine. But getting her in and out of her car seat is going to take two strong arms. Believe me, she's still nonstop wiggle."

Reese grinned. "I noticed." She smoothed her hand over Tory's bare shoulder and down her arm to clasp her fingers. "My unit was scheduled for recall to the States in a few weeks. Because of my injuries, I most likely won't be going back."

"Thank God." Tory shuddered. "I didn't even consider that might happen."

"I wouldn't be here at home recovering if my father hadn't arranged it. I might even still be in Germany. But I can't do much until my collarbone heals, anyhow."

"I'm really grateful to him for getting you home, and for keeping the press away from us."

"The military isn't all that anxious to tell the public all the little details of what's happening over there. They rescued us so fast, I'm not even sure the embedded reporters with our unit knew what was happening."

"Still," Tory brushed a kiss over Reese's mouth, "I was very glad to have him for my father-in-law this past week."

"I'm sorry it's been so difficult. He can be—"

"No, I mean it. He was very helpful, and I'm sure it was hard for him."

"It's going to get harder," Reese said quietly. "I plan to resign, and I'm going to ask him to move the paperwork through."

Tory closed her eyes, took several long breaths, and then met Reese's gaze. "Are you sure?"

Reese smiled. "I was thinking about it all the way back in the plane. I realized as I was coming home that I've been moving toward that decision for a long time. Even before I met you, leaving active service to come here was the first step in letting go of that part of my life."

"Reggie and I will be very grateful if you do. It was so hard with you away."

Reese stroked Tory's chest and cupped her breast. Most of the fullness from pregnancy had subsided, and she caressed the warm, pliant flesh gently. Tory's nipple tightened and Reese felt an answering tension in the pit of her stomach. "I know. For me too. A lot of the time I just felt…empty."

"You're home now. It will be all right." Tory covered Reese's hand with her own and pressed Reese's fingers firmly into her flesh, stilling the gentle strokes. "I don't think you want to do that. Not until you're bet—"

"You don't have any broken bones, do you?" Reese murmured, working her thumb across Tory's nipple.

"No, but you do."

"I'm not going to move much of anything." Reese slid her hand from beneath Tory's, clasped Tory's neck, and drew her close. She kissed her, tasting her lips slowly while she traced the soft junctures with her tongue, replacing another memory with the wonder of the now. "And you don't have to do anything either. I just want to touch you."

"Oh God, yes," Tory murmured. "Anywhere. Everywhere. Whatever you need."

What Reese needed was to skim her fingers over Tory's breasts and hips and thighs as she kissed her again. She drank her in, slowly savoring her as she continued her explorations. She watched Tory's eyes as she caressed her, recognizing the instant when pleasure became need. She smiled.

"You're so beautiful when you're aroused."

"I feel like part of me has been closed up in a dark room," Tory said breathlessly, "and you just opened a door. The sunlight almost hurts my eyes, but it feels so good to be warm. God, don't stop touching me."

Reese nipped at Tory's lower lip. "I never will."

"Reese, darling, I need you so mu—oh!"

"It's all right," Reese soothed as she swept her fingers between Tory's thighs. "Let me give you this."

"I'm afraid I'll forget and hurt you," Tory said desperately. "Reese, I don't know—"

"Shh." Reese slowly stroked through the heat, massaging the places that made Tory tremble, easing inside, a little deeper with each stroke. "You feel so good. I need you."

Tory tilted her hips and took Reese in completely, one exquisite millimeter at a time. "Oh that's so good. Deep. I want you deep inside."

When Reese was completely sheathed, she lay still, only her lips moving on Tory's. As her tongue met Tory's and they gently teased, she felt Tory tighten around her fingers. Still she did not move. As the contractions came faster, harder, she whispered, "I can feel you coming."

"Yes," Tory whimpered softly. "Coming. Just for you."

"I love you."

"Oh," Tory cried softly as her orgasm washed over her. "I love you."

❖

Rica dropped the book she'd been pretending to read as she sat for hours on the sofa. She'd read and reread the same few pages over and over. She regarded the phone on the end table as if it were a loathsome creature rather than an inanimate object. It had rung only once in the last twenty-four hours, and she'd been reluctant to answer it, knowing it was likely to be a call about some problem at the gallery in New York. But then, what else would it be? Carter wouldn't call. *She* had sent Carter away, and Carter would respect her wishes. Carter was the first person in her life who had ever really listened to what she had to say, and believed her.

She picked up the phone, finally admitting it was time to do what she'd been avoiding all day, and pressed the familiar numbers.

"Hello," her father said.

"Papa? It's me."

"Hello, Rica. I was just about to call you."

"I need to see you," Rica said, feeling an unanticipated surge of relief at having said the words.

"Yes. I have some things to discuss with you, too. Let's talk tonight."

"Tonight?"

"Why wait. I'll send a car."

"But—"

"I'll see you later, *cara*."

Surprised by her father's oddly abrupt tone, Rica wished that she could see Carter. Just being with Carter made her feel as if she had a real life of her own, one worlds apart from the one she'd been born into. But wishes, she had learned, were only painful indulgences, and she didn't have time for that luxury at the moment. She needed to get ready for the most important meeting of her life.

CHAPTER TWENTY-NINE

It was well after midnight when Rica arrived at her family home, but her father was waiting for her in his study, dressed in a suit as he always was and looking far fresher than she felt. He rose when she entered, came around his desk, and kissed her on the cheek.

"Let's walk in the gardens, *cara*," he said.

He wanted to talk outside, Rica realized, and immediately braced herself. Although the house was routinely swept for monitoring devices and the phone lines checked, she knew that her father never took chances when he discussed business. She took his arm and followed him out as if they were going to take a leisurely stroll. He didn't seem the least bit tense, but she doubted that she had hidden her own anxiety very well from him. It felt as if someone were kneading her insides with an iron fist.

As soon as they were outside, Rica said, "There's something I want to tell you, Papa."

"Let's sit."

Her father led her along a subtly lighted flagstone path to a secluded seating area with a wooden glider suspended from two tall trees in its center. She had often spent hours during the summer curled up on that very glider, reading and dreaming. She sat next to her father, who extracted a cigar from his inside jacket pocket. She waited while he went through the ritual of clipping the end with a small cigar knife he carried—a gift from her stepmother—and firing it with a gold lighter. Her father smoked a custom blend of tobacco, and the smoke that drifted into the air was vaguely sweet.

"What is troubling you?" Alfonse asked.

"There are things we've never talked about that I need you to know," Rica said. "Things about me."

"If there is something that concerns you," Alfonse said, "then I want to know."

"I've never wanted to hurt you."

"And you haven't."

"If I do, it's only because I need you to know how I feel. Because I want you to understand." Rica realized she'd forgotten the logical things she'd planned to say, and simply said what was in her heart. "I am never going to be any part of your business. I don't want anything to do with it."

"I understand that such matters do not interest you," Alfonse said quietly. "But you are my daughter, and that is a powerful tie that will always be important. Your husband—"

"Papa, there isn't going to be a husband. I am never going to marry a man. I'm a lesbian."

Alfonse continued to smoke and slowly swung the garden swing with a foot against the flagstone. "We are all complicated people. Love—desire—it is never simple. There are many reasons to marry, and not all of them are about what we feel."

"I'm not going to marry someone I don't love, and I'm never going to love a man. Not like that."

"What about children?"

"I don't need a husband for that."

Alfonse smiled faintly. "No, but it is easier. Would it be so difficult to take a husband who would want children as well, and have the other things you need with someone else?"

"It would be a lie, Papa. I can't live that way for the rest of my life."

"Why are you telling me this now?"

It was a fair question and one that Rica had thought about for hours—no, for weeks. Ever since meeting Carter. "Because I don't want secrets between us. And because Enzo needs to understand once and for all that I will never marry him."

"Enzo. Yes, he thought...we *both* thought...that would be the natural course of things."

Rica detected an edge to her father's voice that hadn't been there before, even when she'd said she was a lesbian. It surprised her that he hadn't had more of a reaction then, but now she could sense his anger. "I never gave him cause to believe that, but he always has considered me his."

"I admit, I gave him cause to believe I supported that idea. I had believed he would make a worthy son-in-law." Alfonse's face in the moonlight was as immobile as the statues scattered throughout his gardens. "I realize now that was a mistake."

"I should have said something much sooner—"

"There's a bruise on your cheek, *cara*. Were there other times he struck you and you hid the marks from me?"

Rica's hand flew to her face. Before leaving Provincetown, she had carefully applied her makeup and had been certain that he would not notice the bruises. They had already faded considerably, and she was shocked that he had detected them, especially in the subdued light. "No. I...I would have told you, but how—"

"A messenger arrived early this evening and brought me an envelope. Inside was a photograph of you—not a very good one, but it was clear enough for me to see that someone had struck you in the face. Your cheek was still swollen and discolored." Alfonse regarded her steadily. "I do not know who sent it, but you may tell whoever did that I am in their debt."

"I...I don't know who..." Rica tried to make sense of what her father had just told her. No one had taken her photograph. No one even knew what had happened except Carter and the doctor. Then she remembered waking up the morning after Carter had brought her home to discover that Carter was already up. She'd had no memory of Carter getting out of bed or moving around the room, but Carter could easily have photographed her then. "I might know who took it. A woman." She held her father's inquiring gaze. "A woman who loves me."

"I believe that, if she is the one who sent the photo. And you. Do you love her?"

"Yes," Rica whispered.

"I want you to do something for me without asking any questions, because I'm your father."

Rica waited.

"I've arranged for you and Angela to take a cruise. Just a week of relaxing in the sun because you've both been working hard."

"When?" Rica asked, wondering why he wanted her far away from Boston.

"In the morning. We've already contacted Angela and she'll meet you at the airport. The tickets will be waiting there for you."

"I can't," Rica said softly. "I can't without knowing why."

Alfonse drew on his cigar, then turned it between his fingers, apparently studying the bright red tip as it flared in the darkness. "All I can tell you is that you are in danger and until I have corrected my part in placing you in jeopardy, I want you somewhere safe."

"I need your word on something, Papa, or I won't go."

"Tell me."

"The women I've fallen in love with. I don't want her harmed, no matter what you might learn about her. Promise me that."

"If she means *you* no harm, Rica, then she will have none from me. What is her name?"

"Carter Wayne."

Alfonse Pareto grunted softly. "The lawyer friend of Rizzo's. I remember meeting her. Are you quite sure of her feelings for you?"

"Yes. More than that, I trust her, Papa."

"Then I will trust you. You have my word, *cara.*"

"I'll be ready to leave in the morning."

"Reese, there's someone at the door," Tory called as she hurried past Reggie's bedroom on her way to the stairs. Reggie was standing up in her crib and demanding to be free in no uncertain terms. "I'll see who it is. Just keep an eye on her but don't lift her."

"Okay, I've got it," Reese replied.

Tory finished buttoning her blouse on the way downstairs and hurried to the door. It could only be Bri at eight in the morning. When she opened the door, she stared in surprise at Carter Wayne, noting absently that the bruises were improved.

"Sorry to bother you, Doctor," Carter said quietly. "I was wondering if I might speak to Sheriff Conlon."

"Reese is on a leave of absence," Tory snapped. At the sound of her own anger, she closed her eyes for a second. "I'm sorry. She's not working just now. If there's something you need, you should probably check with Chief Parker."

"This is on the personal side, ma'am. I won't take up much of her time."

"How did you even know she was here?"

"I had breakfast at the diner in town. It came up in conversation."

"Of course." Tory sighed. The whole town was probably talking about Reese's precipitous return. "It's eight in the morning, Detective."

Carter reddened. "Sorry. I'm still on cop time. I'll come back."

"No, wait," Tory said as Carter turned to leave. "Come inside and have some coffee. I'll get Reese." Tory directed Carter to the kitchen. "Help yourself. The mugs are in the first cabinet above the sink."

"Thanks. Can I pour any for you?"

"Make that two."

Five minutes later, Reese appeared in blue jeans, a short-sleeve khaki shirt, and loafers without socks. She regarded Carter pensively as she picked up a cup of coffee and sipped. "I don't usually do business in my home."

"I don't blame you, and I apologize. I didn't want to go to the station." Carter shrugged. "And it's mostly personal."

"Just the same, let's take it outside." Reese indicated the deck, and she and Carter carried their coffee outside and closed the sliding glass doors. "Looks like somebody kicked the hell out of you."

Carter fingered her sore jaw. "Kick's the word for it. Your wife was nice enough to patch me up."

Reese smiled. "That would explain why she's pissed at you."

"I don't follow."

"She doesn't like patching up cops. Figures we take too many chances and overestimate our own skills."

Carter grinned. "She's right."

"Almost all the time." Reese tensed as a shadow flickered in the corner of her vision, and then she relaxed again when Tory passed through the living room carrying Reggie on her way into the kitchen. "What's the problem? Something to do with that undercover case you were telling the chief and me about a couple of months ago?"

"Yeah." Carter wished she could sit down. Her back still bothered her when she stood for long, but the sheriff looked just as bad as she felt, and if *she* was standing, Carter would too. "My assignment was to get close to the daughter of a Boston crime boss. The daughter has a place here. Turns out, she's clean, and now I think she might be in trouble. I need your help with that."

"Who is it?"

Carter hesitated. It went against her every instinct to share information, but she had no choice, and after thinking about it all night, she decided that if she were ever going to trust anyone with this information, it would be Reese Conlon. "Ricarda Grechi. She owns a gallery in town and lives on Pilgrim Heights."

"I don't recognize the name."

"Her father is Alfonse Pareto."

Reese whistled. "It would've been nice for us to know this earlier."

"Rica is not part of her father's business."

"You're sure?" Reese studied Carter's face as she took another sip of coffee.

"Positive. But I'm afraid the guys who tuned me up might go after her next." Carter jammed her hands in the pockets of her khaki pants. Admitting she couldn't protect Rica was eating holes in her. "I was hoping you'd look after her."

"I don't know when I'll get back to active duty. Someone else is going to need to know about this."

"But they don't need to know *all* of it. If you just ask your people to do ride-bys on her house and the gallery. Tell them she's got a crazy boyfriend or something, and you just want to keep an eye on her." Carter grimaced. "Christ, that's practically true."

"Why are these guys coming after her if she's not part of the business?"

Carter flushed but kept her eyes level with Reese's. "Because of me. I got in between her and a guy who thought she was his property."

"You got personally involved with the subject you were investigating?" Reese asked mildly.

"Not exactly." Carter looked out over the harbor, imagining how this must sound to a by-the-book cop like Conlon. "I fell in love with her. She doesn't feel the same."

"Christ." Reese turned to face the water and their shoulders touched very lightly. "Let me see if I've got this straight. You went undercover to get evidence on the daughter of one of the most powerful men in organized crime. Instead, you ended up involved with her and managed to piss off some *other* guy who considered her his. He sent a couple of enforcers to work you over, and now he might be coming after her."

"That's about right."

"What's *his* name?"

"Lorenzo Brassi."

"Not small-time either." Reese shook her head. "I see your problem, but why don't you have some of your people keep an eye on her?"

"One of the task force leaders is convinced Rica is dirty. I can't trust any of them to see what's really going on. My partner backs me, but he's only one guy."

"So there's two of you who believe she's clean."

Carter gripped the rail hard with the hand that wasn't holding her coffee cup. "Not anymore. I turned in my shield."

"You quit," Reese said flatly.

"Yeah."

"Why?"

Carter faced Reese. "Because I crossed a line."

"Do you think you're the first cop who ever did that?"

"Maybe not. But I'm still on the other side of the line, and I don't think I'm coming back."

"Because of her."

Carter nodded. "Yeah. Because of Rica."

"Even if she doesn't love you."

"That doesn't really matter, does it?"

Reese shook her head. "No. It doesn't." She thought about Tory and the Marine Corps and the war and her daughter. She thought about her responsibility to all of them and understood that some choices were made just because they were right. "What are you going to do now?"

"I'm not sure. I own a place here in town, but I don't think Rica is going to want me around. It's too small a community for us not to bump into each other."

"Maybe you'll want to go back on the job after things settle down a bit."

Carter smiled. "I think I burned my bridges there. I'll figure something out."

"I'll do what I can to see that Ms. Grechi is safe. I don't want you trying to do it yourself. You're not a cop in this town."

"It's mostly my fault she's in this situation."

"Nothing is ever that simple. You know that."

"Maybe it is, and we just don't want to admit it." Carter picked up her coffee cup and gestured toward the house. "I should go. I've bothered you and your family enough."

"Let me have a number where I can reach you—and keep me informed of developments."

"Will you call me if there's a problem with Rica?"

Reese studied her. "I don't know. It depends on what the circumstances are. Like I said, cop or not, you took yourself out of the equation when you fell in love with her."

"Doesn't seem right, does it?" Through the glass, Carter watched Tory play with Reggie on the living room floor and spoke almost to herself. "That the one thing that should bring you the closest keeps you apart."

"If you're lucky, that's not the way it works out. Give it time. Things might change."

"Yeah." Carter grinned sadly at Reese. "Anything can happen, right?"

After Carter and Reese exchanged numbers, Carter apologized once again to Tory for interrupting their morning and left.

Tory settled on the couch with Reggie. "You're not getting involved in anything with her, are you?"

"I'm just passing on information to the squads. I won't be doing anything myself."

"Whatever she's involved with, I saw the results. Both she and her girlfriend have been assaulted in the last few days."

Reese frowned. "You saw her girlfriend, too?"

"Yes. Um…Grechi. Ricarda Grechi. Someone assaulted her. And then went after Carter."

"You saw them both at the clinic?"

"Yes."

"As emergencies?"

"That's what it was, both times." Tory bent down to retrieve the toy Reggie threw on the floor and then regarded Reese speculatively. "You're using that tone of voice like I'm a suspect. What's on your mind, Sheriff?"

"Sorry." Reese sat on the couch on the opposite side of Reggie. "Those two are involved with some seriously bad people. I just don't want you anywhere near it."

"I'm a doctor, darling. I have to do my job."

"I know. But if either one of them ever calls you because of another emergency, I need to know right away. And I don't want you to see them at the clinic alone."

"It's that bad?"

"I'm afraid so."

"You don't need to worry." Tory leaned across the baby and kissed Reese softly. "We've had all the excitement we can stand in this family for quite some time. I'll be careful."

"Thanks." Reese smiled as Reggie climbed into her lap.

"Not so fast. I need you to promise that *you* won't get in the middle of Carter's problem. I saw what they did to her, and you are in no condition to fight anyone."

Reese reached for Tory's hand. "I'm not looking for trouble. I'll pass the information on, and I'll be out of it. The only thing I care about is being here with you and Reggie."

Tory kissed her again. She believed her, but she knew that as soon as Reese's body had healed, she would need to go back to work. Until she did, her mind and her heart would never be well. "And we're very glad you're here. So very glad."

CHAPTER THIRTY

Carter dug her cell phone out from under a pile of unfolded laundry. "Wayne."

"Where are you?" Kevin asked.

"On the Cape." Carter perched on the end of the sofa and surveyed the disaster of her apartment. Half-packed boxes of dishes stood open on the kitchen floor, two suitcases bulging with clothes leaned against the wall by the front door, and the remains of the pizza that had been both lunch and dinner rested in the center of the coffee table next to an empty bottle of wine.

"Got a TV?"

A trickle of foreboding crawled up her spine. "What's going on, Kevin? I'm not in the mood for games."

"Breaking news on the local station. A 'well-known' crime figure just went up in flames. Car crash on some back road outside the city."

"Who?" Carter's hand tightened on the phone.

"First reports are sketchy, but it looks like Enzo Brassi."

"Jesus."

"In spades," Kevin said. "You don't happen to know anything about it, do you?"

"I'm a couple hundred miles away, Kevin." Carter rummaged through several boxes until she found an unopened bottle of wine, then tucked the phone between her shoulder and ear while she searched the kitchen for a corkscrew. "And I don't know anything about blowing up cars."

"Where's Rica?"

Carter's voice went cold. "I don't know. She's not in town—at least the gallery's been closed for almost a week. Just what are you suggesting?"

"Ah, hell. I don't know. I was about to call you about something else when I heard the news report. There was a fire at Rica's gallery in SoHo just after four this morning. That's a little bit of a coincidence, don't you think?"

"Was she there?" Carter asked urgently.

"Place was empty. Most of the damage was in the back offices."

"Professional job?"

"Most likely."

"Why the hell didn't you call me sooner?" Carter growled.

"I didn't call you because I didn't hear about it until just about an hour ago when Allen decided to share the information with the rest of the team. Seems *that* gallery's been closed all week, too."

Carter digested the information as she poured the wine. "If both galleries are closed, Rica's probably out of town somewhere."

"I suppose you checked around there for her?"

"I'm not stalking her, Kevin. I'm clearing out my apartment right now." Carter sighed. He knew her too well. "Okay, I drove by her house a couple times and the gallery a few more than that, just to see if anyone was watching her places. Nothing."

"Allen's about ready to go postal over here. With Brassi dead and the records in Rica's gallery destroyed, she doesn't have a case. At least not from the angle she was working."

Carter had to smile. "Now there's a shame."

"She's not stupid, Carter. She's gonna be looking hard at you for this."

"Let her. She won't find anything."

"It sure looks like someone tipped Pareto about Brassi running a little sideline at that gallery."

"You think?" Carter took a healthy swallow of wine and hoped the satisfaction didn't show in her voice.

"I guess you're not going to tell me anything, are you?"

"There's nothing you need to hear," Carter said quietly.

"That's not the same as there being nothing to tell."

Carter let the silence be her answer.

"You need to be careful, partner. You're walking a very thin line."

"I'm out of it, Kevin. It's all over."

"Don't be so sure. Just keep in touch."

"Yeah. I'll do that." Carter closed the phone as Kevin rang off and stared around the room. Bare walls, boxes waiting to be filled, and the only memories worth keeping were the few minutes that Rica had spent there with her. Not much to say for her or her life.

Rica gave the cabdriver ten dollars for the five-dollar trip from Race Point to the center of town. She hefted her briefcase and carry on, and stepped out into Carter's driveway. "Thank you."

"You want me to wait?"

"No. I'll call you back if I need you."

Carter's Explorer was ten feet away, the back open and partially filled with boxes. When Rica saw the packed vehicle, she pushed away the immediate sense of loss at the thought of Carter leaving. Carter hadn't left yet. That was all that mattered. That was all Rica had thought about on her twelve-hour trip. She stopped at the foot of the stairs as Carter started down with an armful of clothes. Carter wore threadbare jeans, a black T-shirt, and running shoes. Her hair was longer and wilder than Rica remembered. She looked dangerous and sexy, and Rica felt a tiny shiver dance through her.

From three feet above her on the stairs, Carter regarded her with surprise. "Rica. Hello."

Awkwardly, Rica shifted her luggage and then simply put it down on the ground. "Moving out?"

"Yeah." Carter edged past Rica and dumped the garments into the back of her SUV. "You look good with a tan. Bermuda?"

"Aruba."

"I hear that's the place to visit. Been gone long?"

"Five days." Rica realized her linen blouse and slacks were rumpled from long hours on the plane, and since she hadn't slept a full night the entire time she'd been away, she probably looked as bad as her clothes. "I came home a couple of days early."

Carter smiled. "Having too much fun?"

Rica smiled too, but her voice was serious when she replied. "I wanted to see you."

"Why?"

"I don't like unfinished business."

"I think you pretty much finished things the last time we talked." Carter sidled past her to the stairs and gestured toward her apartment. "I've got an open bottle of wine. You look like you could use a drink."

"I know that's not a compliment just at the moment."

Carter lightly touched her fingertips to Rica's cheek. "The bruise is gone." She brushed a stray strand of hair away from the corner of Rica's mouth. "You've got a spectacular tan." She leaned forward as if she might kiss her, then stopped. "You look fantastic."

"I see that your head injury hasn't healed yet." Rica caught her scent—a faint odor of clean sweat, rich grapes, and the sea. Her stomach tightened with the memory of Carter's hands on her, in her. Thickly she said, "I'll take that wine."

"Okay." Reluctant to move, wondering when she might be this close to Rica again, Carter hesitated another second. "Let me get your bags."

"Take the light one. Your wrist must still be sore."

Carter didn't argue, because Rica was right. She grabbed the briefcase in her better hand and led the way upstairs. Once inside, she propped Rica's luggage next to her own, found another glass, and poured wine for them both. Then she set the glasses on the table in front of the couch and cleared a space for them to sit. The open doors to the front deck allowed in enough of a breeze that it was comfortable inside.

"Did you come right from the airport?"

"Yes."

"Not much luggage for almost a week."

Rica smiled wryly. "Well, Detective Wayne, that's because most of it is still at the airport waiting for me to pick it up later. I didn't want to drag it all over here, so I just grabbed what was easy."

"What's the hurry?"

Contemplatively, Rica sipped her wine, very aware of Carter's thigh resting lightly along her own. "I don't know. I woke up in the middle of the night with this...feeling, that I needed to come back. Right away. All I could think about was seeing you."

"This just came to you out of the blue?"

"Not exactly. Just the urgent sense that I needed to come home. I've been thinking about *you* all week."

Despite her resolve not to let her feelings get out of hand, Carter felt a twist of desire. "You're making me a little bit crazy here, Rica. What's going on?"

"I'll tell you. But first..." Rica set her glass aside and cradled Carter's jaw in the palm of one hand. "I really have to kiss you."

Carter moaned at the softness of Rica's mouth and the delicate tease of her tongue along the inside of her lip. She was instantly wet, painfully aroused. "Christ."

When Rica drew back, she was breathing quickly and her face was flushed. "When did you take the picture?"

"Wait...what?" Carter's head wasn't working right, and considering that most of her blood had rushed to a few inches between her legs, she wasn't surprised. Then her brain clicked in. Pareto had obviously told Rica about the photo and, fleetingly, she wondered if he'd told her the rest. She hadn't counted on Rica knowing, but there was really no reason not to tell her the truth. "I took it that first morning while you were asleep. With the camera on my cell phone."

"For one of the reports you were going to turn in?" Rica asked acerbically.

"No. By that time, I knew there wouldn't be any report on you." Carter shrugged. "I took it because I...I don't know. Habit, I guess. It was a crime." She emptied her wineglass in one deep swallow and refilled it. "It was *more* than a crime. I guess I just wanted something on him." She met Rica's appraising stare. "Taking it without your knowing was an invasion of your privacy. I apologize."

The corner of Rica's mouth twitched. "There are a number of things you could apologize for. I don't think this is one of them."

"Maybe you should tell me what the other ones are." Carter held up her hand. "No. Wait. Maybe you could kiss me again first."

Rica laughed softly. "I don't think so. I tend to get too distracted, and there are things I want to know."

"All right." Carter took Rica's hand and was relieved when Rica allowed her to hold it. The small connection made her feel more in touch with herself than she had been all week.

"Why did you do it? Why send it to my father?"

"Because I wanted him to know that you weren't safe." Carter looked away, the muscles in her jaw bunching as she swallowed her anger. "Because *I* couldn't keep you safe."

Rica stroked Carter's face. "It's not your job to do that."

Carter whipped her head back so quickly Rica jumped. "It wasn't about the job. I love you."

Rica closed her eyes. "I don't want to hear that right now."

Right now, Carter thought, feeling a glimmer of hope. *She didn't say she didn't want to hear it at all.* "Let me know when you do. Just in case."

"Don't try to charm me into forgetting why I came here. Why was my father so sure it was Enzo?"

Carter considered her answer, suddenly aware that Rica didn't have all the information. She considered any number of stories before realizing that there could be only one answer. Now. Ever. She told her the truth. "I wrote a note on the back."

"My God, you're a little bit crazy, aren't you?"

"Some. Yeah."

"What did it say?"

"Enzo's handiwork. And there's more at the gallery."

"What?" Unconsciously, Rica looked in the direction of her gallery, as if she could see it through the walls and across the blocks that separated them.

"Not that one. The one in Manhattan. We think—" Carter winced. "Some people think Enzo had a sideline, probably selling drugs or other contraband on his own and laundering the money through your gallery. Maybe even passing the goods that way."

"The bastard." Rica very carefully placed her wineglass on a stone coaster that sat all alone next to the pizza box. "We were about to have an accountant go over the books."

Carter shook her head. "He's not that dumb. You might have found a few irregularities, but I'm sure he didn't leave a paper trail." She looked pained. "Of course, that wasn't about to stop our illustrious leader from looking for one."

"You've been watching the gallery," Rica said accusingly. "God, is there no end to this?"

"*I* wasn't watching it, but it's been watched, yes." Carter put her glass next to Rica's and took her hands. She automatically smoothed her thumbs back and forth over the tops of Rica's fingers as she held them in her palms. "Have you talked to your father in the last day?"

"No. I've been traveling. My return was sudden. He doesn't even know that I'm back."

"So you weren't due to come back today," Carter said, just to be sure.

"No. Not until the day after tomorrow."

"I don't know all the details, Rica, but there was a fire in the Manhattan gallery. I doubt there'll be any records for anyone to find."

Rica leapt up. "A fire! My God." She stared at Carter. "What about the inventory? The artwork?"

"I don't know. I just heard myself."

"I need to call my father. My father will know."

"Wait a minute," Carter said as Rica fumbled in her briefcase for her phone. "There's something else you need to know."

"What more could there be?"

"We think Enzo's dead. A car accident early this morning."

Rica blinked and stared, then dropped the briefcase on the floor. Wordlessly, she sat down again next to Carter and curled her fingers around Carter's thigh just above her knee. Her hand trembled and Carter slid an arm around her shoulders.

"You okay?" Carter said after a full moment of silence. "Rica?"

"My father sent me away. Me and Angie. So no one would be at the gallery this week. So we would be far away when something... happened." She stared at Carter, her eyes dark with pain. "That was the reason for the trip, wasn't it?"

"I don't know, baby." Carter skimmed her fingers through Rica's hair and kissed her softly on the lips. "I don't know, and this is one thing you don't want to know."

"But *you* knew. You knew if you sent that picture what he would do."

Carter shook her head. "I didn't know. I didn't know how much he loved you." She took a deep breath. "I only knew what I would do if I were him."

"What? What would you do?"

"I'd make sure Enzo never did anything to hurt you again, in any way."

"You're a cop, Carter. Cops don't work that way." Rica raised their joined hands and rubbed her cheek against Carter's. The warmth comforted her.

"I'm not a cop anymore."

"What are you talking about?"

"I quit."

"I…you…why?"

"You know why. Don't make me say it, when you already told me you don't want to hear it."

For a second Rica looked perplexed, then she shook her head violently. "For me? No. I can't let you do that for me."

"Not *just* for you." Carter freed one hand and stroked Rica's face. Her fingers trembled as violently as Rica's. "For me too. For whatever's left of my sanity."

While Rica struggled to take in everything she was hearing, she found herself more and more drawn to the way Carter's lips curved as she spoke. To the strength of the fingers holding hers. To the pulse that raced in Carter's throat. Her brain was on overload but her body was singularly focused. "I want you to make love to me."

"Rica." Carter willed herself not to move, because everything in her wanted to take Rica into her arms. "You'll be sorry later, and that will kill me."

"No," Rica whispered. "I won't." She leaned into Carter, drawing Carter's arms around her. She nuzzled Carter's neck and kissed the soft skin of her collarbone. "I've never been sorry that you've touched me. Ever."

"I'm going to take you home. We'll talk some more in the morning."

"On one condition."

Carter grinned wearily. "I'm not sure I want to hear this."

Rica kissed her again, possessively this time, her mouth searing over Carter's. "I want you to stay the night with me."

"I don't know why I ever think I'll figure you out." Carter tilted her head back so Rica could kiss her way down her throat. "Because I'm always wrong."

"Is that so bad?" Rica murmured as she nibbled on Carter's neck.

Carter groaned, her legs shifting restlessly as pleasure rushed through her. "Christ no. It's good. Very good."

CHAPTER THIRTY-ONE

It was close to nine p.m. by the time Rica and Carter collected the rest of Rica's luggage from the airport and reached Rica's place.

"Let me get some air in here," Rica said on her way through the living room to open the windows. "I've forgotten how good it feels to come home."

"It's a nice change to be here when one or the other of us isn't banged up," Carter said.

"Isn't it." Rica smiled at Carter over her shoulder. "Would you mind taking the lighter stuff up to my bedroom? I'll be up in just a second."

"Ah—" Carter wasn't sure the bedroom was going to be such a wise choice. She couldn't even look at Rica without aching to touch her.

"I've been traveling since five this morning and I want a shower." Rica crossed to Carter, who stood surrounded by luggage, and kissed her. "And forgive me for saying this, not that I really mind, but you smell like you've been working all day and might like one too."

Carter grinned. "Is that some kind of half-assed come-on?"

"No," Rica said as she slowly ran her tongue down Carter's neck. "It's an invitation to take a shower with me."

Carter felt her knees weaken and her stomach flutter. "I thought we agreed—"

"No," Rica said once more. She pulled Carter's T-shirt from her jeans, slid her hand underneath, and pressed her palm low on Carter's belly while her fingers skimmed beneath the waistband of her pants.

"*We* didn't agree to anything. I asked you to make love to me and you wanted to wait." She knelt, bumping the largest piece of luggage with her hip to move it out of the way, and unbuttoned Carter's jeans. "We didn't discuss me making love to you." She slid down the zipper, opened the denim, and kissed the soft skin at the base of Carter's belly.

"Rica…" Carter whispered, her thighs trembling. She knew there were things they should discuss. She knew there were dozens of reasons they should stop. She knew…she knew…she couldn't think. "I want you so much."

Rica brushed her cheek against Carter's stomach and wrapped her arms tightly around her hips. She closed her eyes. "I know. Me too. I've been crazy all week thinking about you."

Carter bent and gently grasped Rica's shoulders, guiding her upward. She folded her in her arms and kissed her, slowly and deeply. She felt Rica's hands delve under the back of her T-shirt, one hand racing up and down her spine and the other diving into her pants to squeeze her ass. Carter pressed her thigh between Rica's legs and heard her moan. The sound of Rica's excitement cut through her like a scythe slicing ripe wheat, and as her resistance fell beneath the onslaught of unbearable pleasure, she unbuttoned Rica's blouse. Rica cried out when Carter dipped beneath the satin cup of her bra to close her fingers around Rica's breast.

"Too hard?" Carter gasped.

"No," Rica moaned. "I like it hard. I like to feel your hands on me." She dragged her hand around Carter's side, her nails leaving faint red lines in their wake, and pushed her fingers into the open vee of Carter's jeans. She moaned again when she encountered no other barriers, only Carter, swollen and hot and wet. "Oh my God."

"Don't." Carter slammed one hand over her crotch, trapping Rica's hand beneath the denim. "Don't touch me there."

"Oh, baby why?" Rica's voice was a plaintive plea. Her eyes were wild, her lips shining with their kisses, her breasts tight and firm in Carter's palm. "I want to. Oh God, I want you so badly."

Carter swayed, half undressed, vision hazy, her stomach knotted with excitement. "I want us to make love in bed." Her breath came in irregular spurts and she struggled not to come beneath the pressure of Rica's fingertips. "I want you to make me come slow, while I'm looking into your eyes. I want to see you when I—" She groaned and closed her eyes when Rica's fingers twitched over her clitoris. "Please."

"All right," Rica panted, pressing her face to Carter's chest. "All right, darling. Slow. I'll try. I'll try." She laughed shakily. "I'm usually not like this."

"No." Carter gazed down through half-closed lids to where Rica's arm disappeared into her jeans. "Neither am I."

Rica leaned into Carter, one arm around her waist to steady herself as she pulled her hand from Carter's jeans. "Maybe we should take that shower and cool off."

Carter kissed Rica's cheek, then the corner of her mouth. "Shower sounds good. But nothing's going to cool me off."

"Even better."

The sheets were cool and crisp against Carter's heated skin. She lay facing Rica as they kissed and caressed, their legs entwined, her sex pressed tightly to the smooth skin of Rica's thigh.

"Are you okay?" Rica asked quietly.

"Never better in my life." Carter massaged Rica's breasts, rhythmically brushing over her nipples until they grew impossibly hard.

"Feels so good."

"Oh yeah." Carter skimmed her mouth over Rica's, then worked her way along Rica's jaw to her ear. She tugged on her earlobe with her teeth and traced the rim with her tongue before teasing inside. Rica whimpered and arched against her. Carter didn't think she'd ever been so hard and so ready. "Rica," she whispered. "Open your eyes."

Rica, her flickering pupils wide and black, met Carter's gaze. "Can I touch you now?"

"Please."

Smiling dreamily, Rica skimmed her fingers up and down the center of Carter's stomach, then brushed through the hair between her thighs, then circled three fingertips over the base of Carter's rigid clitoris. She massaged her in slow, steady circles. "You're so wonderfully swollen and wet. Does it feel good?"

"Amazing." Carter gasped and kissed Rica urgently, unconsciously squeezing and twisting Rica's nipple. They kissed and stroked and caressed until Carter could barely breathe. Every muscle in her body was in an unrelenting state of spasm. "Can't take much more."

"You need to come, don't you?" Rica breathed against Carter's mouth, flicking her tongue between Carter's lips as she kept up her firm, methodical strokes. "Tell me what you want."

"I want to come all over you. So fucking hard." Carter released Rica's breast and slid her hand between Rica's thighs. She cupped her sex, her fingertips gliding just inside her.

Rica moaned softly and twitched on Carter's fingers. "Shall I finish you now, darling? Would you like that?" She thrust into the depths of Carter's engorged flesh, switching to long, full caresses.

"Yes. Yes, Christ, please," Carter said, hips lifting frantically. "Make me come, Rica. Rica, Rica—"

"That's right, darling, that's right," Rica crooned, working Carter into a smooth deep climax. "You come for me now."

Carter's head snapped back as her orgasm surged beneath Rica's skilled fingers. She was only vaguely aware of her legs thrashing and her fingers pushing hard into Rica. When she registered Rica's wild cries of pleasure and felt Rica writhing next to her, she roused herself enough to thrust Rica to a jolting climax.

"Oh God," Rica sighed. "At last."

Carter laughed and kissed Rica lightly. "I don't think anyone's ever said that to me after sex before."

Rica slapped Carter playfully on the hip. "If you know what's good for you, you'll keep that kind of information to yourself."

Suddenly serious, Carter kissed Rica again. "I know exactly what's good for me. You."

"Carter." Rica stroked Carter's cheek and brushed her fingers through Carter's damp hair. "I love you."

Carter went completely still. She searched Rica's face and found only certainty. She felt the wariness and distrust that she had carried for years like a tight chain around her heart simply break and fall away. She smiled. "I think *that* would be a matter of some consequence."

"Oh, it absolutely is." Rica caressed Carter's face, her shoulders, her back, pressing closer until their bodies touched nearly everywhere. "For me."

"For me too."

"I'm so glad."

Carter brushed her thumb over Rica's chin and kissed her again. "I can't seem to stop doing that."

"That's just fine with me."

"Are you happy?" Carter asked gravely. Of all the questions she had ever asked, this felt like the most important.

"Oh yes."

"It's going to get complicated, because as crazy as it sounds, I'm not good at hiding. Not something like this."

Rica laughed. "You? The undercover detective who managed to stroll into my father's study without anyone even noticing?"

"There will be other Enzos, Rica. Other men your father will want to see you with. Men who will believe you should be with them. I'm not going to just stand by and watch them try to take you."

"That will never happen." Rica sat up and pulled the sheet up to her waist, turning so that she could face Carter. She wanted Carter to see her as she explained why nothing would ever be the same again. "I told my father I will never have anything to do with his business."

Carter pushed up against the pillows, but did not bother with the sheet. "Telling him in so many words counts for a lot. But that doesn't mean he won't try."

Rica shook her head. "I also told him that I'm a lesbian, and that I don't intend to marry any man for any reason."

"You've had a busy week," Carter said, admiration in her voice. She took Rica's hand and kissed her palm. "How did he take it?"

"He's always known, of course, at least since I've been an adult. But we've never actually brought it out into the open. He tried bargaining, but I think he was convinced when I told him I was in love with you."

"Me!"

"Did you expect me to say someone else?" Rica asked with an amused smile.

"I thought you might tell me first." Carter held her hands wide in astonishment. "Jesus. Does he know...oh man, Rica. He's got to have some idea what I was doing there because he saw me with Rizzo." Carter frowned. "We'll just have to make sure that he doesn't see us together. And we'll have to be sure that—"

"No," Rica said flatly. "No more hiding. From him or because of him. He knows I love you, I told him you wouldn't hurt me, and he accepts that."

"Why don't I know any of this? When did you decide you can

trust me?" Carter ran both hands through her hair. "Do you know what this last week has been like? I thought I was going to lose my mind thinking I'd never see you again."

"I know, I'm sorry." Rica leaned forward and kissed Carter lingeringly. "I know. I needed time to sort it out. I realized after I told you that I didn't want to see you anymore that we both lied, to ourselves and to each other. I couldn't *not* forgive you." She stroked Carter's face. "And God, I love you so much."

Carter pulled Rica into her arms and they settled down again side by side. "He'll probably find out sooner or later that I used to be a cop."

"Are you sure you're not going back?" Rica asked carefully.

"Would it make any difference between us if I did?"

"No," Rica answered immediately.

"I'm not going back."

"Because of me?"

Carter started to answer and then paused. "A little bit, yes. But hear me out before you jump to conclusions. Mostly I quit because I didn't have any kind of a life and sooner or later I'd never be able to. I'd lose myself so deep in the lies that had become my life, I'd never find my way out. And I'm in love with you. And there's no way I could be a cop and be your lover. They'd be all over me to get information about your father."

"I'm sorry," Rica said. "I'm sorry."

"Why? It's not your doing or your choice. It's just the way it is." Carter snuggled Rica's head against her shoulder and stroked her hair. "I'm okay with it. In fact, I feel great. I love you, Rica. Jesus. It feels good to say that."

"It feels wonderful to hear it." Rica closed her eyes and listened to Carter's heart beat, quiet and steady. She felt peaceful, as if she had passed through a storm that had raged around her her entire life. "You're going to have to unpack your car again."

"I know." Carter closed her eyes and felt herself drifting. She heard the foghorn on Long Point sounding in the distance and realized she felt at home. With Rica, she *was* home, and always would be. "I'll probably have to get a job too."

"Well, I suppose I could find something for you in the family business," Rica said absolutely seriously.

Carter opened one eye and cocked an eyebrow.

Rica grinned. "Then again, maybe not."

"Go to sleep, Ms. Grechi. You're starting to scare me."

"Will you be here in the morning?"

"Absolutely," Carter murmured, nuzzling Rica's neck.

"Every morning?"

Carter opened her eyes and met Rica's, which were wide and unguarded. "I'd like that, if you want."

"I want very much."

"Then the answer is yes."

EPILOGUE

Tory sat Reggie in the middle of the living room floor with an array of toys and headed to the kitchen to pour a cup of coffee. She glanced at the clock. 6:55 a.m. Bri would arrive in five minutes. At the sound of footsteps coming down the stairs behind her, she said without turning, "Do you want coffee to take with you?"

"No, I'm fine," Reese said. "We'll pick some up someplace on our pass through town."

Tory turned in time to see Reese snugging the knot in her tie against her crisp khaki collar. She had predicted it would be two weeks before Reese rebelled at the inactivity. She'd been surprised, because it had turned out to be almost *three* weeks before Reese insisted she felt well enough to at least go in to the station to do paperwork. During those weeks when Reese had been home, Tory had worked abbreviated shifts to spend more time with her. They'd even gone out of town for several short trips to visit Tory's family.

Tory knew that Reese had tried hard to act as though she was enjoying every minute, and Tory believed that most of the time that was true. But she had seen a distant look come over Reese's face in their quiet moments, and she imagined that Reese had been thinking about where she had been and those she had left behind. As much as Tory wanted Reese safe at home, healing in body and soul, she knew Reese needed something different. "Remember, you promised me you'd stick to desk duty until I'm satisfied your collarbone is healed."

"I remember." Reese kissed Tory's cheek and stole a sip of coffee from her mug. "I think riding around in the cruiser is pretty much the same as riding a desk."

"No, it isn't." Tory tugged Reese's tie for emphasis. "If you're in the cruiser and something happens, you're not going to just sit there while Bri gets out and handles it alone. You know that."

Reese sighed. "All right. That's probably true."

"Probably?" Tory wrapped her arms around Reese's shoulders and settled against her. She kissed her chin, then her mouth. "Oh please."

Reese grinned, then settled her hands on Tory's behind and squeezed. "Both arms seem to be working pretty well."

"Mmm. I seem to remember that from last night."

"You felt so good," Reese whispered. She nibbled on Tory's lower lip, then kissed her long and hard, still feeling Tory's cries of release from hours before echoing in her bones.

"Oh, fu—sorry!" Bri blurted from the doorway.

When Reese broke the kiss and raised her head, Bri had one foot through the door and a look of abject contrition on her face. "It wasn't locked. I should've knocked. I'll go wait—"

Tory looked over her shoulder and smiled. "Come on in, sweetie. We were just talking."

Bri glanced once at Reese, then let the door close behind her. She gasped and pointed past them. "Whoa! Catch that."

Both Reese and Tory followed her gaze, and then Reese bent down and held out her arms to Reggie.

"Come on, champ. Keep coming. That's it."

With a look of determination and supreme delight, Reggie tottered across the four feet that separated them and tumbled into Reese's arms. Laughing, Reese hugged her and stood, holding her tight to her chest. Tory wrapped an arm around them both and held open the other to Bri. After a second's hesitation, Bri joined the celebration.

"I told you she was waiting for you to come home." Tory's eyes were bright with tears.

"Glad I didn't miss it." Reese rested her cheek against Reggie's head and closed her eyes. "Damn glad."

After five minutes of silence in the cruiser, Reese said, "What's on your mind?"

Bri gripped the wheel so tightly her fingers were white. She stared straight ahead. "Nothing. I was just thinking."

"Thinking pretty hard."

"Not making much progress, though." Bri glanced at Reese and grinned sheepishly.

"Why don't you try breathing now and then and see what that does for your head."

"You'd think I'd know that by now. I'm always telling the students in the dojo to do that."

"Sometimes we forget our own lessons," Reese said quietly.

Bri continued to drive down Commercial Street as far as the Provincetown Inn, then circled around to Bradford and headed back toward town. "What do you do when someone gives you an order, and you think it's wrong?"

"A superior officer?"

Bri nodded.

"You follow it, unless you know it to be illegal by whatever law governs the situation. The law of the land, where we're concerned right now. Military law, where I just was." Reese heard the distant thunder of war and knew the answers were never really that simple. "What made you think of that?"

"You didn't want to go, did you?"

"No. I didn't."

"But you did."

"Yes."

Bri spoke so quietly Reese could barely hear her. "I'm not sure I would have."

"You would have," Reese said with certainty, "if you'd sworn to."

"Sometimes when you were gone, I was mad at you. For leaving." Bri's hands had tightened on the wheel again and her voice trembled.

"Head over to Herring Cove," Reese said. When Bri cut the engine a few minutes later, Reese got out. "Let's walk."

They followed the sandy trail between the dunes until they crested the last swell of earth above the beach, then stopped, shoulder to shoulder, bodies just barely touching. Fishermen stood up to their knees in the surf casting for sea bass, here and there people walked with their dogs along the undulating shore, and far out to sea, fishing boats and trawlers skimmed the horizon. In a few more minutes, Tory would put the red kayak in and start toward Race Point.

"Last week," Reese said, "I left the Corps."

Bri stared. "For good?"

"Yes." Reese met Bri's astonished gaze. "My responsibilities are here now, to Tory and Reggie. To you. To this community."

"Are you okay with that?"

"One hundred percent." Reese saw Bri's body relax, but her expression was still troubled. "And forget about being mad at me while I was gone. I think the job we do is harder on the people we love than on us. Just remember that, when Caroline is giving you a hard time about the job."

Bri smiled. "She doesn't. Too much. She's like Tory that way."

Reese laughed. "Then she worries plenty."

"Yeah. She does." Bri breathed deeply, exhaled slowly. "So we're okay now?"

"We always were. You ready to go to work?"

"One more thing. Tory asked me to make sure you stick on the desk." Bri jammed her hands in her pockets. "Except you're my superior officer, so what'll I do if you decide not to?"

Reese squeezed Bri's shoulder. "I have a stop to make before we head to the station. You can drive me there, deliver me back to the station, and then I'll sit at my desk. I won't put you in the position of choosing, but if I did, I'd expect you to assess the situation and use your best judgment. And I know you would."

"Sometimes things aren't always black and white, are they?"

"No, they're not," Reese said quietly. "That's when you have to go with gut instinct." She tapped Bri's chest where her badge rested above her heart. "And what's in here."

Rica pointed to a blank space on the west wall of the gallery. "Can you hang that up there?"

"Sure," Carter said, carrying the largest painting that had arrived in the previous day's delivery.

At the sound of a knock on the front door, Rica called "We're closed," and turned to point out the sign in the front window that listed the gallery hours. When she saw the figure on the other side of the door, she strode angrily forward, flipped the lock, and yanked the door open. "Look, I've had about enough. If you don't have a warrant, you can—"

"I'm Sheriff Conlon, Ms. Grechi." Reese spoke quietly as she looked into the gallery and nodded to Carter. "I'd just like to speak to Carter. I saw her car parked out front."

"I know who you are. And I don't care what you want." Rica stood firmly in the doorway. "Carter isn't going—"

Carter put her hand on Rica's shoulder. "It's okay, babe. The sheriff's a friend of mine."

Rica turned stormy eyes to Carter. "Well, where was she a week ago when we could've used a little *official* help." She wrapped an arm around Carter's waist and angled her body between Reese and Carter. "You're not taking her anywhere."

"I can talk to her right here if you'd be more comfortable," Reese said, trying to read the situation. Rica Grechi was more frightened than angry, that much she could see. "It might be better for everyone if Carter and I take a little walk down the street, though."

"Better for who?" Rica snapped.

"Reese knows the whole story, Rica. We can trust her."

Rica searched Carter's face. "Are you sure?"

Carter nodded and kissed Rica softly. "Positive. I won't be gone long."

"Take your phone." Rica stroked Carter's cheek. "Call me if there's any trouble. If you're not back in thirty minutes, I'm coming after you."

"I'll be back before then. Don't worry."

Reese waited until the door closed behind them and Carter joined her on the sidewalk before speaking. "Sorry. I didn't realize it would be a problem for me to stop by the gallery."

"It wouldn't be," Carter said as they turned toward the center of town, "except we've had a rough couple of weeks since that business with Lorenzo Brassi."

"When you called and told me you thought the threat to Ms. Grechi was over, I pulled the patrols off her house and gallery. Was that a mistake?"

"That isn't where our problem's been coming from." Carter indicated a coffee shop. "Want anything?"

"Always good for coffee. I'm buying."

Reese ordered two coffees to go, thanked the many townspeople who said they were glad to see her back, and handed a cup to Carter as they walked back outside. "So tell me why Rica Grechi looks like she's ready to take on anyone who comes near you."

Carter smiled. "She's being a little overprotective, I guess."

"Considering someone kicked the hell out of you a few weeks back, that's probably justified."

"It's more than that. The FBI pulled me in a couple days after they confirmed it was Brassi who went up in flames. I guess my quitting right before it happened and the fact that Rica and I are lovers sent everybody's red flags into the stratosphere."

"You must have expected it."

"I did. At least I expected to be questioned." Carter sipped her coffee. "But the lead FBI agent decided if she sweated me long enough, she'd get what she was after. She invoked the Patriot Act and kept me incommunicado for three days. Finally my ex-partner raised so much hell they let me go."

"Jesus," Reese said. "Whether you resigned or not, you're still one of us."

Carter shook her head. "No. I'm Rica Grechi's lover. That makes it a whole new ballgame."

They walked to the end of the pier at MacMillan Wharf and finished their coffee while the ferry docked and a hundred people piled off for a day of sightseeing and shopping. Carter tilted her head back as the wind blew salt spray through her hair. It felt good to be outside and free.

"Rica didn't know what had happened to me," Carter said, "and there was no one she could call. She was scared." Carter's jaws clenched as she remembered just how scared Rica had been. "Now that she's had some time to settle down, she's mightily pissed."

"I don't blame her." Reese smiled briefly, thinking that Tory would have reacted very much the same way. "I stopped by to see if you were staying in town. I guess you are."

"I've got my place here, but I've pretty much been staying at Rica's. I'll probably end up opening the law office for real." Carter eyed Reese speculatively. "But this isn't just a social call."

"I also thought I'd let you know that the FBI gave us a call and requested we put you and Rica on our watch list."

Carter's stiffened. "Why are you telling me?"

"Because I thought you should know, cop to cop."

"I'm not a cop anymore."

"You quit because you had to. Because you had another responsibility, to Rica and to yourself. Doesn't mean you're not a cop still." Reese indicated her watch. "We better head back before your girlfriend comes after me."

"I appreciate the heads-up, but Rica and I aren't going to live looking over our shoulders. We don't have anything to be guilty about."

"I didn't figure you did, which is why there aren't any patrols on either one of you. And that's why we're not really having this conversation."

"Thanks."

"You know, this is a pretty small town. Quiet, most of the time." Reese glanced up and down Commercial Street, which was coming to life with early-morning deliveries, tourists out for their runs, and people picking up coffee and pastries from the bakeries and coffee shops. "But things do get exciting from time to time. You ever feel like trying small-town policing, come by the station and we'll talk."

"You don't think that would be a problem, considering Rica's father?"

Reese shrugged as they turned up the sidewalk to the gallery. "That's his life, not hers."

The door opened, and Rica hurried out. She slid her arm around Carter's waist again. "Everything all right?"

"Fine." Carter circled Rica's shoulder and held her close. "Don't worry, babe."

"I'm sorry to interrupt your morning, Ms. Grechi," Reese said. "I'll try to see that you and Carter aren't troubled any further. If you are, please call me."

Rica studied Reese for a long moment, then held out her hand. "Please forgive my temper earlier. And call me Rica."

"Pleasure to meet you, Rica." Reese saluted with a finger to the brim of her hat. "You both have a good day now."

As Reese turned and glimpsed Bri waiting in the cruiser, she felt the last shattered pieces of her world settle into place. This was where she was meant to be; this was her life. She was home.

About the Author

Radclyffe is a retired surgeon and full-time author-publisher with over twenty-five lesbian novels and anthologies in print, including the 2005 Lambda Literary Award winners *Erotic Interludes 2: Stolen Moments* ed. with Stacia Seaman and *Distant Shores, Silent Thunder*, a romance. She has selections in multiple anthologies including *Call of the Dark, The Perfect Valentine, Wild Nights, Best Lesbian Erotica 2006, After Midnight, Caught Looking: Erotic Tales of Voyeurs and Exhibitionists, First-Timers, Ultimate Undies: Erotic Stories About Lingerie and Underwear*, and *Naughty Spanking Stories 2*. She is the recipient of the 2003 and 2004 Alice B. Readers' award for her body of work and is also the president of Bold Strokes Books, a lesbian publishing company.

Her forthcoming works include *Erotic Interludes 4: Extreme Passions* ed. with Stacia Seaman (October 2006), and the romance *When Dreams Tremble* (January 2007).

Look for information about these works at www.boldstrokesbooks.com.

Books Available From Bold Strokes Books

Fresh Tracks by Georgia Beers. Seven women, seven days. A lot can happen when old friends, lovers, and a new girl in town get together in the mountains. (1-933110-63-5)

Empress and the Acolyte by Jane Fletcher. Jemeryl and Tevi fight to protect the very fabric of their world...time. Lyremouth Chronicles Book Three (1-933110-60-0)

First Instinct by JLee Meyer. When high-stakes security fraud leads to murder, one woman flees for her life while another risks her heart to protect her. (1-933110-59-7)

Erotic Interludes 4: Extreme Passions. Thirty of today's hottest erotica writers set the pages aflame with love, lust, and steamy liaisons. (1-933110-58-9)

Storms of Change by Radclyffe. In the continuing saga of the Provincetown Tales, duty and love are at odds as Reese and Tory face their greatest challenge. (1-933110-57-0)

Unexpected Ties by Gina L. Dartt. With death before dessert, Kate Shannon and Nikki Harris are swept up in another tale of danger and romance. (1-933110-56-2)

Sleep of Reason by Rose Beecham. Nothing is at it seems when Detective Jude Devine finds herself caught up in a small-town soap opera. And her rocky relationship with forensic pathologist Dr. Mercy Westmoreland just got a lot harder. (1-933110-53-8)

Passion's Bright Fury by Radclyffe. When a trauma surgeon and a filmmaker become reluctant allies on the battleground between life and death, passion strikes without warning. (1-933110-54-6)

Broken Wings by L-J Baker. When Rye Woods, a fairy, meets the beautiful dryad Flora Withe, her libido, as squashed and hidden as her wings, reawakens along with her heart. (1-933110-55-4)

Combust the Sun by Andrews & Austin. A Richfield and Rivers mystery set in L.A. Murder among the stars. (1-933110-52-X)

Of Drag Kings and the Wheel of Fate by Susan Smith. A blind date in a drag club leads to an unlikely romance. (1-933110-51-1)

Tristaine Rises by Cate Culpepper. Brenna, Jesstin, and the Amazons of Tristaine face their greatest challenge for survival. (1-933110-50-3)

Too Close to Touch by Georgia Beers. Kylie O'Brien believes in true love and is willing to wait for it. It doesn't matter one damn bit that Gretchen, her new and off-limits boss, has a voice as rich and smooth as melted chocolate. It absolutely doesn't... (1-933110-47-3)

100th Generation by Justine Saracen. Ancient curses, modern-day villains, and a most intriguing woman who keeps appearing when least expected lead archeologist Valerie Foret on the adventure of her life. (1-933110-48-1)

Battle for Tristaine by Cate Culpepper. While Brenna struggles to find her place in the clan and the love between her and Jess grows, Tristaine is threatened with destruction. Second in the Tristaine series. (1-933110-49-X)

The Traitor and the Chalice by Jane Fletcher. Without allies to help them, Tevi and Jemeryl will have to risk all in the race to uncover the traitor and retrieve the chalice. The Lyremouth Chronicles Book Two. (1-933110-43-0)

Promising Hearts by Radclyffe. Dr. Vance Phelps lost everything in the War Between the States and arrives in New Hope, Montana, with no hope of happiness and no desire for anything except forgetting—until she meets Mae, a frontier madam. (1-933110-44-9)

Carly's Sound by Ali Vali. Poppy Valente and Julia Johnson form a bond of friendship that lays the foundation for something more, until Poppy's past comes back to haunt her—literally. A poignant romance about love and renewal. (1-933110-45-7)

Unexpected Sparks by Gina L. Dartt. Falling in love is challenging enough without adding murder to the mix. Kate Shannon's growing feelings for much younger Nikki Harris are complicated enough without the mystery of a fatal fire that Kate can't ignore. (1-933110-46-5)

Whitewater Rendezvous by Kim Baldwin. Two women on a wilderness kayak adventure—Chaz Herrick, a laid-back outdoorswoman, and Megan Maxwell, a workaholic news executive—discover that true love may be nothing at all like they imagined. (1-933110-38-4)

Erotic Interludes 3: Lessons in Love ed. by Radclyffe and Stacia Seaman. Sign on for a class in love...the best lesbian erotica writers take us to "school." (1-9331100-39-2)

Punk Like Me by JD Glass. Twenty-one-year-old Nina writes lyrics and plays guitar in the rock band Adam's Rib, and she doesn't always play by the rules. And oh yeah—she has a way with the girls. (1-933110-40-6)

Coffee Sonata by Gun Brooke. Four women whose lives unexpectedly intersect in a small town by the sea share one thing in common—they all have secrets. (1-933110-41-4)

The Clinic: Tristaine Book One by Cate Culpepper. Brenna, a prison medic, finds herself deeply conflicted by her growing feelings for her patient, Jesstin, a wild and rebellious warrior reputed to be descended from ancient Amazons. (1-933110-42-2)

Forever Found by JLee Meyer. Can time, tragedy, and shattered trust destroy a love that seemed destined? When chance reunites two childhood friends separated by tragedy, the past resurfaces to determine the shape of their future. (1-933110-37-6)

Sword of the Guardian by Merry Shannon. Princess Shasta's bold new bodyguard has a secret that could change both of their lives. *He* is actually a *she*. A passionate romance filled with courtly intrigue, chivalry, and devotion. (1-933110-36-8)

Wild Abandon by Ronica Black. From their first tumultuous meeting, Dr. Chandler Brogan and Officer Sarah Monroe are drawn together by their common obsessions—sex, speed, and danger. (1-933110-35-X)

Turn Back Time by Radclyffe. Pearce Rifkin and Wynter Thompson have nothing in common but a shared passion for surgery. They clash at every opportunity, especially when matters of the heart are suddenly at stake. (1-933110-34-1)

Chance by Grace Lennox. At twenty-six, Chance Delaney decides her life isn't working so she swaps it for a different one. What follows is the sexy, funny, touching story of two women who, in finding themselves, also find one another. (1-933110-31-7)

The Exile and the Sorcerer by Jane Fletcher. First in the Lyremouth Chronicles. Tevi, wounded and adrift, arrives in the courtyard of a shy young sorcerer. Together they face monsters, magic, and the challenge of loving despite their differences. (1-933110-32-5)

A Matter of Trust by Radclyffe. JT Sloan is a cybersleuth who doesn't like attachments. Michael Lassiter is leaving her husband, and she needs Sloan's expertise to safeguard her company. It should just be business—but it turns into much more. (1-933110-33-3)

Sweet Creek by Lee Lynch. A celebration of the enduring nature of love, friendship, and community in the quirky, heart-warming lesbian community of Waterfall Falls. (1-933110-29-5)

The Devil Inside by Ali Vali. Derby Cain Casey, head of a New Orleans crime organization, runs the family business with guts and grit, and no one crosses her. No one, that is, until Emma Verde claims her heart and turns her world upside down. (1-933110-30-9)

Grave Silence by Rose Beecham. Detective Jude Devine's investigation of a series of ritual murders is complicated by her torrid affair with the golden girl of Southwestern forensic pathology, Dr. Mercy Westmoreland. (1-933110-25-2)

Honor Reclaimed by Radclyffe. In the aftermath of 9/11, Secret Service Agent Cameron Roberts and Blair Powell close ranks with a trusted few to find the would-be assassins who nearly claimed Blair's life. (1-933110-18-X)

Honor Bound by Radclyffe. Secret Service Agent Cameron Roberts and Blair Powell face political intrigue, a clandestine threat to Blair's safety, and the seemingly irreconcilable personal differences that force them ever farther apart. (1-933110-20-1)

Innocent Hearts by Radclyffe. In a wild and unforgiving land, two women learn about love, passion, and the wonders of the heart. (1-933110-21-X)

The Temple at Landfall by Jane Fletcher. An imprinter, one of Celaeno's most revered servants of the Goddess, is also a prisoner to the faith—until a Ranger frees her by claiming her heart. The Celaeno series. (1-933110-27-9)

Protector of the Realm: Supreme Constellations Book One by Gun Brooke. A space adventure filled with suspense and a daring intergalactic romance featuring Commodore Rae Jacelon and the stunning, but decidedly lethal, Kellen O'Dal. (1-933110-26-0)

Force of Nature by Kim Baldwin. From tornados to forest fires, the forces of nature conspire to bring Gable McCoy and Erin Richards close to danger, and closer to each other. (1-933110-23-6)

In Too Deep by Ronica Black. Undercover homicide cop Erin McKenzie tracks a femme fatale who just might be a real killer...with love and danger hot on her heels. (1-933110-17-1)

Stolen Moments: Erotic Interludes 2 by Stacia Seaman and Radclyffe, eds. Love on the run, in the office, in the shadows...Fast, furious, and almost too hot to handle. (1-933110-16-3)

Course of Action by Gun Brooke. Actress Carolyn Black desperately wants the starring role in an upcoming film produced by Annelie Peterson. Just how far will she go for the dream part of a lifetime? (1-933110-22-8)

Rangers at Roadsend by Jane Fletcher. Sergeant Chip Coppelli has learned to spot trouble coming, and that is exactly what she sees in her new recruit, Katryn Nagata. The Celaeno series. (1-933110-28-7)

Justice Served by Radclyffe. Lieutenant Rebecca Frye and her lover, Dr. Catherine Rawlings, embark on a deadly game of hide-and-seek with an underworld kingpin who traffics in human souls. (1-933110-15-5)

Distant Shores, Silent Thunder by Radclyffe. Dr. Tory King—along with the women who love her—is forced to examine the boundaries of love, friendship, and the ties that transcend time. (1-933110-08-2)

Hunter's Pursuit by Kim Baldwin. A raging blizzard, a mountain hideaway, and a killer-for-hire set a scene for disaster—or desire—when Katarzyna Demetrious rescues a beautiful stranger. (1-933110-09-0)

The Walls of Westernfort by Jane Fletcher. All Temple Guard Natasha Ionadis wants is to serve the Goddess—until she falls in love with one of the rebels she is sworn to destroy. The Celaeno series. (1-933110-24-4)

Change Of Pace: *Erotic Interludes* by Radclyffe. Twenty-five hot-wired encounters guaranteed to spark more than just your imagination. Erotica as you've always dreamed of it. (1-933110-07-4)

Honor Guards by Radclyffe. In a wild flight for their lives, the president's daughter and those who are sworn to protect her wage a desperate struggle for survival. (1-933110-01-5)

Fated Love by Radclyffe. Amidst the chaos and drama of a busy emergency room, two women must contend not only with the fragile nature of life, but also with the irresistible forces of fate. (1-933110-05-8)

Justice in the Shadows by Radclyffe. In a shadow world of secrets and lies, Detective Sergeant Rebecca Frye and her lover, Dr. Catherine Rawlings, join forces in the elusive search for justice. (1-933110-03-1)

shadowland by Radclyffe. In a world on the far edge of desire, two women are drawn together by power, passion, and dark pleasures. An erotic romance. (1-933110-11-2)

Love's Masquerade by Radclyffe. Plunged into the indistinguishable realms of fiction, fantasy, and hidden desires, Auden Frost is forced to question all she believes about the nature of love. (1-933110-14-7)

Love & Honor by Radclyffe. The president's daughter and her lover are faced with difficult choices as they battle a tangled web of Washington intrigue for...love and honor. (1-933110-10-4)

Beyond the Breakwater by Radclyffe. One Provincetown summer, three women learn the true meaning of love, friendship, and family. (1-933110-06-6)

Tomorrow's Promise by Radclyffe. One timeless summer, two very different women discover the power of passion to heal and the promise of hope that only love can bestow. (1-933110-12-0)

Love's Tender Warriors by Radclyffe. Two women who have accepted loneliness as a way of life learn that love is worth fighting for and a battle they cannot afford to lose. (1-933110-02-3)

Love's Melody Lost by Radclyffe. A secretive artist with a haunted past and a young woman escaping a life that has proved to be a lie find their destinies entwined. (1-933110-00-7)

Safe Harbor by Radclyffe. A mysterious newcomer, a reclusive doctor, and a troubled gay teenager learn about love, friendship, and trust during one tumultuous summer in Provincetown. (1-933110-13-9)

Above All, Honor by Radclyffe. Secret Service Agent Cameron Roberts fights her desire for the one woman she can't have—Blair Powell, the daughter of the president of the United States. (1-933110-04-X)